THE TEMPTATION of MAGIC

THE
TEMPTATION
of MAGIC

MEGAN SCOTT

HARPER
An Imprint of HarperCollinsPublishers

The Temptation of Magic

www.epicreads.com

Library of Congress Control Number: 2024935585

ISBN 978-1-33-500695-0

Typography by Jenna Stempel Lobell

First Edition

To the twelve-year-old me who cried when she was told that it would take over ten years to get published. It did, but I'm so glad you never gave up.

We're finally here.

And I'm crying again, just happy tears this time.

I am dragged along by a strange new force. Desire and reason are pulling in different directions. I see the right way and approve it, but follow the wrong.

—Ovid, *Metamorphoses*

PROLOGUE

NICOLE

When I was a girl, my mother tried to explain how vicious I'd become.

I was only three years old at the time, so didn't yet understand the depth and darkness of my immortal urges. But my mother knew.

And she warned me.

"Our kind was made, darling girl, at the dawn of time, when the Goddess of Death crafted us from the stars. To hunt. To kill. To keep the world safe. Which is why, when you grow up, your hunting instinct will make you one of the most powerful supernatural predators in this world.

"An Empyreal."

She'd said it gently as I sat on her lap and clutched a lock of her dark hair so that it curled, shining, over my chubby fist like a maternal gauntlet.

With her bestiaries, she showed me the supernatural creatures that existed, hidden among humans, and how we could transform into their greatest predators.

The ancient pages crackled as she turned them, revealing the research she'd compiled, the sketches she'd made. They told of long, paradisical golden ages when creatures had lived in harmony with humans, back when the world was ancient and new. Then dark storms of time, when the deadliest of those supernaturals massacred their way through civilization until Empyreals had stopped them.

Some of her drawings frightened me. The anarchic variation of creatures, the very reason our strange metamorphic powers were so necessary. When I think of her sketches now, I realize they're why I love art so much, having spent those formative years cuddled in my mother's lap with her scent and the cape of her hair around me, my heart fluttering like a little bird's. They proved there was *so much more* to our world. And while its history and myth were hidden from humans, it could be captured in art, keeping alive irreparable inhuman truths. From then on, I was captivated. Not quite—not yet—understanding that the beings she depicted were *real*. That they could hurt me.

Or, more accurately, that *I* could hurt *them*.

She had seen this dangerous and sometimes violent world, fought it; and though it had scarred her in numerous invisible ways, she had emerged as immortal and indestructible as a piece of ancient sculpture.

But there was one thing, despite our deadliness, that could threaten her.

"If you ever see another Empyreal, my love," she would ask me every night, "what do you do?"

Even now, I remember my learned replies. "Play pretend."

She would sigh and kiss me. "Yes. But what if one of the Wake's Empyreals discovers that you're also an Empyreal? If I'm not there and your father isn't there, what do you do?"

Sometimes, in my dreams, I see her dark, haunted eyes so clearly they wake me with a catch in my throat. Hers had seen eternities;

eons in which she'd slaughtered to stay hidden, to stay alive. To keep a world of ancient secrets.

But when she asked me again, her gaze was as clear and as serious as I had ever seen. *"What do you do?"*

"I run."

I got my first glimpse of that threat less than a year later, when our secret lives collided with it in the deadliest way. When the Wake, the organization that was supposed to keep our world safe by using Empyreals as its loyal hunters, sent one to hunt down my mother, and kill her in front of me.

I learned then, in a way she'd never been able to make me understand, that Empyreals were the most dangerous predators in the world. No human nor creature could compare. That was the way they—*we*—were meant to be. Urged on by an ancient, wild hunt within.

But there was one thing as deadly as an Empyreal's hunting urges: the hunger of the Wake. To them, the information my mother had accumulated, the secrets she'd uncovered about the very workings of our society and the organization that ran it, were just as deadly as her goddess-given powers.

After that night, I hoped to never discover the breadth of my metamorphic nature, yet wished with a desperation born of grief and curiosity that one day I would.

I didn't know which would be worse.

Now, I do.

1 NICOLE

The painting felt, in the dark gold light of Estwood's Museum of Art and Antiquities, like glimpsing the immortal urges slumbering inside her.

It was just a glossy poster, displayed in the marble foyer and lit by a spotlight. Most visitors had walked right past it. But then, Nicole had always felt a palpable draw to paintings of Empyreals.

The Wild Hunt of Odin, read the cursive gold script, *painted by Peter Nicolai Arbo in 1872. Being generously loaned by esteemed mythography professor Diana Westmoore.*

Nicole raked her eyes over the painting. In it, Empyreals streamed from the heavens on an endless metamorphic hunt, riding a sky cleaved by wicked clouds. The cold gleam of the moon illuminated one corner and its inky battlefield, while the archaic gold of the sun in the other backlit the descending warriors.

This was the title piece of Nicole's undergraduate art history dissertation. But it also had, hidden within, the last message from her mother. One that might keep her family safe from the Wake forever.

"There you are!"

Nicole blinked, tearing her attention from the painting's lure. She stilled the thoughtful back-and-forth movement of her thumb over the broken button on her cuff. The sharp edge tested her skin, but little could pierce it. Her fingers slid from where they'd been tucked under the sleeve to the silky, blood-colored lining, and she turned to see her best friend, Remedy Winters, strolling through the crowded foyer.

No matter what Remi said, the melody of her voice always drew attention, and her beauty kept it. The low lights brought out undertones of gold and purple in her brown skin and a sharp lick of black eyeliner accentuated the dark eyes she scanned over Nicole.

"How did I know I'd find you here?" Remi asked with a smirk, coming to a stop, her violet perfume and the camel-colored coat draped over her shoulders brushing Nicole's tweed jacket.

Nicole smiled, recalibrating. "Probably because I've been visiting it for days. The curator has asked me to stop 'loitering' in front of the poster."

Remi laughed. "Didn't he run away from you last week?"

A few human visitors turned toward the sound of a Siren's joy. Humans knew nothing about supernaturals: not that they lived among them in every town and city in the world, or that the Wake kept supernatural society safe and secret. They believed the supernatural was something that belonged in paintings or movies. And yet they still sometimes looked a moment longer, their senses whispering that there was *something* about certain things or people.

Nicole wondered if, as some sensitive humans could, the curator knew on some level that she wasn't human: that she could hear the bloody rush of his pulse beneath his skin; that she could kill him in an instant. Not that she would, or wanted to. She was a predator of deadly supernaturals, not humans. That didn't mean, as her teenage years spiraled closer to her twenties, that she hadn't noticed how

5

some people found it difficult to keep eye contact with her apparently *intense* dark gaze.

It would be even worse if she ever had her first transformation. Until then, her Empyreal power felt like a being separate from herself, and Nicole could keep telling herself she was just like a human.

Gentle. Safe.

And always in control.

"All I did was check on the progress of the painting being moved here. Yet every time he sees me, he acts like *I'm* the harbinger of the Wild Hunt."

Remi shook her head, eyes sparkling with mirth. "He's probably just jealous you get to work with Westmoore's whole collection while he's having to bend over backward to have just one of her paintings in the museum. How long has he been asking her?"

"Almost as long as I've wanted to see them, too." Nicole returned her attention to the painting and sighed. "Ten years."

"And here it is." Remi looked up, her soft curls brushing Nicole's cheek. "It's so . . . vicious."

Nicole said nothing as a complicated twist of fascination and longing went through her. She'd spent years combing through the pieces in the museum, looking for paintings of supernatural origin that might fit her mother's last clue—"*divino artista*"—which meant, among other things, supernatural art. But besides the Celtic artifacts she loved, and the nineteenth-century paintings of ships in dark storms, the museum didn't hold what she was looking for. So she remained convinced the answer lay in Westmoore's infamously secret art collection, and the sprawl of supernatural antiquities kept private in her local coastal manor.

Tonight, Nicole would finally find out if she was right.

"Come on," Remi said. "I want a coffee, and you don't want to be late for her first lecture, do you?"

Nicole smiled, letting Remi steer her toward the glass entrance.

Warm sea air breathed up under her jacket and loose white satin shirt as they came outside. Estwood felt gorgeously academic this morning. The sky had turned overcast with a slowly encroaching storm, giving the air a warm magnetism and muting the golds and grays of the historic stone buildings. It made the distinctly nonmagical place feel almost mystic and even more ancient and Celtic, set as it was between Devon and Cornwall on the south coast of England.

"How did the meeting with your supervisor go?" Nicole asked as they headed down the museum's wide steps and onto the cobbled streets.

"He approved my dissertation, thankfully," Remi said. "So don't forget, when you see the collection, let me know if there are any Siren or Mermaid paintings with instruments in, okay?"

"Yes, of course."

Remi's research into the history of music often had her poring over old texts describing the world's most ancient instruments, lost to time. Nicole didn't know the full extent of the reason Remi and her family also hid from the Wake, but it had brought them to Estwood and bonded them tighter than Nicole had ever dared to wish for.

"Great." Remi squeezed Nicole's arm softly. "Thanks. What about you, did you catch Westmoore this morning after our folklore class?"

Nicole sighed, thinking of the enigmatic professor who'd been in Oxford for ten years. "No, I tried her office, but it was locked. I think the lecture or tonight will be my first chance to properly introduce myself. I just want to see her as soon as possible."

They passed the old church where Nicole's father worked, which housed the university's library. The lantern-guarded entrance to the university's oldest buildings was next, along with its grassy quad where students milled about, their bikes tied up beneath ancient Victorian streetlamps. Then, headed down a narrow adjoining alley that branched onto the next street.

Estwood was the perfect blend of ancient and new: pale, ornately carved townhouses circled a great Mermaid fountain, and the surrounding shops featured delis, bakeries, and other essentials. It had everything you'd expect of a little Cornish town: ancient-looking teahouses nestled alongside art galleries and crystal shops. Then the academic necessities: bookshops, art supply stores, and cheap coffee and wine bars where students could get drinks all hours of the day and night. More modern glass buildings sat between the old ones like invisible extensions into the present, inextricably interlinking the campus with the town itself.

After retrieving their coffees—a lavender oat latte for Remi and an Americano with cream for Nicole—they approached the glass-fronted lecture building, nestled between the folklore and art history townhouses, where a flood of students waited inside.

"I'm going to try and catch her," Nicole said as they stepped into the cool, modern interior.

"Good luck," Remi said, turning to head to her own lecture. "But let me know how it goes tonight, okay? I know you'll figure it out."

Nicole smiled, thinking of the wealth of supernatural artifacts and the academic excitement of figuring out her mother's last clue. The one she'd let *nothing* come in the way of. She shrugged softly. "I have with all the others."

Remi smiled. "She'd be proud of you. Her little mythographer."

An unexpected knot of heat formed in Nicole's throat. She'd only been three when her mother had been murdered. In some ways, too young to remember her—as powerful and mythic as she was—and yet those simple words meant so much. "Get out of here before you make me like you even more."

Remi laughed and waved, and Nicole watched her go. She'd never had a friend other than her siblings before. Being hunted, fleeing from one safe house to the next fearing the Wake were just over their shoulder, had made it impossible. Especially to find another supernatural who understood not just their plight, but how it felt to hide the very essence of who you are. To shrug on humanity like a coat every morning before leaving a house full of supernaturals.

Nicole's fingers rubbed against the rough hem of her mother's jacket as she turned back to the bank of students. They were strangers, all of them. But all humans.

She took a breath and raised her chin slightly. As a child, she'd been paranoid in a crowd like this, unsure if someone in her midst was a creature capable of triggering her first transformation.

Nicole paused in the entrance to the colossal lecture theater, her breath catching with anticipation.

The room was dark and tiered, the seats circling a giant screen like a crescent moon. Laptops were gleaming to life where people had found their seats. She looked over at the empty podium where Professor Westmoore was due any minute. On screen, gleaming darkly, was a mythological oil painting and the words "Introduction to Art History."

Nicole headed up the steps, excited for the anonymity of university. She'd been craving the freedom this year of research offered her over the more rigid types of undergraduate degrees.

It was a foundation course offered by Estwood University—the specialized arts school—allowing teenagers who'd just left sixth form to pick a dissertation and study any humanities classes they desired to complete it. It meant Nicole could take classes like Celtic History, Mythology and Folklore, Gothic Literature, and of course Art History. All of which allowed her to study the supernatural in some form or another. If she couldn't be around it in real life, this was the next best thing.

She'd managed to design a dissertation that allowed her to straddle both worlds, using human-made paintings that—unknowingly to the humans—depicted real creatures. It gave Nicole the excuse to leaf through every human folkloric text as well as works of literature and art, searching for real supernatural truth: from dark fairy tales to steamy paranormal novels. Even a few shockingly made, yet mysteriously bingeable supernatural TV shows she'd laughed herself hoarse watching with her sister and Remi.

Nicole took a seat, scenting the rough fabric of the chair, various types of coffee, new books, and every person in the room. But she was used to overstimulation after nearly nineteen years of heightened hearing, strength, sight, and speed, so tuned it out as she pulled out her laptop and set it on the attached folding arm. She tried to smile at the people who sat in the seats around her, their eyes snagging on her a little longer. She scanned her reflection in the unlit screen of her laptop, finding the same dark eyes and dark hair as her mother.

The same deadly urges.

Sleeping, she reminded herself. *Controlled.*

As the lights dimmed, Nicole sat up straighter and her senses unfurled. There was a gleam of movement by the podium and a moment later one word pierced the darkness.

"Mythography."

Professor Westmoore's voice was unhurried and elegant, with the gentle rasp of age and subtle power of someone inhuman. It caused the hairs on Nicole's body to rise. She hadn't heard this voice since the stormy night her father and siblings first came to Estwood, fleeing an encounter that could have ruined their lives forever.

"The research of mythological art is a seriously understudied specialty." A short, gleaming cap of silver hair became visible as a spotlight bloomed on the stage, revealing a woman who appeared somewhere in her eighties.

Even from across the lecture theater, there was something Elfin about her features, yet Nicole knew the art collector and professor was actually a powerful Seer, like Nicole's father and sister, and likely much older than she appeared. Nicole had an unusual flicker of Seer abilities, so she'd never had much practice with them. It was unheard of for an Empyreal to have any other gift than the deadly reflex to transform.

"During this year," Westmoore continued, "my lectures will take you through a myriad of supernatural images, some from my own collection."

Artwork flooded the dark, lighting students' faces in flashes of bloodred or royal blue. On the screen, moon-eyed Pre-Raphaelite nymphs tugged Hylas into violet water thick with lily pads, their red hair drenched to an ancient rust color. Next, nineteenth-century oil paintings of Mermaids and Satyrs appeared. Delicate watercolor illustrations of Faeries. Armored men spearing great dragons and gallivanting scrawny devils in fiery depictions of the Last Judgment. Then, pages from jewel-toned bestiaries from the Middle Ages with chimera-like creatures—rivaling the bestiaries in Nicole's family library.

The array concluded with a Celtic cauldron, raucous creatures dancing around the bronze rim, and a twisted torc that snagged Nicole's attention. The ancient gold necklace swirled with anthropomorphic patterns, made to look like slowly moving creatures.

"Today," Westmoore said, "I encourage you to forget what you think you know of the world. Because if these artists didn't believe such creatures were real, they entertained the supernatural through allegory, fairy tale, or religion, and with such artistic fervor that might make you believe they were. You will be shown that beneath the human history of the world, art reveals a secret, seething, supernatural one."

The professor looked directly at Nicole in the crowd. They were the only two in the room that knew the creatures in these paintings were real, knew how magic and vicious the world truly was.

Except in Estwood, Nicole reminded herself as her excitement bittered. *We're safe here. Hidden.*

"To these artists," Westmoore continued, "the temptation of magic was too strong to ignore. Let me show you why."

2 KYAN

Kyan McCarter's latest hunt had taken him to a dark, coiled forest in the Fae heartlands of Dartmoor known as Wistman's Wood. Its ancient, eerie trees and mossy boulders were lush after a long night of late-summer rain, yet the silver sky glimpsed above the tangled canopy was burnished and threatening as an ax.

Kyan felt quite the same, stalking the woods.

His transformation hadn't taken hold yet, but even with his heightened senses he was all too aware of every crack and brush of life, every pulse of the forest. It almost made him remember his earliest and most intimate history in Ireland; almost focus on the fact that just over the Irish Sea was the place he'd once called home.

Almost.

Kyan slowed, his tall, muscled form primed with power and tension, gently straining. He stilled, his boots darkened by the wet blades of flora, and closed his eyes.

The Fae he was hunting had killed three humans before Kyan had been given the mission. It lured its prey with unnatural beauty, seduced them, then left their bodies bordering the woods. He had tracked this one across the moors, its usual scent permeated with what the Wake had dubbed the "kill hormone." It led him on an unmissable path, spiraling through the hunter-green density, and was the only thing that would truly begin and complete his transformation.

He inhaled it deeply.

Empyrean power surged through his body. A welcoming heat, edged today with viciousness.

He felt the transformation in his arms first as Fae magic flooded his veins, turning them proud and dark beneath the skin. Then his mouth filled with the taste of earth, sweet and heady. This power felt archaic; perhaps he was becoming one of the most ancient type of Fae, those so removed from humanity they allowed their incessant hungers free rein and their deadly magic to bloom.

He never knew for certain what he'd transform into on a hunt. Every time was different, because his Empyreal would remake him into the natural predator of whatever it was he was hunting. He could guess, after so many centuries, yet the change was always accompanied by a rush of intense relief and a rightness so true it wiped any essence of fear from his mind.

He hadn't felt fear in centuries: he trusted his impulses too much.

Kyan opened his eyes.

They would be completely black now. His ears newly pointed, his dark hair suddenly longer than the efficiently short cut he usually favored.

He turned to scan the trees with new vision. They seemed to pulse, alive and four-dimensional. The great trunks and branches were like broken fingers, draped with ancient moss. Long-handed ferns stirred and brushed against his body. Above, the wood's canopy was sloped, as if it had been bent long ago by a supernatural force. Now, he could *see* the power in the wood.

And he could feel his prey.

Kyan moved slowly, silently. He couldn't risk being spotted by his target, not until the last possible moment when it went for the kill and the change in its hormones fully unleashed Kyan's transformation. Otherwise, he risked the life of the newest girl it had stolen.

And Kyan didn't accept casualties.

Stepping into the small, twisted glade, he found them at the base of a great tree. The girl almost looked human, but he knew she was not. She was young and pretty with dark red hair, but he could see the fear in her eyes as her panicked gaze flittered over the looming creature's shoulder, finding him. The Fae hadn't noticed, too busy murmuring into the girl's neck.

Kyan motioned for her to remain quiet, showing her the circular scar of the Wake on his forearm. Her eyes widened and then closed in relief.

His target made the killing decision a moment later and the scent coiled through the wood. Kyan's transformation stole through his body like a knife. There was no pain, no scream of metamorphosis; his body was made for this.

So, he gave himself over to the hunt.

He flung out his arm and an inky spear of power shot through the woods. The Fae staggered back, unable to breathe as its throat gushed with clear blood. It gave Kyan the moment he needed to cut close enough to grab the girl as she staggered and slipped in the roots of the tree. He hauled her from the mossy ground and shoved her with enough force she'd know to run for her life.

"Run!" he ordered as he allowed the Fae behind him to strike a vicious, desperate claw across his shoulders. Kyan grunted at the force of it. Pain seared his skin as a rush of hot blood and magic slickened his back. Sometimes it made the hunt faster and more effective to allow his prey to believe it might escape him.

They never did.

The girl, however, got a few feet before she slipped and fell hard with a cry, striking her head and passing out.

Kyan threw himself in front of her as the Fae lunged. He caught it by its bleeding throat and slammed it against one of the ancient trees, gritting at the splinter of bark and strike of the Fae's claws across his chest. Kyan bared his teeth as the creature roared. It should have looked beautiful. White hair, sharp features, an otherworldly lure. But right now, it exposed its rawest hungers and Kyan thought of his missions of late and how creatures were becoming more and more bloodthirsty.

"There's no point," Kyan growled as it clawed at him, dousing his body in blood. Hunger, bright and wild, burned behind his eyes as a rush of deathly Fae magic rose beneath his skin.

"Dog," the Fae spat in its language.

The veins in the back of Kyan's hand pulsed as his body tugged magic from the woods and funneled it through him. With his temporary Fae abilities, he located his target's life-force and drew it out. Its power flooded into Kyan's body slowly and fueled him with longings, whisperings. But he forced the magic back out into the earth and felt the splintered trees knitting themselves back together.

Then his prey slumped and stilled in his grip, a quick end to a murderer that hadn't given that grace to his victims.

Satisfied the creature it hunted was dead, Kyan's Empyrean power began quickly returning him to his normal form. The urges lessened and the heaviness of unfamiliar magic bled away as his body shifted back to his natural state. An Empyreal again. Not the being he'd just been or the thousands before that. Just him and the gilded power inside, eternally ready for another transformation should the need arise.

He let the creature's body slip to the ground and turned to find another Fae leaning against a particularly coiled tree, his black hair long and loose, his skin pale as moonlight. He had the thorn-sharp, untrustworthy beauty of an ancient one. And the amusement of one not usually held accountable.

"Watch where you hunt, Empyreal. You're in sacred woods." The Fae stroked a long finger down the still splintered, slowly healing bark. "Damaging these trees is a terrible omen."

Kyan bared his teeth, but no creature had anything to fear from him unless it planned on killing. He couldn't transform his body at will.

"Take it as an omen not to kill people," Kyan suggested, heading toward the unconscious girl.

"Says the hunter with blood on his hands."

"Most creatures are grateful that I rid them of killers," he said over his shoulder.

"He was ours to deal with."

Kyan shook his head, checking the girl's vitals. Alive. Just a bloody welt on the head. Irritation and anger simmered as he turned toward the Fae. "It's almost like you've forgotten what an Empyreal is. That the Wake send us to protect people."

He suddenly recalled first kneeling before the Wake all those years ago, when the world was so different. When his heart had been broken by loss and his powers had been so new. When vengeance had made him a hunter.

The Fae's lips pulled back. "I haven't forgotten. We just don't like them fucking in our business."

Challenge welled up in Kyan's body as he stalked closer slowly. "I don't give a shit about your politics."

"No," the Fae said, with renewed interest, glancing at the unconscious girl. "You don't, do you? That's going to have to change."

"Keep your people in line," Kyan warned, "and I won't have to."

The Fae smiled, sharp as a threat, a dangerous intrigue glimmering in his ancient stare. Then he was gone.

The girl stirred, and Kyan heard the quick flurry of her heartbeat galloping with panic.

He walked back to her and knelt at her side, ducking his head to catch her fluttering gaze.

"You're safe," he told her calmly. He rarely used Influence unless he needed a human or creature to forget they'd seen him, but in instances like this, the mind-altering tone was even more useful. She relaxed and her heartbeat slowed. Hesitantly, she lifted her hand to try and give him something. When he realized what it was, his blood cooled.

"No, it's all right." He'd received gratitude a few times, and yet it always made him uncomfortable. He wasn't doing anything he should be thanked for. Hunting, protecting—it was his entire purpose. He couldn't deny the impulse if he tried.

Being so close to the ancient Druid sites only made that clearer.

"Please," she insisted weakly, forcing her eyes open and closing his hand around the offering.

He looked down at the acorn. To Kyan it was a reminder of the trees of the Druids, the ones he'd once had to watch burn, his people slaughtered beneath them. But to her kind, it was a talisman of sorts

18

that would return you to your family if they were lost.

"It's worked for me," she whispered. "You're taking me home. Now—it's yours." She attempted to push it into his bloodied fingers.

Kyan's jaw tightened so much it felt liable to crack. "I . . . don't have a family to return to. Keep it."

"Then it will find you another," she whispered as her eyes flickered closed.

He wasn't supposed to keep things. The Wake didn't encourage it. Items meant attachment, and he couldn't afford to be anything but focused on his missions. And yet Kyan couldn't bring himself to discard the gift, either.

The hunt was his purpose, killing deadly creatures to protect others. That was all he needed. So Kyan lifted the unconscious girl and began the trek to a local village where he could leave her safely and disappear, but the acorn burned a hole in his palm the entire way.

His townhouse had been built over a century before, its dark, red-brick facade blending easily with the identical houses of Rodney Street.

There were other locations he could have gone to debrief. The Wake had buildings and connections in every city in the world: Edinburgh's windswept silver city; or historic Bath, which had been closer; and yet Liverpool had called to him.

He barely came here anymore. The Wake preferred their hunters to stay in their own way houses, and he preferred it, too. Yet he found himself unlocking the front door.

Kyan only allowed himself this one place. It wasn't a home, so much as the only building he'd ever owned.

He took the stairs three at a time and shouldered open the door to the upper living room.

It was dim with overcast light; the walls painted a dark hunter green. It hadn't been redecorated for years, so the remnants of Victorian furniture gave the room a sense of history he usually avoided. He'd done mindless chores and renovations with his own hands to keep out anyone other than his housekeeper—a little Irish woman, who also happened to be a Hearthea, and who refused to do half of what he asked, doing tasks her own way. Otherwise, he'd had to Influence any others he'd needed to come in to forget what they saw. In this room especially.

Kyan went to the fireplace, its mantel heavy with ancient artifacts. He hesitated before placing the little acorn among them, nestling it between a battered gladiator's helmet, the coiling gold of a two-thousand-year-old torc, and a few Celtic Revival pieces from the Victorian period.

The Wake warned that remembering the past was dangerous. It could make Empyreals mad with regret and longing for those they'd lost. Every time he was here, he was reminded of the ages of his immortality and wondered if they were right. Yet something deep, or perhaps quietly confident, was sure he would manage. History was something he could use to learn and better his hunts. It had already served him well.

As long as he didn't think of family.

Nothing here had been given to him by them, not even the torc; the one his mother had originally gifted him had been lost to time. No, these were items from past hunts, periods that felt like past lives, or gifts from grateful creatures that he couldn't bear to throw away.

Kyan tugged at the dark curls at the nape of his neck. His hair had grown with the transformation. He ran a hand through it, his back and chest no longer smarting from the slash of the Fae's claw marks, completely healed. His fingers gripped the curling lengths and a small unease coiled in his stomach: any longer and it could be plaited.

He'd have to cut it.

Kyan removed his other hand from where it gripped the dark marble, the knuckles white.

Then, locking the door, he walked away from the memories, and went in search of his next mission.

3 NICOLE

Driving down the long tree-lined gravel path toward Westmoore Manor, Nicole's breath caught as she peered up through the windshield.

The manor rose from the sand dunes like a sea-girt palace. The sky had darkened quickly tonight, so the building's pale Jacobean facade was lit by violet twilight. The gold grasses of the beach behind it swayed beneath the heavy purple storm moving inland and the sea thrashed, white-tipped as if laced.

Nicole had borrowed the family Jeep for the short drive, after reassuring the gilded trio of her father, brother, and younger sister that she'd call with news if she discovered anything. She thought of them as the car rolled to a stop, crunching over gravel. They weren't as desperate to discover this final clue. Perhaps because they'd been safe here for almost a decade, perhaps because they weren't convinced there was still a clue to be found. And yet, Nicole couldn't ignore the last line of her mother's message, how it tugged at her, whispering that there was something *more*. Something undiscovered in this coastal haven.

Even if that was just a whisper of a connection to her mother in the form of Professor Westmoore.

Nicole checked her reflection in the rearview mirror, smoothing down her carefully done hair and wiping away a bit of stray mascara. She wasn't a little girl anymore, her sweaty hand in her brother's, staring wide-eyed up at the supernatural paintings behind Westmoore, and the Seer's knowing eyes the first and last time they'd met. She'd grown, she'd researched. And if she was right, after tonight she would have the key to keep her family in this blissful nook of the world. Her heart swelled at the mere thought.

Nicole got out of the car and was immediately struck by strong, warm sea air. Late-summer rose petals, so pale they were almost white, drifted across the stone with the scents of coastal flora and the strong salt of the sea.

Nicole hadn't caught Westmoore after the lecture, nor had she spotted her on the tour of the art history department.

The last time she'd been to the manor had been the night her family arrived in Estwood a decade ago. Westmoore had been a trusted friend of Nicole's mother, and had agreed to help them where she could. But she hadn't allowed them access to her paintings, not then. Westmoore had claimed it "wasn't the right time" and that Nicole's mother only wanted them to uncover the final clue at some unnamed date. Shortly after, she accepted a teaching position at Oxford, taking some of her paintings with her and leaving the others locked up in the manor. But this year, she'd come back to Estwood University, and the fact she'd agreed to be Nicole's advisor told Nicole that now, finally, must be the time.

She came to the manor's grand doors, tracing the Mermaid-shaped handles, and rang the doorbell, her finger burning from its cool pebble-like press. She clamped her lips together to stop from smiling, reeling that she was finally here.

There was a great echoing clack as the door opened to reveal an older woman with pale skin. She was dressed in a smart navy dress, and Nicole realized she must be the housekeeper.

"Miss Palmer?"

Nicole nodded and the housekeeper moved aside, allowing her entry.

She stepped into the polished stone foyer, the roar of the sea muting as the door closed behind her, and her breath caught as she looked up into the bronze dark. The coving was heavily detailed in gold and marble, while the ceiling itself was a dark depiction of gods and monsters gazing down past a heavy, glittering chandelier.

A little sigh escaped her.

"Please, come this way, the professor is awaiting you in the study."

They headed through an elaborate drawing room and into countless rooms of art and antiques, the myriad of supernatural artifacts winking in the lamplight. Nicole felt like she'd been let loose in a treasure trove and tightened her fingers around the strap of her satchel so she wouldn't start inspecting. If there wasn't art on the walls, there were murals of reclining creatures and mythological characters.

The manor was hushed, other than the sound of the storm outside and the distant crackle of a fire, so Nicole's heeled loafers gently clipped on the polished wood.

Soon enough, they came through a great ballroom with glass doors overlooking onto the beach, and finally reached the study.

Richly furnished, the rectangular room had paintings of supernatural women adorning the wood-paneled walls. Gray silk armchairs shimmered from the glow of the enormous, ornate fireplace, where life-sized stone Nymphs supported its mantel. The fire bathed Nicole in golden heat as she stepped inside, and subtly scented the place with smoke and salt and the stalks of lavender crumbling within. Tall glass doors on the right led out to the sand dunes and were swathed by luxurious curtains. The burnished wood gleamed and the murals between them gave an eternal depth to the room.

And there, sitting in the room's center, backlit by the fire, was Professor Westmoore.

Nicole suddenly felt like she needed to curtsy.

"Thank you, May," Westmoore said to the housekeeper, who nodded and closed the door behind them. "My," the old Seer said, "you look so much like her."

Nicole knew, intellectually, how much she resembled her mother, but meeting a relative stranger who could say that . . .

She swallowed, her throat burning. "Thank you."

Westmoore smiled. "Tell me, Nicole. What is it you hope to discover within my paintings?" The question was gentle, and yet it felt like a test.

She met the professor's eyes, which had the ability to look both piercing and cloudy, then turned to the satchel at her side and gently removed the illustration within.

"This was the last clue we have from my mother." She had always left them clues like this: paintings, sketches, pieces of obscure supernatural history that would lead them from one safe house to the next. Two things had been scrawled on the back of this one in her mother's hand.

"Estwood" and "*divino artista*."

Estwood was easy enough to understand, and when they'd arrived they'd discovered Westmoore, who was not just one of the only other supernaturals in town, but one with a mythological art collection to rival any museum.

The illustration was an exquisite pencil drawing by Marianne H. W. Robilliard from 1909 of a woman on a seashore. In it, the figure's dress and long dark hair were wind-whipped to look like the thin garb of ancient Greek statues.

"Mum talked about *divino artista*, the divine artist, for years. Humans think it has a religious meaning: God—the Divine Artist that created the world. But for us, for supernaturals, it explains why some artists have an intimate relationship with the supernatural world. Writers, poets, painters, sculptors, and symbologists notice things other humans don't, can see and spot creatures, thus paint them like their inhuman counterparts.

"But it also represents supernatural art and any paintings that depict creatures. Your manor is full of them. It's safer and more guarded than the museum and gallery in town. And you knew Mum. She trusted you enough to send us here, I was sure that your collection held the answer. That she'd left something with you. Some . . . piece of information?"

Nicole didn't want to voice her theories too soon. Westmoore was still, despite her help, a stranger.

The professor rose and went to a panel in the wall where a door had been cleverly hidden by a painted fold of red drapery.

"Come, I have something to show you."

A dull click sounded, and then part of the wall swung back. Nicole glimpsed weak moonlight streaming into the colossal, dark space and glinting off gold frames. Curiosity and unease swirled in her stomach. And then she felt it: the supernatural essence of the artworks like a wall of power.

"Welcome, Nicole, to my gallery."

Westmoore flicked a switch, and lamps about the room slowly gleamed to life.

Around and above were several mezzanines containing thousands of books. She'd never been around this many nonhuman publications before. To buy them you needed to use your supernatural ID,

26

to ensure information about supernatural history didn't end up in human hands. She could make out three more stories, two great chandeliers splintering light. Multiple silk-upholstered seating areas made up reading spaces, and golden, glass-boxed Celtic artifacts glinted on the shelves.

Nicole looked up to discover a fresco of a supernatural apocalypse on the ceiling: swirling creatures and heavens and gods, the Wild Hunt raging to life at its edges. On the wall opposite were several glass doors leading onto the beach, and another door she noticed in the paneling to her left must lead to Westmoore's private rooms.

But the real allure was the paintings.

At each interval between the dark, glossy bookshelves was a painting, gently illuminated with a picture-light. The gold frames were all engraved with supernatural and Celtic patterns. There was a painting of winged boys with curling horns peeking through their tousled hair; one with a flush of copper wings, the other with small, budding teal ones. Another painting showed a trio of nude Nymphs tugging a Satyr into ancient woods. Then, nineteenth-century paintings of Mermaids, all languid and lovely, their heavy tails like a spill of silver coins.

A sudden, powerful sense of belonging stole her breath. It was like the paintings were watching her; recognized her as one of them. They preened, full of secrets and details to interpret.

I'm here. Tell me everything.

But amid the paintings of creatures, there were others that drew her focus. Scenes from the *Metamorphoses*, the ancient Roman stories of transformation. And painting after painting of—

"It's a timeline," Nicole said softly, "of Empyrean history?" She turned to the professor for confirmation and saw a small smile on her lips.

Westmoore began to walk around the room, taking them past paintings of the Dark Ages, past images of Druids and Sirens, then to Empyreals transforming, hunting, and being inducted into the Wake—kneeling in columned, temple-like spaces.

Two millennia ago, the Wake had risen, believed to consist of powerful supernaturals with the desire to keep the world safe from deadly creatures. They had searched out and practically collected Empyreals for their cause. Their argument being they could help Empyreals, and would pay them for their missions, grant them resources and connections to better travel and hunt. In return, Empyreals would swear fealty to them. Now, the Wake was the most powerful organization in the world, and every discovered Empyreal joined their ranks of loyal hunters.

"I curated this collection carefully over many years. Supernatural history is well guarded by the Wake, as I'm sure you've discovered in your mother's books. They use art as propaganda, yes, but they have done things to keep control of our society that would shock you. Atrocities, assassinations. And of course, collecting every Empyreal they could find to hunt for them.

"Your mother knew that one day the truth would need to be outed, so we curated the collection together, carefully choosing pieces that spelled out this hidden history or commissioning artists to paint special pieces.

"But, Nicole, this collection holds much more promise than a single clue. This is not the location of another safe house."

There it was, the very thing Nicole had suspected.

"The Wake will do anything for these paintings and their secrets, do you understand?"

After the night her mother was murdered, Nicole knew that

28

better than anyone. She nodded softly. "The only thing I can't understand is, why now? Why didn't you let us see it sooner?"

"My dear, you were all but eight when you arrived in Estwood. And though your father is more than capable, your mother distilled something in you. I don't know if she hid it in your mind through the things she taught you, or left it for you to unravel. I couldn't tell you because I don't know what it is. That, and the Wake know of me, so I couldn't risk communicating with you until a certain point in case they ever sent anyone to check up on me. Hence why I've spent the last decade in another town.

"Your mother made it very clear, and I agreed with her, that this art could only be revealed to the public at a certain point in our history, and that you wouldn't be able to uncover the truth behind her message until then. It has taken centuries to put the right people and information in the right places to try and guarantee the events that will come forth. To make sure they lead to success, over defeat."

Nicole frowned. Success? Defeat? Relief swooped through her stomach at the thought she was right, but it swiftly morphed into worry.

"I say this to make sure you understand," Westmoore continued. "To make sure you're ready, and to tell you that whatever this information is, you could use it to barter for your own safety one day. Your mother has hidden a secret so far-reaching and ancient that it could threaten an institution like the Wake. A supernatural art conspiracy kept alive and secret through centuries.

"But the Wake are killing in search of it. Collectors. Creators. Anyone who still remembers the ancient truths or wishes to share and unearth long-slumbering legends. So, I have no more time to wait."

Dread pooled through Nicole. "Do they know about you? Are you in some kind of danger?"

Westmoore waved a hand. "No more than any other time in my life. You make a surprising number of enemies collecting artwork."

Nicole thought of the night her mother was murdered—murdered for . . . this secret?

She felt a dark tremor of reluctance. If she uncovered this, what would stop the Wake from killing her, too? But then, her family lived in hiding because of that very concept: the idea that if the Wake discovered who and where they were, they would assume her mother had passed this information on to them.

The night her mother was killed, Nicole, Dylan, and Bells had been hidden by her mother's Influence. The Wake's Empyreal had been in the room with them and not seen or heard them. They'd survived for their father to come home and discover not just his three crying children, but that his wife was dead and her body taken.

Nicole looked at Westmoore's paintings. If the Wake would hunt them down anyway and kill them, believing her mother had passed on that dangerous information, it was better if Nicole actually had it and the promise of using it.

"Why did you do all this?" she asked. "Keep these paintings? Agree to help us if it put you in danger?"

The professor's eyes softened, and she looked out over the collection. "Your mother saved my life once, a long time ago. And the Wake are not the paragon of safety they claim to be. It's time the world knew."

"Is that why you're allowing the painting to be shown at the museum?"

Westmoore inclined her head slightly. "Partly."

Nicole realized they'd come to the end of the timeline and found herself standing before *The Wild Hunt*. It was enormous—a sprawling, wicked piece that made it seem as if the Empyreals within could pour from the canvas.

Humans had sensed the violent edges of Empyreals' hunts in the past and written of their wildness. Because they were hidden to humans, hunts were thought to be the haunt of spirits, and yet they were frequent enough that the idea of a supernatural predator had permeated the folkloric psyche, resulting in stories that led to paintings like this. It was a truth despite the ages. A truth that waited, sleeping in its legendary essence, inside Nicole, too.

She'd expected to feel intrigue when finally faced with the painting; instead, Nicole found herself completely bewitched, almost unnerved.

But there was another piece beside it, like some dark, violent secret that opened that maw wider.

"Is this a *Bouguereau*?" Nicole's lips parted as she came to stand before the scene from hell. In it, two nude men were fighting, one with red hair, the other dark. They were locked in a vicious embrace with the fire-toned light of hell around them and a winged creature swooping above. It was dynamic, aggressive, and she could barely look away.

"William-Adolphe Bouguereau's *Dante and Virgil*, yes."

"I thought this was in the Musée d'Orsay. In Paris?"

Westmoore gave a quiet chuckle. "A *copy* is there, one safe for the humans to view."

Nicole's brows rose. There were many supernatural paintings out in the public, painted both by creatures or humans who knew about their world, the most famous being the *Mona Lisa*. Humans just had no idea.

But the longer she examined this Empyreal painting, the more her supernaturally heightened senses began to make out its shimmering glass-like pane of supernatural varnish. Layered over paintings, supernatural varnishes could keep the true appearance of creatures hidden from human eyes. Some were posthumously varnished, if a human painter had stumbled onto a creature and their painting would have exposed them, but most were varnished by the artists themselves. It changed anything from a figure's eye color to its entire form and was how supernatural stories had been passed down through the ages, with variations and levels of magical varnish. Some had been designed so only the owner of the painting could see the true image beneath; some allowed every creature true sight but kept humans oblivious—like the paintings in famous museums around the world.

The varnish in *Dante and Virgil* cracked like old paint under her gaze and the ghost of another painting appeared beneath.

Two key differences became apparent.

The dark-haired man losing the fight now had a twisted gold ornament around his neck that glinted, intricately made: a torc. And the vicious red-haired man had his almost clawed hands around it, to tear it off.

Nicole's eyes began to burn. Unnerved, she wiped one, trying to concentrate, until ice shot through her body. The world tilted sharply, and she was thrown from the present into the past with such intensity, she lost her breath in the process.

Visions didn't plague her the way they did her sister, so Nicole was never quite prepared for the bloody veins they would paint in her eyes, nor the feeling of being dragged by the throat into another time and place.

Her boots slammed into the give of soil as air rushed back into her lungs. She sucked in a breath, scenting blood and earth and musk.

Her sketchbook was gone, her bag, the gallery.

Her *time*.

She scoured her new surroundings.

Amber grass scratched at her legs and dampened her clothes. A mist thick with an unnerving tinge of magic transformed hills and boulders into looming shapes. Horrified, terrified screams raced through the void around her. Nicole spun, trying to track the sounds.

Then she felt someone charging toward her, sensed the strength in their body, could hear cries and groans as they cleaved a path through enemies that were little but shapes in the mist.

And then he burst through the white.

Nicole froze as the violence of his being shuddered over her, forcing her to stare up at his height.

He stilled in the clearing, his bare chest heaving with deep barreling breaths, his dark hair partially braided. Blood spattered in frantic handprints over the brush of hair on his chest, like someone had either gripped him for help while dying, or to try and stop him from killing them.

A gold torc sat around his neck, winking in the dim, supernatural gloom.

It wasn't his barbaric appearance that made her stomach clench and the Empyreal inside her bristle with anticipation, but the dark fire of his eyes; the wild passion in that unnervingly direct gaze that made her body throb with the ratcheting of her heart.

A bolt of heat went through her as he met her gaze, and it cooled to panic as a frown deepened in his brow. As if he saw her and couldn't understand why.

The stranger's eyes warned her of his movement before the muscles in his thighs jumped with a step closer.

Then he began to move.

To *stalk*.

Nicole's instincts kicked in like a slap. She reached for the hilt of a blade stabbed into the ground beside her. Her heart was beating so frantically she couldn't make out any other sound.

He couldn't see her. It wasn't possible. No vision allowed a Seer to be seen.

Yet he was looking *right at her*.

He closed the distance between them, his chest heaving millimeters from her face. Sweat rolled down the thick muscles of his chest, streaking through the dirt and blood. Wicked heat rolled off him. The taste of blood and supernatural power prickled across her tongue. Now, she could see that he wasn't as old as he'd appeared, slick with battle and simmering with fury. He was a few years older than her, at most. And there was agony in his eyes along with suspicion. Youth; a tinge of mercenary magic.

And a worry that speared her like a blade.

Nicole's lips parted—to speak? She didn't know what she'd say.

And then he was gone.

Nicole slammed back into herself with a force that had her staggering backward. She hissed at the stinging in her eyes, before blinking at the floor, her teary vision clearing to see her satchel lying by her boots on the dark red carpet.

A soft hand on her shoulder made her whip out to grab their

wrist, immediately clamping on the thin arm of the professor.

Westmoore Manor.

She was here, safe, and being guided to a luxurious chair in the gallery room.

Nicole released Westmoore gently, cursing herself for losing track of her surroundings. What if she'd hurt her? "I'm sorry, I—"

"Are your visions usually so intense?"

Nicole swallowed. "No. I . . . I barely ever have any. Bells and Dad are the Seers; this doesn't usually happen." Her heart hadn't yet calmed, and she clutched at the delicate wooden arm of the chair with clammy fingers.

"May I?" asked Westmoore, her hand hovering near Nicole's temple.

Seers and a few other creatures could view a Seer's visions through physical touch. Nicole tried to speak, but her throat was too tight. She gave a small nod, getting her bearings as Westmoore's cool fingers brushed her temple, and the old Seer's eyes went blood-dark with Sight.

Nicole tried to manage her breathing while the vision played out for Westmoore.

"I see," the professor said softly.

"Who . . ." Nicole tried, swallowing hard. "Who was that? I didn't realize this painting depicted someone real."

But Westmoore gasped in a breath as other images overcame Nicole, these from Westmoore's mind as a vision took over the professor.

Someone reaching out, pleading, their fingers singed, trying to pull their priceless paintings from the burning wreck of their house—

They disappeared as Westmoore snatched her hand from Nicole.

Nicole pushed up. "Professor, are you all right?"

The vision still raced behind Westmoore's blood-dark eyes for a few moments, and when she blinked, she looked suddenly weak. She reached for the glossy table behind her and Nicole went to help her, but Westmoore waved her off with a faint smile.

"I think that's enough for tonight."

"But what did you see? Is someone in danger?"

Westmoore gave a tight smile. "Don't worry about that, it . . . it wasn't for your eyes."

Perhaps not, but she'd still seen it.

"Here." Westmoore dug something from a deep pocket and then placed a cool, ancient key in Nicole's hands. "Tomorrow you'll begin. I've organized with the museum that you'll have full access to *The Wild Hunt*, so you'll be able to work on your dissertation and this research. This art is intertwined with the past, the present, and the promise of a future. Use this key to stay in the manor for as many nights as you need to find the answer. But for tonight, go."

Nicole stared, the key warming in her palm. Stay in the manor? They had been due to research together at night as well as in Nicole's free periods thanks to her busy daily schedule, but—

She nearly asked more, but took in the professor's wearied posture. Nicole backed up. When her sister or father had visions of death, sometimes they needed to be alone to recalibrate. So, she nodded gently and picked up her satchel from where it had fallen, the illustration and her mother's words spilled out onto the floor.

"I'll see you tomorrow," Nicole said. "And thank you, Professor."

Westmoore's veined eyes met hers, and she gave a soft smile. "Remember what your mother taught you, and trust yourself, my girl. No doubting."

Heat pricked the backs of her eyes. She turned and walked shakily through the dark manor, past its moonlit artifacts and flashes of luxury.

When she burst outside, she felt breathless, trapped by the lure of history and visions of a two-thousand-year-old artifact. She took a deep breath of coastal air, despite being immediately pelted by warm rain. Then reached up, absently, to her throat, where the heavy torc had sat around the warrior's throat; a throat corded with muscle.

As if he would release either a roar of battle, or something vicious and intimate.

Nicole had known Westmoore's paintings would hold secret messages, but she had never had visions looking at art before. They'd had to piece together the history behind paintings and artists with the knowledge they'd gleaned from human and supernatural lore. Evidently, she would need both to uncover the spiral of mysteries in the collection.

She looked down at the ancient key in her palm. Perhaps staying at the manor would be a good idea. That way she could research the paintings all hours of the night, too. Resolved, she headed for the car. Tomorrow, when she was feeling less shaky, she'd find out what Westmoore had seen and make sure she was all right.

But tonight . . . tonight she'd been given a glimpse into an artistic conspiracy that spanned thousands of years. That could repaint their world.

So she put aside her unease, and drove through the glinting dark toward home.

4 Kyan

At 3:15 in the morning, Kyan was summoned to the Wake's Liverpool headquarters.

St. George's Hall sat amid the modern city like an ancient temple, the sky above inky with clouds and a few bright stars despite the distant rumble of thunder. Its pale columns had been a steadfast visual over the years as the city curled and changed around it. Now, traffic, giant electronic billboards, and a train station of steel and glass gleamed opposite.

Kyan ascended the steps and angled his scarred forearm to the giant gilded doors, which opened soundlessly to reveal the ornate hall. He'd been here earlier, to debrief and wash away the energy of the previous hunt in the Wake's secret underground baths, but they had been waiting for confirmation about another mission before assigning it to him.

He'd bided his time in the Philharmonic pub, wanting a few quiet hours nursing a pint. The historic bar had been populated by creatures as well as humans. That hadn't been a problem, until a group of Empyreals began needling him, calling him the name they gave him for being the best of them: the Wake's dog.

He didn't care about their opinions, but he did care that the name reminded him too much of a title from his past. One he'd tried to train himself to forget.

To a degree, they were right about him.

He preferred the eternal hunt.

But while other Empyreals might have hunted for the thrill or the power, Kyan hunted to protect.

He strode over the circular mosaics, beneath the vaulted ceiling and past columns of red granite, and came to the end of the hall where two statues of the Greek Titan Atlas held up a platform. On it were three awaiting Messengers.

Used as go-betweens—as no one had ever met the leaders of the Wake—the Messengers were unnaturally still in the low light. Though they looked human, they were as unnerving as the dead and almost as quiet, with no pulse to give them away and no physicality. Kyan had walked through one many a time.

He knelt, the stained-glass window of Saint George slaying the dragon behind him.

"Location?" Kyan asked of the staid, holographic-like beings.

"Estwood, Cornwall."

"Creature?"

"A Specter. Michael Lynch. He's evaded three other Empyreals and all attempts at imprisonment. Vicious, smart, and deadly. We need our best."

Kyan looked up. *Their best. The Wake's dog.* He'd become so out of necessity, out of the desire to never repeat past mistakes and by trusting his power. Because if he'd been quicker, if he'd only listened harder to his Empyreal, maybe his mother would still be alive.

He recalled the feeling of bathing away his previous mission, cleansing him for the next one. The water had stroked up his face and head, lifting his hair, lightening the weight and ghosting his scalp like his mother's braiding fingers. He'd recalled her Druid magic and the sacred patterns of life and history she'd taught him and sunk deeper. When he'd reemerged, it felt like an almost emotionless, ruthless return to purpose.

He went to rise.

"There's one more thing. There's a supernatural painting that must be secured at your new base. Your instructions and new identity have already been sent to your phone. This is to be kept quiet."

His interest flickered. Art had been a part of his missions before, even his last one in Liverpool. But it often made a situation more complicated, brought in more eventualities and need for control, all of which Kyan had experience with.

He inclined his head and accepted his latest hunt.

"Consider it done."

5 NICOLE

The beach had been washed clean by last night's storm, so Nicole's six a.m. jog was over sand as golden as an ancient artifact, packed wet and compact.

To her right, waves crashed along the curved shore, their steady rhythm matching her heart and the push and pull of her breath. The sky was beginning its slow metamorphosis from a soft rose dawn into blue, tinged out over the water with the violet memory of a late-September storm. It beat back the dark, smoothing away the essence of the supernatural that had haunted her after coming home from Westmoore Manor.

She'd barely slept, dreaming instead of the warrior from the vision, embers of burning paintings swirling around him.

It had startled her awake earlier than usual with fingers of heat.

Now, she paused atop a sand dune and looked around the sweeping beach, the imprint of a waning crescent still above, and took in the rhythm of the sleepy university town that had stolen her heart. Seeing that all was well, she berated herself for feeling tense and skidded back down the sand dune.

She'd already been jogging for an hour and hadn't broken a sweat. Her legs worked without strain as she hiked up the next dune, each stride sure, but then, there wasn't much in this town that would strain her. Here, there was no vicious risk of discovery, no temptation of transformation. Just the academic quiet, the cobbled streets, and the ancient comfort of the sea.

In other words, it was perfect.

Nicole cut up into the next bank of dunes. Sand shifted beneath her, marram grass needling her thighs through the sleek dark training gear. She came to stop at its peak and sucked in a great breath of cool morning air, her long, dark ponytail whipping in the wind.

A prickle of awareness had her turning to find her brother jogging toward her.

"And here I thought I could catch you distracted." He said it with a grin, but she could tell he was relieved that, even though they'd spent ten safe years here, her senses were still sharp.

Dylan's dark gold hair was mussed by the wind as he smoothly hiked up the dune. He wore similar dark, sleeveless workout gear which exposed his toned form, tanned after a long summer. While he looked like their little sister and father, Nicole was the dark-haired twin to their lost mother.

Nicole smiled back. "Hoping to spring another surprise attack?"

Dylan grinned and his eyes, the steely blue of the coast in shadow, warmed. He was classically handsome in a way that intimidated most people, with the same full lips they all shared. But when he let his defenses down enough to smile, it softened those sharp edges.

"It's good to be prepared," he said.

She gave him an arch look. "You don't need to tell me that, Dylan."

He looked back out over the beach, and said, almost too quietly for her to hear, "Still."

Dylan had been the least interested in their mother's final clue. Every time Nicole mentioned it, he went cold. It was traumatic for him, the memory of their mother, but then he was the one that remembered her death the most clearly. Now, he didn't want them getting embroiled in *anything* that could threaten their tentative safety, even something as promising as this clue.

But Nicole was convinced it could keep them safe forever.

Her lips parted to say more, to try, for the hundredth time, to drum into him that they were able to consider this place their home. That they were in a position of power here: safe and within reach of an answer. Even if a creature did pass through the wards Remi's mother, Lawna, had placed on the entry points around the town's boundaries, they had multiple protocols to manage them. It was a hell of a lot better than living in a city where they couldn't control the variables of the many supernaturals living hidden among humans; where it was harder to avoid coming across a dangerous one that could trigger her or Dylan. If that happened, if they had their first transformation, and the Wake found them . . .

They won't, she reminded herself, tugging her cap back down to shield her eyes from the rising sun. They hadn't had a run-in with the Wake since that fateful night.

And Nicole would do anything to make sure that if they ever came across another Empyreal again, they'd all come out of it alive this time.

Her heightened senses distracted her for a moment, picking up a car full of students driving down the winding coastal path into town, a new summer track and their laughter carrying on the wind.

Nicole sighed, thinking of her own classes later.

"You know," she said, forcing the tone to shift. She snatched up a bit of sea grass and ran it through her fingers. "I saw that Tomás is taking some of the same classes as me—"

Dylan looked at her sharply at the mention of his ex-boyfriend. "So?"

Nicole hiked slightly up the sand dune to be closer to his tall frame. "We've been safe here for so long. Now I have access to the art." Nicole turned, scanning the array of great coastal houses, skipping over the little fisherman's hut she used as a painting studio out on the dunes, until she spotted Westmoore Manor. The closest to the sea, it sat sheathed in morning light, its windows glinting.

Nicole turned back to her brother. "You don't need to break things off with every person that manages to get close to you."

Dylan's fingers rubbed together—an anxious habit he had when he had no dough or pastries to work with, no baking to keep his mind calm, like Nicole with her painting.

For a moment, she thought she'd gotten through to him.

"Let's just see, shall we?" He nudged her shoulder with his elbow and grinned. "Race you back to the house. If you can keep up."

He sped down the dune and Nicole cursed, skidding nimbly after him and beginning the run home.

She caught up swiftly, pushing with a laugh into the suppressed inhuman speed she usually kept locked away. With so few humans on the beach, she could indulge for a few minutes. If they'd have jogged past their house, the beachfront homes would have become older and more extravagant until they reached historic, sea-view mansions like Westmoore Manor. But when the ground solidified from the coastal paths to wide, tree-lined roads, she made sure to slow to a human's pace.

Nicole waved to those few neighbors who were already about

in their pre-autumn gardens or walking dogs, while Dylan gave the occasional curt nod.

Their house looked like many other homes along the street, if not a bit more modern. Its exterior was painted white, and its black-framed windows gleamed. A pretty balcony sat outside Nicole's bedroom. But hidden within the French doors and hardwood floors was soundproofing and bulletproofing, their garage had all the latest training equipment, and their hidden library had a wealth of information on every known and unknown supernatural creature in the world.

Nicole darted past the waist-high bushes of white hydrangeas and fragrant lavender, squeezing between the neighbor's garden wall and their garage before Dylan could. Then slammed her palm onto the hidden access pad.

"Beat you," she said with a laugh.

"I was weighed down," Dylan said as he kicked off his sandy running shoes.

She scoffed. "By what?" The pad clicked, and she pulled open the glass door to their gym.

The moment she did, Dylan dived.

Nicole dodged quickly, expecting his surprise attack now they were back in the house.

She glimpsed the garage space, sleek and white, mats on the ground and a wall of mirrors on her left with row after row of weights. Her brother kicked out his legs in a quick, smooth arc, hoping to take her down. Nicole jumped over them and swung around the boxing dummy.

Dylan punched it from one side, and it lurched toward her with a rubber shudder, the nails that kept it reinforced to the floor to withstand their supernatural strength screeching with strain.

Nicole used the moment to drop low and dart back out. She jumped up and grabbed him from behind, getting her legs around his back and hands around his neck.

"Dead," she whispered.

There were only two things that could kill Empyreals: being killed when they'd taken on another creature's weaknesses during a transformation—which was practically unheard of, as they became a prime specimen of that species.

Or another Empyreal.

Only another of their kind was strong and fast enough to inflict a fatal wound, like breaking the neck. It was the way they'd suspected her mother had been killed. A quick, visceral horror caught in her chest at the flash of memory, and Nicole shoved the thought away quickly, but it gave Dylan a moment to hook his foot beneath a broken bar she'd used too much strength on last week.

He kicked it up into his hand and her breath caught as he angled it back over his shoulder and aimed it at her throat. The cold, sharp edge pressed into her skin, but didn't puncture.

They'd trained with weapons before, but not surprise ones.

"Always expect them to have some kind of angle," Dylan said, strained.

"Empyreals don't need weapons," Nicole panted. "We are the weapon."

"That doesn't mean they won't use whatever advantage they can. The Wake train them to be ruthless."

Nicole released her grip to drop back to the floor, but as she moved a quick slice of pain scraped her throat.

Dylan threw down the bar and spun to face her. "Are you all right?"

Nicole's feet met the mat as a bead of blood welled up at her neck.

She wiped at the cut, finding it had already healed. Though neither of them had had their first transformations, they possessed all the other Empyrean abilities: heightened speed, strength, hearing, and healing. And the extremely useful skill, the power to Influence: a form of mind-control like a Vampire's glamour.

"Don't worry," Nicole said, reading the guilt in his eyes. He was right to surprise her with things like this. They needed to be prepared for anything. He shouldn't hold back, and neither should she, they'd just be doing a disservice to one another.

"I'm fine, see? Not a scratch."

His jaw worked, angry at himself. She knew what he'd be thinking: *I should have controlled my strength better, I should have—*

But that was one of the reasons he worked as a trainer in the local gym, to know how a range of humans moved, know their strengths, so they could better blend in.

Nicole stepped over and hugged him. "Good session," she said into his chest. "But maybe let's not try this method on Bells, okay?"

Dylan relaxed with a laugh, his arms circling her. "Deal." He squeezed slightly and held on a moment longer to apologize.

The echo of those old bruises on her arm where he'd held her when their mother was murdered pulsed with a dull ache. He'd gripped her so tightly that night; had tried to cover her eyes as she clutched Bells, who was barely a year old.

Had warned her not to look.

"We're a team," she said against his arm. "Unconquerable."

Dylan pulled back. "Always." But a shadow darkened his eyes at the word. Empyreals were supposed to be immortal.

And yet their mother was gone.

He forced a smile. "Let's go. I heard Bells asking Dad last night if we had blueberries for pancakes."

He headed up the few steps to the adjoining kitchen door. As it opened, the metallic scents of the gym dispersed with the soothing scents of home, Bells's tea, and . . . burning?

Nicole gave her brother a knowing look.

"What are you making, Bells?" Nicole asked as they came into the kitchen.

Their fifteen-year-old sister looked up from a lightly smoking pan, her doe-colored brows pulled together in concern, her dreamer's eyes blinking. She stood in the middle of the pale gray kitchen, drenched in morning light from the front bay windows, backlit like a Da Vinci sketch. If Dylan looked like an avenging angel, Bells was as pretty as a grown cherub.

Right now, her sister's creamy skin was flushed, her dark gold hair loosely braided as she searched the white countertop, covered with bowls, flour, eggs, a tumble of blueberries, and a dripping whisk.

"I was trying to make celebratory pancakes for your first proper day working with Westmoore, but . . . something went wrong." Bells brushed her cheek with the back of her hand, smearing it with flour.

Nicole was struck by a glow of love. "They smell great," she lied.

To their right, past the fridge, the room led into an attached greenhouse where Nicole could hear their father pottering. On the other wall, a sweeping archway revealed the hall and living room. All soft shades of cream and white, the house had a perpetual sense of comfort with its dented cushions on the couch, countless art sketches on the coffee table, and an array of crystals.

"Why don't I do that?" Dylan offered, going over to Bells. He looked enormous next to her, over a foot taller than her petite five-foot frame. He gently nudged her away from the bowl, and she drifted to her pink mug of pale tea instead, frowning as she took a sip, no doubt finding it cold. Her glossy plait was loose from sleeping, so the trailing ribbon at the end fluttered as she walked.

"Did you manage any sleep?" Nicole asked, cold marble sticking to her forearms as she leaned on the counter.

"The usual," Bells said, avoiding the question.

That and the subtle purple beneath her sister's eyes told Nicole that Bells had barely slept at all. As a Seer, Bells was like unwritten parchment, old and new at the same time, plagued by strange, intense dreams and visions: a palimpsest of a girl, lovely as a dusk or dawn and just as haunted.

"What did you see?" Nicole asked.

Bells's visions were usually obscure, dark, and thankfully tended not to be related to the family. But Seers didn't often see clues into their own lives, mainly other people's.

"Paintings burning," Bells said softly. "But they—" Her delicate throat worked. "The owners of the paintings were being killed, too. And burning with them."

Unease prickled Nicole's skin at the similarity to Westmoore's vision. She could imagine it all too easily: the bubbling oils, the bleed of varnish and paint, the gold leaf peeling, gilded frames snapping like broken bones. . . .

She took Bells's hand, finding it cool and soft, and stroked it, trying to bring back the warmth. "I'll find out more from Westmoore today. Don't worry, okay?"

Bells nodded, distracted, and Nicole felt that eternal resolve harden.

She would do anything to keep them safe.

Determined to soothe her sister, Nicole headed to the coffee machine, picked up one of the singed pancakes on the way, and took a big bite as she turned it on.

"Delicious!" she said, around the claggy middle.

Bells smiled, perking up slightly as she hiked onto one of the kitchen stools.

"Nicole, why is there blood on your neck?" came their father's gentle voice.

She turned as he walked up the few steps from the greenhouse, cuttings in hand. He brought a light warmth with him from the sun-baked room and the faint, bitter scent of the mutant herb he grew for their tonics.

Though their father was tall, toned, and looked to be somewhere in his forties, Ronan Palmer was actually a 978-year-old Seer. The only hint was a brush of silver in his light-brown hair. He met her eyes with concern, his a more storm blue than the color her siblings shared.

Bells's tired gaze snapped to Nicole's neck immediately. "What happened?"

Nicole looked down at the smear on her fingers. "Ah, we did a quick session in the gym."

Their father arched a brow as he dropped two of the curling red petals into a mortar on the kitchen's central island. "I thought I told you two to take the morning off and sleep in?"

Dylan shrugged. "I like our jogs. Besides, this one"—he nodded at Nicole—"was pacing around the library till the wee hours of the morning, so I could hardly sleep for all the noise."

Nicole sent him a smirk. "I like to be prepared."

He grinned. "So do I."

She laughed, washing off the blood, the cool trail of water down her neck dampening the collar of her workout top. "I was trying to figure out if the vision was a clue, but no luck."

"How does art threaten something like the Wake?" Bells asked, shaking her head.

"Well, in the human world art is propaganda," Nicole said. "It was used by the Church to teach illiterate people the stories of the Bible, steeping them in their faith. And royalty, of course: look at the paintings of kings and queens throughout history. Art showed off the might of a country, certain symbols chosen to portray power, religion. Supernatural art is used to tell stories, real histories that humans think are myth, but it also has secrets painted beneath the varnish."

Like the *Dante* painting.

"Which means that if the paintings were shared, people would get thinking," Dylan said. One more reason he didn't want them looking into it or drawing attention.

"Here," their father said, reaching for the fridge and pulling out their daily tonics. He handed Dylan and Nicole theirs, and Bells hers to help keep her worst visions at bay.

The tonics helped Dylan and Nicole curb their Empyrean natures, affecting their epigenomes and stopping the hormone and chromosome interaction before it triggered a transformation. In case they ever, by some fluke, got near a deadly creature, it would help them resist transforming long enough to get away. But nothing could stop their power unleashing once a creature decided to kill.

Nicole unstopped the chilled glass vial and prepared herself for the bitter taste. She swallowed the thick herbal texture with a grimace.

"Save me some pancakes," Nicole said, "I'm going to shower."

"Don't use all the hot water," Dylan called.

Nicole shook her head with a smile as she headed up the cream-carpeted stairs.

"Try one," Bells said eagerly to Dylan.

"Mmm, better than last time," he said around a mouthful.

Nicole laughed softly.

At the top of the stairs, she glanced to her right, into their library. Usually, the hidden door with its adjoining secret room was sealed off, but Nicole had left it open last night so could see into the large, temperature-controlled space with its unusual vaulted ceiling. It was where they stored their most precious items and everything they needed to keep hidden from the Wake: bestiaries full of knowledge, ancient supernatural texts, weapons boxed in glass, paintings, and her mother's handwritten books. Living here for so long had finally given them the space to house more of the collection, having brought items from multiple secret storage places around England.

But the main feature was her mother's portrait above the fireplace.

"Morning, Mum," Nicole said, walking past on the way to her bedroom.

Her room was at the front of the house, and while the balcony doors were shut against the morning breeze, they let in plenty of light, which prevented it from feeling dark, despite the deep burgundy she'd painted the walls.

Her feet sank into the cream carpet as she stepped into what felt like her cave of mythological treasures. Books on folklore and nineteenth-century art were piled in most corners, and posters of mythological paintings were framed on the walls. Her mother's jacket hung proudly on one of the wardrobe's crystal handles, a pair of heels beneath it with an overnight bag she'd packed after West-moore had told her she could stay nights in the manor.

Nicole perched on the edge of her bed and picked up her mother's old copy of the *Metamorphoses*, where it lay open on the white sheets. It was a very delicate copy, with its cover precariously hanging on, easily a hundred years old.

She'd been looking at it the night before as many of West-moore's paintings seemed to depict scenes from the ancient tales. Nicole opened it again, finding her mother's inscription on the first page and the quote that had always unnerved her.

The secret art to transformation, is death.

Nicole sighed, stroking over the script, mentally promising her mother that she'd find the answer.

Her phone brightened on her bedside and Nicole reached over, finding a ranting series of messages from Remi about accidentally seeing a spoiler for their favorite show and an email . . . from the curator? She huffed, preparing herself, but when she read the curt few lines, she went cold with dread.

She'd planned for everything.

Except this.

6 NICOLE

A short September rain had turned the flagstones to dark, gleaming mirrors as Nicole hurried up the steps of the museum and burst inside.

She discovered the curator hightailing toward the back entrance, which happened to be directly in her path. He cursed when he saw her, and promptly swerved around.

Nicole launched after him. "Mr. Alborough!"

"Nicole, I can't discuss this right now."

She hauled the overnight bag over the strap of her satchel, as if to waggle it before him and prove that he was wrong.

"What did you mean: '*The Wild Hunt* is no longer available for your research'?" Was Westmoore unhappy with something she'd said and changed her mind? Had the vision of burning paintings spooked her? Why else would this happen? Surely she would have told Nicole personally, not through the curator.

The museum was almost empty this early, the place echoing and colossal. Sculptures she'd sketched hundreds of times flashed past as she followed him through the marble exhibit.

Nicole forced herself to slow as she darted fluidly beneath the high, arched halls and around the figures. Her satchel dug into her shoulder, the heavy art books inside slamming against her thigh. She had everything she'd need to begin researching between lectures—floor plans, sketch pads, multiple pencils (even though she was sure to use her laptop), and of course, one of her mother's bestiaries in case a supernatural in the paintings defied her knowledge.

But evidently, that research might not even be happening.

"All actions with Professor Westmoore's paintings have been halted," he said, over his shoulder.

Stunned, Nicole could only gape.

"Which includes loaning *The Wild Hunt* to the museum, so that means you're no longer involved. I'm going to the manor now. It's a nightmare, a great loss."

Nicole didn't care that it was a nightmare for the museum, it was a nightmare for *her*.

A spark of panic flared in her gut, reminding her of the vision Westmoore had last night: burning paintings. If she didn't get to see them . . .

I will.

"Sir," Nicole began calmly. "There must be some mistake—"

"I'm sorry, Miss Palmer, but it's not going to happen, her nephew has decided."

Nicole halted on the rickety parquet, her instincts sparking with unease. "Her *nephew*? Professor Westmoore doesn't have any family."

"I can confirm that she does, and he's due at the manor"—he checked his watch and glanced over his shoulder—"any minute now. Maybe you can convince him to continue his aunt's wishes. Perhaps the poor man won't mind sixteen emails each week."

Embarrassment warmed her cheeks. It swiftly sharpened into annoyance.

Make him give it to you.

Nicole startled at the whispered temptation. She hadn't Influenced anyone in years. But if the curator wasn't going to properly explain what the hell was going on, then she'd just speak to Westmoore herself. After what the professor had revealed last night, how could she go back on her word now?

The curator stopped and turned to her fully. "Really, Miss Palmer. This is so unprofessional, on today of all days."

Exasperation had her huffing. "What are you talking about?"

He blinked. "You don't know yet?"

Nicole shook her head. Had she missed something in the email?

The irritation on his face faded as pity and regret replaced it. "I'm sorry, Nicole. Professor Westmoore is dead."

For a long moment, his words didn't register.

Dead.

Nicole tried to swallow but found her throat too tight. "I don't understand. I—I saw her last night. She was fine."

"It was a heart attack, I'm afraid, quite sudden."

A wave of surprising grief took her breath away. Westmoore was . . . dead?

Gone?

"No," Nicole whispered. That couldn't be right, there'd been some mistake.

The curator reached out and patted her awkwardly on the shoulder. "This is why her nephew is coming to sort everything out. Give it a few days and perhaps we can see. As I say, I'm heading there now to meet him. I'll email you if he has anything more to say."

Nicole stared after the curator as he bumbled back through the museum. When she numbly unlocked her phone to call her father, the first thing she saw was the news already whispered over social media:

Esteemed Professor Rumored Dead

Nicole sank onto one of the gallery benches. It was *true*? A heart attack . . . Could that be possible? Seers could indeed die of natural causes, but still, the timing was suspicious. She'd granted Nicole a key to the manor just before her death, told her to keep coming and researching the collection and its secrets. What if this was just the curator's way of keeping her out of it?

Nicole pushed up shakily. She was going to follow him and find out who this nephew was. Nothing and no one would keep her from finding out what happened, or those paintings. Not if they had the power to change her family's life.

She quickly texted her father to let him know. Likely, he'd take Dylan to the coroner's office to Influence information out of the humans and confirm.

As she burst back into the colossal foyer, a quick, creeping unease overtook her, so intense it almost felt supernatural. Nicole ignored the looming poster of *The Wild Hunt* and headed past the front desk toward the long corridor that housed the curator's office. But as she started down it, the feeling worsened.

Nicole slowed as her skin tightened painfully and all the fine hairs on her body stirred. Warm power awakened from the bottom of her spine, her gut, her *soul*, as if it could flay the human disguise from her skin and reveal the immortal canvas beneath.

The predator.

She'd *never* felt her power before. Not like this. But then she'd never been close enough to a creature that could trigger her transformation. Only ones that meant to kill out of sadistic or cold-blooded brutality could do that.

It meant one thing: There was a creature in Estwood that called to that ancient, vicious part inside her. The part that wanted to hunt.

That would rip her open to get out.

Remi's mother and Nicole's father had warded the town and its boundaries so that they would know if a creature passed through. Somehow, one must have gotten past their defenses.

Her splintered reflection stared back from the broken glass in the curator's door—her fault, from rapping on it a little too excitedly last week.

And that wicked lure breathed from behind it—

It—whatever *it* was—was in the curator's office.

Nicole scrunched her eyes shut at the heady rush of power, so intoxicating it almost took her breath away. She wrapped her mother's jacket more tightly around herself and tried to calm down. The rough herringbone fabric always reminded her of supernatural academia: parquet, warm whispered mythologies in her ear, and the suggestion of magic. Nicole almost backed up a step.

Then she heard low murmurs from inside the office.

"I'll ask you again, what do they *mean*?" The voice seemed to sink beneath her skin and scrape along her veins. And yet it wasn't ancient. In fact, it sounded young. But the unmistakable energy to the words was what cooled her to the core.

The curator's bumble followed. "I have no idea, that's not my specialty. Really, I must be going, I just forgot my—"

"*Stop.*" The supernatural command would have stilled the curator.

Her breath caught. Whatever type of supernatural it was, it could affect a human's mind.

Nicole caught sight of another poster of *The Wild Hunt* outside the office. That painting represented everything she was afraid of in her power. Its viciousness; its lack of control. But she'd been trained to control hers. And if she found out what type of creature this was, they could wait out its stay in Estwood. They could be prepared. Safe.

She took a silent step closer.

"Well, what about the collection now?" asked the supernatural. "Who has access?"

"I . . . just one of the new undergraduate students. Her name is Nicole Palmer. Westmoore was her advisor."

Nicole stilled. The supernatural was here for Westmoore's paintings. If this had something to do with the professor's vision, she needed to figure out what had really happened. There had been no reports of fire, but that didn't mean there wouldn't be.

Nicole heard a door open and close—the office, she knew, had a separate exit that opened onto the alley outside—and the voices receded. She didn't like the curator—hell, sometimes she could barely tolerate him—but she couldn't leave him to the clutches of some horrific creature. She was in control; she could deal with this. Perhaps if she just called his name, the creature would flee.

Their family protocol in this situation was to let the others know, and retreat immediately. But they'd never been this close to answers before.

Nicole cursed, reaching for the door handle and stabbing out a text to her father:

Something's going on, have you Seen anything?

Then one to Remi:

Have the devices picked anything up? I think there's
    something here.

"Mr. Alborough?" Nicole called warily, letting her overnight bag drop to the office floor in case she needed to move quickly.

She crept out of the museum onto the slick cobbles to discover the sky had clouded over, making the morning feel dark and preternatural. The hairs on the back of her neck rose as a ray of light slashed over the alley with a sharp diagonal shadow, dipping over the cobblestones like ink. *Chiaroscuro*, she distantly noted: a contrast of dark and light.

Nicole rang her father as she drifted closer, fascination, need, and an impossible impulse awakening every muscle. The alley forked ahead, and tendrils of scent drifted down the left passage in an elegant smog. Her hair tousled her cheeks in the supernaturally scented breeze and that deadly lure unfurled in her stomach.

For the first time in her life, power rallied and yearned inside her. It *moved* under her heart where she'd always imagined it to be, almost a being of its own.

Get closer.

Nicole reared forward in a wave.

The phone cut out, and the severed call cut through the pull of her Empyreal.

After calling the family, the next step was always to leave: depart as smoothly and with as little attention drawn to you as possible. She didn't want to leave anyone with a vicious creature, one whose deathly energy called to her so strongly, and yet if she took a step closer, that hunter's thrill would set her on a path she could not go back from.

So, she spun on her heel and abruptly crashed into a wall.

"Shit." Nicole reeled back as a strong hand caught her elbow. She blinked at a broad chest, softened by a dark jumper, realizing she hadn't run into a wall but a person. She looked up, surprised, her neck craning. "I'm sorry, I didn't—"

She was struck by his height first, then the width and shape of his solid, rounded shoulders.

Dread crawled through her as she realized who—*what*—stood in front of her. Not the type of creature she'd expected.

So much worse.

"I wouldn't go down there if I were you," the stranger said, some subtle, lyrical accent in his low, bewitching voice.

The tone was so soothing Nicole immediately recognized the supernatural flutter it set under her skin.

He seemed only a few years older than her, but power shivered over his muscled form—a brute strength, present even in the dark, curious eyes looking down at her.

Eyes laced with suspicion.

His gaze lifted to look down the alley, and it gave her just long enough to peer through the cracks in his facade, like the ghost beneath a painting. The line of his nose was slightly curved—broken and rebroken from years of fighting. His skin was subtly tanned from long hours outside, hunting. His hair short enough that its dark wave didn't fully curl over his brow and a strong jaw that drew his face into an age of primal desires.

But she Saw his past as well as his present. Saw him colliding with warriors and ripping through countless transformations; Saw death and pain and bloodied handprints splayed over his chest. And she realized who he was: the warrior from the painting's vision.

The power inside her reared its head in recognition of another of her kind when his gaze dropped back down to hers.

He was an Empyreal. A rare, immortal hunter owned by the Wake.

The one thing that could ruin her perfectly crafted secret life.

And he had found her.

A line formed between the Empyreal's brows as panic screamed with the impulses in her blood. This was it. He was going to drag her away to be scarred and bound. It was the moment she'd feared her entire life: She would be taken from her family. Made to forget them. Brainwashed into being the Wake's faithful huntress by the people that killed her mother—

Never.

A cool, controlled calm came over her. Her father had trained her for an instance like this; she'd gone through countless scenarios in her head during sleepless nights when the fear from her mother's murder returned. She'd just never expected to uncover both a creature and an Empyreal at the same time. But it was her mother's instructions she recalled.

Pretend.

An Empyreal could usually sense another, but it was almost impossible that he could sense her true nature, because she'd never transformed. That meant he was likely here hunting the creature with the curator, not her.

Nicole tugged her arm to get him to release her. She would fight him if she had to, but it would be better for both of them if she remained inconspicuous.

Thankfully, his frown deepened, and he gently let go. But his eyes were dark and intense, focused on her in a way that made her blood run hot.

"I'll handle it," he said quietly.

Suddenly, she sensed the quiet scrape of footsteps behind them, and her back met the wall of the alley. The Empyreal was in front of her, blocking her view, his hand splayed against the brick wall, his coat creating a dark, warm curtain between her and the approaching creature.

Nicole blinked, finding her own body had reacted in a defensive maneuver and her hand was fisted in his jumper to shove him away. But above the roar of her heart, she realized he wasn't trying to take her anywhere. He was keeping her hidden as the creature returned, making it look like they were nothing but a couple in the shadows.

Through the gap in the Empyreal's coat, she almost saw it as it passed. It was human-looking, but she got no glimpse of a face or even hair color, just black clothes and a smooth gait. Her body locked, her fingers tightening against the Empyreal's chest, suddenly registering the strength beneath. The heat. The fact she was *touching* an Empyreal.

Her senses were immediately overwhelmed. The Empyreal's breath steadily ghosted the top of her head. She looked up from beneath her lashes to find the shape of his jaw above her eyeline and the concerned lock of his eyes. And his *scent*. It nearly stunned her speechless. She couldn't describe its deep masculine tone if she tried, nor the hint of the coffee, and something fresh that cut through it all.

The creature cleared the alley, but it felt like they stayed in their impasse for an eternity.

Then the Empyreal asked the question that had caused them to leave other places and avoid other creatures.

"What are you?"

The last time she'd been asked that, they'd had to flee their homes in the middle of the night.

Nicole made her fingers uncurl, surprised at herself, and tore her eyes from his jumper and the body she'd felt underneath. She moved away shakily. By the way he tracked her she realized that whatever he was becoming was something blooded for the nighttime.

Heat bloomed beneath her skin, stirring her own hunter's instincts, and Nicole wondered if she should run. Because if he figured out what she was, he would hunt her next.

But then his lips parted, and he warned, gently, as if reading her mind: "Don't make me chase you."

7 KYAN

Kyan's senses were heightening with this new hunt, so he could feel everything more palpably than usual as slow transformation tingled up his spine, narrowing every nerve ending and coating his mouth with venom. Shallow puddles reflected the sky and the alley's old walls, misted with moss. Tiny details stood out easily, even in the shadows.

But he could feel his prey best of all, slinking onward through town.

Kyan listened to the creature's steps, the tips of his ears warm as cartilage shifted and snapped, re-forming into subtle points for enhanced night hearing. Kyan inhaled deeply, but no kill hormone coiled in the air, so the curator was safe.

The Specter he was hunting was an unusual breed, perhaps something new—it wasn't uncommon for new supernaturals to be discovered, but it meant that sometimes Kyan didn't even know what he was becoming in response to it. Venom, increased night vision, and a growing hunger for blood were all the Vampire-like traits of a Specter, but there was an underlying feral nature to the transformation that made him realize his prey was powerful, so his body was turning him into something just as vicious.

And then there was her.

The girl lingered, meeting his gaze with confidence. She had daring dark eyes framed by black lashes, but a careful coolness went through them at his question. She wasn't going to tell him what she was. Her reaction when they met had told him enough: she didn't trust him. There were many creatures that—for whatever reason—didn't trust Empyreals. But in a mission like this, with something as volatile and intelligent as the Specter he hunted, Kyan needed other supernaturals to stay out of it.

Before he could ask her again, Kyan sensed movement behind him and the curator appeared from down the alley.

"Nicole?" began the old man, not paying him any attention. "I told you to head back to your classes, I'll discuss your dissertation with Professor Westmoore's nephew—"

Nicole.

That was the name the curator had given to Lynch. The name of the only other person who now had access to Professor Westmoore's art collection. The Specter had been asking about it, about *her*, and if it was going to try to locate her, then it was good Kyan had first.

"That," Kyan interrupted, "would be me."

Nicole's attention was on him like a brand. Most likely she knew his "aunt." Kyan wasn't related to Westmoore in the slightest, but taking a role in her supposed family and stepping in as the new owner of the manor gave him the perfect cover, and the perfect base for his hunt.

The curator blinked, mouth dropping open in surprise as he took him in. "Mr. McCarter? You didn't have to come to the museum, I was just on my way to the manor!"

"It's no problem," he said smoothly. "What's this about a dissertation?"

Confusion and a small amount of irritation had the curator waving the question away, and Kyan couldn't help his own annoyance at the action.

"We don't need to discuss that now: the more important thing is your dear aunt. The museum is so saddened by her passing, and we are honored she chose us to show her painting. I'm assuming that will still be going ahead, as it was one of her final wishes?"

Nicole's eyes narrowed at the man's lack of empathy, her full lips tightening into a line.

"Really, the collection is so unique," continued the curator. "Canceling its move to the museum altogether is surely too extreme—"

"*Be quiet and listen to me carefully,*" Kyan began, Influence limning his words, deepening his accent and allowing that ancient whisper of Irish through. He was suddenly conscious of Nicole watching him with the fascination of a scholar and the elegance of someone remaining collected despite the unusual scenario. He wondered if she'd been around many creatures.

"The move of her artwork will go ahead unless I change my mind. We need a sufficient period of grieving and organization."

"How long?" asked the curator, his resistance lessened.

Kyan barely restrained his answering growl of annoyance. "A week at least."

"But—what about her?"

They both turned to look at Nicole. *Good question.* A twist of her scent on the warm air found him: something darkly sweet and subtly addictive. Kyan's jaw tightened, but the action bled venom through his teeth and along his tongue. Whatever she was, she was adept and brave enough she'd homed in on a creature and come to personally investigate, and now she was embroiled in the artwork the Wake had sent him to secure.

"How well do you know this collection?" he asked her, removing the thread of Influence from his voice.

"I was to begin researching today," she said carefully.

Usually on a mission, he wouldn't interact with the players around his prey. His target couldn't know he was here, which was why he'd initially shielded Nicole to keep both of them inconspicuous. That way the Specter would stalk and go for the kill sooner rather than later, allowing Kyan to do the same—like a paranormal sting operation.

However, the Specter might now turn its attention to Nicole. And if she had crucial information on the collection he needed those answers *now*, before the Specter discovered who she was and stepped into her life to find out what she knew. Or, get them out of her another way if she refused.

In which case, Kyan would be inches away, ready for the kill.

His protective urge reared.

Kyan canted his head slightly, eyes skating over her neck as those new hungers stirred.

"Goodbye, Douglas," he said to the curator, leaving a trace of Influenced order in the dismissal.

The old man huffed and headed back into the museum, muttering about what to tell the museum staff and newspapers, before giving Nicole a departing glare.

"I'm headed to Westmoore Manor," Kyan said to her. "You can either come with me, or we can talk here. I'll give you a minute to decide. Just . . . don't go anywhere."

He ducked into the shadowed interior of the curator's office, his increasingly sensitive eyes immediately adjusting and relaxing.

He retrieved the coffee he'd left on the desk to follow Nicole. Even from the museum coffee shop he'd been able to feel the Specter's power as it undulated through the air, up the curator's nose, and threaded into his brain. Now Kyan was on the hunt, his Empyrean instincts could hone in on him so closely that when he concentrated on his prey it was if he hovered behind it. It happened with every hunt, allowing him to not just know the general area his target was, but also get familiar with its patterns.

Kyan took a sip of his lukewarm drink, cautious of his newly sensitive teeth, which ached with a new flood of venom. It was sweet as syrup and blended quite well with coffee. But, not using the venom for a kill, it went like acid to his stomach.

He pulled out his small, battered notepad and detailed the creature's actions and the stages of his own transformation.

Estwood was a mishmash of Cornish roads and sleek Parisian influence. Laid out in a spiral, its tiny streets coiled off like the septa of a nautilus shell, creating oddly shaped, shaded places for murder and manipulation. The Specter looked human, so the locals of Estwood wouldn't even know to fear it, and a university town was the perfect place for it to nest. It would be easy for the humans to unknowingly write off supernatural manipulation as too much partying, too much stress.

But Kyan would know, and he'd be incapable of stopping the creature until it decided to kill. The longer the Specter waited, the longer Kyan would have to stay, and the more drawn out his transformation.

He took a moment to sink into the familiar rhythm of another hunt, to quiet those new rising hungers and the unusually loud hunter's instinct that had perked up when Nicole's eyes had met his own.

He picked up an old newspaper from the desk—its bold headline reading "Never-Before-Seen Mythological Art to Be Unveiled at Estwood Museum"—and ducked back out into the alley, swiping up the bag Nicole had left on the floor.

She had been pacing, texting someone. Her dark hair spread over her jacket but the wings of her shoulder blades beneath were tense. Her full lips parted before tipping up in a tight smile that didn't meet her eyes.

"I walked into town this morning," she said, "so I suppose we'll have to take your car."

He thought of her unusual scent, glanced once more into eyes that were now guardedly polite and said, with a tilt of his head, "After you."

8 Nicole

The drive to Westmoore Manor was the most uncomfortable, acutely supernatural thing Nicole had ever experienced. The sleek confines of the Empyreal's car accentuated how controlled he seemed. It wasn't a frilly vehicle, it was black and gleaming, like a knife, where he was like a sledgehammer.

Westmoore's nephew.

It was a bald-faced lie.

There was a tracker on her phone, so her family could find her if he tried to drive out of town, but she hadn't been able to let him go on to the manor without going as well, so getting in a car with him was a risk she'd had to take. That vision of Westmoore's she'd glimpsed kept playing in her mind—art, burning. Clearly by taking on this identity, the Empyreal meant to keep every gorgeous mythic oil painting for the Wake. They might be shipped off before she'd even had a chance to study them.

Considering her mother had died for this information, she wasn't going to be kept from that house by anyone, especially not someone who worked for the organization that had killed her.

Nicole had no choice but to smile and follow.

But now she had to convince him to let her stay on and study the paintings, and she couldn't give him a reason to think she had something to hide. It was going to be a delicate balance of seeming open while lying, mixing truth with diversion, and she needed to get to grips with what type of Empyreal he was immediately. Stupid and bulky? That didn't seem the case, despite his size. Ruthless?

She eyed his honed form, noted the new-car smell of his rental.

He wore dark jeans that strained over his thickly muscled legs, and he'd removed his coat and jumper before they'd set off, revealing a charcoal shirt beneath. The sleeves were rolled up slightly to mid-forearm, the tendons shifting as he drove, revealing a curious woven leather bracelet around his wrist in a pattern that looked . . . La Tène? Definitely Celtic. And then his hands: wide and large but completely controlled, his firm grip wrapped around the wheel. Hands ghosted with the deaths he'd dealt for the Wake.

She thought of the sharp attention in his eyes and the gentle way he'd released her. Perhaps he wasn't ruthless now, but she hadn't really seen him around his prey, yet.

The idea stroked a soft warning up her spine.

She sent a quick text to their family group, including Remi:

Meet at the house in half an hour x

The x meant one thing: Empyreal.

Part of her had twisted with worry when the Empyreal had stepped back into the curator's office. What if more Empyreals had come? What if they *were* here for her family? She didn't know what she'd do if they were taken, they were everything to her. They were why she cared about this damn art collection in the first place. But every one of her loved ones texted back quickly, and it allowed her to relax a little into the deep seat of the Empyreal's car, even if she'd snuck one hand into her satchel and gripped a pen to use as an impromptu weapon.

They drove smoothly through the streets, past groups of students with their morning coffees and Nicole's anger steeped. Usually, she enjoyed driving up this hill, seeing the sandy expanse and sparkling waters of the English coast unfurl, or the darkening of twilight gild the waves. It had been their first real home since their mother died, and now it was crawling with both a creature and an Empyreal.

Now it was *compromised*.

She risked a glance at his severe profile.

"Did the creature you're hunting kill Westmoore?" Nicole asked.

Those serious eyes scanned her face and her stomach jumped as she was struck again by his fierce, sensual features.

He frowned slightly at her question. "If it had, I would have killed it already."

"Then . . ." She cursed herself for the tightness in her throat. "What happened to her?"

"As far as I'm aware, she died of natural causes."

Nicole pressed her lips together, hopefully her family would know if that was true. Her father had an aptitude for reading death. If she knew him, he'd be checking the body already. But if Westmoore had been killed in some supernatural situation and felt she was in danger, why wouldn't she have reached out to them last night? They could have helped her. . . .

"How do you know for sure?" Nicole pressed.

"A creature releases a kill hormone when, or just before, it kills. It's what allows me to transform."

That she knew. "So the creature didn't have one?"

She had felt such an insistent, wicked pull toward it; such a deep stirring of her Empyrean power that the idea that there *wasn't* a kill scent worried her. What would it be like if the creature did try to kill? How would she resist that? How much worse would the temptation become? Her fingers tensed around the smooth leather-wrapped door handle.

You have your father's tonics, she reminded herself.

"Not from this kill," the Empyreal said, answering her.

She looked at him sharply. "What does that mean?"

The Empyreal almost didn't answer as they pulled up to the manor, and the moment of tension grew as he cut off the engine.

"It means Lynch has killed before, but Empyreals haven't gotten there fast enough to stop him, so the scent has faded and no longer remains powerful enough to trigger an Empyreal's transformation. But it leaves a type of . . . malignant aura around the creature. Makes them smell and feel different."

Lynch, that was the creature's name. She tucked it away for later.

She knew the intention behind the kill was what determined if a kill hormone was released: if a creature killed for sport or malice, as Lynch seemed to, it triggered the hormone. If it was in self-defense, or to protect others, it didn't. Hence why an Empyreal never triggered the kill hormone in another Empyreal—that and the fact they were already the supernatural world's best predators, there was nothing else they could become.

"So that's why you're already transforming slightly?" Nicole asked.

He appraised her. "That's very perceptive."

That's because she knew so much—too much, to him?—about Empyreals. "It's just a guess. You said other Empyreals haven't been fast enough. What makes you think you will be?"

If he wasn't and *she* was too near the creature if it tried to kill, then she would be the one to transform. He was duty-bound to bring in any new Empyreals to the Wake, so he'd hunt her after she'd bitten or stabbed or ripped apart the creature. Nicole wasn't sure if that was what made her shiver, or the Empyreal's next words.

"Because I always am."

He believed what he said—but there was something underlying the statement she couldn't read.

They got out of the car and the Empyreal grabbed his bag from the back while she grabbed hers. As they headed to the door, he reached for his key at the same time Nicole reached for hers.

A shadow appeared between his brows. "What is that?"

"I could ask you the same thing," she said, eyeing his. "How did you get one?"

"I'm her nephew, remember. Next of kin."

Nicole's narrowed eyes shot up to him. How had he done it? Influenced the people in the coroner's or the solicitor's offices? Or was it merely the weight of the Wake's resources that got him what he needed? Either immediately annoyed her.

The Empyreal pushed his key into the lock, tense again. "How, exactly, do you have one?"

"Westmoore gave it to me."

His shoulders stiffened as he stepped inside and Nicole came into the shadowed great hall after him. To make sure he couldn't pick her up and deposit her back outside, she quickly started to walk through the house.

"Perhaps you don't understand how these things work," the Empyreal said as he strode after her. "This will be my base of operations; you won't be able to come in as you please."

Nicole's anticipation built the farther she walked, feeling his eyes on her. There was no scent of burning, and yet the sense of foreboding grew worse. Westmoore was *gone*. Nicole suddenly felt like she was trespassing, despite the key in her hand.

"I'm not leaving," she said firmly, heading right into one of the luxurious sprawling bedrooms and dropping her bag on the bed.

"Yes, you are," he countered from the doorway with a scowl at her bag. "Right after you've answered a few questions."

Nicole pushed past him, heading to the ballroom where she stopped, realizing what he'd said. "Is that why you allowed me in here? To Influence me like you did the curator?"

If he tried, she'd have to pretend his powers worked. They didn't work on other Empyreals, not unless the one doing the Influencing was particularly powerful.

"I brought you here because I suspected you didn't want the curator knowing what you are. *You're* the one insisting you stay. You're welcome to leave anytime you want. *With* your belongings."

But she was so close to the paintings.

He took the lead now, striding past her into Westmoore's study.

Nicole followed. "That didn't answer my Influencing question."

"It depends," he said.

She laughed flatly. "On?"

"On whether you're going to tell me the truth or not."

"About?"

"Anything and everything that's pertinent to this mission." After a moment he located the painted door and opened it, stepping into the gallery room.

Nicole hurried after him.

She scanned the supernatural gallery quickly, shoulders relaxing to see the *Wild Hunt* painting still hung on the wall, as majestic and wicked as it had been last night. There were no signs of a struggle; nothing was singed or scented of smoke.

But then the Empyreal turned to her. "Like this."

She frowned as he stepped out of the way to reveal that where the *Dante* painting had been—the one that had given her the vision of *him*—was now a bare space.

"No," she whispered. "Where—"

The Empyreal motioned for her to stop and slowly approached the wall with a mercenary prowl. Nicole moved closer, stepping around an expensive seventeenth-century table with a glass-boxed bestiary on top.

A flash of rage had her looking around the room. "How did he get it out? Did he just carry it out the door?"

"No, I can feel the wards on the place. Most likely it's warded against supernatural theft."

"Then how?"

His gaze raked over her. "That's what I'll find out."

Nicole blinked. "You think *I* stole it?"

His arms crossed over his powerful chest, the shirt curving over the body beneath. "You could have had a hand in it. And why not? You have a key; you want to study these paintings."

"Yes. *This* one," she said, pointing to the *Wild Hunt* piece. "My dissertation is called 'The Lure of the Wild Hunt: Paintings of the Supernatural in Nineteenth-Century Art.' Your *prey* stole it."

"What makes you think that?"

She blinked, incredulous. "He was asking the curator about it!"

The Empyreal's brow arched slightly. "How did you know that?"

Shit, she'd overheard with her Empyrean senses. Nicole recovered quickly. "I heard some of their conversation through the closed door. Besides, why else would he be hounding the curator of the museum? The important thing is getting it back. And if you don't—"

"What? *You* will?" There was no incredulity there, just a warning.

She glared at the dark interest in his eyes then shook her head, feeling a surprising knot of frustration and upset burn in her throat. "These paintings . . . they meant everything to Westmoore. The fact even a single one has been taken and might have something to do with her death . . ." Nicole swallowed, before steeling herself. "We need to get it back."

"There is no *we*. This is my hunt."

"And it's *my* research. That painting could still be crucial."

"Oh? Why is that?"

Her lips parted before clamping shut. She couldn't admit that it was involved in a century-old conspiracy that his organization was killing people for. But then, wouldn't he know? He'd been sent on this mission to kill a creature and . . . what?

"You tell me," she said carefully. "Why do you care about paintings? Isn't your focus supposed to be protecting people against dangerous creatures?"

The muscle in his jaw worked. "That *is* my focus." He prowled closer. "But what I now need to know is, are you going to be a help or a hindrance on this hunt, Nicole?"

"That depends," she said, mimicking his words from earlier.

"On?" He leaned on the priceless table between them, bringing himself closer to her height. It creaked gently under his weight and her breath caught to be so much closer to the frowning planes of his face, the lush mouth, the strong arc of those shoulders.

The top two buttons of his shirt were open, allowing a glimpse at the column of his neck and the hint of a solid chest. It seemed dangerously intimate in the glow of the gallery room.

A flush of heat surprised her.

He was handsome, but the kind that was rougher around the edges and a little more . . . deadly.

"I'll be staying here when I work late," Nicole said, her throat thick. There was no way she would spend any longer away from these paintings than she had to. If she was here, as much as possible, she could protect them. He couldn't move them out under her watch. "That's why Westmoore gave me a key."

The Empyreal's body seemed to strain as if he might start pacing. "This is a supernatural investigation. I'll be *hunting*."

A shiver teased over her skin at the slow threat of the word. "And I'll be researching quietly, out of your way."

He shook his head as if amazed, and Nicole dared to take a step closer. His nostrils flared slightly and he grew predatorily still.

"I'll *help*."

"How?" he gritted out.

"I have a job to do. Every painting in the collection is important, not just the missing one. Besides, I might be useful with what I know about art."

"That's all fine, but I still don't know one crucial thing. What are you, Nicole?"

She felt a swift, surprising moment of breathlessness under the weight of his attention. There was a heavy, explicitly masculine energy to him that made him feel entirely capable, and entirely lethal. Something hard and still and easily controlled that she envied. That set a low pulse of intrigue tapping through her body like a warning.

"You can't tell?" she asked quietly.

The muscle in his jaw ticked. "No. Empyreals are better at reading dangerous creatures."

He doesn't think I'm dangerous. She had the strangest urge to prove him wrong.

"So, what is it?" He frowned as he tried to puzzle her out. "Nemfer? Vorin? Hearthea?" They were good guesses. All creatures who looked human and had strong protective instincts.

But they weren't Empyreals.

His gaze raked down her face and rested a moment on the pulse thrumming in her neck.

"I'm a Seer," she said, so quietly it was almost a whisper.

That perpetual frown deepened and he shook his head slightly. He raised his eyes to hers and said, just as softly, "You don't smell like a Seer."

Heat rushed to her face and she pushed backward, attempting to cleave some of the tension, but her legs felt shaky.

"Must be my perfume," she lied.

His eyes were still locked on hers, but they flared for a moment, the pupils darker, and she realized they weren't brown as she'd first thought. They were hazel, threaded with dark green.

"It's not," he said, his voice was slightly rougher. He pushed off the table and took a long breath that shifted the lines of his shirt. "Have you had any current visions of this creature?"

Nicole shook her head.

"Empyreals often work with Seers; it allows us to track creatures and locate them before they kill. You can share your visions with me. Is that something you'd be comfortable with?"

"I thought Seers could only share visions with creatures like other Seers."

"I'm becoming a Specter, so I'll be able to access them."

A Specter. Creatures who drink blood. Now his glance to her neck

80

made sense. But he would have to touch her to see the visions. She had no problem seeing her sister's or father's visions, but having the Empyreal's hands on her . . .

"Let's just see, I . . . My visions are a little unpredictable."

He watched her for a beat, and she suddenly feared he would see right through her.

"Fine, but I don't want you to seek the creature out. You can't do what you did today, understood? You let me handle it. Other supernaturals getting involved can make the prey feel cornered and they're then likely to lash out. I won't accept casualties."

The earnestness in his tone relieved her, despite everything. He was serious. But serious about what? Protecting people, or protecting the Wake's interests?

Nicole nodded, trying not to chafe at the fact the words had sounded like an order. She couldn't risk being too close to the creature anyway, not after the way she'd felt in proximity to it today. "Fine. What are the first steps?"

The Empyreal sighed. "I'll check out his lodgings and make sure he hasn't stashed the painting there. It's unlikely due to the size of it, but it will also give me an idea as to how long he intends to stay and what his plans might be."

If there was a chance the creature had the painting there or made any notes or sketches, she couldn't risk the Empyreal seeing them first. "I should come with you."

His frown returned. He looked like he'd refuse but then said, "Fine. We'll go tonight, when he's feeding."

Feeding. The word sent a chill of disgust under her skin.

"One more thing. The research you do on these paintings, I want to read it. If the creature has picked this painting, there's a reason for it, and I need every bit of recon I can to understand him better."

Nicole clamped her teeth together. Surely she could just give him an abbreviated version of information on symbols in the paintings; art-historical interpretations and the like she'd be writing into her dissertation? She could keep the rest, the important information and theories, secret easily enough.

"Deal," Nicole said. "If you do something for me."

His brow lowered. "That's not—"

"You make sure he doesn't hurt anyone. This isn't a game to me. This isn't a thrill or a hunt and it's more than a painting on a wall. This is life and death. I won't have my family in danger."

He watched her, and something deep and earnest went through his eyes: respect.

Interest.

He pulled out a little notepad and quickly wrote on it, then tore the paper and passed it to her. "I'll pick you up later."

It was his phone number.

She paused before taking it, thinking of the vision she'd had the previous night. All the heat and muscle of him stalking through that fog. The blood. The glint of the ancient decoration around his neck. And now the reality: a hunter surrounded by artifacts and art, so different from her vision even though the promise of the warrior hadn't left his body, or his eyes.

He would be deadly, she had no doubt. Her mother's books had warned her of that; the *Dante* painting, too. But with his calmness and grudging acceptance of her into this investigation, he was not what she expected.

Nicole took the piece of paper, careful to avoid touching him.

She would *never* be the Wake's loyal huntress. But to keep her family safe, the cost was working with an Empyreal. She found herself strangely glad they'd sent *him* and not someone else.

"What should I call you? Mr. McCarter? Mr. *Westmoore*?"

The Empyreal watched her for a moment longer and an almost imperceptible tug pulled at the corner of his lips. "Call me Kyan."

9 NICOLE

Nicole strode into her family's secret library. The scents of parchment, ink, and the metallic cloy of weapons, both creature and human, whooshed out to meet her.

Her family and best friend waited, her mother's immortal, painted eyes watching from behind them.

"An Empyreal?" Remi asked, rising.

Nicole sighed. "Yes."

She passed the shelves of her mother's books, the aged spines all the colors of copper and bronze, each one containing knowledge that was just as precious.

There was a quick, tense moment of silence, during which her father's eyes turned murderously calm. "Are you all right?"

"I'm fine," she said reassuringly.

"Who is he? What do we know?" Dylan asked, beginning to pace.

"He seems capable. Curt. Likes to be direct."

"He's the best the Wake have," Bells said, her eyes bloody with Sight.

It echoed what Kyan had said about himself. Which meant he wasn't cocky—he was *truthful*. Another curious trait considering the lying and truth-twisting of the Wake.

"And he's—" Bells's eyes drifted to Nicole.

"What?" she asked, her brow tugging into a frown.

"N-nothing."

"Did you follow protocol?" Dylan asked before Nicole could prompt their sister further.

She'd had to adapt after the adrenaline and feeling like her legs had been knocked out from under her, but: "Yes," Nicole said. She felt more secure now. In control. It soothed the rawest parts of her. "He thinks I'm a Seer."

"That's smart," Remi said. "Empyreals aren't known to have more than one supernatural power like you do."

Nicole kept it to herself that she'd heard the creature—Lynch—asking about her.

"But, Nicole," began Bells. She was sitting beside Remi, her cardigan tugged around her. Evidently they'd pulled her from school. "Did you hear about Westmoore?"

Nicole nodded softly and filled them in on the Empyreal's false identity.

"Those scheming bastards," Dylan cursed. "Using Westmoore's death for their own gain."

"But what *happened* to Westmoore?" Remi asked. "If she has a collection that was, supposedly, so threatening she feared the Wake were killing to find it, how do we know the Empyreal didn't kill her to get her out of the way?"

The Wake's Empyreals would do anything for them. Nicole's mother had discovered that meant occasionally acting more like assassins than the protectors the rest of the supernatural world saw them as. *Had* Kyan killed Westmoore and made it look like a heart attack?

"He didn't kill Westmoore," Nicole's father interrupted. "Dylan used his Influence to find out that Westmoore let go of her house-keeping staff last night after you left. Then, he got us in to see her body.

"She used a herbal poison and took herself out onto the sand dunes so ions from the storm would wash away the evidence and no other supernatural would be able to use magic, or a vision, to see how she died. It would look to humans and creatures like a heart attack. I only know because she asked me to brew that poison years ago as a precaution and the symptoms were the same. She presumably didn't want to be tortured for the information on the paintings, or what she knew about the collection, before they—"

"Before they killed her," said Bells, eyes bloodied as if another vision shimmered.

"Hence why she made sure no humans would be there to get hurt either, if she'd Seen an assassin coming for her," Dylan said.

"Westmoore told you last night," her father continued, "that the Wake have been hunting down collectors, searching through their pieces, stealing or destroying the rest of their art and killing them. Evidently, the same creature that's arrived here has been sent systematically by the Wake to those they suspect have what they're looking for. The creature uses its power to get into their heads so that, even if they can withstand torture, it can retrieve the knowledge it seeks. Then, it kills them afterward."

Nicole remembered Westmoore's vision: the person reaching out, pleading. "So you think the creature killed another curator and got Westmoore's name from their mind?"

Her father nodded. "It seems the most likely. If it had gotten to Westmoore, it would have known all about us. Your mother, which paintings to pick, and perhaps even more details about the message itself."

"So that's why she made sure you had the key before she sent you away," Bells realized. "She couldn't risk calling or warning us in case it tracked the call, so made sure you'd be able to get into the house to access the paintings after she died. Then, she took the poison."

"The poor woman," Remi whispered, shaking her head.

This, *this* was what the Wake did, and the world believed they were saviors.

Nicole looked up at her mother's portrait. Yes, theirs was a life of secrecy, but she was glad she knew the truth. Most of supernatural society thought the Wake kept creatures and humans safe by guiding Empyreals' hunts. Empyreals were accepted hunters because their bodies could only transform when another murder was imminent, granting them a kind of biological morality the Wake used to their own advantage.

"Then this is proof of what Mum discovered: that the Wake uses other creatures to kill and manipulate, not just Empyreals," Nicole said.

Their father shook his head sadly. "They've been doing this for centuries, love. This isn't enough proof. Not without evidence."

"Do we know what the creature is?" Dylan asked.

"No, but this might help," Remi said, removing something from a deep pocket of her suede coat. "I went to check the perimeter when I got your text and found *this*." She threw a charred piece of metal onto the low table. "This was one of my mum's best pieces."

Before Remi and her family had come to Estwood, her mother, Lawna, had been a part of the Fae royal family's security. As a Hearthea—a creature concerned with the hearth and protecting the home—Lawna was able to create force fields, wards, and apotropaic objects to repel dangerous creatures. But it was because she combined her powers with her STEM knowledge that she was so good at her job. Not just anything could usurp her defenses.

Nicole shot a worried glance at Dylan.

"Nothing seemed out of the ordinary until I found a few frazzled pieces of tech," Remi continued. "I've replaced them, even the untouched ones, just to be on the safe side."

"Is it an electrical creature, then? A Nazen, maybe?" Dylan asked.

"No," Nicole said, a frown cutting her brow as she rubbed her face, thinking of the electric blue eyes and static, spark-inducing skin of a Nazen. "I would have felt that."

"What if it's a different kind of energy?" Bells asked, more to herself. "If it gets into people's heads?"

"Like magic?" Remi suggested.

"Ky— the Empyreal is becoming a Specter, so it could be something similar."

"Whatever it is, it's powerful," Nicole's father said, his eyes narrowing in on the tech. "May I?"

He held out his hand, and Remi laid it in his palm.

"Mr. Palmer—" Remi warned.

"I don't think you should try, Dad," Dylan added.

Their father gave a small smile and his eyes flickered with power. "Don't worry, son, it shouldn't be able to track us within the house's wards."

With the tech in his hand, her father's eyes closed.

Nicole's skin grew clammy with nerves. She didn't see her father use his powers often. He mainly focused on making their tonics and gardening the rare herbs they needed, but as he sank into it, she was drawn to the ebb and flow of power, noting how the others leaned closer too.

Her father's head tilted to the side.

Ice shot down Nicole's spine the same moment his face creased with a frown. "It's leech-like. Not a Vampire, closest I think is . . ."

A terrible feeling singed Nicole, stinging down to her fingers as a ghost of the creature's scent slipped beneath her nose.

Her father opened his eyes and the blood-darkness of them swirled away. "A Specter. It's also a Specter."

Dylan cursed, no doubt thinking of all its array of wicked abilities.

"Tell me what you know about them," her father prompted, testing them.

The painting drew itself in her mind before her lips formed the words.

"Specter," Nicole said, slipping an art book from a shelf and flipping the heavy thing open to the glossy print within. She set it on the coffee table between the armchairs and couch, weighing down the open pages with a dagger and a hunk of white crystal. "This is *The Silent Voice*, a painting by Gerald Moira from the late 1800s."

In it, a dark-haired, wide-eyed woman sat shellshocked in a teal gown, staring off the canvas, her hand lifted to her chest. A ghostly being bent next to her, one hand over hers, its mouth to her temple. There was a blue-green wash on the painting like they were underwater.

"Usually Specters like to nest; situate themselves somewhere and poison it slowly. They siphon energy from negative human emotions,"

Nicole continued, meeting the scared eyes of the woman in the painting. "But they also need blood."

"Specters can access a Seer's vision," Bells said. "When they bite someone, they form a short-term psychic connection with them. Hence why Westmoore wanted to be dead before it could find her, and why she was adamant we know nothing, not see the paintings, until there was no other option. That way her secrets died with her, left only to someone who might be able to figure them out."

All eyes slid to Nicole.

Dylan took over gravely. "Natural enemies include other Specters, extremely strong witches, or Baobhan Sith." The Scottish word for Banshee.

"Since the Empyreal is a Specter, too, he'll also be venomous," Remi said, typing into her phone. "I can adapt the wards, but it'll take a few days."

"So . . . the Empyreal might not know what he's standing in the middle of?" Bells realized.

Her father nodded. "The Empyreal's been sent to clean up the mess and hide their attempted assassination. I assume because the Specter failed its mission when it arrived to discover Westmoore was already dead, which will likely be why the Empyreal was sent here so quickly."

"So, the Specter . . . what?" Remi asked. "Stole the painting the Wake wanted for leverage?"

"It would be the only thing to do in this situation, other than run and hide," her father said.

Nicole wished it had taken the second option. But she rose from where she'd perched on the edge of a couch. "We have the upper hand. There are more of us, the town can be re-warded, and the

Empyreal thinks I'm a Seer. I'll find out what's going on, keep an eye on the progress of the hunt and avoid the creature. Then the Empyreal will kill it and be on his way. But I'll make sure we get the painting back before he tries to take it with him."

"How are you going to do that?" Remi asked, worry and warning in her voice.

"We have our ways," Nicole's father answered. He'd taken a seat on one of the arms of the armchairs, beside the portrait of their mother. She thought of the long life he'd lived with her before Dylan had been born. Moving from one place to the next. The things they'd done to stay hidden. Lied. Killed. Used everything in their joint arsenal to keep each other and their future safe.

"Do you think this stolen *Dante* painting is the one you need, then?" Bells asked softly.

"I thought the clue was in the *Wild Hunt* painting because it depicted an Empyreal, but clearly there's something about the *Dante* painting, too. I had a vision about it, and then the Empyreal arrived. Plus, it's the piece the creature stole. There must be a reason."

"And if the Empyreal figures us out?" Dylan asked tightly.

"We leave," their father said smoothly.

Nicole fought her mild panic at the idea. "He won't, however. So, we go about our everyday lives."

"We should let your parents know," Dylan said to Remi. "I know they're doing important research, but we can't keep them out of the loop—"

"No!" Remi sighed. "Do you know how hard it is to get into the Siren archives? What they're looking into right now, they can't leave. Besides, my dorm room is warded better than a Fae queen's bedroom. Trust me. I'll be fine."

Bells looked like she'd argue.

Nicole glanced again at her mother's round portrait. She sat proudly in a historic dress of darkest rose and watched the viewer with intent eyes. While the shades of their eyes and hair were the same and she shared that full Palmer mouth, heart-shaped face, and pale skin, their eyes were different. In her mother's there was a weight like nothing Nicole had seen in anyone else. The weight, she suspected, of immortality's secrets.

And Nicole would do anything to find the last one.

"We can do this," she said, gaining their attention and squaring her shoulders. "We've kept under the Wake's radar for years. We know what we're doing. Besides, the Empyreal will be busy with the Specter, he won't need to look twice at us."

Bells's eyes threaded with blood. But a Seer couldn't purposefully look into their own fate, or the fate of the ones they loved, which meant there was little chance she'd be able to find out anything that could directly help them. Her lips pressed together so they'd almost drained of color.

"He *might*," she whispered.

10 NICOLE

"Wait," Remi said, "you're going to do what now?"

Nicole sat back from the sketches she'd been showing Remi. She'd roughly drawn what she could remember of the paintings from Westmoore's gallery to make sure she had some mental backup. Now, the mythological images were splayed over the pub's slightly sticky table and a small candle flickered over them amid coasters of an illustrated Mermaid holding a lyre shaped like a heart.

They were sitting in their favorite booth in the Siren's Wife, the oldest pub in Estwood. The place was crowded with students and locals, but in a comforting way, a way that reminded Nicole that life was steadily going on around them despite the paranormal undercurrent. Thankfully, their usual table was warded, so humans wouldn't be able to see or hear unusual parts of their conversations.

She had to abide by their new plan and try to seem as normal as possible, so after their talk in the family library, she had returned to classes, bought some books, and gone on a long twilight walk along the beach with Remi.

But her mind had returned to darker things.

"I'm going to scope out the Specter's place with Kyan," Nicole said, taking another drink. "That is, if he responds to my text."

She'd texted him over an hour ago asking where they should meet, but nothing. She tried not to check her phone again.

He'd best not go without her.

"Kyan—the Empyreal? Have you not courted danger enough for one day?"

Nicole arched a look at Remi. Her best friend wore a cream turtleneck jumper, which was bright against the wood-paneled walls behind her, her wet coat gently dripping rainwater onto the floor from where it was draped over an opposite chair.

"I didn't do it on purpose. Besides, I'm hoping it might give me a chance to figure out who the Specter is, so we're not walking around blind."

Nicole looked around the pub, its sense of ease and warmth and laughter, and shivered, tugging her sleeves over her cold fingers. She angled her drying boots closer to the crackle of the flames in the low, ancient fireplace where a giant dog was curled up—a stately Irish wolfhound with fur the color of soot and sand, and sleepy black eyes.

Nicole picked a few nachos and took a thoughtful bite before taking another swig of her beer, which glowed in the low light. Cold bubbles burst over her tongue, the liquid turning hot as the alcohol seeped into her bloodstream.

Remi sighed. "You worry me."

Nicole turned her body toward her friend. "The sooner we get the painting back, the faster we can move on and get back to normal."

Remi huffed but nodded, scanning Nicole's eyes like she almost had something to tell her. Instead, she sighed. "Show me again, then."

Glad to be focused, Nicole looked back down at the sketches.

"Almost all the paintings show ancient supernatural history, but I think it's laid out in some kind of timeline. Perhaps it has some information on what happened in the first Dark Age and how the Wake rose to power."

These were not the Dark Ages human history referred to, though they did coincide in some instances. These were supernatural ones that peaked at different times and almost wiped out humans and creatures—deemed plagues, natural disasters, and the like to keep them secret from modern humans.

"That would be extremely valuable information," Remi said thoughtfully, taking a nacho.

"Do you see anything, knowing what you do about Sirens?"

Remi had lived the first few years of her life in supernatural society, until the mysterious circumstance that forced her family to hide, too. One that had been under lock and key since they'd met shortly after Nicole and her family had arrived in Estwood.

Remi made a thoughtful noise. "These look like lyres," she said, tapping a cream-painted nail on the edge of a sketch.

Nicole glanced to the shining handheld harp perched against Remi's leg, waiting to be played. It was neoclassical in its ornate decoration. Elegant stems of gold flowers coiled around the edges and a butterfly was carved at the base so the strings shot up through its wingspan.

"Do they mean anything to you?" Nicole asked.

"Well, it means they're more ancient, depending on the culture. This one, though . . ." Remi pulled closer a sketch of an unusual piece featuring a blindfolded woman sitting on a dome, hunched over a harp-like instrument. It was too dark to make out anything else. "This one makes me think of celestial harmony, the harmony of the spheres. It's said to be the ancient music that keeps the universe balanced."

An electrical buzz interrupted them as someone plugged their guitar into a speaker. Remi glanced over to where a group of musicians had set up in the corner. Where Nicole could exercise or train to release pent-up Empyrean energy, Remi could only sing it out.

"Go," Nicole said, scooping up the sketches. They'd been going over them for at least two hours. "You don't have to sit here baby-sitting me."

"I do if you're going to read in a pub, you heathen. Pubs are for raucous singing. Besides, we have a mystery to uncover."

"You need to sing, Remi," Nicole said softly. "I'll be right here, enjoying your music. And so, I imagine, will she."

Remi looked over at the girl sitting at the bar with her friends. She had snuck Remi more than one curious glance, the long black braids down her back shifting like rain.

"I take it that's the girl in your dorm?" Nicole asked.

"Uh, yeah." Remi smiled slightly.

Nicole relished that light in her friend's eyes.

"I think her name's Hannah. But there'll be no singing tonight, not now there's an Empyreal and Specter in town. I can't risk it."

Worry threaded into Nicole's chest. Every Siren developed their own song. It wasn't one they wrote, or even consciously uncovered; it was something that, with enough singing, would develop its own melody and dictated who among their kind became royalty. Powerful Sirens could captivate anyone who heard them and use their song for all manner of means, both wonderful or sinister.

But Remi only smiled. "Don't worry so much," she said, brushing the frown on Nicole's brow with a thumb cold from her glass of wine. "The vibrations from my harp should be enough."

Nicole pressed her lips together, concerned, but nodded. "Then, go, be merry," she said, fanning Remi away with the papers. She was only going to sit here brooding over the sketches until Kyan responded anyway.

Her heart jumped into her throat as a text suddenly lit up her screen:

Where are you?

It was from Kyan. She knew it even without seeing the name. Curt. Direct.

Dangerous.

A shot of adrenaline bled through her. "Looks like he'll be here soon, anyway." She took a last swig of beer to coat her suddenly dry mouth.

Remi pecked Nicole on the cheek and rushed off to meet the musicians.

Nicole texted Kyan back and nipped to the bathroom.

Usually she enjoyed sitting in the pub and listening to Remi play—her harp an unusual but beautiful addition that blended well with the other Celtic instruments. Even now, right at the start of their set, Remi's shoulders visibly relaxed as her tension unwound.

But as Nicole moved through the room, she only felt her own power simmer. Since this morning she'd felt so much more *aware* of everything, even cutting smoothly through tipsy students felt easy, more like a predator, despite there being no immediate threat. And yet the desire to use her Influence pooled on her tongue, the preternatural whisper to *hunt* sitting in her blood.

Nicole shook herself as she entered the bathroom.

Just ignore it, you're in control.

And yet the temptation remained, like some wicked magic hidden in her soul.

She washed her hands and pulled her hair loose from its ponytail, then shut her eyes and rubbed her fingers over her aching head. She was a huntress. Whether she wanted to be or not, it was a physical compulsion.

Like Kyan.

The thought almost made her recoil. No, she wasn't like him. He worked for the Wake, and she would never. But where she knew so little about the realities of her power, he moved with such supernatural control. He'd been so silent in the alley today, she hadn't even realized he was right behind her. That worried her. Being prepared could mean the difference between discovery and safety. So she wasn't taking any chances; she had to be prepared before seeing him again.

Nicole glanced warily at her satchel, thinking of what was inside, and when she resumed her seat on the padded bench, she gently pulled out the ancient book.

Her mother's bestiaries were her lists and findings on the creatures she'd come across throughout her life, a life so long Nicole didn't even know how old her mother had been. All different sizes and materials, most of them would have fallen apart if Nicole's father hadn't mended them. They ranged from scraps of papyrus to animal skins and aged parchment, their edges gilded brown, some in glass boxes in their library as they were little more than brightly illustrated sheaves of paper from the Middle Ages.

Nicole opened the leather bestiary to find her mother's slanted handwriting:

Empyreals.

Her writing was neater in this book than others. More stable. Nicole traced it thoughtfully. Any scrap of her would never be enough; she'd seen it in her father's eyes yesterday and knew it was the other driving force that made her so determined to decode this final clue.

She couldn't help but wonder how different their life would be if her mother was still here to tell Nicole all this in person, to train her as only a millennia-old Empyreal could. But she pushed the thought away and began to read.

How to Resist.

An Empyreal's charm mainly affects humans, but particularly powerful ones can even Influence other Empyreals.

1. Remain calm. They can sense, and practically taste, hormonal changes in your body, giving them the power to know exactly what you will react to. There's a fine line between real and Influenced emotion, so try and ground yourself. Think about your surroundings, your checklist for the day if you have to, anything to get your mind off the Empyreal.

2. Breathing deeply doesn't help if you're in close quarters with them. An Empyreal gives off an intoxicating scent—different from an Empyreal's newly turned one, though both are rife with pheromones. Breathing deeply will only draw it in. Breathe normally (fresh air if you can) and try to keep your heart rate steady. They can hear it, so they'll know they're succeeding.

Okay, no deep breathing. She'd try that one.

3. Don't forget who you are. In the moment with them, you will want to forget everything else. Your instincts will be geared toward them. We're rare. We're drawn to one another.

The next section caught her eye:

Sexual impulses.

A shiver of awareness had her looking up as Kyan stooped to enter the pub. Her heart lurched in surprise as his eyes locked on hers. Not many people looked her in the eyes. She wasn't used to the directness. It felt—brazen. Risky.

But then she'd spent her entire life trying not to draw attention, and now she had all of his.

He nodded in greeting, taking his immortal bulk over to the bar. Nicole tried to banish the alcohol's sleepy warmth and quickly hid her mother's bestiary as he placed his order, then made his way over to her.

"May I?" he asked, a dark, almost black pint in hand, a thick white layer of foam closed over its peaty scent.

Nicole nodded at the seat. "Where's the Specter?" she asked, trying to scoot farther away, but the pub was full now, loud students on either side.

Kyan dragged his gaze down her loose hair. He frowned, and, looking away, took a drink. "He's leaving soon, we'll have to wait until then."

"How do you know?"

He slid his eyes to her. "I've been doing this a long time, so I can sense him."

Nicole's immediate thought, like in every supernatural lesson her father taught them, was, *Tell me more.* And yet she didn't want to seem too keen to learn about him or the Wake.

But he seemed to sense her interest. "When an Empyreal begins a hunt, we identify the prey's scent and energy and form a kind of . . ." He seemed to struggle to put it into words. "Connection, that the prey isn't aware of, like an energetic tracking signal. It allows me to sense his movements and actions even from a distance. It takes a while to get the hang of."

The dog that had been dozing by the glowing fire approached Kyan and whined. It bent its head to rest upon his thigh and looked up at him with big eyes. Kyan frowned and picked up the tiny braid woven into the dog's wiry hair. He hesitated for a moment before he began distractedly massaging between the dog's ears, the tendons in his hand jumping.

Nicole took another drink, watching carefully.

It felt dangerous, being closer to his height, to feel the forbidden brush of his leg against hers as he shifted to reach his beer, sending sensations roaring through her body. Her power unfurled, curious and drugging. The strangest thing about her Empyreal was how persuasive it was. How it made her want to luxuriate in it, made it feel like the most natural thing in the world, despite her arguments.

Calm down, she cursed it.

Kyan's head turned slightly like he'd sensed her inner struggle and he moved his gaze from her mouth, to search her eyes.

"Would answering questions help you trust me?" he asked.

Trust you? That was never going to happen. But perhaps she could glean some useful information. So she opted for one that seemed innocuous but had burned in the back of her mind since she'd had the vision of him bloodied in battle. That had, long before that, returned every time she'd wondered what a transformation might be like.

"When did you first . . . when did you know what you were?"

Kyan didn't look up from the wolfhound as he answered. "When I transformed."

Her lips parted. Not all Empyreals knew what they were. Many were born to human parents and lived their lives thinking they were human, if not a bit extraordinary, being stronger and faster and healing better than others. If they had no one to explain what they were, they wouldn't know until their first transformation.

Nicole could barely imagine not knowing what was happening. She'd read her mother's notes on transformation many times. But if he hadn't known . . .

"How old were you?" she asked.

He frowned, thinking. "About seven years old."

Her breath hitched, finding it incomprehensible to imagine a little boy's body tearing itself apart to kill another being. To see *him* as a seven-year-old rather than somehow springing into existence just like this.

An Empyreal could transform at any age once they were physically strong enough to withstand a transformation, but that usually meant puberty. Clearly, there'd been exceptions. Once you transformed, you were granted a lot more control over your body and power—not enough to ever willingly transform yourself into a supernatural, but enough to transform your age and, if you were particularly powerful, your features, hair color, and so on. You could even stop or reverse your aging; you could just never regress back to an age before your first transformation.

Thinking of him as a boy made him—human. And filled her with a thousand more questions: *Were your parents human? Why do you work for such a horrific organization?*

And yet the image of him as a boy was the strongest.

"I'm sorry," she said softly. "That must have been awful." She remembered being eight years old and coming here, clutching her brother's hand. How helpless she'd felt even then, but at least she knew what she was. "You . . . didn't know what had happened?"

He shook his head. "My mother seemed to understand to a degree, but there was no name for what I was at the time. We just thought I was gifted by the goddess."

Her ears pricked up. Supernatural religion was as complex as humans'. "Which goddess?" she asked, and yet she had a feeling she knew.

"The Morrígan and her sisters."

A whisper of foreboding made her shiver. The Morrígan was the Irish Goddess of Death, Fate, and War. Her mother had told her that Empyreals were created from the earliest stars by the Goddess of Death, housing all that ancient fire within them.

All that potential for annihilation.

103

But if that was what his people had believed, what world had he lived in? What *time period*? Had he been wrested off into the Wake as a boy? Was that why he felt as solitary as those islands to the north of Scotland? Hunter green and isolated, waves crashing against the rock. Remaining resolute and . . . lonely?

He met her gaze, and she searched his inscrutable eyes, recalling one of her mother's notes: *Sometimes your greatest weapon is their underestimation of you.* But she didn't feel underestimated in his gaze. Quite the opposite. The realization was like the light stroke of a finger up her spine.

Kyan's eyes dipped to her mouth, and for a moment she thought he might add something.

Instead, he frowned and set his glass down, and she found herself strangely disappointed.

"Let's go," he said, "Lynch is on the move."

11 KYAN

"Can't you just arrest Lynch or something?" Nicole asked as they walked toward the ancient buildings around the quad.

Most of them were buildings for lectures and seminars but were so elegant and Jacobean in design they drew the eye. Streetlamps burned golden in the dark and the sounds of students hurrying to prep for a night out echoed down the streets. Nicole's loose hair tousled gently in the wind and her deep red jumper looked like a bloody target. He had half a mind to drape her in his coat.

"Unfortunately, Lynch has escaped before, which is why I'm here."

"Because you're here to kill him."

It wasn't quite a question, so Kyan nodded slightly, searching her gaze for disapproval. Instead he saw impatience, which was curious.

Nicole looked away. "What are we doing here? I thought we were going to Lynch's house."

"We are. He's staying in student accommodation." Kyan watched for the moment Nicole realized what that meant: that Lynch, like her, was a student at the university.

"Why?" she asked, hurrying closer as Kyan headed toward the arched stone entrance across from the quad's green lawn. Warm light shone from within, casting a glow over racks of bikes and student notices. This was one of the oldest buildings used for students, newer ones built farther out of town. Lynch must have chosen it for easier access, and, Kyan thought, glancing up at the large lead-paned windows, size.

But mostly, *Because of you*, he suspected, glancing at Nicole.

Instead he said, "That's what I'm going to find out."

"Won't he have wards on the place?"

"No. He's cocky and I doubt he's stashed the painting here, not where so many people could have seen him, but it's worth checking."

They headed into the old building. Students chatted in the stairwell and outside their rooms. Music played and scents merged— alcohol, perfume, sex. Kyan pulled Influence over himself to look less conspicuous. At the end of the top-floor corridor, he finally located the Specter's rooms and pulled a vial of blood from his pocket.

As a Specter, he only needed a drop. Fresh was better, but he'd rather not start Influencing people for it. Though, the thought of a dark bead of it on the tip of Nicole's slim finger made heat stir through him.

Kyan ground his teeth, gums throbbing. *It's just the pheromones in this damn building*, he told himself, unstopping the vial. He put his finger on the opening and turned it upside down, then righted it, leaving a smear on his finger. He tried to ignore Nicole's curious glance as he rubbed it over his teeth, feeling the ache in them relax before returning the vial to his pocket. It tasted dead when it wasn't fresh. But unless things got complicated, it should last him the entire mission.

The effects took hold quickly, spreading through his body like a dream, allowing him to step right through the solid door. The matter tugged, resisting, but he breathed through it, finding himself in the Specter's dark room. It was unusual to be able to access the powers of a creature before he'd fully snapped into the transformation, but it only warned him how much more dangerous Lynch was, and how powerful a Specter Kyan was becoming if he had access to these abilities already.

He unlocked the door and opened it, amused to find Nicole's surprised expression.

"Specters are particularly good at getting into places. Especially at nighttime," he explained.

"So you really can just walk through walls?"

He wasn't sure if she looked impressed or worried as she slipped in after him.

"Only with blood. And technically it's the plasma I need, but I absorb it easier when it's mixed with blood."

Nicole's scent brushed past. When he'd been sitting so close to her in the pub, whatever it was had tugged at him. It was familiar, but also wildly unfamiliar. He found himself more attuned to it in the dark, to the fluttering pulse at the base of her throat. The little glint on her lips when she'd just licked them. They'd taste of beer and subtle salt, but more importantly, that delicious scent of hers. He recalled the flush in her cheeks in the heated pub when she'd turned all that curious attention on him. He smoothly slid his eyes away to scan the hallway before closing the door.

The room was supposed to be for two students, built originally to be something much grander than student accommodation. The ancient stone windows granted arched views of the quad below and a glimpse at the night gleam of the sea beyond. The place felt stale, but Specters often did. There was nothing special or eye-catching, just drab, lifeless colors.

Except . . . an unusual scent. Kyan zeroed in on it as Nicole looked about the room.

"Do you See anything?" he asked as he started over toward a pair of black boots with that coastal, sulfuric essence on them. Kyan used his own shoe to tip up the boot so as not to touch it, discovering a spray of sand beneath, and a dark liquid smeared into the tread.

"No," Nicole said, looking about the moonlit space. She sniffed. "What . . . what is that smell?"

Kyan squatted to get a closer look, but the scent confirmed it. "This, is Finfolk blood."

He glanced at her to find she'd paled in the darkness. "What?"

He rose. "Are Finfolk common on these beaches?" He thought of the great serpentine bodies of the ancient creatures. Some said they were Mermaids that had mutated over millennia, giving them a similar look, but making them more vicious. They sometimes dragged themselves across dark beaches to moonbathe in the unearthly quiet. But they could also give omens and prophecies.

Nicole shook her head. "No. The last time was a few years ago, and we had to watch it from afar."

Kyan went to ask why when she came closer, looking at the blood.

"Specters need blood," she said. "Did he kill one for it?"

"It's very unlikely he lured a Finfolk from the deep merely for blood when there are hordes of human students he could drink from."

A flash of fury and frustration went through her eyes. "Has he bitten anyone yet?"

"No." Kyan wasn't about to tell her what he'd read of his prey. How sadistic he could be. He didn't want her to be afraid. But then, with her charging after the creature earlier today, perhaps she should be.

"If he was to bite me," she said, "what would you do?"

The question was a test, he could see it in her dark eyes. And yet he felt his protectiveness surge, even while his own body thought of the idea of *biting*.

Evidently, the urge for blood was growing stronger.

I'd stay in the shadows and let him, he nearly said. That was what he was supposed to do. He couldn't interfere unless the creature was going for the kill.

"If he bites you, he'll find out all your secrets, you know that, right?"

Nicole's gaze turned suspicious, worried.

So, she *did* have something to hide.

"But if you told me, I could help you."

Her eyes narrowed, and yet she seemed fascinated, as if she couldn't tell if she *could* trust him or not. "I'm not the only one with secrets. You want to know what the painting the Specter stole looked like? It looked like *you* and another Empyreal. A big guy with red hair, vicious looking. You were locked in some kind of fight."

There was one person that could be, and memory of them flared through Kyan with cold surprise.

"Does that sound familiar? Ever posed for a nineteenth-century mythological painting?"

He wasn't going to get into the past now, not if it didn't directly impact this mission. "Is that all?"

"No," she said, watching him carefully. She took a step closer, raising her hand as if to touch his face. "When I looked at it, I had a vision of you with a torc around your throat."

109

He couldn't read her now. Why she was suddenly cooperating if not to distract from herself?

He caught her wrist before she could make contact and show him the vision. Kyan inhaled slowly. Though his eyes were on hers, his attention was on the pulse that beat beneath the pad of his thumb.

"You were fighting through a mist," she said softly.

Kyan fought the flash of panic; the deep, ancient grief. "If it's not relevant to the mission, I don't need to know."

"You don't want to see it," she realized.

"Remembering can be dangerous for an Empyreal. It can bring back the days when we felt emotions. It clouds judgment."

Her brow arched. "You don't feel emotions?"

"I do. But emotions aren't helpful when you need to be rational."

He felt suddenly restless, like the gentle throb he could sense at her neck, her wrist. He was so much more aware now he was touching her in the dark. She could have Seen that vision just because he was about to come into her life. But right now, she was trying to distract him from *her*. So, with his thumb still on her pulse, he tugged her gently closer.

She came through a panel of moonlight with a staggered little breath and their bodies almost touched.

"Why is it, Nicole, that you think the worst of me?" His voice had deepened.

Her soft, shapely mouth parted, then pressed into a frustrated line. For the first time since they'd met, she was speechless. And he found he wanted to know why.

He'd encountered all manner of creatures. Some were afraid of him, but that wasn't it: he'd practically tasted her surprise the moment they met, and the darkening of her eyes with purpose when she realized what he was. There were plenty of creatures that didn't trust Empyreals, even though he was there to help them. He accepted that. But then there were those that were worried he might find some reason to hunt *them*. And her behavior around him, he had to admit, was the most similar to theirs.

She was a Seer. Yet there *was* an almost imperceptible darkness amid her distracted sort of elegance that, when she locked eyes with him, set his blood thrumming, low and hot. Made a scowl sculpt itself onto his features.

What was she, that she made him feel this combination of suspicion and . . . desire? He couldn't deny that she drew him, and he hadn't been drawn by anyone for as long as he could remember. Was it possible she wasn't a Seer but just believed she was because that's what her family might be?

"You said your visions are unpredictable," he continued. "Why?"

Her pulse had jumped beneath his thumb, and he felt almost vindicated to see that her pupils had dilated. Yet the question made her twist her wrist within his grip. He released her, but she didn't move too far away.

"I don't know," she said. "I'm secluded in a coastal town. Not much happens here to prompt visions."

Yes, Seers usually needed triggers, but that didn't track.

"Are you afraid I'll hunt you, Nicole?"

Her breath faltered and the knot in his stomach tightened. But then her chin raised, dark eyes glinting in the unlit room. And he realized with relief that, no, she wasn't afraid of him.

"Do I feel like a threat to you?" she asked.

He looked down at her thoughtfully, the pale lines of her jaw, her direct gaze. Felt that strange, coiled energy in her and a tug of memory, mystery. Thought of the words she'd said earlier today: "It's more than a painting on a wall . . . I won't have my family in danger."

Something about her drew him, and he wondered if maybe she *was* a threat and that was why. He thought of all the things she could unearth in him, long buried. And an Empyreal's weaknesses.

So he said, softly, honestly, "I don't know yet."

They continued their examination of the room, discovering nothing more to aid his hunt. As they left, he realized that while he knew what his update to the Wake would say later, he wasn't sure if his fingers would still burn from the delicate heat of Nicole's wrist as he typed those three words.

The hunt's begun.

12 NICOLE

Nicole and Dylan found the body of the Finfolk on their morning jog and she immediately called their father. She'd barely slept after insisting on staying at the manor after reading everything she could about Finfolk at home.

But sleeping in that giant unfamiliar bed had been nearly impossible, that and the knowledge Kyan could return from his nightly hunt at any point. She'd hoped the jog would clear her head and yet it only uncovered more mysteries.

Majestic, ancient creatures, Finfolk were blind and pale as the moon. This one's curving, ten-foot tail glistened like a silver river to the crashing surf, starting, in places, to disappear with natural camouflage. It was the first nonhuman-looking creature she'd ever seen and was beautiful, even in death: strange and half-human-looking. But her horror was louder than her fascination.

Its talons hadn't retracted, so they curved from its webbed hands, the bone sharp and forearm-length, gouged deep into the sand. It wasn't clear if it had clawed itself from the water or been heaved on land to die.

Both were highly unusual.

Nicole had wanted to stay, but she'd had to call Kyan as well and let him know. If they didn't, it would look suspicious. Remi had joined in order to summon another Finfolk from the depths to take away the body before humans saw. As Finfolk were such territorial creatures, she couldn't risk being too close.

Now Nicole could barely get the image out of her head as she hurried across campus to her morning folklore lecture, anxiously awaiting Remi, who would join her when she was done.

Mist had flooded the quad, obscuring the elegant arches of its architecture as if it was sketched through tracing paper, its time-darkened stonework worn by the salt in the sea air.

She scoped out the passing students for supernatural energies now she knew the Specter was masquerading as a student, recalling what she had discovered last night:

Finfolk blood, thanks to its camouflaging properties, can be used to strip supernatural varnishes from paintings. It is an old tool, crude, and cruel, as much blood is needed.

If the Specter had stripped the painting of varnish, that meant he knew there *was* some hidden message in it, something more than the vision of Kyan it had stimulated. Her own blood cooled at the thought of the Finfolk being drained, and the fact her mother's secret could be in the hands of a sadistic killer. Who knew what it would do with that information?

It meant that Lynch could have killed the Finfolk. That had been her initial thought on seeing the body, but her father, being so adept at Seeing death, didn't think so. It only made the body more of a mystery and they hadn't had long enough to deal with it before having to call Kyan.

Nicole started over the smooth flagstones and up the stone steps into the echoey foyer of the older departments. She felt ridiculous coming to class when there was a mystery she should be solving. But her research so far had gotten her nowhere. She needed to get the painting back as soon as possible and couldn't risk its secret being in anyone's hands but hers.

Resolved to make a list during the lecture of where else the Specter could have stashed it, Nicole hurried inside, pulling out a pad and a red pen to scribble down a few ideas.

The lecture theater was already dim, so her senses heightened automatically.

Halfway to a seat, something preternatural and dangerous threaded through the air like blood in water.

Nicole sank into the first chair she could, examining the crowd.

The feeling swirled hot and cold under her skin until the slow dread became an uncomfortable buzz. There were several dozen students in various stages of wakefulness, checking their phones, chatting, opening laptops and copies of the Gothic fiction they'd be discussing. Nicole scanned their faces, their energies, tasted the bitterness of black coffee and the early fragrance of pumpkin spice. One wore too much cologne, another not enough. One was tense, but not dangerous. Most of them were tired after a Freshers' night of partying.

But that wasn't all.

No. Not this again. Nicole gritted her teeth hard enough she felt her jaw ache.

One of the students had their back to her. They talked in a low, intent tone. She stared at them until they turned slightly and she could see their face, feel their energy. She exhaled in relief. Human.

They were all just human. Nicole tried to swallow, finding her throat had dried up.

The Specter was here, somewhere.

She'd wondered why it would masquerade as a student, but in the night had recalled that it had asked the curator about *her*.

Nicole sent her senses through the building, scanning all the entrances and exits. All she could hear was the clatter of people walking over old wood, and the muted chatter of classes. If the Specter was close, then surely Kyan would be, too, if he and Remi had finished with the Finfolk.

Flutters of adrenaline pulsed through her muscles. She pulled her copy of *Frankenstein* from her bag and tried to swallow. She should leave, the feeling was only worsening—

"'The more we study, the more we discover our ignorance'" someone quoted behind her, and she immediately recognized the voice.

Her senses twisted with knowing.

Lynch, Kyan had called him.

She closed her eyes for a moment, cursing everything. Then turned slightly, coming face-to-face with the Specter.

Hunt.

Kill.

The intensity of the urges nearly took her breath away.

She was struck first by the darkness of him: his inky hair against pale skin and lean frame draped in an ebony coat. There was an unnerving intelligence in his eyes, which were a dim kind of ancient silver, pale and cold. And then there was his scent: a metallic whisper like blood spatter, and something musty. He appeared her age, and yet she could feel his supernatural energy.

His smile was sharp enough to cut and his features viciously beautiful enough to hurt just as much. She almost expected him to have an ink-stained copy of *The Secret History* tucked beneath the dark wool coat.

"Can I help you?" she asked, her mouth dry, her pulse tapping an eager rhythm beneath her skin.

He slowly leaned closer to scan her face, then smiled, as if pleased with what he saw. She could scent the echoes of a kill on him, or rather, the immoral aura of it. It was strong enough she had to lock her muscles to resist doing something violent. Her body wouldn't transform now, not unless he tried to kill, but that echo told her enough: this stranger had killed before.

An icy peal of panic snaked through her stomach.

"I hope so," he said, voice following some kind of dark music, "Nicole."

She could barely form a thought through the noise of her impulses. She smiled stiffly. "Nice to meet you, but I . . . have to go." She turned, and started to pack her things into her satchel.

"Come now," continued his smooth voice. "We both know that's not true, unless you're off to Westmoore Manor, seeing as you're one of the few people with a key. Why is that, I wonder?"

"I'm not going to talk about this with you."

"No?"

"No," she gritted out, standing up, her back to him.

"Wouldn't you like the painting back?"

Nicole stilled in surprise and twisted carefully. "You're admitting that you stole it?"

He smiled and leaned back, draping one arm over the back of the next seat, his hand startlingly white; the bones slim as a sparrow's. "I never said I stole it, I just said I could help you get it back."

Nicole's eyes narrowed. Reluctantly she sank back down to avoid drawing so much attention. "Why would you do that?"

"Because, dear Nicole, there's something I need . . . help with. As Westmoore's special little protégé, you would know her paintings better than anyone else in this town."

His unnerving eyes were trained on hers in a way that made cold sweat slide down her spine. But she didn't falter; she couldn't risk him figuring out the vicious urges his presence stimulated. Would Kyan be listening? She couldn't sense him, but then her every nerve was trained on Lynch, each one screaming in warning.

"Nicole!" Remi called.

Nicole spun and her worry grew as Remi sashayed down the aisle toward their seats. The Specter could toy with Nicole, but there was no way she was putting Remi in his line of sight.

Too late, she realized, as the Specter's attention drifted to Remi. *No—*

"There you are, I thought I'd be late— Oh!" Remi halted as Nicole grabbed her bag.

"We need to go," Nicole said.

Remi's dark eyes went serious as she scanned the room for danger. "Okay. All right."

She tried to peel Nicole's fingers off her arm but every muscle in Nicole's body had snapped taut with a powerful new desire.

Protect.

And yet she couldn't. This whole lecture theater of chatting students was exposed to Lynch and she couldn't do anything about it.

Nicole leaned back toward the Specter. "The quad, tomorrow morning at six a.m.," she hissed. "I'll answer your questions, just bring the painting."

That grin flashed again.

Another student brushed past Nicole as they headed out, turning to close the door. The student looked at them expectantly. "You two coming in or out?"

"Out," Remi replied. "I forgot my books. Come on." She grabbed Nicole's hand and tugged her out of the building.

Nicole gasped in the air, but it didn't yet have the crispness she needed to slake away these new hungers. She ripped off her coat with a growl of annoyance, and suddenly there was movement and heat behind her.

She spun, her shoulder bumping into Kyan's chest.

"Do you have a death wish?" The words were little more than a growl in her ear.

Nicole shivered, her body roaring, so alive and sensitive even in the dim sun struggling through the bank of overcast skies. She stepped away. He must have been waiting just outside in case Lynch tried anything, which meant he'd also heard every word.

"This way we're both getting what we want," she hissed back.

"Woah, what the hell is going on?" Remi interrupted, setting a furious gaze on Kyan and looking him up and down.

"I leave you alone for an hour and you set up a meet with the Specter?"

"You *what*?" Remi asked.

"I get the painting," Nicole said, then nodded at Kyan, "and you get a chance to see if he'll try to . . ." She thought of the razor fangs of a Specter, and her eyes darted to Kyan's mouth, wondering how far along his transformation was at this point. He hadn't had a problem sleuthing in the dark with her last night. ". . . kill me," she said. "Killing him first and completing your mission."

"Yeah, I vote no," Remi said.

"I thought I told you to stay out of it?" Kyan said to Nicole.

"I didn't exactly go seeking him out. *He* found *me*."

A nerve in Kyan's jaw flickered, then he seemed to get himself under control. "Fine. Good. It will show me where he's hidden it. And then if he tries to kill you . . ."

I'll kill you myself, warned his dark eyes.

She huffed a laugh. "What's that, Mr. Stoic Hunter? An emotion?"

Kyan smiled tightly, but it didn't reach his eyes. "You'd best hope not."

"I'll call my family, it'll be fine."

"No, absolutely not," Kyan said. "The last thing I need is more creatures involved."

Nicole shook her head. "Sorry, but I can't just lie to them."

"Do you want this painting back?"

Nicole bit down. "Yes."

"Do you want your family to be safe?"

Her eyes narrowed. "Yes."

"Then they *don't* get involved." That, it seemed, was the final word as he turned and strode away.

Nicole's breath rushed out. This was good. It was confirmation Lynch had the painting, and if the meet went well, they would have it back by tomorrow morning and she would finally have that last scrap of her mother's ancient wisdom.

So why did she feel off? Jittery?

"Okay," Remi said. "You best start explaining or I'm next in line to wring your neck."

Nicole shook her head, watching Kyan stalk back across the quad. "Come on, I have a plan."

13 NICOLE

"What the *hell* is the Specter doing in our class?" Remi hissed as they entered one of the soundproof rooms in the library, away from where Nicole's father could see them. She dropped her sleek bag onto a chair and flung her caped coat over it.

Estwood University's library was a converted church. With modern pass-lock doors and dark granite, it was the perfect merging of new and old. Glittering lanterns hung low, and glass-paneled reading rooms lined the arched stone walls. It had deep-red carpet, cloister-like study alcoves, and shelves filled with books on folklore, mythology, and every artistic style in history. A stained-glass window let in some weak light and the intimate glow of old desk lamps lit the main room, but the overcast day made it feel more like twilight.

"Taunting me? He knows I have a key to the manor." Nicole sank her fingers into her hair and tugged. She could still feel the seductive slink of power under her skin, so *tempted* by Lynch's presence.

Tempted to rip his fucking throat out.

"I should have noticed," Remi said, shaking her head.

"No," Nicole said. "Empyreals are hypersensitive to dangerous creatures, that's how I knew there was something there in the first place. I just didn't know who it was until the last second."

Remi bit her lip thoughtfully. "Even though you haven't transformed, you could feel him?"

Nicole nodded. "It's our one and only compulsion, to hunt." Her lips almost pulled back at the slick return of her Empyreal's confidence.

Let's go back, whispered her power. *Let me out. Let me* play.

She remembered her mother's words from childhood: "The Goddess of Death made us, darling girl. The temptation will be difficult to resist."

Nicole growled against it. "No."

"What?" Remi asked.

"Nothing, sorry."

Remi's dark eyes softened. "Are you sure you're going to be able to deal with him in such close proximity?"

"Yes, I'm in control." She had to be; she couldn't be anything else. But if he decided to kill, no amount of tonics or training would help her. Worry poisoned her confidence and she reached for her satchel, pulling out a tonic and downing it in one slick gulp. "I know I fucked up. I'll get more controlled before tomorrow and take a few more tonics. It will be fine."

At the silence, Nicole looked up.

Remi was scowling at her. "Only you would think that right now. You didn't fuck up, you survived an encounter with a psychopath and managed to get some key information."

"Which is?"

"That he has the painting."

Nicole sighed. One thing that Remi's parents had taught her was that there was always a clever way to get through a situation.

It didn't always have to be, well, murder. There were wards, favors, supernatural tech, and even Fae bargains to get you around a situation. It was a smart way to live, and had been learned through years of being integrated into the supernatural world in a more cohesive manner than Nicole and her siblings.

"You're right," Nicole said with a nod.

Remi smirked softly. "Of course I am."

Nicole huffed a laugh, calming slightly. "Okay. So it means that if he needs my help then he can't figure out whatever he's discovered in the painting. . . . It can't just be the painting beneath the varnish, the one of Kyan with the torc. There has to be something more."

"What did that image mean?" Remi asked, pacing slightly. "What does it have to do with anything?"

Nicole thought of Kyan's reaction to her last night when she'd offered to show him the vision; when she'd told him what the painting represented. From his reaction, he knew more than he was letting on.

"I don't know," she mused. "Something to do with Kyan, evidently. The Wake, certainly. Why else would the Specter pick that painting?"

"I guess we'll find out tomorrow," Remi said.

"Uh, no. You're not coming."

"Why not? He's seen me now."

"Yes, but hopefully he doesn't know who or what you are from that glance."

"I can use my voice if he decides to get a little handsy."

Nicole recalled asking Kyan what he would do if the Specter bit her, and shuddered, realizing he hadn't answered.

Remi huffed. "You can't protect everyone, you know."

"I can and I will."

"Nicole—"

"Please don't say that I can't. It makes me panic. I need to believe I can control this because otherwise . . . what am I?"

Remi's eyes softened. "You're someone who is still figuring things out, like we all have to." She paused. "Are you going to tell the others?"

"I don't know. I might just tell them I'm spending the night at the manor for research. But I can't keep secrets from them."

"Well, if you do, you won't have to for long. I don't like this idea any more than you, but if you tell them, you know they'll come."

Nicole chewed on her lip, knowing Remi was right. "What happened with the Finfolk?"

"I was able to call one up from the depths and it removed the body, but the Empyreal doesn't think the Specter killed it, so he can't take him out."

Nicole made a frustrated sound. "Then what killed the Finfolk?"

"That, we don't know yet. So how about we look at what we *can* do? Which is figure out how to deal with a Specter. I'm guessing you have your mum's bestiary on you?"

Nicole smiled. How had Remi come to know her so well? She dug into her satchel and pulled out the text. She had flipped to *S* just as Remi came around the table to read alongside her:

Killing a Specter is particularly tricky. Even if they are mortally wounded, they can still heal themselves, so must be killed instantly. This can be done in any manner of ways, including dismemberment, burning, or complete destruction via bombs or other explosive devices.

The best chance you have is to be faster and

stronger. You need to transform into their mortal enemy; that is the only way to successfully eliminate them.

Frustration simmered in her muscles as Kyan flashed into her mind. She would let him do his job, she had to. That way, everyone would win: her family would remain a secret and the Specter would be killed. But she didn't trust him.

She could never trust him.

She read the last few lines of the entry.

But they can be wounded. Stab a Specter with an aura crystal and they will be incapacitated for days if it's not removed quickly. It will not kill them but will feel like it can.

Be warned, if using one on a Specter, it may encourage them to lash out, or use the plasma from human blood to heal themselves. So, strike true, my loves.

And be ready to kill.

Even years before Nicole and her siblings were born, her mother had penned a lot of her books and entries to her future children. Nicole didn't know how her mother knew the three of them would one day arrive, perhaps a Seer told her. But it still warmed her heart to see her mother address her, despite the time and death that separated them.

"An aura crystal, I've never seen one of those," Remi mused.

Nicole sighed, realizing what she had to do. "I have."

14 NICOLE

Warm rain cut through the muggy air, pattering her umbrella as Nicole hurried to the beachfront to meet her brother. The sculpted lines of the buildings were dark against a clotted, pearly sky—a slightly cold blue with a hint of lilac.

Normally the beach was flooded with people, but at ten thirty on a rainy morning, students were in classes and Estwood was quiet, save for the caw and swoop of seagulls like quick pencil sketches, their echoey song coming from somewhere above.

Perfect for what she was about to do.

She hadn't told her family about the plan, and wasn't sure if she would, but she supposed she had till six in the morning to figure that out.

The supernatural senses lurching and coiling under her skin reminded her of one thing: she couldn't risk a transformation. If Lynch got angry or violent, she needed a way to protect herself that didn't expose her urges or her physical strength so she could run. Because evidently Kyan really was always there. And she needed to make sure that nothing damning came out in either her conversation with Lynch, or through her actions at the meet.

It would be no use if they got the painting back, only to have revealed herself to Kyan. Then he'd be taking her *and* the painting with him to the Wake.

Over her dead body.

Dylan waited for her outside the narrow alley, his eyes cool and steady.

"Ready?" he asked.

Nerves jangled in her stomach, but she nodded.

Nestled at the back of a narrow alley was the crystal shop. It wasn't easy to find—there was only one old-fashioned sign: a disembodied, gloved hand pointing the way into the shadowed entrance—but Nicole had been here many times before.

She gripped the strap of her satchel and started over the cobblestones, her nerves turning to nausea. She breathed out steadily as she neared the fragile-looking glass entrance, the alley narrowing enough that her umbrella scraped the walls. Putting it down, Nicole opened the door.

Inside, seashells, fossils, and crystals glittered. The walls were covered in shelves and drawers, some of which were open to expose hunks of iridescent rocks and sea glass.

Jerren shuffled through from the back. He was a burly man in his sixties, always wearing dungarees, his skin reddish from eternal wind or sunburn and his salt-and-pepper beard kept short.

Though he was human, he knew about the supernatural world, and had several pieces of supernatural stock, including exactly what she was looking for. He was a good man, believed them to be Seers, and had kept them updated on any new supernatural acquisitions, so she was already regretting what she was going to have to do.

But she'd do it, to keep them all safe.

To keep that measure of control.

"Mornin', Nicole, Dylan," he said, but she could see he already knew there was something troubling her. He leaned on the counter. "What's wrong?"

"Jerren, I need a favor." She briefly told him of the new supernatural in town while Dylan pretended to peruse the shop's treasures.

"A Specter?" Jerren shook his head, rubbing his rough jaw. "Christ, I can't sell it to you, Nicole. All aura crystals need a Wake permit."

"But it's an emergency."

"I know, and I'd give it to you if I could, but I have to report each one."

Nicole had avoided Influencing people for years. She and Dylan had had to do it plenty of times as kids, as they could never be too careful. When their mother had been alive, she had Influenced whoever she needed to if their excuses to leave a town overnight weren't good enough, or if people simply needed to forget they had ever existed in order to leave no trail the Wake could follow.

But when she was gone . . . their father was brilliant, but nothing could really beat Influence. Even as a child Nicole could do it. She just hadn't had reason to in years, and only ever used it in dire situations. After looking into Lynch's eyes today and feeling her Empyrean power shift, she couldn't risk it awakening.

She could feel Dylan keeping an eye out from where he leaned against the wall near a case of glittering sea rock and crystals.

So Nicole reached deep into herself and tapped into her power. After so long unused it bloomed up like a wave, warm and intense.

"I'm sorry, Jerren," Nicole said. Then her Influence warmed her throat and lips. Her voice lowered, turning dreamy and inhuman. *Please go and get me the aura crystal and put this in its place.* She put a chunk of almost identical pale quartz up on the counter. *"And forget we spoke about this."*

Jerren's eyes glazed over as he turned and headed to the back of the shop. Then, as if rewarding her for using some of her Empyrean power, a flood of endorphins banked her. She tamped it down the best she could, and the intense satisfaction quickly turned to cold guilt. Heat glared in her cheeks and her fingers ached as she gripped the counter.

Jerren came back out, staring over her head, and set the cloth-wrapped bundle on the table with a dull *thunk*. Nicole reached for it, taking the weight steadily. It was cold, even through the wrapping.

"I'm sorry," she whispered again, taking in his hazy eyes. Then she turned to hurry back through the shop.

"Just like old times," Dylan said, pushing off to open the door for her. There was no sarcasm or joy in his tone, it was more . . . comforting. Regretful. Like he knew they'd have to return to these ways eventually.

Nicole pressed her lips together and hurried from the shop.

Outside, she closed her eyes as they walked back down the damp alley, letting the mist of fine rain stroke over her features. She opened them again to see the gray waves, dotted with the dark specks of surfers, roiling past the beachfront restaurants.

Nicole breathed in the ocean air, hoping it would wash the guilt away. But the power was still swirling in her blood; warm, convincing. The other reason she avoided Influencing people was it seemed to stir her Empyreal even more, unlocking the intoxicating lure of power she'd always controlled.

Do it again, it whispered.

She considered skipping her next class and going to try and get herself together in the painting studio. But looking out over the dunes to the fisherman's hut she didn't want to feel like she was running away.

"I would like to think that you won't need it," Dylan said, "but considering the creature has stolen a painting the Empyreal is looking for, and you're in the middle of it, then I'm glad you're prepared."

Nicole looked up at him, finding he'd opened the umbrella over them, the clear fabric immediately pelted with rain.

"When aren't I?"

He gave her a fond, if worried, smile.

"I just don't want to be . . . tempted," she said quietly.

"Were you?"

Nicole stared out. How could she admit it? It would make her sound like she wasn't in control, and she couldn't bear the thought of giving him more to worry about.

"I haven't got close," Dylan said, "because I don't know if I would be. I'd like to think that with our tonics and everything I could resist, but I'm not risking it, and I don't think you should either."

"He has the painting, Dylan. We need it."

"I know you love this place," her brother said, looking out at the dark silver waves. "But we can find a new home if we need to."

The backs of her eyes burned with the threat of tears. "We could *try*. But without Mum's clues, it would be a losing effort. Besides, I just . . . this place is special. And I don't want to do this forever. Don't you want to be settled?"

She'd seen his bedroom; sparse and undecorated, whereas she and Bells had embraced their spaces, embraced this place. She thought of all the things in the house: the badly hung paintings she'd put up to prove they would stay here long enough to hang artwork. The dying fern called Gerald that Bells insisted she could keep alive but frequently forgot about. Even her brother's reluctant stamps on the house, like the cookie cutters Tomás had bought him that he'd left on the side table, intending to give back, but never managing to. He was afraid to commit to this place, perhaps afraid to fall in love with a home or person and have to leave again.

Perhaps it had been easier for Bells because she was younger, less jaded, despite the nightmares that plagued her. More willing to find hope in the waking hours. She had, after all, known this town as home since she was five years old.

Nicole went to tell him about the meet with the Specter when her phone began to vibrate. She plucked it from her pocket and showed him the screen. Dylan shook his head with a smile.

Try hiding anything from a Seer.

"Hey, Bells," Nicole answered, slipping the crystal carefully into her satchel.

"What did you just do?" demanded their little sister.

Nicole sighed. While it was unusual for a Seer to have visions of their family, if they involved other people like Jerren, it was possible. Clearly this moment was important enough to break through to Bells.

"Did you just use your powers on Jerren?"

Nicole could hear the chatter of Bells's fellow students in the background. She must have had a vision in the middle of class. Nicole rubbed her temple; she hadn't even thought it might affect her sister.

"Jerren is the sweetest person in this town," Bells said. "He replaced my pink quartz scrying crystal for free once when I lost mine."

131

"Don't make me feel worse."

"Why did you do this?"

Nicole sighed again, stepping into a particularly glassy puddle to shatter her reflection. "It's just for security, okay? I'm not even going to use it, and I'm going to put it back as soon as the Specter is dead and gone. Jerren will never even notice it was missing."

"He could get in trouble! It's illegal. And what about the Empyreal? He could have sensed your powers!"

"I'm by the beach, the ions will smother any lingering power. Besides, he's tailing Lynch." Nicole had allowed the knowledge that Kyan watched over the lecture to placate some of her guilt for leaving. Not that there was anything she could do to stop Lynch if he tried to feed off anyone. Not without exposing them.

Bells sighed. "It's risky."

"Everything's risky with a Specter on the prowl," Nicole said, hushed.

"I don't think it was a good idea."

"Why leave it to sit in a safe when we might need it?"

"Why do you think we will? Have you had a vision?"

Nicole didn't miss the tension in her sister's question and her brother's curious glance.

"No," she said. "Have you?"

Bells went quiet on the phone.

"What have you Seen, Bells?" Nicole pressed.

"Nothing, I just . . . everything has consequences." She paused. "Remi isn't with you, is she?"

Nicole smiled and she looked up to find that Dylan was smiling, too. She was pretty sure Bells had been enamored with Remi for a year or two now, even though she had never said anything about it, just blushed profusely whenever Remi looked in her direction.

"No, don't worry, she isn't complicit in my evil schemes."

"Good. But, next time, just tell me, okay? I'm already feeling useless—"

Nicole frowned, worry clenching her chest. "What? You're not useless, Bells."

Dylan seemed about to say something.

But Bells said, "I . . . I need to go. Don't do anything else or I'll tell Dad."

Nicole huffed. "Deal, but we're not done talking about this."

"I love you," Bells whispered.

Those tears almost brimmed in Nicole's eyes. "Love you, too, little oracle."

15 KYAN

It was five in the morning when Kyan returned to Westmoore Manor.

He hesitated outside Nicole's temporary bedroom. She'd chosen one in the guest wing, separated from Westmoore's quarters by long corridors and the ballroom.

And yet, it didn't feel far enough.

He'd felt her in the house since he arrived back, knew she'd been studying in the library, her unique scent ghosting through the house.

But now there was silence on the other side of the glossy door, aside from her steady breathing. She must have fallen asleep with the light on—he'd seen it shining across the sand dunes like a beacon as he'd made his way back. It reminded him, uncomfortably, that there was someone waiting for him.

He thought about leaving her asleep. Letting the hour of the meet glide past, keeping her safe.

Usually, he would let events proceed—after all, she'd organized this herself, and he would be near to stop a kill. But if she didn't cooperate, Lynch was likely to torture her for the information he wanted. And Kyan would have to listen and not interfere until that killing blow. . . .

Her breathing changed on the other side of the glossy door. A hitch.

She'd awoken.

He knocked softly.

He heard an intake of breath, the rasp of clothes against covers, and a small curse as she asked, "Er . . . yes?"

For a moment he didn't know what to say, or how. So said, somewhat gruffly, "It's me."

Papers rustled, as did a heavy silken-sounding comforter, then came her quiet steps.

She pulled open the door a moment later, cheeks flushed from sleep. He was punched by the scents: paper, graphite, and the lingering fragrance of *her*. Delicate, yet heady. That perfume that was beginning to feel a little addictive in its mystery.

The room behind her was cream-colored and luxurious, with glass doors onto the night-shrouded beach. The ornate bed was covered with notes and a slumbering marble fireplace sat opposite, paintings of ships and coastal dawns hanging about the room.

"Did you follow him and see where the painting is?" Nicole asked.

His lips almost curled up at her tenacity, but a low frustration stopped them.

He sighed, lingering in the dark hallway. "I'm going to give you another chance to back out of this."

She blinked and the last of the sleep in her expression evaporated. "What?"

"You don't have to do this. He will slip up eventually and I'll get the painting and kill him."

She searched his face before turning and striding back toward the bed. "I'm doing this whether you want to be there or not."

He followed, his boots sinking into the plush carpet. "I'll be there."

She looked over her shoulder from where she was shuffling an array of crumpled sketches, a crescent of charcoal staining the edge of her little finger and hand. He felt the strange urge to stroke it, to have some of it rub off on him.

"Using me as bait grating you, Empyreal?" she asked, with a smirk in her voice.

"Yes."

Nicole faltered and there was a vulnerable flicker of confusion in her dark eyes. It bothered him that she'd think so little of him, and yet he didn't know how to change her mind. Didn't know why he cared.

He snatched up one of the papers—notes on the paintings. "What have you found, then?"

She went to take it back. "We can talk about it later."

"We have time," he said, running his gaze over the page to take his focus off her. He wanted time to think of some other way to get around this.

Nicole made a frustrated sound and climbed back on the bed, sitting semi-tucked beneath the covers. He flicked a glance at her crossed legs, heard the rasp of her tights, and felt the urge to pace, to knot and unknot the leather bracelet on his wrist.

Instead, he perched on the end of the high bed and read her notes, letting his long legs cross at the ankles.

"I don't know why you need to read them," she groused quietly. He stole another look in her direction as she looked down at the last of a cold coffee, then began to braid back her loose hair.

Subtle lavender veins traced her eyelids, those sharp eyes fanned by dark lashes. Low-lit by the lamplight, she was every shade of autumn, tinged with nighttime: dark chestnut hair with a few almost indiscernible strands of red, which silhouetted her heart-shaped face and the blush in her pale cheeks.

An English rose.

"And I don't know why you feel the need to integrate yourself into this mission," Kyan said, "but here we are."

He saw her scowl but kept his lips in a firm line. There was one question he needed answered before they left. She'd kept much from him already and he could feel her anxiety as he looked over notes she clearly hadn't had the time to cultivate for his eyes. There were question marks all over the place, threads of ancient history, research on the Druids that made his gut clutch and eyes skim quickly to something else.

But it was her skirting around his questions that bothered him; that made him feel like there was something he was missing. And if he missed something, people could get hurt.

"Why do you want this so much?" he asked.

She paused, a glimmer of vulnerability in her eyes. "Because this is my home."

Ah. *Truth.*

He settled slightly at the honesty. "Then let's get your painting back."

NICOLE

Kyan parked the car a few streets away from the quad with five minutes to spare.

He'd barely spoken during the dark gliding drive into town. She tried not to recall his presence at the end of her bed: the preternatural power in his body, the simmering tension from the moment she'd opened the door to him. The way the sight of him in the glow of her bedroom had stirred heat in her stomach; made it feel like letting him inside was somehow forbidden.

Now she took a breath; the scent of cool nighttime air was still on his dark coat, along with whatever that addictive scent of his was.

"Try not to rile him," Kyan said, frowning at the night before they got out.

Nicole shot him a look. "You just worry about Lynch. I've got this under control." It was only a mild lie. Her insides felt liable to shiver with nerves and she wished she'd told her family. Knowing *they* would back her up would soothe this unease.

She was just grateful she'd had a chance to retrieve the aura crystal from beneath her pillow before they left. It now sat, bulky and cold, in the band of the jeans she'd changed into.

Kyan's eyes narrowed as he shot her a look. "You *should* worry about him. At least have a little healthy fear."

"I do," she said, realizing it was true. But she was more afraid of transforming than hurting. Pain was fleeting for her, her body healed too quickly. But the pain of loss? The fear of being found by the Wake?

Those were eternal.

"Good," Kyan said.

"I'm not reckless, Kyan."

"No," he said thoughtfully. "I don't think you are."

They both got out of the car and he lingered for a moment, leaning on the hood. It reflected the dim streetlamps and the last wink of stars in the sky.

"He'll try to bait you," Kyan said, "but just keep as calm as possible." He paused, like he might say something more, but ended with, "I'll be close by."

And then he was gone, and she was alone in the nighttime street. The sound of the sea called in the distance, but otherwise, Estwood was asleep.

She hoped that would remain the case.

The day would lighten soon, but for now, the early-morning sky was an intense dark navy, made a little paranormal by the sliver of a moon, and so she walked the last of the way.

Lynch waited for her in the great rectangle of grass in the center of the quad, the old buildings around it illuminated by eerie blue lights. She was almost surprised to see he'd actually shown up. But there he was, his scent a palpable, fragrant string leading her, luring and tempting her most vicious instincts.

But he would not win.

Striding toward him, Nicole kept her eyes on his, even though a low pulse of annoyance and worry had already started tapping along her spine.

"Not a minute late," Lynch said.

"Where's the painting?"

His smile flashed. "It's safe."

"I thought you wanted me to look at it. I can't tell you anything if—"

Lynch held up a scrap of paper and Nicole stilled. On it, barely illuminated by moonlight, was a series of numbers.

She risked taking a few steps closer, eyes devouring its details. It was the edge of a page, torn off so as not to reveal any more of the sequence. Nicole reached out to take it, but the Specter pulled it back.

"What," asked Lynch, "is this?"

They were closer now, perhaps too close. She resisted the urge to take a step back. "What's it from?"

The Specter's eyes narrowed. "Now, now. I asked first."

Nicole tried to control her expression. She would bet this was the reason he'd needed the Finfolk, to use its blood and take the varnish off the painting, revealing—this.

Was *this* her mother's message? Not the vision of Kyan, but some kind of cipher? She'd had a tendency to use codes and ciphers, or little historical crumbs that Nicole would have to research to figure out. But her mother only used ciphers when the information was too risky to write plainly. She must have worked with Bouguereau and asked him to paint this cipher into his piece, just as she likely asked him to paint the alternative image beneath the varnish: the one of Kyan with the torc around his neck. Nicole had often wondered if the human artist had known of their world thanks to all the creatures he painted. Now she had her answer.

It meant this was the secret Nicole needed.

But now it was in the hands of a Specter.

She slowly stepped closer, as if approaching a dangerous animal, and raised her brows slightly, wordlessly asking to see it. But his moon-white hand didn't move.

"I wouldn't know what it meant until I saw all of it," she said. But at the suspicious look in his eyes, her senses began to rush.

Her heart knocked a little harder. Her senses a dull roar in her ears.

"Why is it, I wonder," Lynch began, circling her, "that a girl in a small coastal town knows about codes and ciphers and paintings?"

The last thing she needed was him figuring out she had a bigger part to play in all this. That she *herself* was involved. Her mother.

"I study art history; I know how to read a painting."

"That's not enough." Lynch stepped closer. His hand, the one that had held the piece of paper, appeared again.

But the paper was gone.

"Did you just call me here to toy with me?"

"As fun as that sounds, no. I'm on a deadline. Literally." Something more than irritation flashed through his eyes—an urgency she couldn't exactly call fear. "You have an idea what this is and who put it there, but you're not telling me. That, Nicole, is not fair at all. I need answers. So, are you going to help me, or will we have to play this little game a bit more ruthlessly? The choice is yours."

"Show me the rest," she said, "and I'll help you. Better yet, show me the painting."

His hand reached for her neck and she deflected it automatically, cursing her unusual reflexes.

"But touch me and I'll smack that little smirk off your face."

She had no idea what he could learn from his touch.

His *teeth*.

Her blood could tell him a great amount.

Lynch grinned softly, watching her mouth. "So violent. I do like a woman with a bite of her own."

"Is that what your victims had?"

His brow arched. "Interesting assumption."

"It's not an assumption." *I can smell the evil on you.*

"They did," he said. "At the beginning." But he pushed away softly, as if to put space between himself and his past murders. "Besides, 'victims' is such an ugly word. Is that what you're worried about? I wouldn't kill you, Nicole." *Not at the beginning*, was the unspoken rest of the sentence. He'd want to wear her down first, until she was a shade of herself. Until she was out of her mind with fear. "If you need the painting for the same reasons as I do, we would be much better becoming a nice little team. I can share."

"I doubt that."

He smiled, delighted. Suddenly she wondered if he'd been like this his entire life. He could be a few hundred years old, or Nicole's age. But how long had he been systematically killing people in cold blood?

Mirth glinted in his eyes. "Nicole, Nicole." As if daring her, his finger grazed her neck.

Nicole's breath caught as his cold touch trailed downward, his eyes inches from her face.

"You know what this little piece of nonsense is. Perhaps I should just get the information out of you another way." He tapped her neck and gave a white flash of his teeth.

Her power sent an electric current of anticipation through her blood.

Just try it, it seemed to say, causing her breath to hitch.

Perhaps he would mistake it for fear, when it was actually the temptation to rip his head off his shoulders.

"Some people like the drug of my venom. Just think of the evening we'd have. That slow, hot feeling in the blood, relaxing the muscles, the pull of my mouth at your neck. All that sweetness on the tongue, and the knowledge flooding between us. How . . . intimate."

Don't break his hand, she chanted, her eyes fluttering closed as she went to take a shaky step backward. *Control yourself.*

But then his fingers closed around her throat to stop her, and when her eyes flashed open, she was elsewhere.

Suddenly, with the contact, she was *there*, with every mutilated victim he'd created. Every quick spray of blood. Every cry for help; cries that devolved into sobs, into sounds Nicole would hear in her nightmares.

This is the type of thing Bells Sees at night, she distantly thought.

And then she was one of them. She was looking through the eyes of one of his victims, from where they'd fallen in their living room. Somewhere warm and homey. Lynch stood in the light of their fireplace, his thin teeth long as needles, his face a new mask of horror, white and malicious.

In the vision, Lynch launched and his razor-sharp teeth split through the skin of their neck. And pain seared through her. Pain, like nothing she'd felt before, which split her from the person's consciousness.

Suddenly, Nicole was standing across the same room, seeing the attack happening. Then the girl's face changed.

It became Remi.

Then Bells.

The Specter was suddenly behind her, whispering in her ear, "Stop me if you can, little huntress."

Rage and desperation had her launching at him in the vision, to kill, to save the girl and herself. Her best friend. Her sister.

But when she reached for Lynch, her arm was scarred with the

Wake's mark. That perfect circle she saw when she closed her eyes; when she looked at the sun, the moon, the earth; into Kyan's eyes.

A circle.

A cage.

"You can't save them," Lynch taunted. "He'll hunt you next."

A bolt of pure fear ripped her from the vision, like it tore right down the center of her heart.

No.

When her eyes flashed back open, it was to Lynch's grunt of pain and a deep, shocking feeling of satisfaction as her Empyrean powers pulsed and bled through her.

"No," she whispered, looking down to find she'd stabbed him with the crystal.

Hot, dark blood slowly spread over her hand. As she stared, she started to tremble with the clamor of her instincts. Had the vision been a mix of past and future, or had he somehow gotten into her head?

She let go of the crystal and it sucked deeper into his abdomen.

Her fingers shook as she stared at the blood on her hand. Her lips tingled and a strange taste slaked through her mouth as her insides pulled and dropped.

Suddenly, her bloodied hand was around Lynch's throat. His jerk brought them almost nose to nose. Her lips almost pulled back in a snarl.

"What did I tell you?" she warned, in a voice she almost didn't recognize.

His awful eyes had gone black; with pain, with intrigue, and his teeth flashed, no longer plain and white, but those needle-like horrors.

Nicole shoved him with a shaking hand and backed up, fighting every instinct and forcing herself to *run*.

"I haven't been intrigued," Nicole heard him say, "in a long time."

Before she could get through the archway to the street, he had grabbed her arm and almost dislocated it. A second later something hard and cold slammed into her back: he'd thrown her against the wall.

She cried out as pain shot through her skull and shoulder blades.

Then Lynch's hand was around her throat.

16 NICOLE

A hot wave of anticipation crashed through Nicole's blood and a darkness clutched her stomach as she stared into Lynch's vicious silver eyes.

"What did you stab me with?" he seethed.

She jerked her face away, the smell of his blood trying to congeal, turning her stomach and burning her pulse into a rapid, hungry fury. But she couldn't use her strength to get him off her. Kyan was supposed to be here, somewhere, *watching everything.*

"Get. It. Out," Lynch hissed.

The crystal wouldn't kill him, but it would feel like it could.

The faces of the people in her vision returned. Crying. Screaming. Lynch had made sure to wring every last drop of fear from them before they went insane. Before he killed them.

Her lips pulled back in a snarl. *"No."*

Pain and fury bulged the veins in his neck. "My, aren't you full of surprises?"

Several knife-like pricks dug into her where his fingers met her throat and made her hands and head tingle with numbness. She choked on a cry.

"I tried to be civil, Nicole. But fine, let's see just what other surprises you have."

His nails lengthened, piercing her neck. Pain sparked down her veins and she fought a scream, feeling his power seep deep into her energy points, her *being*.

Her Empyreal thrashed like a caged animal.

She struck him in his wounded side with a fast jab. He gave a strangled cry, his nails dislodging, but a drip of blood ran down her throat from his grip.

Followed by the cold stroke of his tongue.

Panic had her hand back at his throat to push him away, her knee coming up between his legs as her thumb pressed *hard* into his wounded side. He drew back, his mouth smeared with her blood, his eyes near feral.

But his pain-dark eyes gleamed with a revelation. "You're an—"

Suddenly his hand was gone.

Nicole slid down the brick, her skin scraping against it, and nausea lurched up her throat as agony singed her neck.

Kyan had Lynch pinned to the wall opposite. His eyes burned dangerously, his chest heaved and his teeth glistened with venom; even his back seemed larger.

"You're lucky," Kyan said, his voice low and deadly, one great hand around the Specter's neck, "that the Wake, that my *body*, has rules."

She'd never seen him like this.

Like the hunter from her vision.

Usually, Empyreals didn't allow themselves to be seen by their targets. If Lynch now knew he was being hunted, it could change everything. He might hide himself and his deeds better. He might take it as some kind of sick challenge. Yet right now, Nicole was just *grateful*. She'd never thought she'd think that about—

Lynch's strangled laugh cut through her thoughts, his eyes still on Nicole. "An Empyreal."

Her blood iced.

She reached up to her neck, wincing. The skin throbbed where his nails had stabbed into her, but while the wounds had quickly sealed over, the backs of her eyes burned with the remnants of Lynch's power. He'd tasted her blood. He knew what she was. She fought the tremors of her power as it crashed over her in waves.

"I wonder if he'll figure it out," Lynch said, gasping a cracked laugh.

Those waves of fear froze.

I'll rip you to pieces, you little—

Nicole tamped down on the anger as her Empyreal lurched painfully inside. She gritted her teeth and smashed a fist against the ground in frustration.

Kyan looked over at her sharply and let Lynch go, shoving him roughly through the archway and into the cobbled street. The morning was beginning to lighten; they didn't have much longer before shops began opening.

"Get out of here," Kyan warned.

Lynch staggered a few feet away.

"What the hell are you doing?" Nicole struggled up, her muscles screaming. "You're letting him go?"

Kill him, now!

Lynch looked between them, a gleam of choked amusement making him laugh before doubling over from the stab wound. He looked up. "Now we've entered this dangerous little tableau, come and find me, Empyreal. You and I have something to discuss."

Something to discuss.

If he told Kyan what she was—

Nicole launched for Lynch's throat and was practically hauled off the ground by Kyan.

Lynch laughed, blood trickling through the fingers clamped to his abdomen as he hobbled down the cobbles and out of sight.

She needed to make sure Kyan didn't go to whatever damned *chat* Lynch had planned. What would the Specter do? Offer Nicole in exchange for safety from the Wake? Of course the Wake would take that offer, what would they care about letting another killer like Lynch go free when she was her mother's daughter—with possibly all her secrets?

She gripped Kyan's bulky arm to stop him going anywhere.

"What did he mean by that?" he asked her.

Nicole let go of him and staggered back against the wall, her harried pulse burning in her neck. "By *what*?" she hissed. "You're the one who's supposed to understand him."

Kyan stepped closer, scowling. "Are you all right? I smelled blood."

She let out a harsh laugh to hide her sudden fear. She'd healed too quickly to admit Lynch had punctured her skin. Besides, what could she say? *I was going to rip out of my skin and kill him, just give me a minute*?

"I'd be a lot better if he was dead," she snapped, shaking.

"There was no kill scent."

Nicole gaped. "*Really?* He just had me against a wall but you're going to let it go? I thought you protected people?" She shook her head and winced immediately. "What are you waiting for?"

"I need *proof*," Kyan said, bending closer, his own frustration burning up the words. "I don't go around killing because the Wake want me to."

Liar.

"What more proof do you need?" she said, throwing her arm out after where Lynch had disappeared, hissing at the way the tendons in her neck pulled. She glared at his fresh blood on her hand. It was *everywhere*, like her secret, spilled and gaping and deadly. Now in the hands of a monster who could use it against her. She shook her head, astounded. "It doesn't matter if there's collateral damage, does it? People can get injured as long as you get him in the end. Were you even going to stop him?"

Kyan's eyes narrowed and anger flared in them. Yeah, well, he could get in line. She was damn angry at herself, first.

"I can't transform until he makes that decision. What did you think you were doing, stabbing him out of nowhere?" She glared up at him and didn't answer. "Didn't you think for two seconds that you might get yourself killed?"

It hadn't crossed her mind. Not once. She'd felt powerful. Panic and fear were there, but for the people in the vision, for her family and Remi. She didn't have the emotional energy to unpack that right now. She knew stabbing Lynch wasn't smart, but her body had *made* her.

For years she'd put the Empyreal part of herself away neatly, had been happy with herself. But nothing had challenged it. Now the rug had been pulled out from under her and her soul perked up and her blood became a foreign animal. Everything stirred and sharpened and grew alive and she didn't know what to do. All her reading fled in the face of impulse. She only knew what her body told her. And that could ruin everything.

Was ruining everything.

"I didn't . . . I couldn't . . ." *I couldn't control myself.* "What do you want me to do? Tell you I'm sorry? I'm *not*." She spun and stalked away instead, the skin of her neck tight and pulsing as it tried to heal. She clamped her fingers around it to hide its progress.

"You know I'm becoming a Specter," Kyan said, striding alongside her. "You remember I can walk through walls?"

She glared up at him. Of course she knew, she wasn't an idiot. "Don't patronize me, Kyan."

The muscle in his jaw flickered. "I'm trying to be clear. I was on the other side of that wall. I was right there. I've been doing this a long time, Nicole; I know what I'm doing. Why don't you trust me?"

Because I could never trust an Empyreal.

Even my own.

"What the hell were you doing with an aura crystal anyway?" he asked.

"I wanted it for protection."

"Because you didn't trust me to keep you safe," he said tightly.

"You said yourself you wouldn't have been able to stop him unless he decided to kill me!"

"But I did!" He thrust a hand through his hair, looked around as if for his sanity. "I'm not supposed to do shit like this."

"So why did you?"

Kyan's attention narrowed back on her. There was a flash of something in his dark eyes that shot heat and intensity through her already overstimulated body. So she hurried away faster. Anywhere to get farther from Lynch, from Kyan and the temptations they raised within her.

I need a tonic, she realized, her shaking hand grappling for her satchel before realizing she didn't even have it and she'd already had three tonics in the last twenty-four hours. She heard a little sound of distress, then realized it had come from her. Her legs seemed suddenly rubbery, the world tilted—

"I—"

Suddenly the floor was gone and the sky came veering toward her.

Then she was still. Blessedly still, and there was something warm and solid against her left shoulder, a kind of delicious heat and scent.

Kyan.

Nicole blinked as he began walking, realizing what he'd done.

"Put me down," she managed.

"Not a chance."

"I'll fight you."

Kyan gave a humorless laugh. "Save it." Then, softer, but still tense with fury: "You can barely walk for trembling. His blood is still on your hands. How about you let me help you for ten seconds."

Suddenly she wanted to cry. She *was* trembling, but with rage, not shock. Or perhaps it was both.

"I get it," he continued, "you don't like Empyreals. Maybe you just don't like other creatures in general, but why—"

"He was going to hurt my sister, the way he'd killed those people." Bile rose at the back of her throat and she wanted to scream. She cursed the warm tears blurring her vision.

Understanding dawned in his eyes. "You Saw something?" He softened. "You should have told me."

"I was in the middle of something. What did you want me to do? Call over and tell you?" She growled in annoyance and wiped her face with her sleeve.

"Listen to me," Kyan said, stilling and getting her to look him in the eye. "I won't let him kill anyone. I haven't lost someone on the job in a long time and I don't intend to ruin that now." His eyes flickered to her bruised throat and the muscle in his jaw ticked. "But I can't be efficient if you don't trust me. So how about the benefit of the doubt, okay? And no more secret weapons unless I know about them. Truce?"

She wanted to trust him. How much easier would it be if she

could just pass the burden to him and leave it there? Not have her whole being swirl with a strange mix of envy, wonder, and desire. But how could she trust someone who worked for the Wake, with everything she knew?

He just broke the rules to protect you, some traitorous thought reminded her.

"Where are you taking me? Please, just . . . put me down."

Kyan's jaw flickered, but he lowered her to the ground.

She tested her weight and found herself more stable.

"This artwork and its history means a lot to you, doesn't it?"

She nodded tiredly. "More than you know."

"Then, come with me."

Nicole looked up at his fierce face. "Why?"

"So I can grab my laptop from the car. I'm getting you something to eat, and then we're looking at the Wake's archives."

17 NICOLE

Lamplight burned as the sky swiftly lightened, creating misted coronas of gold and reminding Nicole of images depicting the power slumbering inside her.

A reminder of the Empyrean fire.

Tamp it down, she told herself as Kyan walked her to a nearby café, open early.

The whole town was starting to feel different. Nicole scowled at the few leaves already settling in the cobbles. She both loved and dreaded autumn's transformation. Right now, she felt too much like a creature hinged on metamorphosis to appreciate it. Above, the slivered moon remained in the sky like an omen: some paranormal eye she'd awakened that now wasn't going back to sleep.

She didn't realize she was shaking until she stepped into the café's tiny bathroom. It wasn't aftershock or fear; she wasn't dizzy or weak.

She was *alive*.

Nicole scrubbed the blood from her fist, recalling how it had seemed to crawl down Lynch's abdomen, congealed, thicker than human blood.

"All the perfumes of Arabia will not sweeten this little hand." Few knew Shakespeare had based that line on an Empyreal, on the fact nothing could cloak their scent after they'd transformed.

That had almost been me.

She didn't want to imagine how differently it might have gone without their tonics or the crystal. It drained energy just like Lynch did. It would pull deep into his body, making it very difficult, and very painful, to get out. *If* he could get it out. She hoped he couldn't. That it would fester and poison.

But his parting words returned: "You and I have something to discuss."

She'd ruined it. She hadn't gotten the painting, or even the cipher, and now Lynch knew what she was. She hadn't even been able to keep herself contained. Her bloodlust had overwhelmed all sense of caution, all thoughts of the consequences.

Nicole wiped her dripping face, checking her neck. It was now a vicious bruise and wasn't healing properly. In fact, she could barely feel it healing at all. A low panic began in her stomach, so she forced herself to breathe deeply, hoping the water sloshing in the sink would drown out the sound.

Bells was safe, so was Remi; she'd texted them both to confirm. But now Lynch knew something about both her and the painting.

Nicole met her eyes in the mirror.

She'd wanted to kill him.

Though she looked the same as she had this morning, something had changed: her dormant Empyrean part had cracked wider with a taste of release.

And it wanted *more*.

Everything seemed sharper when she came back out, like it was three times as loud as usual, including her attention on Kyan.

The café's early opening hours meant there were already a few professors and students here before their classes, so the windows had a dreamy haze of condensation.

Dawn filtered in and strokes of blue unveiled themselves in the sky outside, seeming like the first glimpse of unimpeded daytime she'd felt in days. From her seat she could see down the street to the calm blue of the sea.

"Try and have some water," Kyan said, nodding to the large, gently steaming mug set before her.

Nicole didn't bother resisting, cupping the hot porcelain and blowing softly before taking a warming sip, the action thawing the ice in her chest. She kept her eyes glued to the dark gray laptop he'd retrieved and had set, unopened, on the tiny table between them.

Her stomach nearly growled. She needed proper food and a nap and maybe someone to slap her. She folded her fingers together so he wouldn't see the red crescent marks where she'd clenched her hands.

Concentrate.

A clatter smashed through her raw senses. She felt like a wild creature, something short-tempered and fraying.

Something about to unravel.

To kill.

It was a level of overstimulation that almost made her want to burst into tears.

I can't do this.

She wasn't beginning a slow transformation like Kyan, thanks to the tonics and the fact it was her first. An Empyreal's first transformation was never slow, not in the same easy way as an Empyreal who was used to and accepted their body's metamorphic power over centuries. Even now, he sat in front of her, relaxed, while she jittered.

Just endure it a little longer.

"Have something to eat and then we'll take a look," Kyan said.

She focused on sipping the hot water while waiting for her heaping full English breakfast, unsure how much longer she could bear to be in here as the day began around them. It felt almost embarrassingly intimate to be eating with him. She wondered, as they both started to eat, if he thought she was scared and wired with fear.

Better that than him knowing her Empyreal bounded through her veins, making her ravenously hungry, now it was calming down.

His dark eyes met hers briefly throughout, silently checking if she was all right but otherwise remaining quiet. Despite his preternatural presence and perceptive gaze, he was good at transforming his energy into something she felt she could almost trust. Unnervingly good at it. That, and the fact he *had* been there for her during the attack, made her shoulders reluctantly relax.

"Truce?" he'd asked.

Hmm.

She finished off her meal with a scoop of eggs on buttery toast, and the last foamy remnants of a coffee, feeling sated and warm; less jittery but now sleepy. She'd probably only slept about fifteen minutes last night, and the events were slamming back into her. But the shudders hadn't completely stopped. She closed her eyes, pleading gently with that ancient power within: *I'm tired. Stop now, relax. Too much.*

Nicole eyed Kyan's laptop as he paid, but he didn't open it when he came back over. Instead, he slipped it under his arm and went to leave.

"Where are we going?" she asked.

"Somewhere quieter."

He held the door open for her and Nicole followed, the cool morning air and quiet almost making her groan with relief.

He led her to the old bookshop, its antique bell jingling as they stepped inside. It made her feel even smaller than usual, and somehow more human to notice Kyan stooping to enter behind her.

Lighting was low and glowing in warm pools. They moved past books on Cornwall, rolled-up posters of artwork, glinting shells and sea glass, scented candles, and tins of biscuits. Kyan headed for a small couch in a warm spot, somewhere people wouldn't be able to see what was on his screen.

As soon as they sat down, her attention narrowed to his laptop and the way his strong thigh pressed against hers, thanks to the giant divot in the old leather couch that sloped them closer to one another. And it returned: the confusing feeling of comfort around him. She wasn't sure if it was because he was taking the lead for ten minutes and she wasn't fighting it, or if she was simply tired and he was agreeing to help her. But having watched him move and eat with his economical control made something in her slowly unwind. It caused a flurry of confused signals to her brain.

Get the hell away from him.

Get closer.

She told that one to piss off.

Kyan opened the laptop.

"Why are you doing this?" She desperately didn't want it to be some kind of trick. Were the Wake's archives really so accessible? She'd always imagined they consisted of great tomes in a hidden research facility with passcodes and people in robes. Maybe they needed blood identification to enter. She hadn't expected he could pull them up on his laptop. In a bookshop.

On public Wi-Fi.

"We both need answers. After his questions, we know Lynch has the painting. He'll be more guarded now he knows I'm here. Might even avoid going to check on it and inadvertently leading me to it. We'll find it, it's only a matter of time, but until then, you're the researcher and I have access to key supernatural history through the Wake's archives. But I'm going to be beside you the entire time so the only creatures you can look up are the ones in the paintings." He watched her intently, as he always seemed to, like her secrets would write themselves on her face.

Nicole listened carefully as he typed. Could she tell his password from the sound of the keys?

He pushed up his sleeves, exposing sculpted forearms brushed with dark hair. Veins stood proud in his hands as his fingers worked. Then he held his left arm up to the laptop's camera and she realized what he was doing.

He didn't have a supernatural passport or ID.

His scar was his passport.

Kyan tugged the sleeve back down before she could see it. *That* was how he gained access to the archives.

He turned to her, subtle amusement on his face, and placed the computer on her lap. The cool, humming weight of it was strangely intimate. That, and the fact his arm was no longer beside her, but around the back of the couch so the easy heat of him breathed over her, turning his body into a protective cave.

She swallowed. There was nothing but a dark blue screen and search bar, the bar backed by a white circle symbol. The cursor's line blinked in and out of existence, waiting.

He could look at this whenever he wanted?

He nodded. "Go ahead."

"Wait, I need . . . Can I take notes?"

He hesitated before nodding.

Nicole reached for her satchel—Kyan having brought it from the car. The laptop shifted on her knee as she pulled out a notepad and pencil, resting it alongside them.

Where to start?

Both of the two main paintings, *The Wild Hunt* and *Dante and Virgil*, had one thing in common: Empyreals and their hunting urge. Since Kyan had been so reluctant to talk about the vision the *Dante* painting stimulated, she decided to play it safe and start with the first one. But, just to test, she set her hands on the keyboard and typed "Finfolk."

A second later the page was flush with information. The origins of their names, last known sightings, migration patterns, details of their abilities. There were sketches, photographs, so many things that weren't in her mother's books. But she also noticed details her mother's books had told her that didn't seem to be on here. She could learn so much more. Have every curiosity quenched.

She wondered if the Wake had a database page on her mother and all her aliases. Nicole knew her mother had a few close brushes with them in the past, but would it be enough to be in their archives?

A sharp ache tugged in her heart. She needed her. Wished her mother could tell her how to fix this, what to do. Wished she could be told that, no matter what happened, if she had turned and killed Lynch, it would be all right. And if she didn't, her friends and family would be safe.

After the adrenaline, the anger and confusion, Kyan's jumper, soft and thick against her arm, made her, for an inexplicable minute, want to tuck herself closer. To rest her cheek against it and sleep.

"How badly did he hurt you?" Kyan asked, drawing her attention from the fine print on Fae crowns.

She hadn't realized she'd reached up to her collar. Her fingers flattened on her neck. She'd checked the angry purple flare before they'd left the café; that Lynch had made a mark on her struck her more than she wanted it to.

"Not as much as I hurt him."

Kyan didn't give anything away, his frown forming a dark needle of shadow above his right brow. And she wondered: If he were a painting, could she read him better?

Nicole returned to the archives and typed in "The Wild Hunt."

She'd done plenty of research on it before, fascinated by the idea that Empyreals had skirted the edge of human awareness throughout the ages. The database read:

> The Wild Hunt: Some believe it came into human
> folklore with the Dark Ages, when mankind was
> almost overrun with unnaturally vicious creatures.
> To prevent another Dark Age and Wild Hunt from
> happening, all Empyreals discovered must swear an
> oath of loyalty to the Wake. All must be accounted
> for and available should another Dark Age descend.
> Humanity would not survive otherwise.

This logic was widely known and one of the reasons creatures accepted and mostly felt safer knowing the Wake was in control and that their Empyreals hunted throughout the world. But her mother had been adamant that an oath of allegiance, a blood oath, had done something else to Empyreals. The Wake had forced Empyreals to take it.

And if any had refused, they killed them.

"This oath," Nicole murmured, wondering what he would say about it. "This is your scar?"

Kyan seemed newly tense at her question but nodded.

"But it's different from when you were first drafted into the Wake? Didn't you swear an oath then, too?"

"Yes. The first was to hunt for the Wake. The second was introduced in 1902, to bring any new Empyreals we discover into the organization." He nodded his chin at the page. "To stop a Dark Age ever happening again."

"Were you there for that? Did you see it?"

Kyan nodded slightly and a barrage of questions filled her mind, one standing out in particular, considering she still felt like she was fighting the call of her Empyrean powers.

"I told you," he said, eyes softening, "I've been doing this a long time."

"How . . . how old are you?"

"My physical form right now? A few years older than you. Otherwise, I . . . don't know."

"What do you mean?" A cold, awful feeling began to spread in her chest. In her mother's many books on Empyreals, she had discovered that the Wake almost brainwashed them. She hadn't discovered how, but she knew why.

It kept them alone; it kept them loyal.

But it also meant that in their doctrine of telling Empyreals not to think of the past, they would, in turn, begin to slake away those memories. Forging them into hunters that lived for the next mission;

that didn't think of the past, but the *present*, and only that. Not even the future, she supposed, for all they'd see ahead was an eternity of hunting: no family, no goals other than those immortal urges.

It was one of the reasons she was so afraid of getting taken. What if they did that to her? What if they made her some loyal huntress who didn't remember her family? Who was barely able to see her brother, her father, or sister . . .

Her throat grew hot, and that quick, intense urge to cry surprised her again. She swallowed hard.

"We didn't date the world quite the same way when I was young," Kyan said, drawing her out of those thoughts. "It was a long time ago. Called the Ulster Cycle now."

She blinked hard. She'd been looking at the screen to hide her expression but now she frowned at him in a mix of fascination and amazement. "Isn't that Irish mythology?"

"My turn for a question," he tried instead, but she didn't miss how he wanted to move on. "Where did you get the aura crystal you used on Lynch?"

Nicole turned back to the laptop. She couldn't tell him they had a crystal supply from a Cornish smuggler. She didn't want Jerren getting into trouble when she was the one that had Influenced him to give it to her.

"I need to know, Nicole."

"We had it in the family. I didn't mean to use it; I just kept it on me in case."

She hoped he wouldn't ask her any more questions, but he easily could after handing her a massive secret database. It was give and take, and she waited for him to take. He'd offered her information about himself. . . .

"I'll get us coffee," he said instead.

He rose and she watched him as he moved through the shop.

Leaving her with the database must be a test.

His long legs hadn't been crossed or relaxed when he'd been sitting beside her. His feet had been firm on the ground. Ready, in case he needed to run, to hunt.

She could all too easily imagine him running after her.

KYAN

Kyan watched Nicole from across the bookshop. Her legs were rigid under the laptop, her foot at an angle, like she was trying to not fidget. Like she was going to run away.

Her hair had been in a neat plait this morning. Now tufted bits had come loose and she tucked some thoughtlessly behind her ear.

Sitting so close to her he'd noticed how dark her eyelashes were; how her eyes darted across the information like it would disappear any moment. Her hand had trouble keeping up, resulting in elegant yet almost scrawled notes and loose sketches.

Other little things stood out, too. The scratch of her pale jumper every time her hand moved, the fluttered wrist of her blouse and how it hid half her hand.

The surge of protectiveness he felt with her tucked into his side.

The bruise at her neck and how much it bothered him.

It sat under the lace collar of her shirt, its purple mark half hidden.

How badly did he hurt you? Anger threaded through his muscles, aching with unused energy. Of course Lynch had hurt her. Kyan had been sure the Specter had drawn blood and the scent of it had made his body *feral*. He'd no longer seen reason, heard none of the logic that usually told him, *Wait a little longer. Wait for the kill scent.* Hearing her scream, scenting her blood, his body had moved.

And he couldn't find it in himself to regret it.

But while there had been no blood, Lynch *had* almost cracked her head open against the wall. There was still brick dust in her hair. Kyan had had to force himself not to brush it away by squeezing the damn life out of the back of the couch.

But Lynch hadn't planned to kill Nicole there and then. No, he hadn't yet made up his mind on how he wanted to punish her.

Kyan thought of her pleading, pained eyes, bright with fury: "It doesn't matter if there's collateral damage, does it? People can get injured as long as you get him in the end."

He'd never hated the rules before now, nor the complexities of his Empyreal power. Not like this. And then there was the hunger and an urge for connection that was beginning to form thanks to her.

Yet there was one other issue. The Wake wanted this painting. Why? More often than not he would ask for clarification when tasked with something other than a kill. He wasn't an idiot, and he wasn't blind. Yet Nicole had mentioned oaths, and then Lanhydrock had come up. . . .

Kyan turned as the barista slid their steaming drinks over the counter: dark coffee in two old china teacups. A bitter chunk of chocolate melting gently against the hot porcelain. He headed back over, setting down the drinks on a coffee table, and found Nicole holding her breath. He sat and glanced at the screen. She wasn't reading anything out of the ordinary.

Then, her fingers moved to hover over the keys and she typed in a new entry: "Empyreal."

"You can ask me," he said.

She seemed to battle with herself before quietly asking, "What's it like, being what you are?"

He thought of the mark on her neck.

"Like you're responsible."

The last time he'd felt he'd truly failed surfaced from its long-buried place inside: holding his mother's still body. Kyan jerked out of the memory quickly, disturbed.

"What do you feel when you turn? Does it hurt?"

A swathe of complicated emotions swirled in his stomach. "I've been asked that by many different creatures." *But never like that. With a soft wonder. A tiredness. A note of knowledge and resignation.* "Why do you ask?"

"I want to understand."

It reminded him of the reasons he'd never stayed with someone long enough to truly explain who and what he was. There was too much pain and a lack of passion. Things now glaring in his gut and body thanks to Nicole rushing to people's aid. Challenging him. Unspooling something knotted so tightly over hundreds of years he was convinced it could never unravel. Never *wanted* it to. Nicole, with questions that seemed more deeply rooted than a supernatural scholar's curiosities. That seemed, for an innate reason, like she *could* understand.

It left him uneasy, curious.

"It's different every time," he said, sitting back from her. "It depends on the creature."

"Now? How do you feel?"

A frustrated sigh escaped him. How could he make her understand? If she did, would she trust him enough to let him do his job?

He suddenly wanted to lean close, to show her without words how it felt. Use his venom with a slow sinking bite into her skin, something intimate and gentle that could transfer all his feelings and explain. To slide his tongue over the blood that would pearl up, as if as eager for him as he was for it.

The need surprised him.

And yet, her dark eyes made him believe she could understand. Like he had a home in her attention. While she wanted to know, it wasn't a greedy curiosity.

So, he leaned closer and the warmth of her body heat soothed him.

"I feel venom in my teeth, so they ache."

Her eyes dilated, a dark, slow unfurling. His own burned from the slanted light through the windows and the glinting refractions from the chandeliers.

"I dislike the daytime because I'm now blooded to work and feed in the night. I want blood, but not with the savageness of a Vampire. More like . . ." He drifted; he'd never explained these things before. "Like I'm slowly dwindling to empty, like my muscles are thirsty and slowly tightening. I only need a drop."

His eyes roamed over her skin to the little hollow at the base of her neck, like an inverted arrow. Then to where the jumper on her left shoulder had tugged down from holding her satchel. He knew how warm her skin would be. How, if he bent even closer, so close he could touch his teeth to her skin, the nerves in them would relax and flood with ease and her hair would shield him as he sank his teeth into her. She would smell like cotton and lavender and strange stimulation.

But his bite was venomous. And he was not a Specter, not in his soul, not in his chest. He was just borrowing its hungers.

So why did the mere idea of those things thrum something deeper in him?

"But you stay the same in your head?" she asked, sounding almost breathless. "In your mind? You're still *you*, even though your body is different?"

There had been times when he hadn't been. When the transformation had torn him into something else and remade him. But most of the time he had a grasp on his personality, his consciousness. "I think so."

She stared at him like she wasn't sure of his answer. But then, there it was: reluctant acceptance. A knot of tension in him soothed.

Her eyes dropped to his mouth and he noticed how close they still were.

An alert sounded on his phone that made her jolt slightly away, and he found himself immediately irritated by the interruption.

"Is that about the Specter?"

"No," Kyan said. "When you were in the bathroom I honed in on Lynch. He's put himself into a healing sleep and won't be awake for a few hours at least. It's the curator emailing me again."

Her lips curled up and he realized it was the first time he'd almost seen her smile. It made her dark eyes wink with gorgeous amusement.

"He's infuriating," she said.

"And yet you tried to stop the Specter from hurting him, even though he doesn't seem to respect you or your research. Why?"

Her cheeks gently stained with color. She sat back slightly, and he could almost feel her putting up the wall between them again, one that had felt like it shimmered, growing translucent enough for him to say everything he'd said. "What can I say? I guess I'm protective, too."

Nicole turned back to the archives, and he fought the urge to say something else. This time she pulled up the stolen *Dante* painting. Staring at it, he considered telling her more about it as a low twinge of warning and history went through him. Nicole had said she'd Seen him from that painting.

"Can you tell me anything more about this?" she asked. Her eyes roamed over him and back to the painting, as if cataloguing the similarities.

Kyan's jaw worked. "I know who the other Empyreal is."

Nicole's attention sharpened. "What? Who is it?"

Kyan looked down at the screen, at the two Empyreals forever locked in a losing fight. The one with red hair looked to be transforming into something more vicious. But that wasn't the way Kyan remembered him.

Alexander hadn't been winning in their last battle.

So Kyan chose his words carefully. "An Empyreal I knew a long time ago, Alexander. He's dead now; the last time I saw him was at the oath-swearing in Lanhydrock."

"Lanhydrock . . ." Nicole chewed on her lower lip, deep in thought. "That's close. An hour away, maybe less. It's a long shot, but it might be our only lead as to why Lynch stole that painting, or give some insight into it, if that's where you last saw Alexander and both of you are in the stolen piece."

Kyan hadn't been there since 1902, and he wasn't inclined to go back. But if it illuminated something about this artistic mystery and gave him a one-up on Lynch, then it might be worth it. Even if the idea of spiriting Nicole away from Estwood and Lynch for a few hours made some of that strain in his chest lessen, calmed some of the roaring protectiveness that had ripped open at the sound of her scream.

"Do you want to go?" he found himself asking.

He wasn't sure if it showed a measure of trust in him that she wanted to come, or a focus on the case and whatever secret reason she really had for wanting that painting.

But he found himself relieved, and pleased, when she said yes.

18 NICOLE

Nicole didn't know why Kyan was so tense. His broad shoulders were even more bunched than usual as they strode under the gray granite gatehouse of Lanhydrock House.

Unlike Westmoore Manor, which was backed by the ocean, Lanhydrock sat at the bottom of a sloping hill, its surroundings thick with spearing, ancient trees. Crenelated gray stone made it look like a small castle. It had the bearing of one, too, the large, U-shaped layout drawing you in.

Its exterior was bearded in lush, fluttering plants and the twisted silver trunks of magnolia coiled around doors and windows. The sky above was a pale and lovely blue, the color stark against the sharply cut circular lawn and glinting paneled windows.

Nicole wasn't sure what she was searching for as they followed the little burgundy visitor signs toward the arched front door—a coat of arms carved into its dark wood—and strode inside. While they didn't have the stolen painting, the next best thing was researching its—and the Wake's—history, as her mother might be leading her to something key. What better way to do it than in a place Alexander had been? A place where the Wake had made Empyreals swear their second oath? She hadn't been able to tell Kyan that was why she'd been so keen to come here, and yet discovering the connection to the Wake felt too perfectly like a crumb from her mother to ignore.

What she also needed was to figure out what the numbers were on that piece of paper Lynch had shown her. She'd scribbled them down so she didn't forget, but hadn't seen enough of them to know how they were laid out or what they meant. So for now, the history of the supernatural paintings was all she could work with.

It was a quiet morning and people trickled through the granite archways with cameras hanging around their necks and children trailing after them. Dark wood paneled the lower halves of the walls, the top halves painted in soft blue or clay colors, or papered in the delicate forest-green florals of William Morris. Paintings, old photographs, or the heads of animals were mounted on the walls, adding to the house's historic scent.

Walking down the corridor, an insistent feeling tugged at her. Nicole blinked a few times, a small lurch of panic upsetting her stomach as a vision threw her from her mind and into someone's from the past. Visions were omnipresent, so they used the best viewpoint a Seer needed, for whatever history wanted her to know.

This one seemed to put her in the mind of a serving girl who saw Kyan walking down this same route. The grace with which he carried his body entranced her, and when the cool slip of his eyes washed over her, a wave of heat blushed up her neck. He nodded gently in greeting. His black suit matched his dark hair, which was brushed back neatly but a little tousled like he'd been horse riding; the high white collar accentuated his clenched jaw. A pocket watch chain glinted in time with his long strides.

Nicole reeled as the memory swept away.

"You said you were here for the second oath?" she asked him, blinking hard.

Kyan didn't look at her, but his jaw feathered with tension. "Yes."

"But weren't there humans here?"

"Yes, the Wake used a large celebration the owners of the house were throwing as a way to disguise so many of us in one place. There were dinners, festivities, a ball."

She Saw glimpses of it throughout the house as the edge of her Seer senses spliced with visions of his history. She'd never experienced historic images so easily, and was glad Bells wasn't here. If Kyan's history was so palpable in this place, she didn't want to know what Bells might See with her stronger abilities.

Nicole checked every painting with Kyan shadowing her, tense as a bodyguard. Passing a study, she felt the scratch of initials carved into wood, rough under her fingertips.

Then Saw Kyan and a group of bulky Empyreals dressed in attire from the early twentieth century.

Saw a hunt. Deer scattering past horses. Men racing through the trees, faster than humanly possible.

She blinked out of it, finding they'd come to a long sitting room—its pale ceiling vaulted and adorned with plaster reliefs. An array of decorative screens and couches attempted to break up the long space. She caught Kyan's reflection in a mirror they'd stopped beside. His jaw was clenched and he'd raised a hand, like he might brush something from her hair but thought against it.

"Where was the oath sworn?" Nicole asked, rubbing her eyes and turning to look over the room and better face him.

"The Great Wood, outside," Kyan said.

Relief settled Nicole as a headache began to pound. Hopefully they could leave soon. "Right, perhaps we should go out there."

She stepped to her right and bumped into a table thanks to her burning eyes. She cursed, steadying it while Kyan reached to steady her, gripping her on the inner left arm near her elbow.

"Follow me," Kyan said, voice gruff.

Her fingers instinctively grasped back and she felt the solid, carved muscle of his forearm and the exposed skin where he'd pushed up the sleeve of his dark green jumper. The raised veins reminded her of Michelangelo's *David*, but living, breathing. But there was more beneath her fingers: a circular mark, shiny and puckered, an inch below the crook of his elbow.

What is . . . ?

It wasn't a burn or a brand, it was a scar, the type you could only get from carving slowly with a blade. With patience or undiluted obedience. Now it was a silken ring of raised skin, silvery and present. A reminder of the oath all Empyreals made when they were inducted into the Wake. To honor and hunt for them. If you disobeyed it, you risked execution.

There was no such thing as a successful apostasy.

Alarm slammed in her pulse. There it was—the symbol of the Wake, representing the open eye and "awakening" of an Empyreal. With his scar singed into her mind, a vision shuttered over her eyes.

She Saw a storm of horses.

Mist spiraling over dark, spearing pines.

The dried speckle of mud on black riding boots.

Then a knife at his arm, scoring, marking him body and soul, binding him to a mission he couldn't deny even if he wanted: the oath to bring in all other Empyreals he found.

The snap of someone's neck in his hands.

Nicole jolted as she felt the spatter of water. No, blood.

Felt the eye-watering scrub of a nail brush over his fingertips and nails.

Saw his eyes in a cracked mirror, full of conflicting emotions.

A historic ball with a hundred silk dresses. Tense conversations. Strange dreams.

And a woman in his arms.

In the memory, Kyan gripped the woman in anger and confusion, because the harder he looked, the more her face transformed. Gone was the face of his mother. Her features morphed and dark eyes swirled in the place of forest-green ones. The love, the hope he'd felt at seeing his mother's face again for the first time in centuries dissipated into fury.

The illusion splintered with someone's interruption, and the woman bolted. But when she turned to look back, Nicole's heart shot up into her throat.

The woman who had pretended to be someone Kyan knew and had been in Lanhydrock the day the oath was sworn, damning all Empyreals like her, was Nicole's mother.

19 NICOLE

Nicole reeled out of the vision, a sob escaping, and tore her hand from Kyan's arm.

He'd met her mother.

Kyan frowned down at her as if seeing her for the first time. "The woman in the memory . . ."

He stepped closer and Nicole's body tensed, ready to run or fight. He froze and raised his palms.

He'd seen it, too, because they'd been touching.

Her eyes stung like hell and burned with tears. She couldn't stand here having just seen her mother's face. Alive. Breathing.

Breathing.

Unlike the last time Nicole had seen her.

"I won't hurt you," Kyan said.

The gentleness in his tone nearly undid her. He *would* hurt her if he knew what she was. If not him, the Wake themselves.

"Breathe, you're okay."

"I have to go, I need . . ."

She rushed back through the house, scrambling to find the exit. Her heart warred, angry and confused beneath her ribcage. It felt like her Empyreal, clamoring to get out. To *break*. She tried to reel the grief in quickly, neatly, but it crashed over her so completely she struggled to catch her breath. She clapped a hand over her mouth as tears overflowed.

Being a Seer was different, vulnerable. She couldn't fight visions of futures or make sense of history. They had a taste of certainty about them.

Seeing her mother's dark hair flash out in the vision; Seeing her look over her shoulder . . . Nicole remembered her mother's hair from the night she died. She'd watched from behind the shimmering pane of power as her mother stood between them and the Empyreal who'd come to kill her.

But this was so much worse than a memory. So much newer.

Nicole shut her eyes, tears drowning her lashes. She felt Kyan following but pushed on. She needed to get out of this house and fisted her fingers to squeeze away the memory of his scar at her fingertips.

Bursting outside, she came to a stop on the lawn—the *circular* patch of grass. The Wake's symbol. Her mother had been here for the oath swearing.

But *why?*

"Who was that woman?" Kyan asked.

Nicole couldn't admit it was her mother, but she couldn't risk lying too much either. "I don't know," she said. "It was your memory. Did you know her?"

"No. Do you perfectly remember faces you saw years ago? This would have been over a hundred. Seers can make us remember moments or details. I'd almost forgotten. . . . But then, from the moment I began this mission *you've* been embroiled in it, and now a woman who looks just like you? Who was she? Your mother?"

It was a logical assumption and yet it still made her breath catch with worry. "No."

"Don't lie to me," Kyan warned, his voice a near growl.

"My mother died when I was three," Nicole snapped, tears burning in her stinging eyes. "That woman is a mystery to me."

It was true. Despite everything she had learned from her father, all the books and stories, all the subconscious lessons, her mother had been an enigma. But she needed to change the subject quickly, lest those damn perceptive eyes see her secrets written on her face.

She thought of him in the *Dante* painting. "You want to talk about being embroiled in this? So are *you*. Why exactly were you chosen for this mission?"

Confusion and suspicion sharpened in his eyes, as if the thought had occurred to him, too.

Then he said, more to himself, "I shouldn't be looking into it."

"What are you talking about?"

He turned to her. "This. History. We're not supposed to—" He bit off. "Empyreals aren't supposed to think so much of the past. We're not like other immortals."

He suddenly reminded her of one of the paintings in Westmoore's manor—Bouguereau's *Nymphs and Satyr*: a straining Satyr being dragged through a dark forest by pale-skinned Nymphs.

Kyan stared hard at the landscape around them, at the Great Wood surrounding the house. He'd made his scar there, surrounded by other Empyreals after her mother had slipped inside his mind and shown him someone else's face.

The vision had given her so much insight into his world. So many personal moments. So many secrets.

He knew Mum.

She shook her head, grappling with the thought; with the idea that her mother had come here. Why would she ever risk going into a house full of Empyreals?

Nicole felt a strange parallel. Why was *she* risking it?

For answers.

But if Kyan knew what her mother was, it wouldn't be hard for him to put two and two together. There'd been too much confusion in the vision's energy to know what he suspected, and Nicole didn't dare ask outright.

"I didn't know her," Kyan said. "She got into my head the night before the oath and tried to convince me not to take the oath. I thought it was nothing but a dream until she came to me at the ball the next night, wanting to know if I'd sworn it. Only seeing her then made me realize the dream had been some kind of mental manipulation. But before I could question her, she bolted. Do you know why?"

"No," Nicole said honestly. "Why?"

"We never found out."

Mild panic rose under Nicole's skin. "Who's *we*?"

"Another Empyreal, Callum. He's an old friend."

Kyan strode away and out of the gatehouse to the path that led back up the long hill toward where the car was parked. Nicole hurried after him and the colossal trees spotting the acres of sloped land either side of the path draped intermittent shade over her.

Watching his speedy walk, she got a flash of him running over wet hills in harsh winds, rain pelting his skin and pouring over straining muscles. Nights alone, stalking his prey, buried in the mission to distract from anything else.

He had no time to feel anything else.

Nicole hissed out of the vision, the bright pain of a headache lancing behind her dry eyes. They were on *fire*. She stopped and scrunched her eyes shut to ease the burning, reaching for her bag to pull out the eye drops specially made for Seers. She'd always kept some in her satchel, mainly for Bells, but had never needed them herself.

She sensed Kyan walking back toward her.

Nicole tipped her head back and tried to open her eyes, but the air burned viciously and a drop of the liquid ran down her cheek instead.

"Let me help you," came Kyan's voice, still terse.

"I can do it by myself."

"Yes, but you don't have to. Don't be so stubborn."

The drops disappeared from her hand and his fingers met her jaw. She gasped softly.

His grip was firm. Hot, but gentle.

Nicole grew deadly still.

Kyan tilted her head back. She swallowed and saw—no, *felt*— his eyes glide up her neck.

"Open your eyes," he said roughly.

They fluttered open with a glare of pain, and he darted two quick drops into them. The relief was instantaneous. Nicole blinked and he came back into perfect focus, offering her the dark sunglasses he'd slipped from his coat. She shook her head.

"If I asked you one more time if that woman was your mother, would you answer me honestly?"

She made herself meet his gaze. "I don't know her."

It felt like it was costing her something to say the words. It was safer to lie, but it was beginning to feel wrong.

Something shifted in his eyes. Steeling him.

"Then why do you care?" he asked. "I thought this might have been something about my past; even wondered if that's why I'd been sent here after Lynch and this artwork. And yet *you* are the one who needs these paintings, who wants to hunt this historic trail, who looks exactly like a woman who broke into one of the Wake's most secure, most historic oath-swearings in supernatural history. Why try to find a missing painting and put yourself in this position unless there's a connection here you've got to hide?"

He was right. He was so right about everything, and yet she couldn't admit it.

Her heart pounded as he neared her secret. "I care about the collection, and that woman has something to do with it."

He leaned closer. "Why should I let you continue working with the art? Do I need to remove you from it?"

No. He wasn't doing this, not now. Now, more than ever, she needed answers. "And how would you do that?"

"I'd ask nicely," he ground out.

Nicole fisted her hand in his jumper. "No. You promised me. And if there's one thing I know to be true about Empyreals, it's that they stick to their oaths."

He stared at her, and the heat of his body radiated onto hers. She felt the rise and fall of his breathing and got a rush of that scent that confused and stirred and drove her half mad.

His eyes dropped to her mouth. "Fine."

As he straightened back to his full height, her fingers fell away and the spell of tension between them dissipated.

"Why did they make you take a second oath?" she asked. "After centuries of service?"

"What does that matter?"

Nicole nearly wanted to tear her hair out. Clearly it mattered! This oath had damned her family and her mother had tried to stop it.

"I Saw it, it must be important." There must be something her mother needed her to know about it. Though so far, that thing seemed to be Kyan himself. . . .

He shook his head. "I don't know why they chose then, I'm not privy to the Wake's reasoning. I wondered if our numbers were dwindling, and we needed everyone out there. Before that, bringing in other Empyreals was just a general order despite the fact we're drawn to other newly transformed Empyreals. It wasn't a physical compulsion until we carved that mark."

Her eyes almost dropped to it, now.

Nicole swallowed, adrenaline humming loud in her veins.

If she had come to Lanhydrock without Kyan, she wouldn't have had the same vision—it had been triggered by touching *his* scar.

Westmoore's words from the night before she was killed returned to her: "It has taken centuries to put the right people and information in the right places to try and guarantee the events that will come forth. To make sure they lead to success, over defeat."

Her mother had had reasons for everything.

"Why did she pick you?" Nicole murmured, looking up at his severe face. The one she'd been so shockingly relieved to see drag Lynch off of her earlier.

Kyan slammed on his dark sunglasses and turned to stride back up the hill. "I don't know."

Watching him go, Nicole was no longer wholly convinced he was just blindly following the Wake's rules. He'd bent them to help her; to save her being bitten, or worse. . . .

Whether she could have saved herself or not didn't matter. It meant that they were in this together, coiled like the torc she'd seen around his neck.

And she realized that it wasn't him she was afraid of. The thing that scared her was the Wake finding out her secrets.

But Kyan . . . Kyan she was beginning to trust.

And that shook her just as much as seeing her mother's face again.

20 KYAN

Back in Estwood, Kyan dropped off a close-lipped Nicole, but instead of heading to Westmoore Manor, he drove back into town to Lynch's dorm.

The university was busy for its Freshers' week, which meant there were fewer people in the dorms; instead they were out at classes or exploring the town and beach. Soon, however, they would return in droves, drinking and preparing for the night ahead, filling the halls full of drunk students susceptible to Lynch.

He'd tried not to think of Nicole's vision on the way back, but the memories shimmered.

Later, he told himself, pushing away thoughts of Lanhydrock until he was calm and alone, then maybe he could make some damn sense out of what was going on. He thought of contacting Callum. Gods knew where he was. If he wasn't swiftly completing a hunt, he'd be somewhere thoroughly enjoying his time between missions.

Callum had been the one to go after the mystery woman that night and had tracked her for months, if not years. But she was always just out of his reach. He'd eventually stopped talking about it, but had he ever tracked down Nicole's lookalike? If it *had* been her mother and she truly was dead, Kyan would never know why she'd done what she did.

But how much should it really matter to him? Lynch was his goal. Not the past. Telling Callum about Lanhydrock would only bring him here, and Kyan wasn't sure he wanted his observant friend so close, at least not until he'd figured out what Nicole's relation was to the woman from Lanhydrock—if there was any connection at all. It could just be a coincidence. Maybe time had blurred the woman's face with Nicole's.

He didn't think so.

Lynch's words from the alley returned: "I wonder if he'll figure it out." Did he mean Nicole's connection to his past? Or something else she was hiding? Either way, it gave him all the more reason to figure her out. That and the strengthening lure toward her, the likes of which he'd never felt before, let alone been tempted to pursue.

The scent of blood found him before he'd even arrived at Lynch's room. He listened, hearing two sets of breathing, one labored.

"Come on in, Empyreal," said Lynch from the inside. "I'm not going to bite *you*."

No, Kyan realized, coming into the punching scent of blood and musk and cold.

Lynch was sitting in the center of his large room, a girl, semi-conscious from blood loss, draped across his lap like some reverse *Pietà*. She was clothed, though her neck had been punctured deep by Lynch's bite. Her pulse was steady, though, and Kyan couldn't sense fear or pain. She'd be all right, once the venom wore off and Kyan made sure someone called the nurse.

Lynch grinned slightly, his teeth dark with blood. "I'll give your pretty Seer some kudos. She knows where to aim."

Sure enough, Lynch's side was dark with blood. The wound wasn't clotting, and it seemed like the Specter had tried to get the crystal out with little success.

"It's not like you didn't deserve it," Kyan said, crossing his arms. "You've killed before, I can smell it on you."

"How primal. That's not the point though, is it? You were sent to kill me, but you were also sent to retrieve a painting."

Kyan didn't let his suspicion show. How did Lynch know the details of his mission?

The Specter smiled. "The thing is, I've hidden it. Somewhere nice and secret. And you're not getting it unless I want you to. Unless you get a message to the Wake telling them to spare me."

Kyan's eyes narrowed. He'd dealt with prey that had begged him before, even offered him things. But they didn't usually offer the Wake something. And how could they? The organization's reach was global, their resources almost infinite.

"That's not the way I work," Kyan growled. "I don't make deals with murderers."

"You don't have a clue what you're in the middle of, do you?" Lynch asked with bewildered fascination.

"Why don't you tell me just what you think you've found and I'll let them know."

Lynch shook his head, recalibrating. "No. You tell them that I've got the painting and I have its secrets, and we'll go from there."

"Why shouldn't I just kill you and take it?"

"Because you *can't*."

Kyan took a few steps closer, a thousand years of hunting confidence blooming hot beneath his skin. "I *can* kill you," he warned, looking down at his prey.

"You could *try*. But your slow transformation won't complete unless I kill someone and release a nice fresh wave of that kill hormone." He patted the girl in his lap. "Thing is, I'm good with control, just like you. I don't kill all over the place. I need to feed like any other being on this earth, and supernatural laws allow for every creature to feed, just not kill. So, you won't be able to kill me with a Specter's powers as half Empyreal, half Specter. You'd have to use some other unsavory tactic, and what a mess something like a decapitation would make. What attention it would draw. Even *you* can't Influence a whole town of people, and I should let you know, I won't make it easy."

That was just the issue: it wasn't whether Kyan *could* kill Lynch, it was whether he *should*.

"Rest assured," Kyan said darkly, "no matter what control you think you have, mine's better. You'll slip up, or you'll get too hungry, and when you do, I'll be there to finish the job."

Lynch's smile was cold. Kyan scented the bitterness of fear, but more than that, there was calculation.

"Here's the deal, Empyreal. They've sent you to kill me, but if you kill me, the Wake won't have what they *really* want, which is the painting. And without my telling you where it is, how long would you bother searching for it? Your job isn't to be an art lackey, it's to hunt creatures, and I'm sure you'd much rather run along and get on with the next one. Unless you'd be happy hanging around here with our lovely little Nicole. . . ."

Kyan fought a snarl. "Why are you so fascinated with her?"

The Specter's eyes winked with amusement. "I could ask you the same. She's clearly hiding something, and after the way you seem so invested in her safety—"

"I'm invested in anyone's safety."

Lynch grinned. "Right. Sure. I noted there was no snarling about this poor soul, but I try to sink my teeth into Nicole's pretty neck and you come running."

He was right, and that was the most unnerving part of this situation.

The Specter leaned closer. "You're transforming into a Specter, which means you'll be needing plasma soon. I wonder if Nicole would be able to help you with that?"

A low peal of rage found him. "You're forgetting something," Kyan said, stepping closer. "With that nice little wound in your side, I could torture the truth out of you."

A flash of hatred went through Lynch's eyes. "I'm rather better at it, I imagine."

Kyan allowed a mirthless smile. "You may be unhinged, Lynch. But I've had two thousand years to understand creatures and their weaknesses."

"And yet you ignore your own. I've heard about you. The Wake's best dog. The hunter who's tried to forget his history. Just what are you trying to forget so desperately? A lost love? A mistake? . . . Ah. A mistake."

It was one of the reasons Kyan had tried to rename himself throughout the centuries, keeping the name of one of his grandfathers, Cían, but not spelling it in the Irish way—for fear of that history reminding him every time he wrote it down, every time he looked at his profile and got a new mission on the Wake's database.

Yet he couldn't bear to rid himself of his family, of Ireland, completely.

"Empyreals don't have weaknesses."

"You don't *really* believe that, do you? Haven't you noticed something during our lovely little conversation? Two things." He ran a finger along the girl's still wounded neck, through the blood, and brought it up to the light. "One: you *protecting* Nicole. Two: the restrictions imposed upon you thanks to the Wake's oath. If you really wanted to as a new Specter, you could find out her secrets. Take a bite and discover them. Don't wait too long to have a drink, though, hunter. Or those urges will slake themselves, and we wouldn't want Nicole to see you teeth-deep in some other pretty undergrad, or better yet, Nicole herself."

His laugh followed Kyan out.

"Come find me," Lynch called, "when the Wake have their answer."

Frustrated, Kyan stared down at his phone as he jogged out of the building and ended up hitting Call, but accidentally stabbed the video button. Before he could cancel it, having learned his lesson after the last time Callum had answered in the middle of a more compromising situation, his best friend's face came onto the screen.

He was in a bar, somewhere expensive where the low light gilded his dark skin and infamously handsome face.

"Well, well," came Callum's sardonic voice, the curl of a smile on his mouth. "To what do I owe the pleasure? Still can barely use your phone, I see."

Kyan smiled grimly. "Have you ever had prey that wants you to contact the Wake for them, to offer something in exchange for their life?"

"Color me intrigued. No."

"That's what I thought," Kyan said, ripping open his car door and sinking inside. He felt more like walking, but there was no way to know if he'd need to be back here at a moment's notice. Already he could feel Lynch falling back into a restful sleep. That would give Kyan enough time to rest himself, and try and figure out what the fuck to do about all this.

He scrubbed his face.

"As much as I love listening to your grumpy silences—" Callum began.

"What do you remember of Lanhydrock?"

There was a pause at the other end of the phone. Kyan had spent long enough around Callum to know his interest had been piqued.

"Where are you? Why don't we have a catch-up." His friend's voice had gone smooth and low. *Interested.*

Clearly, the other Empyreal remembered it well.

Warning bells went off in Kyan's head. He couldn't have Callum come to Estwood while everything was still in play. His friend was powerful and had managed to make Kyan smile and laugh despite the eternities they'd lived, but he wouldn't let a situation lie if there was something he'd wanted within it: and he had wanted answers about Lanhydrock for over a century.

"The last catch-up led to you seducing one of the Fae princes and nearly burning down their gardens," Kyan said instead.

"I regret nothing. They needed relandscaping anyway—that really was a terrible place for a lantern."

Kyan huffed. "Forget I mentioned it, I'm just nearby so it came to mind. I'll call you again when my mission's done."

But when he hung up, Kyan looked at the cords around his wrist and thought about home and duty.

And, for the first time in years, *home* was louder than the ancient whisper, and *duty* conjured questions. Doubts.

21 NICOLE

Nicole began systematically checking her mother's journals for the third time. The light was waning, so she'd snapped on some of the lamps in their family library, but her frustration only grew the longer she looked.

It wasn't here.

After Kyan had dropped her back home, she'd made her way upstairs. The previous twenty-four hours with little to no sleep immediately caught up with her and she found herself crashing in bed until the late afternoon. Once she'd awoken and eaten enough to feed a small family, she headed straight to their secret library.

After Seeing that vision in Lanhydrock, she'd hoped her mother had made some note in one of her many journals as to what she'd been doing there and how this all connected to the paintings.

The *Dante* painting had been painted in 1850, *The Wild Hunt* in 1872—years before the oath—but did they have something to do with *why* the oath was implemented? Or were the paintings just a springboard to get Nicole researching Empyreals and oaths, then Lanhydrock, where she could have this vision? The only issue was there *was* no 1902 journal, and the end of the 1901 one had nothing relevant; neither did the beginning of 1903.

A frustrated hitch in her throat made her feel unstable. She needed to figure this out. Nicole looked up at her mother's portrait.

"There you are, what—" came her brother's voice.

She turned, wondering why he had stopped midsentence.

"What the hell happened?" He reached her in two long strides, checking her neck.

"It's all right," Nicole said. "I'm fine." She took his wrist gently, choosing not to tell him or the others about Lynch, or Kyan intervening.

Not yet.

She knew how difficult it was to be faced with a creature neither of them could kill though they desperately wanted to. She didn't want him to feel worse.

"Did Lynch hurt you?" asked a soft voice from the door. Bells stood there looking sleepy and worried. They must have just brought her back from school. "Maybe we *should* leave."

"No, hey, it's okay. I found something today," Nicole said. "I just need one of Mum's journals to check on it—it could be a great clue. Exactly what we need."

Dylan frowned. "Well, you're not doing it on your own."

Several hours later, Nicole found herself working in the university library with Dylan sprawled in the seat beside her. Remi sat across the table with her headphones on, while Bells dozed on an oversized knitted pink scarf and their father passed at intervals with the book cart. Having them around her, knowing everyone was safe, caused that deep and anxious feeling in her stomach to settle.

"That's the twenty-fourth time you've made that little noise," Dylan said. His legs were stretched out, feet resting on the elegant metal bar beneath the table, a book on the early twentieth century open in his hands. The light of the library's dark gold lamps, hazy in her periphery, lit his hair in expensive shades, and she noted more than three people watching him from down the length of tables.

Nicole gave him an unamused look. "And which sound is that?"

Remi made a sad little sigh from across the table and Nicole's head whipped to where her best friend sat typing notes on the Siren paintings for her History of Music Theory paper.

Dylan pointed at Remi. "Spot on. *That* sound."

"Traitor," Nicole whispered.

Remi smiled at her papers, flicking an amused look over her herbal tea, the label fluttering down the side of the glass travel mug. Nicole caught the scent of honey, lemon, and a supernatural herb her father grew especially for soothing Siren throats. But then her friend's eyes went to Nicole's throat—hidden by a black turtleneck— and her lips tightened. They'd had words when they arrived, which mainly consisted of Remi telling her she should have listened and let her help. It had ended in the promise to do so from now on.

Nicole reached for where the cold remnants of her coffee sat in the breathy lamplight. Giant books were spread about, their glossy color prints of mythological paintings gleaming. A slim volume on the houses of the National Trust sat open in front of her. In the book, Nicole had found a black-and-white photograph dated 7 January 1902 with a large group of men staged in front of Lanhydrock House.

Nicole had scoured the lines of characters, halting on a few faces, wondering for a moment if they could be Kyan, but then she found him, standing next to a stunning young man with dark skin and a sardonic smile.

And, there, farther along, was Alexander.

What were you up to, Mum?

This must have been a photograph of the Empyreals there that day, all fifty of them. Her mother wasn't in it, and the lack of women amid the Wake's ranks wasn't lost on her. Her mother had, curiously, never written about that fact—that female Empyreals were even rarer than men, or seemed to be. Nicole often wondered if it was due to the patriarchal nature of the organization, or if, more disturbingly, they had been killed off. . . .

She thought of Kyan again. Her mother wanted to stop *him*, which meant that she wanted him to be swayed.

But what was so important about Kyan?

Nicole gently pulled out the 1901 journal from her bag and flicked it open, checking the pages again. Thankfully, the ever-dark converted church meant she was safe to read bestiaries—or, in this case, one of her mother's diaries—without a human student nosing over her shoulder.

The little leather notebook's edges were gilded with age. Nicole sighed at her mother's scrawl, fighting the urge to touch it, wondering if she'd ever See a vision of her mother through the ages, writing with the old scratch of a pen or feathered quill. Her hope dwindled as she got to the last few pages, several of which were empty.

She shook her head, unsure what she'd been expecting. Her thumb stroked the edge of the notebook, where the leather had been folded around the cover and sewn into place. It had come away slightly, unraveled, and there was a little circle drawn in the lower right-hand corner.

"Dylan," she murmured, showing him the symbol of the Wake.

Her fingers had absently tugged at the thread, which, she now noticed flicking back from the start of the book to the end, was different. Why would you use a different thread? Unless you'd run out of it—or unpicked it once and needed to sew it back again, to hide something?

Nicole cradled the book and hurried through the library, Dylan tailing her.

"Dad, I need a pair of scissors or a knife or something."

"You've already tried to kill Lynch with a crystal, love," her father said, without looking up from the books he was sorting. "If you think I'm giving you another weapon, think again."

"I could kill him without a weapon. That's not what I need it for."

He looked up, realizing what was in her hands.

"I think there's something in the back cover."

Instead of reaching for the scissors on his desk, her father pulled out a needle-thin knife that had been cleverly hidden in his belt buckle. He held out his hand for the book and Nicole handed it over. He shoved everything else aside and laid the journal on the desk, sitting to slice through the thread carefully. Sure enough, when he peeled back the lip of leather, it created a sort of pocket with a sheath of delicate paper inside. Nicole craned over the desk as it slid into her father's hand.

Her heart kicked up.

"Room, now," Nicole said, rushing back over to the desk. "Remi, can you wake Bells? We found something."

Remi plucked out her earphones, on alert, and leaned down to Bells, humming a few notes that had Bells's eyes fluttering open.

"Sleep okay, little one?" asked Remi.

Bells smiled dreamily, her dimples darkening, and nodded.

"Come with me," Nicole said.

They followed her into one of the glass reading rooms and once the door was closed, all crowded around to read the page.

"I can't read this," Remi said, frowning at the page. The note was slanted, almost savagely, quickly written. Nicole doubted most people would be able to, but she'd studied her mother's handwriting since she could read, so she read it aloud:

1902

I do not know how they managed to craft such a damning oath, but they've done it.

They knew that only the most powerful Empyreals could kill them, so in their hunt to track and neutralize them, the Wake have crafted an oath that means all Empyreals who have sworn it will be driven by a new compulsion: to bring in any unclaimed Empyreal they discover to the Wake.

But my investigation into the development of the oath has revealed that, in the first induction, an Empyreal had to swear to defend and protect the Wake, meaning that Empyreals will never be able to physically harm one of the Wake's true leaders.

Evidently, the first oath was implemented to stave off the possibility of Empyreals turning on the Wake in a mass apostasy. Somehow, they worked some ancient magic into the oaths, both of which draw blood and *are thus completely binding.*

This is why no more Empyreals can be discovered by the Wake, or there will be none left that can defeat them.

And this, I fear, may be the downfall of my plans. It is all the more reason I must prevent Empyreals from being taken.

Or this world will truly fall to ruin, and the Wake will succeed in summoning a new Dark Age, with no Empyreals left to kill the true predators: the Wake themselves.

"Oh my god," Remi breathed.

"Why would they want to do this?" Bells asked.

"Control," her father said solemnly. "Control the supernatural world's greatest predators, and you have the society in your hands."

Nicole stared at the journal. She'd known the oath meant Empyreals were bound to bring in new Empyreals, but *this*?

And if this was the issue—how could she stop it?

Preventing herself from being taken was the first step. No doubt her mother had discovered how to rectify this and prevent a Dark Age, then hidden the answer in the stolen painting's cipher. She wouldn't have been able to write information like that in any easily readable way.

But until they got the *Dante* painting back, she only had *The Wild Hunt* to work with. That represented the Wake's goal, she suddenly realized: the Dark Age and Wild Hunt.

More than ever, she needed to get back into Westmoore Manor

to see the *Wild Hunt* painting while they figured out how to get the *Dante* one back from Lynch.

But it raised the question: Was the painting an omen? A warning? Or a prophecy?

Two hours later, Nicole found Dylan at the bar of the Siren's Wife, nursing a pint.

After they'd discovered her mother's message, he'd stiffened up and found some excuse to leave. She'd felt more than a little shellshocked by the discovery herself. While one part of her was exhilarated that there *had* been some answer on this conspiracy-woven path, the answer itself was so huge that she didn't know what to do with it.

"You best be up for talking, or I'll just sit and cock-block you all night," Nicole said, sliding up onto a stool next to him.

Out on the beach nighttime bonfires glimmered and the early sound of music and waves drifted across the shore. Across the pub, Remi sat with the local musicians and gave her a wave.

Dylan gave an amused huff into his beer and ordered her a glass of red wine.

"Why did you leave?" Nicole asked.

It was safe to talk here, there were no other creatures in the vicinity, and she couldn't feel Kyan or Lynch.

"Because Remi needs to sing tonight, she's waited too long." *I'm here to protect her, this is something I can control* was his unspoken addition.

Nicole felt a surge of love. "That's not the only reason, though, is it?" she asked gently.

"It's hard to explain."

"Try," Nicole said, thanking the bartender as he passed her a glass.

Dylan took a drink and sighed. "I was already reluctant about you looking into this stuff. Not because I don't want an answer, but because I'm worried, Nikki." Her brow crumpled with concern at his rare use of the nickname. "I don't want you looking into stuff that could get you hurt. And now it's so much bigger than us. I thought if anything, this was just going to be the next safe house, and now what? We really are sitting on top of information the Wake would kill for. They'd already hunt us down just for being our mother's children."

A bolt of fear and adrenaline pulsed through her at the thought. "All the more reason to *have* that info."

"But, the danger this poses . . . What if they find out? What if they do take you, or . . ." He shook his head, throat working. "I just . . . I can still see it sometimes, you know?"

Nicole's chest grew tight and she reached out to squeeze Dylan's hand.

"And I'm almost angry that she's left it to us. Which makes me feel like a shit son."

"Hey." Nicole rested her head on his arm. "No bad self-talk, okay? This isn't what we thought it would be, but that doesn't mean it's going to end up being something bad. This could be the answer to everything, to the lives we really want."

He gave a sad laugh. "Nicole, *this*: trying to stay under the Wake's radar and avoiding who and what we are is our life."

She frowned, his bleak tone twisting a chord of real worry in her gut, followed quickly by anger. The Wake's grip on their lives would *not* take any more happiness from them.

"No," Nicole replied. "Dad said there might be a time he'd master the tonics so that even if we did transform, we'd be able to stop the scent and be safe. It might take a few years, but . . ."

Dylan shook his head softly, as if he didn't believe her. Nicole quickly tapped into the controlled reassurance she'd mentally built to keep thoughts like this from wearing her down, too.

She tugged on his arm. "*Hey*, I'll make sure we can live the lives we want."

He slid her a look. "By fighting a Specter at dawn without telling anyone?"

Nicole pressed her lips together and swallowed a mouthful of wine. Her father had been more than livid at the news. "That wasn't my wisest moment, I'll admit. But I'd fight whatever I need to."

He laughed, exasperated, his eyes lit with mirth and worry. "After seeing that he'd hurt you, I considered locking you in your room, but then I'd just be some kind of overprotective-older-brother cliché."

She sighed, taking a drink. "Then I'm Bells's overprotective-older-sister cliché. There's nothing wrong with our protective urges, Dylan. We love one another. We want each other to be safe."

"At least you can have visions," Dylan sighed. "I can't even See something that could help, like you and Bells. I just have to bottle up the hunting urge and remain clueless. I've only ever felt this kind of protective rage once, and I was too damn young to do anything about it."

Emotion burned the back of Nicole's throat. "I know how you feel."

He slid an appraising look to her, as if surprised and relieved she'd admitted it. A breath gusted out of him. "The lure of its power is addictive, isn't it?"

"I've never felt anything like it." This unending yearning, this hunter's instinct, this dark temptation.

Even now, her power kept creeping up under her skin. The desire to use it pooling on her tongue. She'd used it too many times in the last few days, been too close to Lynch, and now she itched to feel it spool out. It didn't want to be stopped and started but *unleashed*.

"It's so much—"

"Stronger than you thought," Dylan finished.

Nicole laughed sadly, taking another drink. "Yeah."

He rubbed her back supportively and tears pricked into her eyes.

"Bells is weirdly quiet about all this," Nicole said, focusing on the hot burn and richness of the wine.

"I've heard her muttering prayers to the Goddess of Prophecy when she thinks I can't hear her."

Nicole's heart ached. "What does she ask for?"

"'Show me their futures; help me keep them safe.'"

A twist of worry and love formed in Nicole's chest. "I'll talk to her."

They quietened as the sound of Remi's harp cut through the night, the pub growing silent. It happened every time and always filled Nicole with joy, pride. But tonight, Remi seemed particularly supernatural, sitting there before a breathless crowd on a barstool, the warm light of candles playing over her features.

And then she began to sing.

Her voice was smooth and so mesmerizing a person could listen to her for hours without realizing. She had a tone that seemed to sink right through the body.

Tonight, she must have chosen one of the pieces her father had collected over the years on his mission to track down every ancient Celtic song he could. It sang of mythic warnings and magic, gods and Druids. Love and loss.

Nicole rubbed her arms to stave off a shiver.

"I know Dad said you're like Mum, but just . . . don't be too much like her, okay?" Dylan said softly as Remi finished. "Keep me in the loop. Don't lock me out, even if you think I'll be annoyed."

"Maybe try not to be annoyed then."

He choked a laugh.

"But, deal."

They both looked over as the door to the pub opened, revealing a bunch of students, including Dylan's ex. Tomás locked eyes with Dylan and lingered for a split second. Her brother nodded softly and Tomás must have read the lack of invitation, so he waved at Nicole and headed to a corner with his friends.

"It's not too late, you know," Nicole said. The wine's warmth through her, relaxing her further now she knew Dylan was okay.

He swallowed, face hardening. "It's easier," he said quietly, watching his ex. "To not get attached. Attempting the relationship doesn't even really take the edge off. It just makes you want them more."

Nicole thought of her hand, fisted in Kyan's jumper, and pushed away the surprising return of emotion, frustration.

She squeezed Dylan's arm in silent support instead, as another stranger came into the bar.

He must have been in his early twenties. He was stunningly

handsome, with dark skin and short black hair forming a perfect widow's peak. His dimpled chin gave his face a sense of sculptural beauty and he moved with the type of easy confidence that suggested he owned the pub and everything in it. She almost recognized him, realizing he must be one of the master's students at the university.

When he locked eyes with Dylan, a frisson of energy shivered over Nicole. She tried to smother a smirk.

"Anyway," she said, noting Dylan's gaze. "I'm going to go home. Goodnight, *brother*," she added, loud enough the stranger heard.

Dylan gave a small smile. "Subtle."

"You're welcome," she said. "See you at home."

She nipped around the bar to say goodbye to Remi, but just as she passed a few drunk students, she saw her friend in the middle of kissing Hannah.

Nicole smiled, ducking back toward the door, trying to ignore the small part of her that felt suddenly lonely.

She chastised herself as she went to leave, her brother's words swirling around her mind: "It just makes you want them more." Nicole sighed, thinking of her power; of all these new desires. They were beginning to make her feel like the ghost beneath a painting— the under-image before the artist changed their mind and painted something else. Something new. Something that wasn't so raw with incomplete perfection.

But which one did that make her? Which was her true self? The Empyreal or the girl she felt she was? And did the pentimento of that true self seeping into the foreground prove that she was an Empyreal and not . . . Nicole? What did all her studying add up to if she was just a creature-girl trying to contain herself?

What if that was all she was?

And what if she failed?

She looked back to see the handsome stranger take her vacated seat beside Dylan and realized the people in the rest of the pub were in their own little groups, too: friends, couples old and new. The scents of perfume and pheromones and longing caught sharply in her throat. She tried to shake it off. Relationships should never make or break your identity or fill a void, she knew that. And yet, she couldn't deny the realization that, evidently, she wanted one more than she'd thought.

And that the person who sprang to mind was the person she could never get close to.

"Just visiting an old friend," Nicole heard the stranger tell Dylan.

As she moved through people to get to the exit, she heard a final few words: "You're siblings? I wouldn't have guessed; you don't look much alike."

"No," Dylan said, sounding slightly sad. "She looks more like our mother."

23 NICOLE

"I'm missing something," Nicole said, two nights later, rubbing her eyes. When she blinked them open again it was to see Remi sitting opposite her at an ornate seventeenth-century desk in the gallery of Westmoore Manor.

"You're missing this thing called *sleep*. You've been at this for days," Remi said, brows drawn in amused concern over her notes, gleaming paintings of Mermaids and Nymphs behind her.

Nicole sighed, testing the still sore wound at her neck. She'd had no time to rest, not after they'd discovered her mother's note. Not after hearing her brother's worries, which all too easily echoed her own. He was right, this was bigger than them all, and Nicole couldn't let them down.

But her damned neck was not healing as quickly as it should. It had calmed and cooled thanks to her father's salves but still sat mauve and angry under the skin. He suspected it was because it was a wound inflicted by a supernatural and because she was suppressing her Empyrean powers it wasn't healing. Either way it was a constant pulsing reminder of their situation.

Nicole rubbed her forearm thoughtfully and twisted to look at the *Wild Hunt* painting. She'd been hoping to find something in it that would give them a clue about the oath, but as far as she could see, the varnish wasn't revealing anything beneath, so she'd reverted to good old-fashioned research. Her other option was somehow speaking to Kyan in as subtle a way as she could manage. Yet the thought of bringing up the scar and his allegiance to the organization that killed her mother . . .

It felt wrong. It felt obvious.

Besides, she'd barely spoken to him for days. There was a silent tension every time he checked the gallery room, questions and secrets strung between them, taut and damning. He'd said in a curt word or two that Lynch was still here, still going between feeding and sleeping and plotting. But she was no longer sure if it was those words or his presence that made her blood pump loudly, her body so hyperaware of him that even the brush of her own hair on her skin was maddening.

He'd come to read her notes once or twice, or to look at the *Wild Hunt* painting. But when he stood next to her, his jaw would flicker, his body tense and he would gently rock back on his heels, almost prowling closer before deciding against it, only to shove his hands in his pockets and leave.

She knew, even when his body was aimed away, he was very, *very* aware of her.

And it made her feel . . .

Things you shouldn't be thinking about, she cursed herself. *It's just your body. Hormones, adrenaline.*

The good news was she could control all of that. The thought calmed her in increments.

"You've been just as busy researching," Nicole said to Remi, pushing those thoughts away. "And yet . . . you look great." The low light from the banker lamp gilded her cheek, made her look even softer and lovelier.

"That," Remi said with a smile, "is because I have a date."

Nicole perked up. "You do? With Hannah?"

"Yep, we're going to that little wine bar in town."

Nicole smiled, relaxing at the thought of her friend having a slice of normal; sitting under a white awning at one of the café tables that spilled out onto the cobbles and a new moon above the square. She wouldn't mind a glass of wine right about now.

"Good, you'll relax. Something will be right in the world. How is Hannah?"

"She's good," Remi said as she packed up her things. "I'm just glad she hasn't been near Lynch. Though she is getting curious about other things. What my parents do, where I lived before coming here . . ."

Hannah was human, so there was a fair amount of Remi's life she had to keep secret from her.

"Do you think you'll ever tell her what you are?"

Remi paused, manicured fingers toying with the handle of her bag. "I don't know. Your parents and mine are all supernatural, so there was never the issue of trying to explain that beings like us exist. I think dating someone who already knows would make a relationship easier."

Nicole chewed the inside of her cheek. She'd always planned to lie to potential partners about what she was. It was one thing attempting to reveal the supernatural world to a human, but a whole other when explaining that she wasn't any type of supernatural they'd heard about before.

"But for now, it's about relaxing and getting to know her better, not telling her that Sirens exist. It's not like we're immortal mates, you know?"

Nicole laughed. "Right." Only certain supernaturals could form that type of bond, like Fae and Vampires, and though every type of supernatural had their own beliefs about love and connection, each also wrote about it differently. Empyreals, for example, didn't have such a thing. "But good, I want everyone to relax a little bit."

Remi smiled and leaned on the table. "And when are *you* going to relax?"

Nicole looked back down at her notes and half-finished coffee, her gleaming laptop screen illuminating the sketches of the paintings fanned out everywhere else. "Er . . . soon. But you, go, be merry. Let me live vicariously through you."

Remi shook her head softly. "Don't stay up reading until three a.m., okay? We have another day of lectures tomorrow."

Right.

Nicole looked to the door to Westmoore's private rooms and realized she'd been hoping Kyan would walk in any minute. She told herself she wanted updates on Lynch, or that she was worried that any tension between them might make him edge her out of the house, and away from the art like he'd threatened at Lanhydrock.

And yet, she wasn't completely convinced that that was what was causing the pressure in her chest. While it relieved her that he was close by, she also felt mildly stressed by his ongoing terseness. It wasn't that they were the best of friends, even if they'd . . . well, they'd grown closer. When he'd shown her the Wake's archives there'd been a sense of comfort there. But she'd ruined it by keeping secrets.

Which is what you're supposed to do, she reminded herself sternly. *It's the way you'll survive in this world.*

Remi kissed Nicole on the temple. "Try and get some sleep."

"I'll shower and change into my pj's now as proof," Nicole said, getting up to stretch, noting the darkness deepening over the sea outside.

She sent her senses throughout the house for signs of Kyan. She'd heard him come in earlier and go to his bedroom, so he must be sleeping before night properly descended.

"Good," Remi said. "Then I'll see you at class tomorrow."

Nicole walked Remi out before texting her dad an update and heading to shower. Peeling off her jeans and wiping off any remaining makeup, she tried to run through everything she'd researched as she stepped beneath the hot spray, soothing the lingering ache in her neck.

Thanks to Lynch making himself scarce, her body had recuperated more quickly. Still, she wore jumpers when out, both against the chill of the encroaching autumn—always colder by the sea than elsewhere in the country—and to hide the wicked mark.

Just thinking of the killing instincts that had tempted her during their fight pushed a sense of urgency through her. The art was the answer to everything, including a convenient way for her to *think*, and not feel at all. Resolved and in fresh cotton pj's—a little white cami set with shorts and an oversized cardigan—Nicole headed back to the gallery.

They now had a key piece of information from her mother, something the Wake didn't want people to know.

So, the next question was: How to break the oath? Would her mother have figured that out and hidden the answer in the painting? There *was* something here, even if just in the code Lynch had shown her. And if the Wake knew she had a way to break an Empyreal's oath, that would destroy their control. She could definitely see them killing for that.

Nicole retrieved her lukewarm mug and looked over at the *Wild Hunt* painting.

The other part of her mother's journal entry had been "the Wake will succeed in summoning a new Dark Age."

What could that represent but a Wild Hunt?

She'd felt a draw to this painting from the start, whether it had a hidden message in it was another matter. Her gut told her it had something to reveal, too.

Glancing out over the beach, the moon was barely reflected in the dark water, little more than a luminous sketch that glittered and shifted, its light too dim to flood into the gallery. But that cold, almost paranormal gleam reminded her of something she couldn't put her finger on. Nicole sighed, and looked again at the *Wild Hunt* painting.

There.

The moon outside reminded her of the one in *The Wild Hunt* with its cold, hazy glow. It was painted on the bottom left, below the bank of wicked clouds that cut diagonally across the painting, its swarming darkness spilling with hunters.

On the right was what could either be viewed as the sun, or, Nicole suspected, the star from which Empyreals were supposedly made, seeing as the term "Empyrean" was ancient Greek for the highest fire in the heavens.

Deciding to just check the basics, Nicole scoured the shelves, discovering a book on supernatural symbolism. She flicked through. Perhaps she was overthinking, considering the clue to be more subtle than it was. So she scanned for the items and images in the painting:

the sun, the moon, the battlefield, perhaps demon horses or something equivalent. If they had a section on Empyreals, even better.

Paging through the table of contents Nicole noted each chapter was written by a different supernatural author. And then she spotted one entitled: "The Wild Hunt."

Nicole flipped to the page, revealing glossy color prints of different pieces of art depicting the Hunt. The idea of the Wild Hunt, she knew, was rife in Celtic legends from Ireland, Wales, and Norse kingdoms.

Linked to the origin of Empyreals, the Wild Hunt can depict either that very beginning created by the goddess from the stars . . .

Nicole paused, thinking back to what Kyan had said: that as a child he'd believed the Morrígan, the Irish Goddess of Death, had blessed him. Was that the goddess the book was referring to? She kept reading:

. . . or, some say it is a prophecy: that the Wild Hunt will be unleashed upon this world.

A prickle of unease danced up her spine. A prophecy? Why did that sound similar to her mother's note?

While the moon is a symbol more often used for Werewolves, Vampires, and other such night-prowling creatures, one particular moon does have significance for Empyreals: the October hunter's moon.

A hunter's moon, to bind a mated Empyreal pair.
Some say the goddess created each Empyreal with a perfect
mate, so they could hunt for eternity together.

Nicole frowned. She'd heard of mates among certain immortal beings, but never Empyreals.

She checked the author of the page, and her frown smoothed out as her breath caught. The author was listed only as "*divino artista.*"

She'd bet anything this had been written by her mother and laughed softly until she read the last line.

As a bind of love is the most powerful, and love transcends even
death.

24 KYAN

Kyan startled awake. His skin was damp and chest heaving. No moonlight knifed in, so his navy sheets and the bedroom in Westmoore Manor were barely illuminated. Yet he could see it all with his Specter vision, how large it was, how luxurious.

How different to the one he'd been in in 1902.

The dream skidded and faded away, taking him through a rush of memories, the words of the oath ringing in his mind:

"I, hunter of the Wake, declare that I will, to the extent of all my ability, detain and transport to the organization any discovered Empyreal who is unclaimed. No matter how young, no matter whose bloodline, no matter what piece of the earth they inhabit."

The penalty was death for those that refused to take it, and death for those that didn't obey it.

Kyan pulled back the sheets, déjà vu crashing over him, and looked down to the scar on his forearm as guilt eddied with it.

He'd been in a strange state when he'd taken the oath.

The day before, he'd been plagued with questions: What could the Wake possibly need from their greatest weapons? Why had they summoned them in such numbers? It had been the largest gathering of Empyreals Kyan had ever seen of their rare kind: fifty other hunters.

Yet after arriving at Lanhydrock and an evening of dreams of his mother, he'd been suspicious. Especially as she'd told him that the Wake would want him to swear an oath. The dream had been so real he'd been convinced she was somehow still alive. She'd been a force of nature, and Druids were such incredible healers that part of him had hoped she'd survived the massacre that had destroyed her and the last of the Irish Druids. After he'd killed the creature that had razed their forest home, he'd passed out with her in his arms, waking up afterward on a boat to Scotland.

In the dream at Lanhydrock, she'd come to him in their Edwardian dress in the small church on the grounds.

But when he'd awoken to realize it had been nothing but a dream, it had unearthed his long-buried grief and made him remember that the Wake was all he had left. Not the life he once had in Ulster with his cousins, his people; the echoes of magic that had been slaughtered out of existence. Her warnings didn't drive him from the Wake, but further into it.

The Wake had been the ones to give him an eternal purpose. If they asked of him another oath, he'd take it. He'd told himself the dream of his mother had been nothing, just lingering memories that had flared up thanks to a new publication on Irish mythology that had been released around that time, which mentioned his own ancient names and stories.

But that hadn't been all.

Kyan pushed up from the bed, cursing the memories that were flooding back as he paced in the dark room, remembering the Messenger's words following the oath:

"You may begin the hunt."

Kyan had then hunted down one of the Empyreals that had

refused to take it: Alexander. Kyan had been wary of him for years. The other Empyreal had been as dangerous as their relationship was complex and had gotten reckless and vicious in his killings.

Now, Kyan caught his reflection in one of the luxurious room's mirrors above the dresser, and he remembered standing in front of one after he'd killed Alexander: staring at his hands in the clean white ceramic bowl, dark in their sun-stained color and thick with blood and dirt. It had sunk into the lines of his hands, into his fingerprints, and dried under his nails.

He'd taken a nail brush and scrubbed, tempted to use it on the raw skin of his new scar, the way it itched and fevered. The burn of his oath had hummed through him like a disease; rendering every bone weak with subservience but strong with drive. It was now a mission—his mission—to be obeyed at all costs, and he would.

But that day, Kyan had killed his own kind. Not with his power, with his own two hands.

And he wouldn't forget that.

Nor would he forget the bloody words Alexander had spat in his face when Kyan had tackled him to the bracken after a fight that tore through the woods, shredded his elegant suit and every civil disguise they'd worn in front of the humans.

"There's more to life than their every fucking whim. I'll not bow forever, I never should have in the first place. If you had any real will left, neither would you."

A flash of intuition had almost stilled Kyan.

Then there'd been a crack louder than a gunshot, and birds shot up through the trees. Alexander's head had slumped from Kyan's hands, the neck broken. His mangled body lay staring blindly into Kyan's face, as rain began to fall and the blood on Kyan's arm washed off his newly scarring oath. . . .

Kyan rubbed his face. It had been his duty to take the oath. But was it the same now?

Over a hundred years later he still worked for the Wake. Still killed for them. It was his job. His nature. His body had never steered him wrong before and he trusted that he couldn't make a kill until a creature's own killing hormone was released.

The day of the oath, however, he had killed Alexander without transforming.

But he could do nothing about that now and couldn't allow himself to be dragged too deep into history. Yet there was another mystery at hand, one that might have actual consequences for his current mission: the woman that looked like Nicole. Kyan thought of the brown eyes of the small, shapeshifting intruder who'd disguised herself to trick him.

Eyes just like Nicole's.

He mentally compared the similarities. It was undeniable. They had the same dark hair; same face; were the same size. Was this why Nicole tugged at him? Calling back to some almost-lost memory?

He cursed.

The night after the oath-taking, after he'd killed Alexander, all the Empyreals had to be present at the human ball held at Lanhydrock House, to complete the illusion they were nothing but civil gentleman guests. His mother had come to him again, or at least, he'd thought it was her. But as soon as she demanded to know if he'd taken the oath, Callum had interrupted, seeing through her illusion. Her face had then transformed into someone else's, his mother's slightly pointed chin and strikingly intelligent green eyes changing. And that blade of hope Kyan had nurtured had splintered in his chest with such pain his breath faltered.

If Nicole and this woman were related, did Nicole have the same abilities as her? Could she dip into his mind like the woman had? Push thoughts and dreams into his subconscious and exploit his memories? Change her face and make him think she was someone else?

But she's a Seer.

Was it possible the woman had been a Seer, too? Or some other kind of being like Nicole, one that was difficult to pinpoint? There were many shapeshifting creatures, and she must have used the skill to get past the Wake's Empyreal-and-human-only boundary that day.

Was it possible the woman was an Empyreal?

No. An Empyreal had no way to dip into another's mind, sift through their memories, and find a familiar face, even if the very ancient and powerful few *did* have the ability to transform their features. How would she have known what his mother looked like unless she had a Seer-related power?

Callum had never been able to figure out what the woman wanted. Or why, out of all Empyreals there, she'd singled *him* out.

The events of that day set Kyan off on another hundred years of steadfast hunts. More dark nights alone, another century of suppressing the image of her lest it haunt his dreams. More reasons for him to retain the title of the Wake's greatest immortal assassin.

Kyan stalked from the bedroom, moving easily in the dark. His new night vision was spectacularly helpful in tracking Lynch, but resisting the need for fresh blood was becoming a problem, and the strong urge for it made him head toward the kitchen.

The hallways were mostly dark, save for the odd lamp causing the manor's artifacts and great gilded frames to glint as he passed.

The kitchen had a minimal elegance compared to the rest of the house. The walls were pale gray and the elegant architrave white, matching the sleek cabinets and large multileveled slab of white marble which served as both countertop and breakfast bar. A long, unused mahogany dining table sat perpendicular to it.

Kyan selected a vial of blood he'd left in the fridge. He tipped his head back and used a dropper to stroke it over his sensitive teeth, the cold burning as his body filtered the plasma.

Then he felt the benefits and closed his eyes to absorb them.

He hadn't realized how long he'd stood there, his body reeling from the blood, his energy linking with Lynch's. He was drawn out of it by the whisper of bare feet on the wooden floors and stiffened.

Nicole.

She moved unnaturally lightly, even for someone her height.

Kyan turned and there she was, coming out of the luxurious dark of the house into the kitchen, wearing only her pajamas, her hair loose around her shoulders—all that metamorphic color gleaming in the dim.

He suddenly wanted to sink his hands into it. He gripped the countertop instead.

Her wary eyes sharpened on him with enough intensity he got a kick in the gut . . . and then a kick lower.

Tell me what you see, he wanted to ask. *Tell me why you feel so . . .*

Instead, all he could think about was what *he* could see. A mystery with a supernatural allure. Someone whose very essence called to some deep ancient instinct in him, and whose blood was a mystery of sensations.

"Nicole," he said, bothered by the roughness in his voice.

He glanced to the clock, finding it was eleven thirty. He'd been standing here for hours.

"I didn't realize you were up," she said, lingering in the doorway, her cheeks slightly flushed. "I . . . didn't hear you." She seemed surprised by this.

He nodded, but with the blood in his system he now saw her in more detail, including the pulse at her neck. "You should get to your room," he ground out.

She didn't move, her dark, frowning eyes still on his. "I've been in a research spiral, so I'm hungry."

So am I, he almost admitted. But now was not the time to be thinking of certain . . . hungers.

He focused on the wall, trying to regain control before managing, "What do you want to eat?"

But she was moving toward him, and his muscles wired with awareness when he realized he was standing next to the fridge.

"I did buy food," she said, pulling out a glass container of some pasta dish. "And I brought some from home."

She paused beside him, and he glanced down at her quizzical expression.

"Are you all right?" she asked. "Did you . . . sleep okay?"

He hadn't been asked that in . . . long enough he couldn't remember. Did she really want to know or was she just so used to living with people she loved, people who asked one another those kinds of questions? He scanned her eyes: the way her brow had pulled low over them, turning her expression serious; the way they weren't just dark but had flecks of amber that no doubt lit when in sunlight. Sunlight that currently burned the shit out of his eyes.

She blinked and he realized he hadn't answered her question.

He nodded tightly. "Fine."

"Then you won't mind if I . . ." She leaned closer.

He stiffened as her hand reached for him, as her scent rushed up at the displacement of air. *Gods*, what was it? Darkly sweet. His body drew taut in answer: whether to want or to hunt, he couldn't tell. He'd always been able to tell. The insistent urge made him almost angry. He wasn't this person. He'd practically been celibate for centuries unless the aftereffects of a transformation pushed him over the edge. And here he was, almost driven to a base, insistent temptation by the shape of her mouth. Forget about the curved slope of her shoulder. Her bare legs in those shorts . . .

Desire surged through his body.

Her staying here was a bad idea. He'd speak to the curator, the vice chancellor of the university, someone. Anyone. He'd Influence whoever he had to, even if that was Nicole herself, in order to get her out. He couldn't afford to be distracted.

So slake the need. The thought had his jaw clenching so hard it felt liable to crack.

Nicole looked up and he was momentarily stunned. What was it about her gaze that perpetually knotted something in his gut? And what was she doing? He waited for the soft press of her touch, wondering why now. . . .

Until he realized what she was reaching for.

The kettle he was currently standing in front of like a giant gargoyle.

Kyan forced his fingers to release their grip on the edge of the marble counter and angled himself away from her, taking a step back, then another; watching as she gave a small, unsure smile and moved to where he'd been, bending over the counter slightly to reach for the kettle, which was tucked back against the wall. He looked away as she filled it at the sink.

The loud crack of the kettle snapping back onto its base made his sensitive teeth grind together and bleed a warm rush of venom.

"I was just going to work some more on the *Wild Hunt* painting," Nicole said, as if to make conversation.

He nodded. "I'll get my laptop, then."

She turned, surprised; the little teacup she'd selected clipped against the counter. "Oh. I thought you'd changed your mind since . . ."

She thought he was angry with her after Lanhydrock and was going to withhold the information? He'd threatened to, after all. He felt a rush of shame and shook his head.

"No— I . . ." *I thought you'd come to me.* "I don't know how to—" He wasn't used to being around anyone when he was on a hunt. The protective instincts were heightened. The idea of someone waiting in the place he was to call his base was throwing him off.

So come and go as you please and don't even think about her presence.

Tell her no.

But how could he ignore her, or the mystery of the art, when her unusual scent ghosted through the halls? When he could hear her in the night on her phone to her friend, leafing through the research in Westmoore's study, or sighing that lush little sigh she didn't realize she made every time she stepped into the gallery room.

"No, it's fine. We're trying to figure this out together, after all," Kyan said.

But to do so, he needed to clear the tension that had been building between them since Lanhydrock, and after his dream, he wondered if he knew the cause.

25 NICOLE

Nicole turned back to the kettle to hide her expression, wondering what to say. She hadn't expected Kyan to be in here. When she'd stirred from the revelation about her mother, she'd thought Kyan had left, no longer hearing him in his room, which was why she hadn't put her cardigan back on.

Yet here he was. "We're trying to figure this out together," he'd said.

She should ask him more about the oath and the passage she'd discovered about Empyreals. But she was surprised and a little off balance seeing him like this. She mustn't have heard him because he'd been so still.

Nicole tried not to tug at her sleep shorts or the small top. She'd seen him avert his eyes, even as a muscle ticked in his temple, and was seriously reconsidering the little pajamas she'd brought. In her defense she'd expected to only ever wear them hidden in the manor bedroom, not while standing before a hulking immortal hunter.

Before *Kyan*.

He still had that haunted look that had followed him since they'd been at Lanhydrock, and she didn't know how to approach him with this sleepiness about him. Like he'd just woken up, hair tousled. He wore a short-sleeved white T-shirt that stopped at the bulge of his tanned biceps and a pair of pajama bottoms. A complicated warmth spread in her, so Nicole stared at something else, anything else.

She poured the boiling water into her cup, tying the label of the herbal tea bag around the handle.

"I also want to talk about what happened at Lanhydrock . . . when I brought up your mother," Kyan said.

"We don't have to talk about that," she said quickly. She wasn't sure how much she could concentrate with him like this, close and warm and gentle beside her.

"It's just that I understand," he began, "how it feels to lose one."

Her stomach dropped at the sincerity in his words. *No*, she wanted to plead, as the eternal emotions simmering beneath the surface threatened to rise again. It didn't happen so much anymore when people gave general platitudes. But Kyan knew more than a human, and he was being so *gentle* about it.

Don't make me care about your past. About you, she thought desperately.

This was supposed to be clear-cut. He worked for the Wake. They would hunt her. She couldn't think of him as anything other than a stoic, dangerous Celtic warrior. She couldn't risk it.

And yet her heart ached at the thought that he'd lost his mother. When had it happened? When he'd been that little seven-year-old boy? Newly transformed and alone? She nearly couldn't bear the thought. What other family had been taken from him over time?

"We can work on the archives until Lynch goes out," Kyan said quietly.

Nicole stared at her cup. He really was offering her access back into the database that could help solve this riddle. She'd struggled to conceive of a single way she could trust him, and here he was, offering it.

He must have seen it in her eyes when they met his.

An incredibly warm, intimate feeling crested like a wave through her chest. She almost reached up and pressed it, trying to stop it, but put her cup down instead, too hard.

She wasn't used to such delicate china, not when her mind was elsewhere and her body was reeling toward something she had no desire to unravel. But it meant she forgot her strength for one crucial second.

The shatter split through the moment and then Nicole felt the strike of pain. She hissed in a breath, finding most of the porcelain had shot across the counter but scalding water had also splashed over her.

A moment later, blood pooled in a fresh slice on her hand.

Her attention shot up to Kyan as his eyes went immediately dark.

A second later, his hands had clamped around her waist and the floor had disappeared as he sat her on the countertop. She barely had time to register the feeling of his hands or the cool of marble against the back of her thighs.

He reached for her wrist like he was fighting a deep, inescapable urge, his face severe as a sculpture.

"Are you all right? Let me see. Don't worry, I'm in control."

Nicole closed her fingers around the slick blood and hid her hand behind her back. She could feel the skin knitting back together with Empyrean speed, even the searing pain from the hot water gently easing far faster than it would for a human. It reminded her of her father's theory on her sporadic healing lately: that a wound inflicted by a supernatural with magic or power was more difficult for her body to deal with. But a slice on the hand from a teacup?

Already done.

She couldn't let him see that she'd already healed, and she had to make sure he didn't *taste* it, no matter what he said about control.

Because if he did, he might discover the truth about what she was, just as Lynch had.

She needed a distraction. Something . . . *anything*. If she ran, he'd only follow.

The thought had barely formed before Nicole grabbed Kyan's shirt with her uninjured hand and dragged him to her mouth.

She hadn't really meant to. She'd only ever kissed one person before, on a night out with Remi the summer before classes began, and it had been so . . . disappointing.

But the moment all six feet plus of Kyan collided with her, staggering into the space where her legs had parted, and his lips met hers, some strange alchemy flooded her system with a molten *need* like she'd never known.

Kyan stilled completely.

For a moment, so did she.

Oh god, she hadn't even asked him. She should stop immediately and apologize and—

But as her lips moved to pull away, he snapped into motion with a low sound of desire and her body answered it with a shocking lurch of its own.

There were urges, she'd been discovering, that could short-circuit her brain. One of them was the urge of her Empyreal that told her to *hunt*. That told her her body needed to do something it had never done before.

226

This was another.

Nicole found herself relaxing against him, into the surprising flood of sensation. At the incomparably warm luxury of Kyan's lips parting against hers and the slow, hot glide as his tongue joined the kiss, pooling warmth through her body. Every part of her honed in on that liquid touch and she made a sound against him, somewhere between a moan of surprise and pleasure as a world of sensation opened up inside.

She reached, as if on reflex, for his shoulders, suddenly desperate to touch him; her fingers finding the warm stretch at the back of his neck between his hairline and shirt. Drowning in that earthy, masculine scent of his.

And then his hands were on her.

They closed around her hips, fingers long, palms wide and warm. He pulled her closer until they were flush, her legs hooking naturally around his hips. The immediate thrill of her almost bare thighs against him turned more heated and drugging when his head tilted, and the stroke of his kiss deepened into something inky and inescapably sensual.

Then her back was arching, crushing her breasts against the carved strength she could feel beneath his thin T-shirt, sending sensation and relief spiraling out. Every part of her body he touched seemed to come alive, especially when he stroked around her backside then up her spine, hands diving into her hair and slowly fisting a hold.

Nicole whimpered against the feeling as he kissed her again.

Deeper, faster.

More.

She needed him *everywhere*. Her legs tightened as heat pooled between them and Kyan made a low, pained sound.

Suddenly his lips ripped from hers, but he didn't move away, as if he couldn't. His chest heaved, rising and falling against hers.

"Go to bed, Nicole," Kyan said roughly against her mouth.

She felt such a rush of heat at his words, her lips formed around a no.

But then she realized just how close he was to losing that infamous control.

And just how much she wanted him to.

He seemed to release her by degrees, but it was too slow, each graze of his fingers a luxurious torture, leaving her feeling soft and hot and wanting.

"I should go," Kyan said, taking a few steps backward, breathing heavily.

Nicole reeled, almost careening off the counter. Her lips burned; her skin was suddenly bereft of his heat. Her body was sensitized in places she'd never allowed herself to give much thought to. And it felt *good*.

No, it felt so much better than good.

"Are you all right?" he asked, gaze tracking over her breasts to the place she had fisted her hand against the counter.

Right. Her hand.

"I'm fine," she said, still breathless.

He nodded slightly and turned. Then she saw the blood she'd smeared on the shoulder of his T-shirt.

Shit, she'd been so overwhelmed she'd touched him with her injured hand! What if he smelled it, tasted it? Lynch had discovered what she was through it. After what she'd learned about the oath, she couldn't take any chances.

"Wait!"

She cringed as he stilled, not sure what to say. Alarm and desire pulsed through her.

"Nicole . . ." he growled.

She shivered, clambering off the counter on weak legs. "I got blood on your shirt."

"It's fine."

"No. I . . . Give me your shirt."

Oh my god, what's wrong with me?

His dark eyes met hers over his shoulder.

"I . . . I'll get the blood off."

"I know how to get blood out of a shirt, Nicole."

Of course, he was a hunter. He'd probably had enough practice with that.

"Still. Won't it be tempting?"

Tempting. God, she couldn't even think of that word right now. Not with him looking at her like that.

Like temptation was the very hell they were both trapped in.

"I can control myself," he said thickly.

Still, she held out her hand. "It's no problem."

"I'm not going to make you wash my shirt while your hand is bleeding."

"Kyan, please," she whispered, hardly able to stand it, unable to lie for a moment longer, to think *straight* when her body was screaming at her to stay. To step back over, to—

As if he knew how much she needed it, even if he didn't understand why, Kyan turned to face her. He didn't break eye contact as his thick bicep flexed, and then he was pulling the shirt over his head, ruffling his dark hair. Her mouth dried at the sight of that heavily muscled stomach, stroked with dark hair, up and *up*, past solid pecs and over wide shoulders.

He took a step or two toward her, his chest so close she felt dizzy from that masculine scent, and handed her the shirt. Her fingers closed around the soft, warm fabric.

"Anything else?" he asked roughly, and god help her, her eyes dropped briefly to the band of his pajama pants before heat scored her cheeks.

"No," she breathed.

She backed up shakily.

Oh my god, that was a mistake. Now she'd have that sight scored into her mind for the rest of her *life*. She banged into the counter with a yelp, and he lurched closer, every bloody muscle in his body suddenly outlined with strength.

"I'm fine," she gasped, not sure if her whimper was from the pain, or need. "I'm good."

He gave her a warning look as she backed out of the kitchen, still clutching his shirt. It was like walking away from a wolf, but she couldn't tell which one she was in that scenario. Because while she felt his own desire like pulses of magnetic energy, and felt deliciously *wanted*, she also felt her own hunger.

Just as adamant to be fed.

Nicole staggered back to her room through panels of lamplight, for once blind to the luxuries of the manor. The minute she crashed into the guest bedroom she beelined for the sink in the adjoining bathroom, washing her hand to reveal nothing but a shiny pink mark that was quickly fading.

She met her eyes in the mirror. Her pupils were dilated—not from the blood, but the great well of *want* that had cracked open inside her. She whooshed out a breath, her kiss-plump lips tingling, feeling too physical. The tile against her bare feet was cool and prickling, her top trailing sensation across her shoulders, her breasts.

Oh god, she thought, *I want him.*

He was an Empyreal, her greatest threat and her greatest fascination. Everything she'd been warned against.

And yet, she wanted him, still.

She was supposed to be in control. But she was not in control around Kyan. She argued with him, she wanted to know about his life, she felt confusingly safe around him, and now she ached for his touch, too?

What's happening to me?

She should leave. She should pack up her things right now and put as much distance between them as possible. And yet her every impulse rejected the idea. She wanted to be here, and if she hadn't stayed late tonight, she might not have been on the right tangent to find that information about Empyreals.

She might not have kissed him.

Nicole clambered into the high bed with its cool, expensive sheets and stared at the ceiling. At the night beach. At the door.

He was a hunter. That was the only way she was allowed to think of him. Not a guy. Not an option. And *not* something she suddenly wanted to call back.

Not at all.

KYAN

Kyan wasn't sure he should move. He stared, shirtless, at the dark doorway Nicole had gone through, and he had to force himself not to follow, not to haul her back toward him and continue feeling every curve, every toned inch. He cursed the new memory of her breasts against his chest as desire roared beneath his skin, hot and loud.

How was it that she managed to surprise him at every turn of this mission?

When he heard her bedroom door close, he forced his mind back to Lynch. *That* was his focus here, not Nicole. Not tonight, not *any* night. But as he finally forced his body to move, to the simple task of turning around and leaving—

He stilled as a knife of a different kind of hunger drew his attention. Kyan breathed deeply, scenting that newly delicious, addictive fragrance. It clutched at his gut, and he looked down at the broken shards of Nicole's cup still lying on the floor.

Blood.

He stared. Nicole had said she didn't want her blood around him in case it was a temptation. He frowned, part of him wanting to leave it. Tasting her blood after being close might . . . complicate matters. And yet it offered him the perfect opportunity to understand something that had puzzled him about her from the first moment they met.

What was she hiding?

Kyan squatted. He hesitated before stroking a finger through a spatter of blood. Lynch's attack had changed the playing field.

And then she'd kissed him.

This mission had a fine, deadly balance, and if Kyan failed, Nicole might get seriously hurt. She might scream, she might be *afraid.* . . .

He allowed the blood to meet his tongue.

Sensation exploded. She tasted like she smelled: some unusual liquid ambrosia that called to his Empyreal beneath his slowly transforming body. Any kind of vampiric creature took years to develop and understand the taste of different creatures' blood. Kyan had never been one long enough to learn the differences. But he knew one thing. The taste of Nicole's blood was . . . *more.* It pulsed with a promise that made his Empyrean senses roar to life. Perhaps she *was* some kind of unknown creature and that was why she was so defensive about her visions, why she moved and smelled so unlike any Seer he'd ever met.

Could that explain his draw to her?

But it hadn't been a Specter's hunger that had made him want her with an almost wicked desire.

No, that had been purely *him.*

Kyan swept up the shards slowly, to prove to her that he wasn't now some raging beast for her blood. For *her* though . . . he had felt it in those moments she was crushed up against him. But it wasn't just the soft press of her body that set his teeth on edge and his urges murmuring with need. It had been her eyes, just before she'd cut her hand. Those lovely, concerned eyes after he'd told her about his mother. She cared. She knew that grief, and he'd never told anyone the things that had suddenly wanted to pour from him when he'd seen it.

How sweet she was. How vicious when she needed to be.

Whether she had tried to keep that wall up between them or not, it had been cracked tonight. He thought again of sending her away and decided against it. He couldn't feel untethered by both the Wake and Nicole, so he went back to his room and put on a new shirt and jeans, his body still raw, and opened up his laptop to log into the Wake's database and send them a message:

What is the importance of this painting?

He paced for a few long moments before it made him want to hunt, before it made him think of Nicole. . . .

Then came the reply:

Information not necessary.

Kyan frowned, his intuition flickering coldly. Not necessary? *I'll decide that*, he nearly wrote back before hesitating.

Whatever was going on with this painting, he and Nicole were winding tighter and tighter together. So he forced himself out of the house, onto the night-swept beach, and toward the sleeping university town after his prey.

Otherwise, he wasn't sure he could resist tracking back through the house for Nicole instead.

26 NICOLE

"I told you to not work too late," Remi said the next morning in their folklore lecture.

Nicole blinked her gritty eyes a few times, hoping to clear them enough to better concentrate on the professor, the unnecessary bandage around her hand rough against her propped-up jaw.

She'd been excited about this class, hoping it would give her a few useful tidbits on the Wild Hunt, and yet she was ready to close her laptop and rest her head on her crossed arms like the girl three rows down. She'd go blissfully unconscious in about a minute.

Nicole reached for her double Americano, finding it long gone. She made a small sound of distress and sensed Kyan stiffen where he sat sprawled in one of the tiny lecture seats two rows behind, his dark eyes watching over her.

Remi slid Nicole the last of her mocha.

She took it gratefully. Her supernatural metabolism rarely allowed much of a hit from caffeine, but it was better than nothing.

"I *tried*," Nicole said just as quietly. "Besides, *you* were up late, you said you didn't sleep till three."

Remi laughed softly. "That's because I was busy doing *other things*."

Nicole shook her head with a smile, catching Remi's smirk.

I was busy too, Nicole almost admitted, thinking of being pressed up against Kyan in the kitchen, the hot brush of his mouth, those words that sounded all too much like a plea: "Go to bed, Nicole."

She shivered, resisting the urge to look over her shoulder.

After she'd lain awake in bed for a while, she'd had a terrible realization, throwing off the sheets and rushing through the house. But when she got back to the kitchen, she'd discovered the bloodied shards of the broken teacup—the shards with her blood on—were gone.

And so was Kyan.

After that, sleep had evaded her completely. Had he cleaned it up and gotten a deeper read of her from her blood?

She felt Kyan's gaze on her, warm enough, intent enough it brought the memories back. Pressing her fingers to her gritty eyes, she damned her razor-sharp memory and supernatural senses.

The good thing was that he was so direct, she imagined he'd ask her about it if he had. But there was little she could do about that now; instead she had to try and get her head on straight and *focus*.

Remi leaned in again and whispered, "So, what? Is he your bodyguard now or something?"

This morning, during a ridiculously tense run-in in the kitchen while she was halfway through a large breakfast in the hopes it would wake her up, Kyan had stepped into the doorway.

"Now you're Lynch's target and he knows what I am, there's no more element of surprise," he said. "So I might as well come with you."

"Come with me . . . where?"

"To your classes."

There was no talk of the kiss, although she didn't miss Kyan's

236

glance to the counter where he'd sat her, and heat had rushed through her in response.

"No," Nicole said, answering Remi's question. "He's just thorough, evidently."

Remi made a thoughtful noise. "He can hear everything we say, can't he?"

"Yes," Kyan answered behind them, quiet enough humans wouldn't hear, but that Remi and Nicole could.

"Cool. Great." Remi turned back to the lecture, sliding Nicole an almost amused look.

When it was over, Remi walked with them to the exit.

"I'll see you in the library tonight," she said. "At seven. *Promptly.*" She eyed Kyan up and down before swanning from the building.

Kyan's lips twitched slightly. "Are all your friends and family this protective?" he asked as he held the glass door for Nicole.

"It's a trait of ours."

"If only you'd follow my orders as well as you do your friend's."

Nicole's eyes narrowed as his lips lifted in a shadow of a smile. She nearly did a double take. A kiss and now . . . a *smile*?

She rushed through the door.

They walked together through town to the library—it was so strange to see life continuing: classes going on and professors strolling down the street. Nicole couldn't help but notice Kyan's completely natural physical confidence and the gazes of people as he walked past.

She hastily swiped her student card at the arched stone door of the library. Last night they hadn't looked at the archives again because they'd been . . . distracted. But today, she was determined to stay on track.

She chose a seat in the center of the dim space and Kyan took the seat beside her, thigh brushing hers. A flush began a slow creep up her neck and lust as ruthless as her Empyreal tugged at her.

Focus, remember?

And yet, she felt his arm as it draped over the back of her chair. For a moment it tugged some of her hair and her breath hitched, remembering the feeling of his hands in it. . . .

She snuck a look at Kyan and found that he was already looking at her, his eyes swollen and dark with dilated pupils. And he wasn't breathing. His attention slowly slid to her mouth.

He was asking her without words: *Are we going to talk about the kiss?*

"How's your hand?" he asked roughly.

"Good," she whispered.

He made an agreeable noise at the back of his throat. Then he moved, leaning closer. Her heart took off and she suddenly felt lightheaded. Since they hadn't discussed it she hadn't known how their interactions would play out after last night, if kissing would become . . . normal or not. It had been an accident. A spur-of-the-moment thing.

And yet, anticipation clutched in her chest. He was close . . . so close.

Kyan angled his lips to her cheek as if to whisper something, but they stroked across it, featherlight. She shivered as her breath hitched.

"And your throat?" he murmured.

"That's good too," she said on a shaky exhale.

Just then, a student drifted past, and their scent caught Nicole's attention. She looked up, startled, to see them ashen and barely awake. They smelled like—

"Lynch," Kyan explained, stiffening and sitting back.

The lingering desire flooded away with her rage and she twisted to face Kyan. "He's been feeding off more people?"

Kyan nodded tightly.

"What are we going to do about him and the painting?"

"I'll meet with the curator and we'll check the museum."

She didn't need to ask to join him, she realized, because he'd said "we." Something about it warmed her heart, filling her with relief.

"I'm thinking we might be able to use this Saturday to draw him out if we need to."

"You mean the day that *The Wild Hunt* was supposed to be on show in the museum?"

Kyan nodded. "I might offer another painting, something inconspicuous. It will get a meeting with the curator and get us in the museum without too much Influencing."

"Okay, good plan." She paused, wondering if she should ask him about what she'd discovered in the symbology book in the manor, deciding out of everyone, an Empyreal would probably know.

"Do you know anything else about the Wild Hunt that could be useful?"

Kyan forced his eyes to the laptop. "They say our best Empyreals, if they're ever killed, are recruited by the goddess should the Wild Hunt ever manifest."

Nicole's brows rose, fascinated. "Is that what you believe?"

"It's what my people believed. Just as they believed in the Druids, in souls, in soulmates."

She blinked. "Soulmates? Like mated pairs of supernaturals?"

"I suppose, though Empyreals don't have mates."

Her curiosity sharpened. That was what she'd thought and

what she thought was general knowledge . . . and yet the book she'd found last night had claimed the opposite. She was almost certain the entry had been written by her mother, but if that was the case, why wouldn't she have written it in one of the many journals in the house? Why keep that a secret from the family until Nicole found the book in Westmoore's library?

She frowned, and Kyan mistook it for confusion.

"To hunt and be immortal, there's no room for a partner; the Wake have known this for years."

The Wake might have lied, she thought.

But then, why would the Wake tell Empyreals they were unable to be mated? Was it to keep them loyal? That made sense. If Empyreals believed they could find a partner and wouldn't have to be so alone, would they be such dedicated hunters?

Suddenly she wanted to reach out to him, to reassure him, but she curled her fingers into a fist instead and pushed away the thought of him finding a mate, and the way it made her feel—irritable.

Remi was right, she did need sleep.

27 NICOLE

The next night, Nicole expected to find Kyan in the manor's kitchen, but when she came into the sleek dark gray space with its antique accents, she wasn't prepared for the sight. She'd been working on the paintings all day, drafting up ideas for her dissertation—though working on it had felt so inconsequential next to the real work she had to do. But knowing they'd be getting news tonight in a meeting with the curator had made her edgy.

Kyan was cooking. Two steaks sizzled in the pan and an arrangement of vegetables were laid out beside it with herbs, spices, and sauces, and she could smell potatoes browning in the oven. It was weird watching him cook—such a human thing to do.

And she wasn't going to lie, he looked good doing it.

"You're full of surprises," Nicole commented.

One of Kyan's brows raised and a rare smile pulled at his mouth. "I need to eat like anyone else."

Why did those words make her blush? His eyes raced over the deepening color, then he nodded to the stool across from him and resumed chopping.

"I thought we could eat before we go," he said, voice rougher.

They were due to meet the curator tonight at eight to check the museum's archives and make sure Lynch hadn't stashed the painting in plain sight. She had a feeling Kyan hoped that if they found the painting and took it back, Lynch would be angry enough to kill and he'd be able to eliminate him.

"Do you really think he stashed it there?" Nicole asked.

Kyan took a thoughtful pause. "Hunting usually requires you to understand your target. Their way of thinking, their way of killing. But Lynch is—"

"A sadistic piece of shit?"

A smile flashed over Kyan's face, and then he laughed. A rough, delicious sound that made her breath catch. "I was going to say complicated. But at the same time, this is one of the easiest places he could have hidden it."

She huffed, clasping her neck. Suddenly she was exhausted.

What if it wasn't there? What if Lynch had hidden it elsewhere? Then she'd be back to square one; to pieces of research that could spiral off in any direction. How would she know which of them to follow? Her mother's clues had never been this complicated before. But then this was the biggest and most important piece of information she knew. She couldn't very well leave it to be easily uncovered.

The only pieces that seemed to make the most sense were those that had led them to Lanhydrock and shown her a vision of her mother. If that wasn't a sign she was on the right track, Nicole wasn't sure what would be.

She glanced at Kyan. He looked like the man in the *Dante* painting and her mother had tried to persuade him not to take the oath, so maybe uncovering some of *his* secrets would be the missing pieces she needed. It had been testy enough of a subject and she hadn't wanted him to ask more questions about her mother, but she couldn't avoid it forever.

"Will you tell me about your past? About why the woman from 1902 used your mother's face?"

Kyan dropped a scoop of butter into the pan and sprinkled in some herbs. He chopped spring onions with quick, precise bites of his knife and threw the vegetables in, removing the steaks and letting them rest.

Nicole thought he wasn't going to answer, then he started, reluctantly.

"I was born in Ulster—a province in Ireland. That time has been branded the Ulster Cycle by modern people. Few records remain and I don't even know if it's accurate considering no written sources from the time are left, but it's thought to have been the early first century AD. Stories of that time are myths now. My cousins and I are in some of them."

She couldn't help her surprise. He'd mentioned the Ulster Cycle before, but had studiously avoided talking about family. "You have cousins?"

"I did. They . . . they weren't immortal. Any other family I had—died."

Nicole cursed. She shouldn't have assumed. "I'm sorry." She wanted to say how much family meant to her, how she wouldn't know how to exist without them, but stopped herself. The mere thought of losing them made her ill. Kyan had already suffered through that, and he'd been slowly showing her that he wouldn't use her love for her family against her. "I would do anything for my family. I can't imagine . . ."

His shoulders relaxed slightly before tensing again. "I had different names then."

"Tell me," she encouraged softly.

His gaze turned so intent she felt a blush stain her cheeks. "My first name was Sétanta. But after my first transformation, my name became Cú Chulainn."

She sounded it out, *coo-hull-in*. A calming, quiet, almost intimate name. Her skin prickled.

It wasn't just a name steeped in ancient magic and the love of his lost family.

It was a name steeped in blood.

KYAN

Kyan hadn't spoken those names for at least a hundred years. The last time had been in Lanhydrock's tiny church, hidden up the hill behind the house, when the woman from the vision had used the face of his mother.

"Were your parents human?" Nicole asked.

She was wearing a delicate gold necklace of ancient design. It rested on her chest, framed by the sweetheart neckline of a thin black jumper, and drew his attention. He found himself uncharacteristically pleased to see her in an Irish design. The jumper didn't touch the dimming bruise on her neck and she'd tied her hair back into a ponytail, he imagined to keep any irritation away. She looked soft, warm. So opposite to the feelings incurred in him when he remembered his past.

Kyan frowned down at the food.

"My mother was a Druid. I didn't know my father. I suppose he could have been human. Empyreals are mostly born to human parents, though many mutate and develop powers out of necessity. But I imagine he was an Empyreal."

"You never met him?"

He shook his head. "No. My mother was a very independent woman. But I had many foster fathers who were friends of my mother's and taught me everything they knew. My family wasn't just her and the Druids, but people like my uncle, the king."

Nicole's lips parted slightly, a flash of realization going through her. He hadn't thought of that title himself for many years.

"My mother wasn't just the king's sister but his charioteer. She

would take him into any battle. She had a way with horses that—"
He shook his head. For a moment the memory didn't sting or fill
him with regret. It was just fondness. "I haven't seen anything like
it since. When I think of her, I think of all the Druid women who
raised me. Their knots and patterns and how they braided my
hair. How they taught me the cycles of life and the ways of their
magic."

The cords around his wrist suddenly felt like a weight.

"What happened?"

The past shuddered over him like it had been lingering over
his shoulder, waiting for permission to take hold. He rarely allowed
himself to think of those times. When he had a different name, a
different way of viewing the world: like he was indestructible. And
he had been. He was.

Others weren't.

He met Nicole's gaze and could already see the mirror of the
events in her Seer eyes.

"There was a war. They now call it the Cattle Raid." His smile
was bitter. "The real motivation had nothing to do with a prized
bull. The ruler of the next province, Queen Medb, set out to destroy
my uncle. It was one of the most intense battles of our time; thousands of men were slaughtered. Thanks to an old curse, all the men
of Ulster other than myself were incapacitated. I was seventeen, just
back from my training. I thought I could hold off an army in single
combat."

She blinked, but instead of disbelief, there was worry in her eyes.
Something about it twisted his gut. Had anyone worried *for* him,
since then?

He carried on swiftly. "So I did. It was a matter of honor, then, to accept that kind of challenge. I held them off for a while. But by the time the Ulstermen were able to fight alongside the other warriors—" He cut off, remembering the unnatural white mist that had sheathed the battlefield, obscuring his Empyrean senses. To this day he felt a deeply engrained suspicion of mists like that, so thick you can barely see a few feet ahead of you.

And that, he suspected, was the vision Nicole had Seen of him from the *Dante* painting.

One of the last times he'd worn a torc.

"When I got to the Druids' settlement at the edge of the forest, they'd been slaughtered by a supernatural. I don't know what kind. It hadn't been one of the mythical beasts I'd hunted before or after. I don't know if that would have made it easier. This one looked like a man."

The memory gripped him by the throat with that old twist of anger, horror. Guilt.

"I fought and must have killed it, but I don't remember much, just holding my mother afterward. Next thing I knew I woke up on a boat to Scotland. I couldn't go back to Ireland for a few centuries."

Tears blurred in Nicole's eyes. "I'm so sorry."

His mother's almost-black hair had spilled out over his legs, her snapped staff splintered and limp in her hand. Her tall frame had been so small in his arms. The last time he'd seen her face had been through a blur of ravaging tears and he'd felt little but the rawness of his throat as he screamed. Then someone was dragging him away.

He swallowed, sternly shoving the memory back deep down into himself.

"It was a long time ago. I'm sorry I don't have a happier story."

Nicole shook her head, a complicated emotion washing over her face. "Don't be. You told me the truth. That's worth more than a happy story."

He didn't add that he'd never fallen in love after that. Never allowed himself to get close enough to someone again that he could call them family. He would always think of the last person he'd loved in any capacity, gone. He couldn't risk being too late to save someone he loved again.

He couldn't risk his emotions or selfish goals blinding him. He'd wanted glory in that battle, he'd wanted to protect his people, but it had meant he'd returned to his own family too late. And he had received glory, at a cost that had haunted him through the centuries but carried his ancient name on.

It was better to have his life guided by the Wake. He didn't make the decisions about where he went and what missions he took. He couldn't pick the wrong one if they chose for him. Then, he hunted his dictated prey like no other Empyreal in their employ.

Sometimes with an unfeeling ruthlessness.

Kyan nodded to the cupboard, diffusing what he could of the memories. "Want to grab some plates?"

Nicole blinked and got up, setting the plates down between them, and resumed the spot opposite as he finished the food.

"Would you like some wine?" he asked, going for it for himself.

She sighed, something lost about her gaze now. "Sure, thanks."

He pulled his favorite from the cupboard. Pouring the red liquid made him think of the vial of blood he now carried everywhere. He'd need fresh, soon, to make sure he was prepared for any new games Lynch had up his sleeve.

Nicole took a bite of food. Her eyes closed briefly, enjoying the taste. He felt a strange swell of pride, and then the rush of a different kind of hunger.

Keep it together, McCarter. It's blood hunger. That's all.

Except he knew it wasn't. It hadn't just been the kiss, or the strange allure of her scent, or the fact that hearing her get hurt had cracked open a viciousness that made him wild.

She was beginning to wear him down. The more he got to know her, the more he found himself getting attached, the more he noticed little things. Like how she often tried not to smile at him, pursing her mouth instead, eyes flashing. Like allowing her lips to lift was somehow forbidden.

He cut another slice of steak, trying to keep his attention from the seam of her lips as they darkened with the wine. To keep his body from obeying the urge to close his mouth over hers.

His ancient heartbreak had taught him to innately trust his instincts and impulses, because while the world changed, those hadn't. So he found the words leaving his lips despite wondering if he truly wanted answers.

"Nicole, I need to ask you something."

28 NICOLE

Nicole cleared her throat as her defenses bristled.

The meal had seduced her senses: the peppered steak; the thin slices of creamy potato, the edges crisped and brown. The flare of spices contrasting with the cool, smooth choice of wine.

But her Seer side had been seduced, too. She could taste his history like the food before her. The wild landscapes of Scotland and Ireland, dark nights around campfires, legends and stories, hunting to survive. The soothing stroke of someone's fingers in her hair.

He's ancient royalty, she realized. He had the bearing of it. The energy of someone who could lead people and keep them safe. Shoulders wide enough to be cloaked in purple, his neck encircled with a golden torc. Even if he felt more like a wearied bodyguard to a king.

She wanted to know more. What had that time been like? What more did he remember of the creature that had killed the Druids? Could she somehow help him discover what it had been? Perhaps her mother would have answers in one of her bestiaries. . . .

The face her mother had worn at Lanhydrock flashed in Nicole's mind. *Kyan's* mother.

Her insides shifted and a ghost of his loss tore through her heart. That cry he'd let out, that echoed on the ravaged forest site of his memories, had made tears burn in her eyes. For some reason she'd thought Empyreals wouldn't appreciate loss, were conditioned against it or used to it after killing so many creatures.

He was not.

Had her mother thought about how it would make Kyan feel to give him such hope? Nicole dropped her gaze as a bout of shame turned her stomach. Her mother had done it to try and save other Empyreals from the Wake's clutches. She had a reason; she wasn't playing games with people's grief. But it still made Nicole knot her hand in her jumper. She couldn't tell him the type of truths he'd just told her or give him the satisfaction of answers, and she knew, so painfully, what wanting them was like.

She was going to have to lie, despite everything he'd opened up and told her.

Ugh. Why was she now developing an aversion to lying?

What if he asked her again what she was? Did he feel the difference? That she was something more? Something like him?

He scoured her face and heat swirled in her stomach with a bout of frustration. It looked like he almost didn't want to ask the question.

"Can I see your visions of Lynch?"

Nicole tried not to show her surprise. Kyan seemed surprised at himself, too, the muscle in his jaw flickering.

He'd have to touch her for her to share the vision, and the realization was followed by a quick, warm anticipation. But the visions from that night in the quad had been twofold: the first part had been a tableau of Lynch's past victims, morphing into a threat against Remi and Bells; but in the second the Wake's mark had appeared on her arm as she lunged for the Specter. She'd have to keep sharp control over what she allowed him to see and only reveal the first. The second was too full of her own fears and could reveal what she was.

But if this meant Kyan had more power over Lynch and could take him out faster . . . She wanted to help, somehow. To have some power in this mess of a fight that she couldn't actually fight in without hurting someone else she loved.

But this she could do.

So Nicole nodded.

They finished their meals and he slid the plates aside. Nicole took another gulp of wine.

"Did he touch you anywhere in the vision?" he asked.

"My neck," she whispered. "He bit the girl. That's where I felt it the strongest."

Having Kyan's attention zero in on any part of her made her feel like he could uncover everything.

He pulled his stool closer, until he was sitting directly before her.

"Concentrate on the vision," Kyan said softly. He lifted his hand and hesitated.

Nicole nodded, giving him permission.

The warm pads of his fingers touched just below her collarbone and slipped beneath her jumper's shoulder and bra strap. Her breath caught.

His eyes met hers in question.

She nodded again and her hand fisted on the leg of her jeans. Shivers ran over her skin, sending a tremor up her arm and across her chest as he tugged gently to reveal a bit more of her shoulder and neck. The feel of her bra shifting and the fabric grazing her breasts made it seem like he would undress her, like he was touching her there, too, causing a low, liquid thrill. Even just his proximity had her powers swimming almost drunk in her veins, as if relaxed and satisfied by his closeness.

He paused, eyes meeting hers, his dilating darker. He closed them briefly, seeming to curse something under his breath. Then he lifted his hand, but he didn't go for her neck. Instead, he reached around for her hair tie and tugged it slowly and smoothly down, so her chin tipped backward until her hair flooded around her shoulders.

Kyan leaned closer, almost close enough to kiss her, and breathed deeply. Then slowly, gently, his fingertips grazed her throat where she'd felt Lynch bite the girl in the vision. Where she still now had a slowly healing bruise.

But, oh, how different this felt. It made the delicious heat in her limbs pool to one particular place and begin to throb. Suddenly she was so wildly aware that they were alone. Over the last few nights, the manor had developed this sense of forbidden indulgence in her mind. A shadowed, art-choked luxury with a hundred magnetic moments.

And she wanted them *all*.

"Breathe, Nicole," Kyan whispered as his eyes closed to concentrate.

But breathing had turned into a heady thing. How did he do this every time? Awaken her body in a whole new, addictive way?

His dark shirt was open at the neck and one of his legs rested between hers. Not touching, but close enough that the heat of his body breathed over her. His other arm rested on the counter at their side, curved protectively beside her. She took in little details, the fragrant dip at the base of his throat, the stubbled line of his jaw. His mouth. He had a beautiful mouth. She'd kissed it, had crushed herself against it, and yet never really allowed herself to *look*.

Nicole squeezed her eyes shut and focused on the vision. It came back in sharp shots. Her eyes opened to see Kyan's do the same, his pupils swelling a dark, intent red and taking over the hazel of his irises, even the whites. A shiver of alarm ran through her.

She shut off the vision before she showed him the rest, just as she jolted at the memory of Lynch's razor teeth splitting through her skin with a hiss of ghostly pain and allowed the first glimpse of Remi and Bells to explain why she'd stabbed Lynch.

Kyan's fingers grazed her neck softly, as if to soothe, as his eyes swirled back to their normal color.

"I'll kill him before he kills anyone." His voice was a warm, intimate murmur. But there was a lethal promise in that deep, subtle gravel, and for a moment, his Irish lilt was back.

A shiver whispered over her skin, leaving sensitivity in its wake. His words held more weight after what he'd told her. No wonder he'd become one of the Wake's best hunters—his mother's murder had made•him want to ensure something like that never happened again. It was a strange, awful parallel to why she fought *against* Empyreals, after what happened to her mother.

But if he killed Lynch before he killed anyone else, it would stop her turning. It could save her family.

She stared up at his sculptured face—those eyes that could transform from aggressive and animal into pools of softness. The slightly skewed line of his nose. How had he broken it? Why had it never healed? Only something traumatic could have kept the break. Had it happened at that battle he told her of, or during his first transformation?

She wanted to run her finger along the shape, sketch it into the notebook she'd left abandoned in the gallery. Her eyes drifted to the subtle crease in the middle of his lower lip. Every part of her growing sensitive, interested.

For a split second, knowledge was in his eyes. Would he admit it? Whisper it? God, she wanted him to say it like a prayer. *Just tell me.*

Tell me you know who I am. What I am, and you want me anyway. That you'll protect me.

He didn't know the truth about what she was, that they shared an origin of Empyrean fire, but something simmered between them. It changed the air. The rhythm of her heart.

They'd drifted closer. So close he only needed to lean forward slightly.

"He threatened you," Kyan said, into the hollow of her neck.

A moment later, his teeth grazed the sensitive skin. A full-body shiver made her shudder in his arms, those pulses of heat between her legs turning low and aching. She couldn't help the little sound that left lips.

Kyan ran his tongue along the bruise, before placing a kiss there. "All better." He pulled back, and suddenly the sight and feel of him filled her with the knowledge that she *was* shockingly safe in his arms.

And then Kyan's lips brushed hers.

They were so smooth. His kiss was a searching, curious graze that made her entire body flare and home in on the staggered touch. A blush of pleasure unfurled as his lips pressed onto hers, firmer this time.

Part of her wanted to help him forget all he'd told her; part of her wanted to help him remember. Because if he had that tether to family, he would understand her more. But at the same time, she tasted his ancient grief, rust-worn and bitter.

Nicole reached for him as desire bounded through her, new, immediate.

And it needed *more*.

She slipped off the stool to stand between his thighs, pressing against him, reaching up to grip his shirt. She felt a kind of madness when her fingers grazed the hot skin of his chest, remembering the glorious sight of him shirtless, filled with a new, desperate desire to know how that body would feel over hers.

His hand slipped to her lower back, the other cupping her backside in an explicit hold that felt so *good*, before his hands ran up to thread into her hair.

Sinking against him, into the liquid heat of his tongue's slow play against hers as his fingers tugged her hair, her self-control snapped like a twig. Whatever this feeling was, she wanted—no, *needed*—more of it.

She could fight her Empyreal, or she could fight this.

She couldn't fight both.

This kiss wasn't like the other. The first had been born of a distraction, but this was slow and purposeful and filled her with the kind of rising heat that could incinerate, that made her want to crawl onto his lap and stay there, that made her want to move with him in ways that curled her hips. A raw sound left her lips, mingling with the relieved one he made—

"Well, this got interesting quickly," came an amused, unfamiliar voice. "My apologies."

Nicole jolted against Kyan, her lips ripping from his. The hot skin of his jaw scolded her cheek, scratching with stubble. They breathed heavily together; his arms drawn around her protectively.

She blinked hard and twisted back to find out who had

interrupted, and saw . . . the handsome stranger who'd been chatting to Dylan in the pub a few nights ago? Puzzled, embarrassed, she took him in.

He leaned in the doorway, a bag slung over his shoulder. His grin was not apologetic, it was like a cat with cream. Stunning and confident and dangerous.

"Callum?" Kyan asked, voice rough.

Callum? Nicole stiffened with shock, and panic swamped away her satisfaction so quickly she felt sick. That was the name of the Empyreal who had searched for her mother for over a century.

Oh god, if he sees your face . . .

Nicole turned away and slammed her cheek against Kyan's hot shoulder, squeezing her eyes shut.

Kyan's large warm hands fanned on her back and the sudden shift in him was palpable. The strong arc of his shoulders grew rigid as he rose, towering over her.

"What are you doing here? How did you know where to find me?"

"You told me on the phone, remember?"

"I didn't, actually, which tells me you've either got a bug in the Wake's database, or on me."

"I guess you'll never know. Now, why don't you introduce me to your new friend?"

"Er . . . I'll just . . . nip to the bathroom first," Nicole said, before rushing out into the wide, dark-paneled passageway, hung with a line of heavy chandeliers and paintings.

She heard Kyan say something and then felt him moving after her.

"Nicole."

She stopped in the hall, turning to him.

His perceptive eyes dashed over her quickly, worried. "Are you all right?"

Nicole stared at his mouth. She stood there a few seconds too long. Forcing herself to step away felt so unnatural a rush of complicated emotions warmed her cheeks. She wanted to stay in his arms.

What's happening to me?

I can't control myself.

She swallowed hard, her body aching. "Yes. I'm just embarrassed. I'll be back in a minute." She made herself smile but it felt wobbly.

He hesitated before nodding and ducking back inside. She watched him walk away with an unsatisfied desire that made her stomach flip. Anger surged up that they'd been interrupted, that she was *annoyed* they'd been interrupted. That they'd been interrupted by another *Empyreal.*

What the hell was going on?

She lingered before moving farther down the hallway, trying to calm her racing heart.

Should she run? No—no. She couldn't make this seem like a big deal. She wasn't supposed to know anything about the woman from Lanhydrock, even though it *was* her mother. Acting suspicious about Callum's arrival when Kyan mentioned he was the one who had been looking for her would just increase this new Empyreal's interest.

But why was he here? Had Kyan . . . had Kyan brought him here to meet Nicole and see the similarities? To prove that the woman from Lanhydrock was her mother? Callum had said he'd spoken to Kyan on the phone; did that mean they'd discussed Lanhydrock?

Nicole felt suddenly nauseous.

Then she thought of her mother.

How long had Nicole craved her? Pored over her books and advice for years, and now she'd just gone and thrown it all out the window. She bit down as guilt blurred her vision with tears.

But as she made herself walk farther along, she realized that, thanks to her Empyrean senses, she could still hear their conversation. And eavesdropping would allow her to figure out whether this was going to be an emergency, or something she could lie her way through.

Either way, she couldn't risk running if they were going to the museum later to check on the painting. Resolved, Nicole slipped into the nearest powder room—a luxuriously furnished little bathroom off the main hall—and listened.

29 KYAN

Kyan went back into the kitchen.

"Callum."

His charming friend sat back at the head of the dining table in one of its ornate armchairs, wearing a smile that had caused more trouble in the sixteenth century than the influx of Fae into the Milanese royal family. His legs were stretched out and crossed and his fingers gently cupped a glass of wine from the bottle Kyan had left open.

"This place is nice," Callum said. "Better than that dump in Positano, remember? Christ. How long's it been?"

"A few years," Kyan said, coming in cautiously. "How did you get in? This place has supernatural wards."

Callum's smile flashed. "Come now, Kyan. When have you known a place or person I can't get to tell me their secrets?"

His words were true as well as teasing, which told Kyan that he recognized Nicole.

"Can't a friend come and enjoy some wine? Catch up?"

Kyan played along, even though he always preferred directness. "How have you been?" he asked, trying to put off the inevitable conversation.

"The usual. Been over to the Netherlands for the new Velek election." Callum rolled his eyes and swiped up the bottle to add more to his glass, pouring some into Kyan's, too. "Messy. So messy. Why they always insist on dancing under the orb-rain, I'll never know. Took me days to get it off."

"You're not supposed to dance under it naked."

Callum grinned. "Still trying to spoil my fun, McCarter? You haven't changed."

Kyan shook his head but his lips curved up into a smile. Telling an Empyreal they hadn't changed was akin to saying they were useless—not transforming.

"But *that's* not why you called me." A sharp gleam had entered Callum's eyes. The intrigue, the hunt. "You found her."

Protectiveness shivered through Kyan. "She's not the woman from Lanhydrock. I only just realized the connection."

"I know we're supposed to let go of the past, but it was only the 1900s, Kyan."

"Not all of us tracked her for a decent amount of those."

Callum gave him a look. "Someone breaks into the Wake's oath-taking, they don't let it go. The girl will know something."

If Nicole did, he'd be the one to find out. He wanted more time with her, alone. To figure out the connection. But it only made him remember the feel of her mouth on his. Not only his venom-laced teeth ached thinking about it.

He took a long drink.

"It's not *her*," Kyan repeated. "The most logical conclusion is it was her mother, but if that's right, she's dead. There's no way we could find out what she knew."

"How do you know she's dead?"

261

Kyan paused. That . . . was a good question. "That's what Nicole believes." As he said it, he knew it to be true. She'd been too upset when he'd initially asked her.

Callum made a thoughtful noise as if he highly doubted that. "Can she do what the woman did?"

"She's a Seer, Callum. I've watched her have visions."

"So close to Lanhydrock . . ."

"It's a coincidence."

Callum gave him a flat look. "You know better than I do—"

"I know," Kyan said, exasperated. *There are no coincidences.*

"Is that why this mission has dragged out?"

"It's only been a few days."

Callum shrugged, taking a sip of his wine and rising to stab a leftover asparagus from the pan, his white teeth flashing as he took a bite. "So, what's the problem?"

"My prey is fascinated by her. He hurt her, but is smart enough not to trigger the kill hormone. He's a little piece of shit." Kyan didn't miss the returned accent in his near-growled words.

Callum's brow arched. "You exposed yourself to your prey?"

Kyan's jaw clenched as he glanced at the door through which Nicole had left. Callum's gaze followed as a subtle frown creased his face, but his eyes twinkled with amusement.

"I see your infamous ease in the hunt is getting . . . torqued." Callum smirked. "What happened to being impartial on a mission? 'Don't get emotional, Callum,'" he began, mimicking Kyan's voice. "'You're here on a mission, why are you smiling and having fun? What is this, the sixties again?'" He tutted.

Kyan grabbed his glass of wine and swallowed another gulp, the image of his own ancient torc haunting him. It represented everything he'd shied away from since his family was killed: love, the risk of feeling so much for someone else that their loss could gut you.

"Why don't I stay?" Callum said. "I can play lord of the manor while you kill the Specter. Let's just call her back, have a little chat. No harm, maybe a little Influence. We all get the answers we want, and everyone has unburdened themselves."

"No Influencing her," Kyan growled.

Callum's brows rose and his eyes glinted. "Does this have something to do with the heat wave of sexual tension in here? Do you plan to seduce the information out of her? Ah! Did you want advice?"

"I don't want your seduction advice."

Callum slapped his hand on his chest in mock offense. "Why not?"

He teased like he damn well knew why not. He could read Kyan like a book, just like he had from the first time they'd met. Callum had been the first person who had been able to drag him out of his grief. He was sharp and intelligent, but he was also stubborn and—

"I'm a savant, a hedonist, a lover of men and women, a—"

"Exactly," Kyan said flatly.

A wicked smile lit Callum's features. "And *why* exactly do you think that means I won't have valuable seduction advice?"

"Because I'm not trying to seduce her."

At least . . . that hadn't been his intention. He'd been intrigued by Nicole, enjoyed her protectiveness, felt she was a kindred spirit in that way. He liked that she looked him in the eye—not in awe of his Empyreal nature, as many creatures were, but not afraid of him either. She made him *wake up*, readdress ideas and rules he'd long accepted. Even if waking up from the pattern of his missions and

263

routines meant awakening long-dormant hungers that slammed into him with the teeth and ferocity of centuries of denial. No one else had stirred him like this. Now he wanted her in the most explicit—

Kyan pushed the wineglass away. "This is . . ."

What could he say? *It's not serious*? That was a lie. He was serious about figuring out her secrets, but he was just as damn serious about Nicole. It made him uneasy, and he hadn't felt uneasy in a long time.

Callum placed a warm hand on Kyan's shoulder. "After being a practical monk and ruining my fun with your disinterest in parties and lovers for centuries, I'm pleased for you." Beneath the amusement, genuine relief lit in Callum's eyes, even if it was mostly smothered by intrigue. "However, that doesn't change the fact that she's involved in your mission. Now, if you're feeling conflicted, *I'm* charming enough to have talked Mahaela out of their third Trepid. I think I can get some answers from a pretty Seer."

Kyan shook his head. "That woman in 1902 used my mother's face. She could have also robbed the face of someone in Nicole's family to hide her true identity. She might not be related at all. I need you to let me deal with this."

"You want answers and so do I. Thank the gods we're on the same team," he said, clinking his glass to Kyan's. "But all right. We'll play this your way. For now."

They both stilled as a door opened in the distance and the soft patter of Nicole's footsteps could be heard coming down the corridor. She appeared a few moments later, gilded by the light of the kitchen. Her hair—the hair he'd fisted his hands in—was still fanned around her shoulders, somewhat hiding the mark there. It only reminded him what was at stake.

Nicole smiled at Callum in greeting and Kyan's breath caught.

He wasn't sure she'd ever actually smiled at him, not like that.

"Hi," she said, confidently coming in and offering her hand to Callum. Her shock seemed to have gone and in its place was a calm, controlled openness. "I'm Nicole."

Callum lifted her hand to his lips. "A pleasure, Nicole," he purred.

A flicker of danger shot behind Callum's eyes and Kyan remembered the few other times that look had passed over his friend's features; all of which had ended with Callum getting the answers he wanted, whether by elegant carnage or something more secret.

"I can't wait to learn *all about you*."

Pulses of power emanated from Callum. Nicole had no idea how she hadn't noticed he was supernatural when she'd first seen him . . . unless he'd Influenced himself to dim it? The thought only led to a bigger question: How hadn't *Dylan* noticed?

Oh god, Dylan!

She had to tell him as soon as possible. He hadn't come home the night he met Callum, had they spent it together?

"Unfortunately, we have a meeting," Nicole said, looking to Kyan.

He was watching her strangely, a frown on his brow and his eyes fastened on her lips.

"Right," he agreed, focusing. "Yes, at the museum. There's a painting."

"A painting?" Callum asked, intrigued.

Nicole mentally cringed. The last thing she needed was more of the Wake's Empyreals knowing this artwork was important.

"Is this like that mess with the Pre-Raphaelites?" Callum asked.

They knew the Pre-Raphaelites? Her lips parted with curiosity, questions pooling on her tongue.

But Callum said, "I'll join you, then. Little family trip."

Warnings went off in her head. "Oh, you don't have to. Surely you've traveled a long way. Why don't you rest and . . ."

But as she looked to Kyan for assistance, she saw his eyes had glazed over. He was homing in on Lynch. A moment later, clarity swirled back into them and his voice regained that hard hunter's tone.

"Lynch is headed to the museum," Kyan said, striding from the room.

Nicole hurried after him. "I'm coming!"

He slowed for a moment as she ran after him but burst out of the house into the night. His car sat just outside, its gleaming black exterior highlighted by the crescent moon. The sea was loud tonight, the rushing waves beating like a heart. Fragrant sea air crashed over her, prickling her overheated skin.

He reached the car door first. "Nicole, I don't know what he's going to try. If the painting's there I'll find it, but you're a Seer, not a hunter. He's a Specter who's been killing for decades."

No, I'm not! she wanted to shout. *I'm faster and stronger, I can protect myself.*

"How about Nicole and I search the archives while you deal with Lynch?" asked Callum coolly.

Nicole spun, surprised by his silent approach.

Kyan looked between them but nodded before sinking into the car. Nicole climbed in the passenger side and Callum folded himself into one of the back seats. Then they were speeding for the gates. The sudden roar of the car set her back against the seat and flared her adrenaline as they raced down the private path.

Kyan shot her a quick glance like he was battling to understand her. "Can I trust you not to try and stab him again?"

Her jaw clenched. "Maybe. I don't have any more hidden weapons, if that's what you're worried about."

Truce, remember? her eyes said.

Kyan looked ahead, jaw tense.

The museum was quiet as they pulled up outside. Its austere face lit by spearing white lights from below. Stars winked in the sky above and seagulls glided, ghostly against the dark.

"Where is he?" Nicole asked when they jumped out of the car. A short rain had made glassy puddles, reflecting the old Victorian streetlamps and trapping a few fallen leaves beneath the water. Autumn, already.

She tried not to think about that eternal metamorphosis.

"Inside," Kyan said. He was looking up at the museum as he slipped something back into his pocket, a swirl of red darkening in his eyes.

Blood.

"Does it help?" she asked. His eyes were already on her and as they walked under a streetlamp, they shone like an animal's in the dark.

"Yes. And—it distracts me from other things."

A shiver ran under her skin.

"You two go in via the back," Kyan said. "I'll deal with the curator and security."

Nicole nearly argued. She wanted to hear what the curator had to say, but she knew he was more liable to want to please Kyan as Westmoore's nephew, and her priority was the painting, not the curator. So, she followed Callum down the alley where she'd first sensed Lynch, her unease growing as they came to the back entrance and the security guard stationed there.

"Sorry, you can't—" he began.

"Actually," Callum said smoothly, Influence limning his voice. *"We can. Come with us."*

The security guard blinked as if dazed and stepped aside. Callum waved a hand to allow Nicole to enter.

Any other night she would have been thrilled to be in the museum at this time. But now, knowing there were two Empyreals and a Specter here, the difference between humans and supernaturals made her nervous.

The museum at night was all gilded and nude tones. The sculptures cast deep shadows, and the only illumination came from the great glass ceiling panels that filtered in moonlight.

Why would Lynch have brought the painting here? Unless he wanted to try and Influence more information out of the curator, or maybe to hide it amid the archives? That would be smart. The curator and his team might just bypass an unusual crate or another glinting frame.

But Nicole wouldn't. *Couldn't.*

She was very familiar with the museum after spending years combing through its paintings, so knew the way to the archives even though she'd never been inside. She led the way to some glass doors, behind which lay the off-limits section.

"Open the doors, please, and take us to the archives," Callum said, and the security guard let them in.

Once the doors opened, Nicole felt the subtle, distinctive tug of the supernatural. She made herself inhale, scenting something. . . . Finfolk blood?

The painting. It was here, somewhere.

The archives were held in one long room with mesh stacks for paintings and shelves for items. Checking through each approximately sized painting would take at least half an hour.

Plenty of time to be interrogated by an Empyreal.

Nicole squared her shoulders and began the inspection, listening as Callum took the security guard's keys, told him to leave and forget what he'd seen, then released him from his thrall.

Everything felt too quiet and still, too charged. Was it just because she was walking alongside a mysterious Empyreal who knew her mother? Or was it because the Specter was here, somewhere?

"Do you feel Lynch about?" Nicole asked.

"He's not my prey," Callum said. "I'm not as deep in his head as Kyan is, so no. Not yet."

If Lynch came near her, she'd have to resist every fighting instinct she had and run, but after seeing the slow decline of her fellow classmates, that was getting harder. It was better to be in here, even with a highly intrigued Empyreal, than near the Specter.

"Something dangerous is here, though," Callum said. "Perhaps it's you."

Nicole huffed slightly. She was trying to follow her senses, follow the scent of the Finfolk blood, but she couldn't help but be overwhelmed by Callum's presence.

Stacks of paintings flashed by as she walked past them, scanning for ones that were the right size and feel.

"So . . . what is this a painting of?" Callum asked.

Nicole hesitated to tell him. How much did Kyan trust him? Had Callum *also* been sent by the Wake and Kyan just didn't know it? From what she'd overheard of their conversation, that didn't seem to be the case, but then Callum *had* admitted how capable he was at keeping secrets.

"Come now, Nicole, you can trust me."

She turned back to look at him. He was even more elegant and charming standing amid stacks of artwork. "I don't know that. Did you tell Dylan what you were?"

Callum's eyes winked with lust. "Ah, of course, your brother. No, it . . . didn't come up."

"Why should I trust you if you've lied already?"

Callum smiled. "Do you trust Kyan?"

Yes. The thought was so quick, so instinctual, and yet it went against everything she had been taught. "I . . . well . . ." *Maybe I do, maybe I'm starting to.*

"Interesting," Callum murmured.

"Two Empyreals fighting," Nicole said, pushing that thought away firmly. "That's what the painting is. Humans think it shows a scene from Dante's *Inferno.*"

She couldn't trust *anyone* other than her family and Remi. Kyan was proving himself capable and . . . kind. Kinder than she'd thought one of the Wake's Empyreals could be. And she couldn't deny how attractive he was to her. "Attractive" didn't even feel like the right word to describe the feeling. But she still shouldn't trust him, and had to remember that.

"One looks like Kyan, strangely enough. He mentioned that the other looks like another Empyreal he knew, someone called Alexander."

"Alexander?" Callum's intrigue increased as he ambled through the stacks of paintings.

"Who was he?"

"A vicious alpha asshole, that's who he was," Callum said smoothly, long fingers skimming priceless works of art. "Always thinking he was better than others, always hungering for another hunt, and not in a good way." Callum picked up an artifact. "Let's just say the world didn't miss him. Though his death was still, well, unexpected."

"How did he die?"

Callum put the artifact down. "Kyan killed him."

Surprise cleaved through her. Had Alexander become dangerous or tried to hurt someone? Was that what the painting really represented? That moment?

"When? Why?" The tone of her voice caught his attention, because Callum's dark eyes turned to her with interest.

"Apparently that's news," Callum mused. "Yes. In Lanhydrock, actually. I hear you two took a nice little trip there so I assumed he'd mentioned it. Alexander refused to take the oath, so Kyan was instructed to kill him."

Her surprise turned to iced shock.

"Kyan killed another Empyreal for not taking the oath?"

What would he do to her if he discovered what she was? If she refused to be taken in and swear the same oath? Her stomach flipped with dread.

"He did. I might say that it was out of loyalty to the Wake, but your mother's mind games had fucked him up a bit the night before."

"I doubt she did it for that reason," Nicole snapped. Her worry twisted into panic as she realized what she'd said.

But before she could add on the words *whoever that woman was*, Callum continued.

"You and I, dearest, need to have a little chat about your mother. You may keep playing the 'I don't know her' card with Kyan, but

I knew Freya. And you are her spitting image. You have the same gleam in your eye, whether you know it or not. So, either you tell him, or I will."

But she couldn't, could she? Could she admit it *had* been her mother? The only problem would be if Callum knew *what* her mother was. If he had no idea what she was and just believed her to be some miscellaneous creature, then it wouldn't matter.

But if he knew she was an Empyreal then it would increase the suspicion over Nicole's strange scent and abilities. Thank god she'd had visions in front of Kyan—enough to convince him she was truly a Seer. It was a cloak that would keep her true nature hidden . . . unless Lynch decided to expose her and ruin everything.

She thought of her father, how he'd started to research possible poisons that could affect a Specter. "Just a precaution," he'd said. Part of her wondered if they *should* just kill Lynch. But then she remembered her mother's note—*strike true, my loves*—and knew nothing short of transforming would ensure a kill. Frustration wound through her.

"My mother had a long, *long* life," Nicole said carefully. "However, she's gone now. And even if the woman at Lanhydrock *was* my mother, that wouldn't help this situation at all. The focus here is the painting and the Specter. Not some woman from 1902."

"There's one thing you will learn very quickly around immortals, Nicole. And that's that the past never stays dead." Suddenly a noise had Callum stilling. "Stay here, it sounds like our dear Kyan has found his prey."

YAN

Kyan took the museum's steps two at a time while Callum and Nicole went around to the back alley. He watched her go, her hair shining in the moonlight, and it made him think of the dust in her plait from when Lynch had rammed her against the wall.

He found the curator in the main hall, a security guard was with him.

"Oh, Mr. McCarter, I'm sorry but we're having a situation. There seems to be an intruder in the museum."

"Yes, I'm sure there is," he said, turning to follow the paranormal pull of Lynch.

He heard the curator mutter a comment to the security guard before rushing after Kyan.

Kyan traced the corded bracelet around his wrist as he walked, rough against his fingers. He could still taste the blood in his mouth and the metallic aftertaste it had left on his tongue, even though it had already been absorbed into his teeth. The surge of plasma banked through his body and change throbbed in his skin, making his mouth slick with venom.

Lynch was sitting in the curator's office behind the man's desk with that infuriating look of entitlement on his face.

Kyan breathed deeply, scenting the wound at the Specter's side. It was still unhealed and leaking dark blood beneath his jacket.

"Ah, finally," Lynch said. "You were taking *forever*."

"What are you doing here, Lynch?"

"Security!" the curator called, bumbling in a moment later.

"Oh, shut up, Douglas." The Specter waved his hand and the

curator's mouth snapped shut immediately, his face going pale.

"I wanted the Wake's answer. So, what did they say?"

"Nothing. I didn't ask them. I don't bargain with murderers."

Lynch's eyes narrowed with displeasure. "I'm disappointed in you, Kyan."

Kyan made a sound like a rough laugh. "I don't give a shit."

"Well, *I* do. If you're not going to cooperate, this changes my plans."

Lynch opened his jacket to expose the bloody mess of his side. His nails elongated and he winced as he dug them into the wound with a wet sound, roaring as he tried to pull the crystal out. Kyan's lips drew back over his teeth. Why would Lynch be trying to remove the crystal again, now? Here?

Lynch strained, pulling as the veins beneath his skin pulsed and lurched. Then the crystal broke free.

He laid it, bloody and glistening, on the desk, and shot Kyan a dark look before picking up one of the heavy paperweights on the curator's desk—a geode.

"What are you doing—" began Mr. Alborough.

But Lynch brought the bookend down on the crystal with a loud crack and it splintered down the middle.

It would likely take a while for the Specter's wound to heal, but it seemed he'd gotten his anger out, until he raised his eyes to Kyan's.

A shiver of instinct had Kyan's body ready as Lynch dived across the desk to the curator.

Kyan moved at the same time, tearing Lynch's jacket to stop him reaching the human.

But the Specter still managed a bite.

The curator shouted in pain, but before Kyan could tear Lynch

275

away, planning to just *drag* him back to the Wake, white-hot pain knifed into his side.

He looked down in shock to see Lynch's bloodied fingers where he stabbed Kyan with the crystal.

He had wanted to know where Nicole had found it, not just to help him figure her out, but because he wanted to make sure Lynch couldn't get one and use it on *him*. As he was becoming a Specter, it would wound him like it had Lynch, and he couldn't afford to be incapacitated. Not now.

The crystal buried deeper into Kyan's side and he struggled not to buckle, clutching the wound. He tried to dig his fingers into the bubbling gash, but it was already too deep.

"If you won't bargain with the Wake," Lynch said, teeth bloody, "I'll have to end this my own way. Don't make me ask again, hunter. I'm ready to make this so much worse."

The security guard skidded into the doorway, but must have just seen Kyan looming over the curator, who was swooning with a bloody neck. A needle of pain went through Kyan and suddenly he was jolting with the electric shock of a Taser.

Lynch laughed, blood on his teeth.

And then he was gone.

NICOLE

Nicole fought the urge to follow Callum when he ran to Kyan. What could Lynch say in that time? But with Callum out of the archives, she could concentrate. Her senses fanned out in the silence, and she felt the supernatural essence of the painting sharpen.

It pulled her straight through the rest of the archive, through another glass door, and into a large room where paintings were cleaned.

A movable light arched over a large table, bright and cold and still lit. Someone must have been in here recently. . . . But it was the gleaming frame on a large central table that made her rush closer.

The *Dante* painting.

Around it were little jars, some with supernatural-smelling liquid inside, and a magnifying arm hovered over the stolen painting.

Did this mean the curator had taken it?

There was a particular glint to the canvas, as if it was wet. Perhaps Lynch had set this up tonight to get more of its secrets? Perhaps he'd only uncovered a small piece of the cipher and was now attempting to get the rest of it.

The frame itself was a piece of luxury, burning bright as the Empyrean fire under the lights. Nicole took a step closer, scanning it for clues, marks. Perhaps the code Lynch had found had been inscribed into the frame? But on closer inspection, that didn't seem the case.

Besides this painting, she'd only seen a supernaturally varnished painting once or twice, but it reminded her of the glass-like sheen of her mother's Influence; like the barrier that had separated

Nicole and her siblings from her mother's murderer. It had gleamed and distorted the image on the other side as their mother had collapsed in their nursery, an Empyreal towering over her. The Wake's Empyreal would have seen nothing but the rug, when in fact Nicole and her siblings were huddled there a mere three feet away.

She'd seen through some of this painting's varnish to the image of Kyan with the torc. Focusing on it now, she could still make it out, but no lines of code. Perhaps there'd been a second layer of varnish beneath, and it had been reapplied to hide it?

A moment later, Nicole's hackles rose as the scent of strange, poisonous blood seeped into the room. She spun, finding Lynch.

"Hello, Nicole."

She looked down to see his black turtleneck was wet with blood and hoped it wasn't Kyan's. But it didn't smell like him. It smelled like that awful darkness that had spilled over her hands the night she'd stabbed Lynch in the quad.

"What do you want, Lynch?"

"Why can't you see that we're on the same side, Nicole? Neither of us want to be owned by the Wake."

"That's not looking too good for you, though, is it?" Nicole said, trying to push the conversation away from her. What he was saying would sound highly suspicious to Kyan and Callum. "Having them send an Empyreal to kill you. Perhaps *two*?"

Lynch's pale eyes narrowed and that cold moodiness that breathed off him took on a sharper edge. He came closer and Nicole stifled the urge to snarl. Instead, she gripped the edge of the restoration table and moved as far back as she could. In the light, the cold grace of his face was white as marble.

"Why wouldn't I just offer them *you*? I'm sure they'd be happy with a little baby Emp—"

Nicole had covered his mouth with her hand before she'd even thought it through. She couldn't hear either Callum or Kyan, but that didn't mean they couldn't hear her and Lynch.

The Specter's white jaw flexed as his mouth opened. A moment later his teeth scraped along her palm. She hissed as horror stroked down her spine, drawing back and wiping her venom-tingling hand on her jeans.

Lynch chuckled, the vicious wink in his dark eyes electrified. "Don't worry, the venom doesn't do much unless it enters your bloodstream. And the Empyreals are a little preoccupied. I wanted a moment alone to talk about our mysterious cipher."

"If you're just going to play games, leave me alone," she growled. "If you don't give me something more to work with, I can't tell you anything anyway."

Lynch's unnerving eyes gleamed. "Rest assured, huntress, I won't let you snap, I'm not an idiot—even I couldn't survive you if you wanted to kill me." He leaned closer and her body arched backward slightly over the painting. "But do you think your hulking hero will help you if he finds out what you are? The Wake don't allow apostasies, not after that cultish little oath. And they certainly won't let an Empyreal like you go unbound. Not with all this . . ." He inhaled and her lips pulled back in a disgust. ". . . potential. Perhaps I should mention it the next time Kyan comes to see me."

Cold surprise cleaved through her. "He came to see you?"

Intrigue darkened his eyes. "Oh, yes. We had a lovely little chat about you."

What the hell had they talked about? Nicole thought of Callum mentioning that Kyan had killed Alexander. How deep did his loyalty to the Wake really run? Yes, he had helped her so far, but after the story he told her of his mother, how could she hope to have him on her side if things got worse? She needed to at least *try* to back off from Kyan emotionally and make sure she had what she needed: the painting's secret.

"Give me a bit more of the cipher," she said.

Lynch must have heard the subtle plea in her voice, because his gaze turned almost fascinated, and he pulled out the little piece of paper he'd shown her in the quad. "This?"

Nicole stiffened as he leaned in, her power drawing up, as if preparing to transform.

But then his lips met her cheek and she squeezed her eyes shut, fingers finding the piece of paper even as disgust and metamorphosis warred in her.

"I'll come and ask you again when we have more time to be alone," he said against her skin. The threat sank into her like a cold lake. He pulled back. "But just to give you a little motivation, I can say hello to your dear friend Remi if I must. I noticed she lives practically down the hall from me. Or perhaps your pretty little sister. 'One a smiling babe full of innocence and joy; the other far more dreadfully murdered,'" he said, quoting *Frankenstein*.

He must have seen the blood drain from her face, she could barely control the reaction.

Satisfaction and viciousness darkened his eyes. "Until then, enjoy the painting."

"'Devil,'" Nicole quoted back. "'Do you dare approach me? And do you not fear the fierce vengeance of my arm wreaked on your miserable head?'"

"I do love it," Lynch said, looking unnervingly satisfied, "when you quote a killer."

Then he kissed her on the cheek and disappeared, leaving the paper in her hands.

She couldn't help but think of another *Frankenstein* quote: "As I imprinted the first kiss on her lips, they became livid with the hue of death."

KYAN

Kyan found himself running to where Nicole was, the sound of Lynch's bloody laugh echoing in his ears and his side a bright, agonized burn. Just thinking of the Specter near her dug deeper into the predator that had been seething beneath his skin for days.

Callum almost smashed into him as he rounded into another gallery.

"Where is she?" Kyan roared.

"What the hell happened?" Callum asked, smoothly swerving and sprinting back in Nicole's direction.

The wound was on *fire*; he could barely run.

He saw her in the lab room through the glass door, looking shaken, blood on her face.

Callum opened the door as Kyan tugged his coat over his wound. He didn't want her to see it and think he couldn't protect her.

"What happened?" he demanded, pain and a quick lurch of worry going through him. If Lynch had bitten her . . . "Why is there blood on your face?"

He moved closer, the low peal of worry in his gut heightened. But it wasn't a cut, it was as if Lynch had brushed his lips across her cheek. The following surge of protectiveness was almost as vicious as the vampiric longing his transformation was causing. Kyan stroked away the blood with his thumb.

"Did you go to see Lynch without me?" she asked, her cheek still cupped by his hand.

He clenched his jaw and stepped back.

Hurt and worry went through her dark eyes. She spun to face

the table, her hands shaking. "I'm taking the painting."

Kyan reached around her, his own side glaring with such pain his vision almost blurred.

"Nicole, I need to check it before it goes anywhere, and I need to deal with this shitshow."

"Well, I need some answers, especially if you're keeping things from me!"

I've told you more than I've told anyone in years. "Like *what*?"

"Like how you went to see Lynch. Like the fact you *killed Alexander*."

Kyan's mouth clamped shut. That one was fair, and yet he'd only kept it from her because he felt guilty about it. She already believed him to be a brutish follower of the Wake, why give her the one real reason to think that was true?

"Let's not start keeping score on who's keeping secrets."

Guilt and anger flashed across her features. "I . . . It's not like . . ." She pressed her lips together so tightly they almost bled of color. "Well, we have the painting back now, so you won't have to worry about keeping me around and getting in your way for much longer."

"That's not what—"

"Goodnight, Kyan." She stormed past him and out through the door.

He wanted to follow, but Lynch's little stunt biting the curator would have stimulated enough fear and pain to seal over the Specter's wound, maybe give him some pain relief. Kyan knew his prey, and warnings were ringing in his head.

Lynch wasn't finished yet.

"That went well," Callum said.

Kyan groaned and winced, checking his side by peeling up his shirt to see the angry wound.

"You'll need someone with more delicate fingers than either of us to get that out," Callum said pointedly.

"She doesn't want to speak to me right now."

"So don't speak, just *do*."

"Just help me with this painting."

"Listen to me, you stubborn bastard," Callum began.

Kyan frowned, arrowing a look at his friend.

"You don't have to do everything by the book all the damn time."

"If I don't then what?" he growled.

"Then you start *living*. You've never had a problem trusting your impulses. Your decision making, yeah. But not your protective instincts, so don't start now. You made a mistake *once*, Kyan. Let it go."

"Are you telling me to bend the rules?"

Callum grinned. "I'm always telling you to bend the rules. Maybe you should actually listen."

31 NICOLE

Nicole daubed another hasty lick of paint on the canvas. The night was black outside the window, the rain heavy against the panes. She hadn't wanted to go home and face her family's questions and she couldn't bear to go back to the manor, so she went to the only other place she knew she could be alone: the beach hut.

They'd rented it for years: an old fisherman's cottage that was practically falling down, with just one room and a tiny bathroom, but it allowed her to paint without making a mess of the house.

The hike over the dunes nearly made her give up and circle back but she powered on out of sheer stubbornness, and no small amount of spite.

Sitting at the table before the windows, the old wood smeared with paint and an array of paintbrushes, Nicole looked at the paper Lynch had given her.

It was indeed a piece of a cipher, and yet it was also a way to irritate her further, because she didn't have enough of it to know what type of cipher it was. She needed Lynch to tell her, or she needed to find out from the painting, but the painting was still in the damn museum with Kyan. And she had a sneaking feeling that Lynch had only given her this much because he'd done something to ensure she wouldn't be able to get any more from the painting. He'd given it up too easily.

Sadistic bastard.

Nicole stuffed the cipher back in her pocket and slashed more paint on her newest piece, dabbing her brush into a selection of smooth oils, applying, testing, applying again. She was working on a portrait of Remi with her lyre. Painting was supposed to be calming. She'd started teaching herself thanks to her mother's sketches and bestiaries, but mainly because of the portrait of her hanging in their library. It was a hobby she could take wherever they moved to. And usually it worked to keep her happily focused for hours.

She forced herself to focus on color, texture . . . the warmth of Kyan's lips. The stroke of his tongue over hers . . .

Damn it!

Nicole threw her paintbrush and it clanked across the table, leaving a splotch of paint.

She let her head fall into her hands. She needed to calm down; she didn't want to go back to the house in a panic, or the family would think she couldn't handle this. She had to remain calm and collected at all times. And she definitely couldn't think about Kyan. It was almost like she could still hear his labored breathing from their kiss. And her own, now fevered for a whole other reason: that he'd killed another Empyreal for not taking the oath.

Like the Wake might do to her if they ever found her.

Wait . . .

Nicole stilled. She *could* hear labored breathing.

She stood abruptly, closing her fingers around a palette knife. Whoever it was, they were staggering. Wounded. Could it be Lynch?

Kyan fell into view against the door.

286

Nicole ripped it open and a gasp of night air blasted over her.

"What are you doing here?" She didn't want to talk or argue—but he didn't look in any state to. Her anger suddenly morphed to worry. "What happened?"

Kyan looked like he was using the last of his strength to stand. His hand pressed against his side but rain and sweat meant a dark stain crept from under it. He pulled his head from where it rested on the doorframe and forced himself to stand up.

"I need your help."

He fell inside and stumbled toward her table as she quickly swept the painting up, then reached one arm up to tug at his shirt and pull it off. Heat radiated off him. He towered over her for only a moment longer before sinking onto the table, the muscles of his stomach clenching and the—*Oh god*—the open wound of his abdomen glinting.

Nicole nearly dropped the painting, leaning it against the wall.

"That doesn't look good."

He tried to smile. "It doesn't feel good."

"What happened? Why aren't you healing?" She focused on the blood rather than his body, which looked like a living, sweat glistening *Belvedere Torso*.

"Lynch stabbed me with the crystal in the museum. I thought I could get it out"—he gritted his teeth—"but after Influencing everyone I'm drained, and without having blood from a living source I can't even make it budge. Even Callum struggled and now it's festering. Once it's out, I'll should be fine." He grunted as he pulled a knife, sticky with blood, from his back pocket. "I need your eyes, and your hands."

He handed her the knife.

Nicole stared at him. "You want me to . . . cut it out?"

"Can you?"

Some part of her roiled at the thought, but the rest kicked into action. She'd been trained for the likes of this, after all: stepping up when someone needed help, when they needed to be safe. This was what she was made to do.

"Hold on." She set the knife down and angled the desk lamp toward the dark, glossy wound.

Kyan closed his eyes and sat with his head back, body lax with exhaustion yet wired with pain.

"I need you to lean back," she told him.

His hands slid across the table and sent tubes of her paint rolling, knocking over a pot of brushes. He was exposed before her, legs spread, the graze of hair on his chest winding down to where his jeans hid the rest of him. His stomach, slick with blood and sweat, clenched in a long exhale.

Nicole rushed to the bathroom and hurriedly washed her hands and the knife. When she came back out it was to grab the box of matches and sanitize the blade.

"That doesn't matter," Kyan said. "My body should fight off any infection."

"Let's not take any extra chances, okay?" She stooped to tenderly analyze the wound. The skin around it was hot. Pulling slightly, she ducked her head and hoped that he'd be too fazed out with the pain to notice she was using her Empyrean sight to see the crystal. It was buried deep. Removing it would hurt him, but it was better than leaving it.

Kyan steadied his breathing and Nicole tried to control her features as she pressed her fingers into the hot wound. She could grip the crystal easily, but it was wedged in deep. She tugged and his muscles jumped.

"Why didn't you tell me about Alexander?"

Kyan blinked through a haze. "We're going to talk about this now?"

"Why not?" It could distract him.

He winced as her fingers probed.

"He's dead and gone."

She pressed her lips together. That might be true, and yet she couldn't help but remember those urges rising up near Lynch and the Specter telling her that Kyan wouldn't protect her.

It was a good thing, she tried to tell herself. It was a reminder.

"I did it because I thought I was doing the right thing," Kyan said.

She looked up at his parted mouth, the sweat running down his chest. His dark, honest eyes. She felt things looking into those eyes. Things she shouldn't.

Nicole reached for the knife and changed the subject. "Why haven't you had any blood?"

Kyan shut his eyes, as if talking about it reminded him of the lack.

"Not that I'm offering to give you any," she said quickly.

"No, I don't want you to. After kissing you, I don't think it's a good idea to mix in blood."

Why? she wanted to whisper as her heart thundered like the waves outside.

"Can't you just drink from an animal like Edward Cullen?"

A pained laugh barked out of him, his stomach clenching. It was the first great laugh of his she'd heard and it caused a warm swell in her chest, until it was followed by his sharp intake of breath. "Edward Cullen is fictional," he said, voice strained. "And a Vampire, not a Specter."

Nicole smiled before slipping the knife against the slick column of the crystal, which had bound the tissue, the veins and organs sticking to it. Quickly, to ease some of the pain, she ran the blade around it. The table splintered beneath his grip as he let out a growling agonized sound, his entire body taut.

Nicole yanked and the crystal ripped free. She stumbled backward but Kyan's hand whipped out to grab her forearm and haul her back, causing her chest to crash against his sweat-slick one.

His warm breath rushed over her ear while his mouth stamped firm at her temple. They both stilled. His breathing was labored so she didn't dare shift, unsure how much pain he was in.

"I should stitch you up or something," she said quietly to his jaw.

But he didn't move, and her breathing hitched for a different reason at the scent of him. Nicole slammed her eyes shut—*don't breathe it in!*—but it was too late.

God, how did he smell so good? Even now?

Get a grip, he's hurt!

They were quiet for a few long moments as Nicole struggled to force her body's immediate reaction to *cut it out*. Kyan moved slightly so his slick temple pressed against hers. The only sound was their breathing and the rain lashing hard against the window. She soaked in the feeling of being held against his bare skin, feeling his heartbeat. Then he straightened slowly with a wince, his mouth grazing close to hers.

And those ancient, forest-colored eyes darkened.

"I got it out," Nicole said, raising the crystal between them. She analyzed it as blood roared in her ears and fear tapped in her chest at how intense these feelings were.

He released his grip on her. "Thank you."

"Yeah, of course." Nicole searched for something else to talk about, wrapping the bloodied crystal in a painting rag.

"I won't bite you," he said quietly, even if he looked like he was fighting it.

"I know," she said, holding up the rag with the crystal.

His laugh was rough. "You're not afraid of much, are you?"

Nicole wiped her hands on the damp towel she'd brought out of the bathroom, and averted her eyes. "Oh, I am."

He brushed some hair back from her face. "What frightens you?"

Her eyes almost flickered closed at the easy comfort he could give her through just that action. One her body craved, but her mind rebelled against. How could she feel this around an Empyreal? It was an action that should make her tense up, push him away. Yet all she wanted was to sink into it.

Was it because they'd kissed? Opened up something inside her she hadn't even known was there?

I'm afraid of getting taken away. Having every dream I've ever had for my life crushed because of one organization's bid for control.

Your *organization.*

But worst of all . . . "Losing my family," she whispered.

"It's a grief I wouldn't wish on anyone."

Complicated guilt rose in her and she found herself reaching for his cheek. Her fingers hesitated before gently touching the warm skin, slightly rough with stubble.

"I'm so sorry, Kyan," she said softly.

He closed his eyes for a moment and shook his head before

291

raising a hand and watching as his fingers stroked beneath her jaw, each one sending arrows of sensitivity through her. His thumb grazed her lip as he frowned.

"It's in the past."

But this is now.

And while every logic she'd ever known was whispering inside her, making her feel guilty, everything he'd done so far had been to protect her.

And protection was everything to Nicole.

So, she found herself inching just slightly closer.

Kyan closed the last bit of distance slowly, that eternal frown back between his brows, as if what he was about to do made him just as conflicted as her.

She held deadly still, lips parting.

Then, gently, breathlessly, he pressed his mouth to hers.

Relief and pleasure flooded her limbs. She reached for his solid, wide shoulders, the bare skin hot and smooth. His hands moved as his mouth closed on hers again, softly, barely a whisper of want. His slight stubble grazed her face and sparked every nerve.

Their kisses were slow and savoring and her body reacted in waves, a crash of pleasure with each one and a deep pulling of anticipation for the next, again and again, almost torturously.

He slipped his hand up under her shirt and his fingers skimmed her back. Suddenly she needed to be closer.

She climbed onto him, thighs sliding over his. He tugged off her cardigan as their tongues met and groaned into her mouth, kissing her back, harder. And then her hips were flush with his and she felt drugged with desire.

"I should stitch it," she whispered against his mouth for a fevered

292

moment, distant logic hammering through her mind.

"It can wait."

Nicole let out a breathy laugh and glanced down to see his wound slowly knitting itself back together. She peered at his bare stomach, warmth blushing up her neck and face.

"You're injured, and you might want to clean that." She nodded to where blood was beginning to settle, darkening the shadowed lines of his sculpted stomach. "And I should . . . er, wash my hands." She looked at them over his shoulders, bloody.

He began to smile. It made his eyes soften, and—was that a dimple on his left cheek? *God help me.*

"I'm all right now," he said. "Thanks to you."

Her chest warmed with such intense affection her breath caught. She nearly scrubbed at it, worried, but he shifted her on his lap and leaned to allow her to reach the floor again, her body instantly frustrated that she was denying it.

She ducked into the little adjoining bathroom to hide her face and Kyan followed.

"How's your hand?" he asked, the massive, semi-naked bulk of him coming to stand behind her.

Right. The one she'd hurt in the kitchen.

Nicole swallowed hard as he cupped it, not knowing it was now healed. She'd wrapped it in a fresh cloth and tucked it securely before painting. Now, she washed the blood from her fingertips in the tiny paint-stained sink.

"It's fine," she whispered as he bent to wash his hands either side of her, his front pressed against her back. Nicole fought the pleasure as the proximity pressed his hips to her backside, enough she could feel *all* of him. Heat roared back through her and pooled low between her legs. Her eyes almost fluttered shut and she fought the new urge to move against him.

She met his gaze in the mirror, his dark with desire. He kept his eyes on hers as he bent and brushed a kiss to her temple.

"Thank you for helping me."

She shivered, her breath shaky, but nodded, not trusting herself to make a damn sound.

Just stay here with him, a part of her whispered. *Be with him. Pretend there are no consequences, that there's nothing forbidden about it.*

Stop resisting.

She reached for a fresh cloth and drenched it, handing it to him. He removed his arms from around her and went to wipe his stomach. Nicole glanced down to the wound's progress.

"That's not very quick," she said, her worry louder than her heated thoughts.

"It'll take some time," he answered. "I'm not only an Empyreal at the moment."

Nicole nodded distractedly and slipped back out, reeling, needing to pace. She could barely get the scalding dash of his tongue out of her mind, the press of his body against hers. What would that feel like, everywhere? She didn't know kissing could be like this. It felt so good. *Better* than good.

But she needed to focus.

"How's the curator?" Nicole asked the wall, not trusting herself to face the bathroom, where he still stood half naked in the shadows.

"He needs bed rest and a blood transfusion, but he'll be fine. I Influenced the paramedics to forget afterward."

"And you did all that with a gaping wound in your stomach?" She glanced over her shoulder as Kyan stepped back into the light and her body gave a lurching peal of excitement that almost made her blush again.

His lips pulled up. "Callum was helping me."

Right. Callum.

"Where's the painting now?"

"We got it back to the manor."

Nicole relaxed slightly. "Lynch did something to it, though. I don't know how to make sure it isn't damaged."

"I called a supernatural restorer; she's coming out in two days to check it."

If the full cipher was still in the painting, she couldn't allow someone else to find it without her.

But before she could ask, he said, "Yes, you can be there when she does."

She met his eyes to see them soften and felt herself smile. He was beginning to know her so well, and it was almost like an apology for their secret-keeping comments in the museum.

Nicole headed for the door as warm emotions bloomed through her. Kyan followed, bending once they were outside to pick up the coat he must have dropped before he came in, his bloodied shirt tucked into the back of his jeans. Shaking off the sand, he put it on, and they began the walk over the dark beach toward the row of houses overlooking it.

"Are you still angry with me?" he asked.

Nicole sighed. "No, I—" *I got angry because you're right, but I can't tell you the truth and it's wearing me down.*

I got angry because I'm damn well confused as to why I have to feel all this for you.

"—No."

"Good," he said softly, and tears filled her eyes quickly as he offered his hand. "Let me take you home."

Nicole tried to tell herself she felt nothing. But she felt two things with a startling clarity as her hand carefully linked with his.

Pain from her not-healing wound, which was its own kind of deeply unnerving.

And . . . affection. That was the only word she'd allow herself. Affection, and an intense, aching lust, for an Empyreal.

She closed her eyes, and cursed it all.

32 KYAN

The pavement glinted with rain by the time Kyan had taken Nicole home. He'd dropped her back off at her family house and was headed back toward the manor, when he decided to confront the person that had been following them discreetly since the beach.

He still didn't feel completely healed, the wound sensitive despite Nicole removing the crystal and the slice sealing over. So he used a bit more blood, discovering he needed extra. It soaked into the vessels of his teeth and his tongue dashed over them again, searching for any more of it, because he could still taste Nicole's kiss; taste the echo of the shaky exhale she loosed when he'd touched her. It did unspeakable things to him, made him want in those visceral, physical ways he felt her want, too.

And he wanted to give her what she wanted. . . .

Damn it, what was he doing?

Kyan turned suddenly, grabbing the scruff of the pursuer's coat, whipping him from the light of a streetlamp and pinning him into the brick post of a house's driveway.

Nicole's brother.

Kyan could hear the hurried beat of the boy's heart, felt him reach for a weapon. Kyan's hand dashed out and ripped it free first, throwing it to the pavement with a metallic ring.

"Why are you following us?"

"I'm keeping an eye on the town. On you," Dylan growled.

That much Kyan had noticed early on. He'd felt eyes watching him coolly and looking away before they thought he'd noticed. But he always noticed.

"I'm not risking her getting hurt. Again," Dylan said.

Kyan thought of the mark on Nicole's neck. But from the look in her brother's eyes, he knew that wasn't just what he'd meant. "I would never hurt her."

"No? How the hell do you know that?" Dylan shoved out of Kyan's grip.

"I don't hurt anyone who hasn't killed."

"I'm not talking about your power, Empyreal. I just saw you kiss . . ." He broke off, as if too furious to speak. He moved closer, vibrating with anger. "What are you *doing*? Are you just going to . . . use her until you leave? It's not like you can be together."

A slow tide of anger rushed up Kyan's chest. "I don't think she'd appreciate us talking about it."

"Don't assume you know more about my sister than I do."

"I don't assume anything. In fact, I'm constantly questioning. Why she wants this. What she *is*."

Dylan stilled and Kyan took the moment to assess. Her brother was strong, almost Kyan's height, and there was power in him, but what kind?

"We're all Seers," Dylan said.

Kyan found himself shaking his head slightly, his powers piqued but his voice flat as he said, "Really?" He tried to ignore that he'd heard more of that lost Irish accent in his words. He was no danger to Nicole, he never would be.

Yet she didn't taste like a Seer.

Kyan stared hard at Dylan. His face didn't hold many similarities to that of the woman from 1902. *Could* it have been a coincidence?

He'd taken the oath because it was all he had left. But discomfort, and something stronger, sat in his stomach as he began to wonder if a lifetime serving the Wake was still all that he wanted.

If that really was all that was left of him.

His phone pinged, interrupting. It was a message from the restorer, confirming her plans.

He looked up to find Dylan stalking away.

"What happened that makes you all distrust me so much?" Kyan asked.

Dylan didn't stop as he said, "One of you killed our mother."

33 NICOLE

When Nicole got into the house, she could hear her father working away in the kitchen.

The lights were low, the house cozy and calm, and she found herself taking a huge breath of relief, but it staggered at the back of her throat.

She hadn't told her family that she was developing feelings for Kyan. But she was beginning to feel like the changes toward him were showing on her face, in the way she moved, the way she spoke. Something glaringly obvious.

Worry twisted her gut. She'd never kept secrets from them. But . . . was this a secret?

Should it be?

Nicole walked into the kitchen to find her father at the island. A bottle of white wine was open on the counter, alongside an array of plants and herbs he was sorting.

Her father's ancient case of supernatural weapons was open on the floor. It was filled with all sorts of things: crystals, poisons, a few wicked blades, some more fantastical ones, a selection of guns, a small mace, and a few stakes.

"Hello, love," her father said, glancing up at her over the rim of his glasses. His blue-gray eyes took her in and Nicole breathed deeply, able to read the tension in his frame.

"So, do you want to have a glass of wine and explain what happened?" he asked. "Or do I have to ask? There's leftover takeout in the fridge."

Nicole's shoulders drooped in relief at the familiarity of the moment. They had a takeout night every week, no matter what home they'd been in or where they'd traveled to. It was one of the little constants her father kept for them. In Estwood, they'd been able to build in a few more routines: weekly visits to the deli with its artisan cheese, local honey, and wine; the farmers market they went to on Saturday mornings; and the fish-and-chip shop opposite the beach they frequented after long walks along the sand.

But this one always thickened her throat with memories.

She got out the box of noodles and poured herself a glass of chilled wine, discovering a line of fresh tonics in the fridge, the little jars rattling gently as she opened it.

"What are you making?" Nicole asked, frowning at the green paste in his mortar.

The black mortar, the one for poisons.

"Poisoned bullets," he said, holding one up before dropping it in the mixture.

Nicole swallowed a scoop of noodles. As a Seer, her father was more than familiar with dark deeds, but she knew that as a husband and father, he had been the one doing them on a great many occasions.

She filled him in around mouthfuls of takeout, savoring the cold greasiness, the spice and flavor, and the chilled glass of white wine. When she was finished, so was her father's deadly concoction.

He said nothing as he loaded a gun, and she was reminded of the story of how her parents had met: in Rome, hundreds of years ago, when he'd been hunting down a creature that had been haunting his visions and killing locals.

He'd been overpowered by it at the last second and would have been killed if it weren't for her mother, who had sensed the kill scent and saved his life.

Their connection had been immediate, he'd told her.

"You're not going to do anything reckless, are you, Dad?" Nicole asked him, knowing that over the centuries, her mother had taught him more about how to kill creatures without Empyrean power. On how to keep people safe.

"Of course not, love. But if Lynch touches you again . . ." The revolver snapped shut. "I make no promises."

After finishing her food, and texting Dylan to make sure he was okay, Nicole headed upstairs to check on Bells. Her sister survived the dualities of light and dark every night. There was a quiet strength in her, and a deep empathy. Out of her siblings, Nicole knew Bells would be the most able to understand her complicated feelings.

But when she got to Bells's room, she discovered that the door was ajar.

"Bells?" Nicole asked softly. Not wanting to wake her if she was asleep, she poked her head inside.

Her sister was sitting on the floor in her room before the little altar she had set up against the wall for the Goddess of Prophecy. It glittered with lit candles. The sight wasn't unusual, but the blood trickling from her sister's nose was.

Bells's lips moved in some sort of prayer and her eyes danced behind her veined lids. *"Speak to me, Morrigan sister, Badb of Prophecy, show me my family's futures. Show me how Lynch will end—"*

"Bells!" Nicole darted inside and her sister's eyes flashed open, fully bloodred.

Nicole's movement created a gust of wind that extinguished one of the candles and her sister's eyes fluttered, slowly returning to normal.

Nicole reached for her, unsure if or how to help.

Bells blinked a few times. "Nicole?" Suddenly she looked guilty as she took in where she was.

"Bells, what ritual were you doing?"

Bells slapped shut an old book beside her, but not before Nicole caught a glimpse.

"You were doing one of the forbidden Seer rituals? Bells, Badb is the Goddess of Prophecy and *Madness*."

Suddenly Bells's eyes filled with tears. "I know! But I can't just sit around and do *nothing*!" Her words dissolved into a hiccupped cry.

Nicole sank down and tugged her into a hug. The brush of her sister's cheek was incomprehensibly soft and a little hot against her own.

"That's okay," Nicole said, "you don't need to. You have enough nightmares to deal with when you're asleep, let us take care of the ones lurking in the daytime."

"But all of my nightmares are *real*," she said, eyes shimmering like the sea. "And I can't fight them. I can't fight *this*."

Nicole stroked back her sister's hair, brushing the tears away. *I'll kill anything that tries to hurt you.* "Not a single one of them will reach you, do you understand?"

Bells's lip trembled slightly. "That's not what scares me. It's that

303

I can't do anything about it. I'm not afraid of the things I See. And it nearly worked—I thought . . . I thought for a minute I heard something. Someone saying my name."

Nicole drew back, worried. "Listen to me, don't risk that, okay? I know we're well warded in the house, but who knows what beings can tap into a Seer's mind when she's open in a ritual like this."

"But you keep leaving me out of everything, how else can I help? I'm even alone in school since you and Dylan graduated. I have no one to sit with at lunch and nothing to do but worry about the Specter lurking around town and you being near one of the Wake's Empyreals."

Nicole frowned. "What about that nice girl you said spoke to you in your English class? You said you liked her."

"She barely spoke to me," Bells sniffed. "I think it's because I See things about them all. Things that will happen to them, anything and everything, even if it's terrible, and I can't warn them or they'd think I was crazy. But it means I always look like I'm having an allergic reaction with my eyes going veined. And yet I can't see anything for *us* and it's infuriating. I want to be able to *use* my power. I want to be able to *live*, not just feel like I'm sleepwalking through life, in my visions or with a girl—" She clamped her lips shut. "I can't even speak to Remi without getting nervous." Bells clapped her hands over her face and cried a little more and Nicole wrapped her closer.

"Hey, it's okay."

"She probably hates me."

"She doesn't hate you. Remi thinks you're adorable."

Bells let out a sad little sound. "Ugh, that's even *worse*. I just feel useless."

"You're not," Nicole said, wiping her tears away. "You train just like me and Dylan."

"Slower," Bells said. "Weaker."

Nicole pulled back. If her sister really was this worked up, there was something she could do about it, for both of them. She pushed up. "Come with me."

She tugged on Bells's hand until her sister blew out the rest of the candles and rose, then led her down through the kitchen to the gym and flicked on the light switch.

"Nicole . . ." Bells started to argue.

"You're right," Nicole said, coming to stand on the mat, legs shoulder width apart. "We do go easier on you."

Her little sister frowned, looking hurt and rumpled.

"You're not an Empyreal, but that gives you an advantage. You have more control. There's no threat that you could transform, which means you're not getting freaked out inside."

"You get freaked out inside?"

"Of course," Nicole said. She smiled slightly, realizing that admitting it, even slightly, didn't feel *so* bad. "But you have more advantages. You're small, which means you can be sleeker and faster. But most importantly, Bells, it means they'll underestimate you. So don't underestimate yourself first."

Bells's lip quivered slightly, but she lifted her chin. "Show me what to do."

34 NICOLE

Two nights later Nicole paced in the ballroom of Westmoore Manor.

The *Dante* painting had been laid out on a large table Callum and Kyan had brought in and chairs were set up around it. Lamps, cables, and anything the restorer might need were stationed and ready.

"She'll be here soon, don't worry," Kyan said.

Nicole huffed. He looked up from where he sat at the table, his laptop brightness low. If they turned all the lights off, his Specter night vision would probably be better than his usual Empyreal abilities. Nicole pushed that thought out of her head.

She had no idea how to be around him, especially not when he looked at her a beat too long; when the air seemed suddenly electric with tension and the new intimacy between them kept luring her attention to his mouth.

Especially not when her brother was also here, arms crossed, scowl on his face. When he wasn't glaring at Nicole and Kyan, he was eyeing Callum, who sat sipping wine like he didn't have a care in the world.

"This is cozy," Callum said.

"You could have mentioned you were an Empyreal," Dylan said.

"Well, it's not exactly first-meet conversation."

They shared a look that went from annoyed to charged and Nicole went out to pace in the corridor instead, leaving them to bicker.

She felt rather than saw Kyan come up behind her.

"You've worked with her before?" Nicole asked, turning to see him leaning in the archway that led into the ballroom. He wore a thin navy jumper and dark jeans, yet she could so clearly remember what was *under* it and had been pressed against her in the kitchen, the beach hut—

"Yes. She's one of the best. Don't worry, she'll tell us what the substance is."

Nicole wasn't just nervous about meeting a supernatural restorer but also because when they stripped the painting she didn't know what it might reveal. They were planning to reapply the varnish to protect it properly, but by that point, the secret would be exposed. She'd played around with the partial cipher as much as she could, yet still hadn't figured out what type it was. Lynch hadn't yet approached her again, but it was only a matter of time. . . .

Before she could stress more, the doorbell rang.

Nicole followed Kyan through the house and when he opened the door, it was to find a young woman who looked to be somewhere in her early twenties.

"Phew." The newcomer blew upward so her black fringe fluttered out of her eyes.

Behind her a taxi drove back down the dark drive, but it was the newcomer that swallowed all Nicole's attention.

"What a ride! I had some Coa in the cab to stay awake and I literally think my head exploded. Hi, I'm Vera!" She grinned. Beautiful, tiny whorls were tattooed on her neck. She'd tied a blue scarf

307

into her dark hair and had done her eye makeup smoky blue to match, with sharp black eyeliner.

"Hi," Nicole said, holding out her hand. Her nerves returned with full force as the woman's cold fingers closed around hers with a prickle of supernatural power. "I'm helping research the collection."

"Oh." Vera's eyes dashed to Kyan.

"She's one of us," he said.

One of us.

A surprising swell of pride tugged Nicole's stomach.

Kyan reached over and took Vera's suitcase as she came inside.

"What a house, huh?" Vera commented, stepping inside the darkly glinting foyer. She swiftly followed Kyan as he strode back through the manor. "So," she said, glancing at Nicole, "you work for the Wake, too?"

Horror made her say, "No!" And her eyes widened at her automatic reply. She cleared her throat and avoided Kyan's curious stare. "No, I'm a student at the university. I'm a Seer."

"Oh, cool. Don't look into my soul without sunglasses, okay? It's bright in there." She winked.

Nicole's smile grew.

"I've set up your room on the highest floor," Kyan said.

Vera grinned. "You remembered."

Nicole was surprised by the honest smile that came over his features.

"Do you want to rest up there first?" he asked.

"No, I'll take a look later," Vera said. "I want to work for a few hours. I'm all buzzed now and I have to be back in Venice tomorrow evening."

Kyan nodded and started walking back toward the ballroom.

"That's where you work?" Nicole asked as they followed.

"Yeah, I trained in the Wake's restoration academies. First at home in South Korea, then New York." Vera shrugged, grinned. "It's cool work." She let out a low whistle as Kyan led them into the ballroom. "Nice piece."

"Why, thank you," Callum said, putting down his wine along with whatever tense conversation he'd been having with Dylan.

"*Callum?*" Vera said with delight. "Last I saw you, you were getting arrested by the Venetian police for that boat chase. How did you even get it into the piazza?"

The Empyreal smiled and shrugged. "What can I say, sometimes I just let them catch me for fun."

Nicole fought a smile.

"But this . . . this is a Bouguereau," Vera said, coming close to the painting.

They all approached, and Vera's pupils split, making four instead of two. Nicole stifled her gasp.

"Half Vulpe on my dad's side," Vera said. She flashed the split-pupiled gaze to Nicole. "Crazy family parties, let me tell you."

Vulpe were a more mischievous type of Fae that dealt in glamours. Nicole didn't realize she was grinning until she felt Kyan's stare, and the curve of his lips, the . . . affection in his eyes quickened her heartbeat.

Nicole cleared her throat, forcing attention back to the painting. "It's, er, been treated with Finfolk blood, we think to remove the varnish."

Vera gave her an approving look and warmth spread through her.

"You want to go into restoration?"

"Maybe, but probably supernatural art history." She smiled to

309

stop herself speaking and ignored the knot of emotion that clogged her throat. In truth, it was one of the dreams she had. One of the many *maybes*. But being an Empyreal, there was little chance she could do it. She couldn't risk working with supernatural paintings. What if she exposed herself by breaking through a centuries-old canvas to kill a murderous colleague? Or was triggered by pigments or oils made from dangerous creatures?

"You're right, Finfolk blood has been used. The camouflaging elements in it dissolve the camouflage in the varnish. It's a cruel and illegal way to do it and it changes the consistency and smell of the blood, so most people don't notice it. We use more sophisticated stuff now."

"Are you sure Lynch didn't kill the Finfolk?" Nicole asked Kyan.

"He didn't make the killing blow," was all Kyan said, but the words were tense.

Spurred by anger, Nicole craned closer to the painting. "Has he damaged it?"

"It doesn't harm the painting, don't worry," Vera said. "But he has layered another varnish over. If I took it off, we'd still find what's underneath."

A breath of hope and relief filled her chest. "Let's do it."

"It's going to take some time. Can I get another Coa?" Nicole thought of grabbing one herself. It was the supernatural equivalent of a bubbly caffeinated drink; give it to a human and they might run into a wall, but she was already feeling too anxious.

"Sure," Kyan said, heading into the kitchen.

Nicole grabbed her notes and settled down as Vera opened her suitcase to reveal cloths, tools, Q-tips, and jars of dried ingredients.

"This is what you do when you start," Vera began.

A few hours later, Nicole tried not to let her disappointment and concern show on her face. Part of her had been worried about what the painting might reveal to Kyan and Callum, but it didn't end up mattering.

Because there was nothing here.

Kyan noticed her mood shift, but thankfully he didn't ask about the cipher. She knew he'd remember from the night in the quad, and yet he hadn't asked her outright what she was looking for. Instead, he made a call.

"Mr. Alborough," Kyan began. "We'll go ahead with displaying a painting of my aunt's tomorrow night for the event. But it will be a copy of a Bouguereau."

Nicole skirted around the great table to try and catch his eye, alarmed.

"I know it's short notice, but it's this or nothing. No, *The Wild Hunt* stays here. Do what you need to." He hung up and turned to Nicole. She didn't even have to ask him to explain. "We'll use the event to lure Lynch, and then I'm taking him in. He's too smart and too dangerous. I can't kill him with spectral powers, as I won't transform unless he tries to kill. So we'll drag him back to the Wake. There's still a risk he could escape, he's done it before, but with two of us . . ."

Kyan looked at Callum for confirmation and the enigmatic Empyreal nodded as if agreeing to help.

Nicole tried to find it within her to be relieved. Tried to smother her confusion, her anger over the painting's lack of secrets. She'd been right in thinking that Lynch had given the cipher and painting up too easily, because whatever message was hidden in the painting, he now had it.

311

And he'd removed its evidence forever.

But that meant that two Empyreals were taking the creature that *had* those secrets right back to the Wake's clutches.

Nicole met her brother's eyes.

Their mother's secret remained, but at what cost?

Now Kyan had a new plan and it meant he might take her chance at an answer away forever, as well as himself. She didn't know which made her feel worse.

35 NICOLE

"Do you think Lynch will give you the rest of the cipher tonight?" Remi asked, sitting in the great bay window in her dorm room. She'd positioned her desk there and laid out her computer, as well as a mirror. The night beyond was dark already, and its swiftly cooling air gently breathed through the ancient panes.

Remi's dorm was in one of the oldest parts of the university, which meant it had carved stone windowsills and rich, old wood paneling. She had, however, made it her own. A great gold gramophone shaped like a gilded flower steadily played a jazz standard. Ghostly white pieces of coral and gleaming nautilus shells were lined up on shelves or tables. Black-and-white minimalistic posters of the cycles of planets were framed and leaning against the dark wood. And delicate sheaves of sheet music, faded with time, were splayed out on most surfaces.

"He better," Nicole said, sitting on the bed and taking another sip of white wine, the glass misted with condensation at her fingers. She glanced at the dress she'd brought to get ready for the museum event. "Or I'll never get it."

While Kyan had stopped the *Wild Hunt* painting from being loaned to the museum, preferring to keep it safe in the manor, he'd allowed them to show off the *Dante* piece instead. Lynch had already had that in his clutches, so it wasn't as much of a risk. The museum board had agreed to an impromptu unveiling to celebrate and Kyan had managed to get all of them on the guest list.

"Lynch hasn't been opposed to risk so far," Nicole continued, "and he's been getting twisted. I think he's losing patience. If he stabbed Kyan, then he's not going to be shy about doing something worse. I'm just relying on there being plenty of other people there, and two Empyreals. He hasn't exposed himself to humans so far, even with those he's bitten. There have been no university reports of missing or attacked students. But Dad said if Lynch tries anything, he's shooting him, no excuses. Hence why they're all coming tonight."

"Oh jeez."

"Yeah." She wasn't averse to shooting Lynch at this point, especially not if that would help wound him and further aid Kyan and Callum taking him in. What she *was* averse to was everyone coming, even Bells, and Lynch being taken to the Wake before she got the cipher. "So, I hope your bag is packed."

Remi nodded toward the small suitcase she'd prepared. She was going to stay with them tonight just in case.

"I don't know what we'll do about Hannah," Nicole said. "I guess we can say you're going on a trip?"

Remi rolled her desk chair over to the bed and tipped Nicole's face up to do her eyeliner. "Oh, er . . . we don't have to worry about that. I broke up with her."

Nicole jerked, causing Remi to draw a wet line of makeup over her temple.

"What? Why?"

314

"Keep still!" Remi tsked and used the edge of a wipe to clean the mark.

"Sorry." Keeping her mouth as still as possible Nicole asked, "What happened?"

Remi sighed. "I sang in front of her."

"But she was there the other night at the pub when you sang."

"No," Remi said. "That was when I was concentrating, just singing one of the old Celtic songs Dad discovered. This . . . this was me. I was just humming while I was making coffee. I wasn't thinking, and you know that's when the melody of my Siren song can begin to form."

"Oh."

"She got this look on her face." Remi paused while she tried to pull herself together. "And obviously, I know humans get mesmerized by my voice, but it was almost like . . . I don't know. Like she just went away, you know? I don't know, it made me feel like . . ."

"Like you couldn't be yourself?"

"Yeah." Remi's lips pressed together. She chewed on them for a second before starting on Nicole's other eye. "And honestly, with Lynch still a threat, I don't want her getting hurt if he decides to come for us separately. I'm sure it's for the best, it's just . . . Do you feel like it's possible for us to find someone when we're living like this? Here, in Estwood?"

The question had plagued Nicole some nights, because, while she was so glad they were safe here, what did that mean for any kind of meaningful romantic relationship? Where on earth would she *meet* someone? And could she risk ever telling them the truth? Humans could probably never know, and while she and Remi could make human lives and be with human partners, would they be

315

satisfied constantly hiding the truest parts of themselves?

"I'm sure if we could trust them enough, it could happen," Nicole tried. "Then perhaps we could have something like your parents. They're so in love."

Remi rolled her eyes. "I know."

Nicole laughed. "It's nice, you know? Seeing the pair of them."

Remi reached out, understanding, and put her hand on Nicole's. "I know." She sighed heavily. "Well, come on, we have T-minus twenty minutes until we're due at the museum."

Remi got up and selected a dress from the rack of glittering clothes as Nicole checked the lipstick Remi had chosen for her, a red that contrasted with her pale skin and dark hair, bringing out the flush in her cheeks.

Then she turned to her dress.

Life in Estwood was *ease* and *comfort*: breakfasts with buttery toast, jeans and oversized cardigans, early mornings with her family and the scent of coffee, hours spent working through the library and reading about art history, watching people surf even on gray days.

Or, it was supposed to be.

Now she felt like she was unraveling, becoming a wild thing slowly against her will. Everything felt darker. So she dressed in tighter things, anything to feel contained. Even if the constriction also grated, made her want to rip through the restrictive pencil skirt, every scrape of her lace bra a slow infuriation.

So, she'd picked a black dress with a slit in the leg, just in case. Something that made her feel in control, but ready to run, because while they had their plan tonight, Nicole had Seen pieces of Lynch's previous kills, and they haunted her all the way to the event.

36 NICOLE

The glass doors of the museum reflected Nicole's black satin dress as it shimmered darkly in the warm glow. Remi's cream backless one gleaming along with the pearls in her friend's ears and threaded into her curls.

Nicole scanned the entrance as they entered, her heels clipping on the foyer's marble floor. Lynch could come to her at any point tonight with the rest of the code. He hadn't been shy about causing a scene before, so what better place to accost her than the most luxurious building in Estwood other than Westmoore Manor? They might have her mother's clue by the end of the event, but she couldn't guarantee no one would get hurt for it, and that had nerves tapping beneath her skin.

They showed their tickets and were offered champagne from one of the many circling trays.

Remi clinked hers to Nicole's with a deep breath.

"Here we go," Remi said, linking their arms as the pair headed into the grand gallery room.

As an arts school, Estwood University had a strong connection to the museum, so a surprising number of people had turned out despite the short notice: professors of art history, the vice chancellor, art students, and even some historians and scholars from London.

Nicole couldn't help but feel cheated. She'd hardly had a chance to attend classes; to truly soak up the atmosphere.

She looked for Lynch, but her eyes locked on the painting instead, standing in the center of the room on a small dais.

"I thought they were showing *The Wild Hunt*?" someone whispered. "This must be a copy of the original—it's supposed to be in Paris, isn't it?"

"I wonder what the rest of the collection is like," someone else said with dual levels of intrigue and judgment.

Nicole and Remi walked through the milling crowd toward the *Dante* painting and took a moment to absorb it in all its vicious glory. Vera had re-varnished it, fixing Lynch's attempts. While it meant the painting was safe, Nicole couldn't help but see horror and missed opportunities. The low burn of rage at the thought that Lynch had taken the cipher flushed her skin as much as the champagne.

"Hi, Mr. Palmer," Remi said, breaking through her thoughts. Nicole turned to find her father and Bells. Her sister was wearing a dress of blush pink, and her father wore a gray suit with a white shirt but she knew there was a gun tucked into the back of his waistband.

"Bells! You look so beautiful," Remi said, gathering her up in a hug.

Bells flushed prettily and Nicole smiled.

"If Lynch comes to speak to you, we're here," her father said quietly.

Nicole nodded, eyes scanning the crowd. Dylan was outside at an exit, and if she concentrated hard enough she could locate his steady breathing.

She caught her reflection in the mirrored bar that had been set up across the room. Remi had darkened her eyes with eyeliner and painted Nicole's lips bloodred. She didn't recognize herself for a second, with her long dark hair softly curled and the black dress hugging her form. She felt like all her inner potential for danger was, for once, revealing itself.

A prickle of heat had her turning to discover Kyan entering the room. Her stomach dropped at the familiar stature, the tension in his shoulders, and a jolt of fire lit in her belly as his eyes met hers. He paused for a moment and his look of unmitigated *want* startled her.

God, she was screwed.

Kyan was beside them in an instant. The tension in his face softened, then heated for a different reason. That forbidden, simmering desire burned brighter, hotter, and she felt her own body react. Eager, *distracting*. His hand came near her elbow, and while she could feel the heat of him, he didn't touch.

"Nicole," he said, voice rough, "can I talk to you?" There was an urgency in his tone. A no-nonsense look in his eye.

She'd only seen him like this once before, when Lynch had pinned her and rooted his power into her neck. Kyan lifted his head to look toward the back rooms like he'd just heard something. Nicole strained to see his eyes, the hazel swallowed with dark pupils, and knew the Specter had something to do with this.

"I'm just going to the bathroom," Bells whispered to their father, and she ducked away, asking a security guard for directions. Nicole fought her anxiety watching her disappear out of sight.

"Where's Callum?" Nicole asked, unwilling to leave her family and talk to Kyan until Callum was with them, even if she was still wondering if they really could trust the secretive Empyreal.

Remi crossed her arms, watching Kyan carefully while her father sized them up.

"Who, me?"

Nicole turned to find Callum looking dangerous in a dark suit. He grinned. "Hello, love."

"I'll be back in a minute," Nicole said, Kyan's solid hand on her lower back, guiding her through the crowd.

They slipped into a shadowed archway in the next art-clad room. Her body came alive with adrenaline in the almost dark, with Kyan's hands on her.

Once he had her in a more secluded space, he gently pressed her against the wall. She studied his face, which had lifted to listen to something. She listened, too, but couldn't hear anything out of the ordinary. Kyan's mouth was a hard line but when he met her gaze, the violent focus in his eyes dimmed. Then he winced slightly, and Nicole looked down to his side. She fought the instinct to dip her hands into his jacket and check where they'd removed the crystal.

"Is it still hurting?" That wasn't normal; he should have healed by now. "Has the plan changed?"

He'd been all right with them coming tonight, but . . .

"Nicole, I've been following him all day. He's bitten most of the security guards, which means he'll be able to get into their heads. I need you and your family to leave. I don't know what he's going to try."

Her lips parted, startled. Part of her wanted to say, *I can't go yet.* She'd even told Kyan that they were willing to use force on Lynch, and he'd agreed to it. Weakening Lynch together might be just what they needed to get rid of him. But not before she got the rest of the cipher. If there was even the slightest chance he would give it to her, she would take it.

At her hesitance he said, "Just trust me."

Those words had haunted her since they first met. Had he not proven himself so far? He was a good person, he listened to her and helped her, despite the Wake. Despite there being another Empyreal here, one that she'd left in tense conversation with Remi and who'd watched her father with interest.

"All right," she said. "Okay. I'll talk to the others. We'll . . . we'll come up with another plan."

Hopefully Bells was back from the bathroom. . . .

"Bells."

Cold horror ran down her spine. Her sister had been pointed somewhere by a security guard. Pointed, now Nicole thought about it, in the *wrong direction*.

Nicole rushed back out into the main hall as the sound of a microphone being tapped scythed through the audience.

"Welcome, everyone!" the curator called, standing on the dais with the painting behind him. "What a magical evening. I cannot tell you how ecstatic I am that this incredible painting has been loaned to our museum. All thanks to the late Professor Westmoore and her generosity. And of course, her nephew, Kyan McCarter. Let's all give him a round of applause."

Nicole pushed through the crowd to get to her father, but something about the clapping began to unnerve her. She could feel Lynch, his scent lingered in the air, but she couldn't pinpoint him and she didn't feel Kyan's presence at her back. Nicole spun, hoping he'd taken the other way around to find Bells.

"Yes," came a familiar voice. "Let's all thank *Kyan*." Lynch strode onto the stage with an ironic clap.

Alarmed, Nicole looked to Remi and Callum, who were now at the bar with her father, but Bells was still gone.

And so was Kyan.

A security guard began to move through the crowd toward her. Nicole tensed, scanning him for any sign of a bite—and there, at his neck, were two puncture marks that made her stomach clench. He handed Nicole something, and she carefully took the folded piece of paper, opening it to reveal more of the cipher.

She looked up to find Lynch watching her from the makeshift stage, the curator confused beside him.

Then Bells was being hauled up to stand beside them both.

Nicole lurched, shoving through the crowd.

"Ah, ah," Lynch warned, pulling Bells toward him and crushing her to his front.

Bells's panicked eyes met Nicole's and rage like nothing she'd ever felt roared to life, almost numbing her to every other sensation, every sound and action in the room.

Yet at the same time, it made her realize why the room felt so *off*. The majority of the audience were enthralled, but there were still those that weren't. They were already chatting to their neighbors, wondering if this was some sort of show and craning to look at her. Her old anxiety of being discovered resurfaced. These were *humans*. They couldn't expose themselves to them without huge repercussions; that alone would bring all the Wake's attention to them, to this little town that had been their perfect refuge for so long.

"Let's just talk about this," Nicole tried, fighting the urge to keep her voice low. She moved closer.

"I don't have time for you to stall any longer, my dear," Lynch said. He jutted his chin to where Callum leaned against the bar. Though the Empyreal's stance was lazy with confidence, his eyes

322

were sharp and watchful. Nicole couldn't tell if that meant he was ready for whatever Lynch planned, or ready to merely watch chaos unfold with interest. "The Wake have sent another one and that changes things."

Remi looked ready to sing a blasting note to knock him away from Bells, but Lynch kept her sister directly in front of him. Her father wouldn't be able to get a shot in and Nicole wouldn't be able to tackle him from this far away.

"I realized something in our little moments together," Lynch continued. "That harming *you* doesn't get you to do shit. Harming your loved ones, though? *That* makes sure you tell me the truth."

He trailed a finger down Bells's cheek and her sister's lip quivered, even as she tried to steady it and raise her chin high in the air. Nicole couldn't help her pride.

"Exposing your family's supernatural powers would be a lot worse for you than me. I don't care if people are suspicious of me. I won't be here much longer, as long as you and I have a little chat. So, last chance, Nicole. There's more of the cipher, tell me what it means."

Nerves crawled under her skin. She met her sister's wide, scared eyes and tried to tell her with her own: *It's okay. I'm here. You know what to do.* But she could see the panic in them, and it set her own heart at a dangerous staccato.

Think, she reminded herself. *Just use your brain, not your impulses.* Because every impulse was telling her to *dive and tear his throat out.*

"Get your hands off my sister first."

Bells attempted the defense move she'd been practicing with Nicole, but Lynch hissed and bared his teeth. They curved out, morphing, thin and horrific and threaded with venom, inches from

Bells's throat. His pale eyes had gone beetle black.

"*Keep still,*" he ordered. "You lot, too."

Her father, Callum, and Remi were now hemmed in by security guards who all had bite marks on their necks. What had Bells mentioned the first time they discussed that Lynch was a Specter? That a bite from one might allow Lynch a measure of psychic control over them?

She had no idea how he was managing to keep them all trained simultaneously, it was only supposed to work on one person at a time. What kind of Specter could do this?

Nicole used all her effort to remain still when a slow, drugging, deadly confidence born of the predator within began to unfurl, hot in her blood. Deep beneath her fear, it was sure it could kill him.

And it wanted to do it *now*.

Nicole's eyes raced over the paper. She wasn't an expert code-breaker, her mother had always used something different each time, so she'd need to research this. But she'd been checking number-like ciphers since she got the piece from Lynch. This looked wrong—it was just a long string of numbers.

"I . . . I don't know."

"Don't *lie*."

"I'm not lying!" she shouted. "Was this the exact way it was written down? Was it spaced out this way?"

His eyes narrowed as he thought. "No, there were dashes between the numbers and spaces."

"Which ones?"

He made a frustrated sound. "Between the two and twenty-six and six."

"In threes?"

He thought. "Yes."

Nicole's breath rushed out of her. "It could be a book cipher. Each number correlates to pages and letters."

"So, translate it!"

"I need a key, the book the cipher is based on."

"Which book?" Lynch growled.

"I don't know! It could be anything!" She racked her brain. What book? A book she would have access to, probably, or maybe a book about Bouguereau? Or that book on supernatural symbolism she'd found in Westmoore's library? "I'd need to check it against several different ones."

"That's not good enough, Nicole. How do I know you're not stalling?"

"Bite me and find out," she growled. With her Empyrean senses she could hear Remi singing a few low notes, something that would interfere with the power Lynch had on the people guarding them.

Lynch grinned. "I have a better idea. I made sure before I stabbed Kyan that the crystal would fracture. Did you know that an aura crystal *moves* through the body of a Specter, especially when in small slivers? They're drawn to the heart."

Nicole's blood cooled as she remembered the only two ways an Empyreal could be killed: as another creature with its weaknesses, or by another Empyreal.

He snapped his fingers, and Nicole smelled smoke. Her eyes flashed to the great, vicious *Dante* painting as flames began to crawl up the canvas and she recalled the vision Westmoore had: burning paintings.

Now this one was aflame.

In the next second she didn't care, because Lynch's teeth flashed,

325

and Nicole's scream was drowned out by Bells's as Lynch sank his teeth into her little sister's neck.

At the same moment, Lynch released his thrall on the human guests. Screams erupted and people shoved others to get out of the way as the painting began to burn in earnest.

Lynch's eyes closed, blissful. But at the sight of his teeth in her sister's neck, a dam of rage burst free in Nicole. She didn't care who saw her speed, who she shoved out of the way, if they were hurt or not. All she knew was she had to get to Bells.

"Now, Bells!" Nicole screamed.

A gun went off and Lynch jerked back in surprise, looking down to where Bells had shot him in the gut. Some relief broke through Nicole's fear. They'd given Bells a gun beforehand, expecting Lynch might go for her as he deemed her the most vulnerable. It didn't make it any easier to watch.

Bells then did the self-defense move Nicole had taught her and Lynch's teeth were ripped from her neck, slaked with bright blood, some running down his chin.

But the damage had been done. Lynch's venom began to work and Bells swayed. Nicole's heart shot into her throat.

The moment Bells was out of the Specter's grip more shots went off: her father fired five times at Lynch and didn't miss once, piercing him repeatedly in the chest and shoulders. Lynch shuddered backward with a laugh, and a second later, Kyan tackled Lynch off the podium, the pair falling to the marble floor.

Nicole caught Bells before she hit the ground, smashing her elbow as she caught her. The bone splintered she realized, but she didn't give a shit.

"I'm sorry," Nicole said, tears in her eyes. "It's okay, Bells, you're okay." Hooking her arms under Bells's knees, Nicole lifted her up, ignoring the searing pain, and pulled her to her chest.

"I got him," Bells whispered, body sliding into the clutches of the venom.

Nicole sobbed behind her teeth, ignoring her sister's blood seeping onto her arm. "You did good. I've got you, you're safe."

I'll kill him.

I'll hunt him down and kill him—

But she forced herself to run in the opposite direction. "Dylan!" she screamed. "Remi!"

"Nicole!" Dylan shouted, motioning from the entrance after punching a glazed-eyed security guard who was trying to stop him from keeping the way clear.

Smoke detectors went off and the gates between the gallery rooms began to close. People jostled and slammed into her and she roared at them to "Get out of the fucking way!"

Remi ran with her, and she felt her father behind as Bells's head fell into the hollow of her shoulder, her bloodied neck gleaming as they rushed ahead.

"Now!" Dylan shouted. He'd jammed himself between the archway and the gate, straining against the bars to hold it open.

But before they got there, someone stepped in their way—a security guard with a bloody neck, aiming a Taser at them. Remi loosed a sound that had him dropping the Taser and clutching his head so Nicole could race around him.

Then, a glimmer flashed in her periphery—someone with broken glass coming at her.

"Nicole!" Remi screamed.

Nicole turned her body to shield Bells, but the pain didn't

come, instead there was the splinter and crack of bone. She whipped around to find her father had caught the attacker's wrist and broken the man's arm with a quick maneuver. But the glass sliced her father's arm instead and blood quickly stained his ruined suit jacket.

Another enthralled attacker dived for them, Lynch's mark at their neck, but they bounced right off a wall of air. Stunned, Nicole's head snapped around, finding Remi's mother by the gate with her hand outstretched. Forcefields were one of a Hearthea's powers and Nicole almost sobbed with relief to see it holding, their attacker sprawled in the chaos.

Lawna Winters wore a fitted top, her black hair pulled up into a bun exposing the beauty of her face. No jewelry glinted against her dark skin except the gold band of her wedding ring. She was soft-featured and sharp-minded and there was a pure kindness in her dark eyes with a note of lethal brilliance. You couldn't tell if she was in her thirties or fifties, but as Remi's mother, Nicole imagined Lawna was somewhere in between.

"Out!" Remi's mother shouted, as their attacker was then thrown across the room by a blast of the forcefield's energy. *"Now."*

Nicole twisted to see Kyan punching the shit out of Lynch. As if he sensed her, Kyan rose and twisted, wincing in pain as his furious eyes met hers. If there was still a shard of crystal in him, the longer it stayed in there, the more likely it was that it could kill him.

The thought was like a stake to her stomach.

"Nicole, go!" he roared.

She flinched at his tone, a hunter's order laced with worry, and something epic seared her chest.

"Let's go," Lawna ordered, hauling her away.

Nicole staggered, torn, but she needed to get Bells out. So, she rushed through the gate Dylan held open, Remi cutting off the defensive Siren sound that kept others at bay and following.

Dylan was still straining to keep the gate open. With a roar, he yelled, "Dad! Lawna!"

They broke from their fights, but the door was slipping. On the other side, Nicole went to pass Bells to Remi and help Dylan keep it open when a hand clamped around the bars and shoved with immortal strength, moving it back by a foot, allowing their parents to get through and Dylan to sag with relief.

Callum.

"I've got them," Callum said to her brother. "Get out of here!"

Dylan faltered a second, eyes locked on the Empyreal with shock and gratitude. Then they were bursting out into the chilled night to find a giant black 4x4 parked in front of the museum, Remi's father in the driver's seat. The moon lit the car and his handsome inky features, and his wide-set shoulders eased at the sight of them.

Nicole had never felt such relief in her life.

"Get in!" he ordered.

37 NICOLE

Their escape protocol had them running to the Siren's Wife pub. It was full for the evening, so Nicole and her family waited at the side entrance, avoiding the noise and people inside.

They'd been exposed to humans. Bells had been bitten, and Lynch had become far too volatile. Looking at her semiconscious sister in their brother's arms, Nicole couldn't bring herself to be furious that Lynch had burned the painting or had the rest of the cipher. Keeping her family safe overrode *everything* else. And if that meant fleeing to the safe house her father had organized for them several miles away, reached through the hidden smuggling tunnels beneath the pub, then that was what they'd do until Kyan dealt with Lynch. She hadn't wanted to leave him in that situation, but Callum was with him, so she had to try and trust he would be all right. The alternative would drive her mad.

She couldn't get his pained look out of her mind.

Instead, she adjusted the backpack on her shoulder and turned to Remi.

"I'll see you soon, okay?" Remi said, the tears in her eyes like stars.

Her parents stood behind her, ready to return to their fortress of an apartment in town.

"Promise me."

"I promise," Nicole swore, heart tearing apart.

Remi turned to Dylan, who held Bells, still semi-unconscious, and clasped them in a double hug.

"Rest up, sweet Bells," Remi said softly, her beautiful face pinched with worry.

She traced a finger down Bells's cheek, Bells's eyes moving behind closed lids.

While Dylan and Nicole had changed and grabbed their emergency supplies, bags, and the most important of their mother's books, their father had managed to get Bells to chew a special herb that had begun to combat the venom and had slathered her neck in a poultice to help draw it out. But they'd still have to carry her from here on out.

"Are you sure you don't want to come with us?" Nicole asked.

Lawna shook her head. "I've rigged our place up. Besides, it's *you* and the painting's secrets Lynch wants. I want to keep watch on the situation from here."

"How did you know to come back?" Remi asked her mother.

Remi's father, Adam, answered in his deep London accent. "Ronan called us. We weren't going to stay away while there's a Specter and two Empyreals in town."

Remi shot Nicole a look and she smiled for the first time in what felt like hours.

"See you on the other side," Lawna said.

"Stay safe," Adam added.

"You too, my friends," Nicole's father said, hugging them both.

Nicole stared as they left and climbed into their car. Then she turned back to her family, numb.

The Siren's Wife's underground smuggling coves were hidden

in the back storeroom under several crates of alcohol. Nicole shoved them out of the way and opened the trapdoor, chilled air breathing up like the breath of a great, cold-blooded beast.

She dropped in first and after a quick moment of weightlessness, slammed into the damp ground below. She reached up so Dylan could lower and drop Bells into her arms. Ignoring the knife of pain in her elbow, she caught her little sister. Dylan helped their father down, then jumped in after them. Bells's hot cheek pressed against Nicole's, and she fought back another wave of tears, trying to support her sister's neck.

Yes, she was furious at Lynch for biting her sister, but most of all she was incandescently angry at *herself*, feeling like she'd somehow let it happen. She hadn't controlled the situation enough. What good was she if she couldn't look after her family?

Dylan went to take Bells again as their father turned on a strong torch that illuminated the darkness.

"No," Nicole hissed, tears in her eyes. This was her fault; she deserved to carry Bells the whole way.

"It's not your fault," her father said.

She choked back the sob. "Yes, it is. Let's just go. The sooner Bells can rest, the better." Then she'd spend all night trying to figure out how to fix this.

They walked in the dark for what felt like hours, their bags of emergency supplies on their backs. Nicole's whole body was in pain; her heart twisted at seeing Remi drive away. She just kept reminding herself that once this was over, they could come back. Neither Callum nor Kyan would leave the humans from the event remembering what they'd witnessed; she just hoped none of the drama ended up on social media.

Besides, they'd need to return for the rest of her mother's books and their weapons. For now, those treasures were locked away with a passcode in the secret library, so even if someone got into the house while they were gone, they would remain hidden.

She was exhausted by the time they emerged through the coves. The edges of the river fanned out before them, black in the nighttime, and a dinghy-like boat was waiting.

Nicole passed Bells to Dylan once he was in the boat and climbed in, too. Her father pulled out a key as she pulled up the anchor and Dylan lay back with Bells against his chest, his arms around her. Then the boat hummed to life and her father began to motor it up the river.

Nicole's breath spiraled, ghostly in the night air as she watched every shadow on the banks and the cold autumn burned her nose. The darkness pressed like a mist, the black water flaring out from the boat in moonlit ripples.

"How did Lynch manage all that?" Dylan asked.

"I think he used the night Nicole got the painting back as some kind of harvesting," her father said. "He revved both Nicole and Kyan up with anger and fear, then used that energy to pull out his crystal and bit the curator to heal his wound. Clearly, he's getting desperate enough to expose us and himself. So, we'll head off tomorrow."

That stole Nicole's attention. "Wait, we're *leaving*? I thought we were just laying low in the safe house?"

"For tonight, we are." Their father looked at her sternly. "But your lives have been threatened and our secret has been shredded. We can't stay here. My only priority is to keep you three safe."

"Where are we going to go?" Nicole asked, panicked.

He didn't answer.

"What about Mum's cipher? How will we know where to go or what to do? Are we just going to make new identities again? Pretend we'd never come across all this?"

"If that's what it takes, yes. We've lived without solving this cipher for a long time. But right now, you're too connected to all this. If we move you out of the equation, hopefully things will cool down, but we'd still have to move anyway. You know this, Nicole: we can't get attached. I'm sorry."

Grief smothered her like an avalanche. She looked at her siblings. Bells was unnervingly still but for her racing pulse and Dylan's jaw was set as he watched the trees gliding past.

Nicole knew he was right. The sensible thing was to leave and go wherever her dad thought they would be safe.

"But there's something else, isn't there?" asked her father. "What else is keeping you here, Nikki? You know we can make a home wherever we go."

"I . . ." Sadness filled her, burning her throat with weakness. "I want to hunt Lynch." She sighed with relief and shame as rage burned her throat. "There, I said it. I want to end him after everything he's threatened, that he even laid a finger on Bells and threatened Remi makes me . . ." She swallowed, tamping down the instincts. Meeting her brother's eyes, she knew he felt the same. "And I know that I can't, but I'm afraid. Afraid of leaving because I've Seen him kill people. What good is it if I See things I can't do anything about? How can I have been so close to Mum's answer, everything she did to keep us hidden, and leave it with *him*? I've failed her!" She slapped her tears away, but the sobs threatened to worsen.

Her father reached out and she let him tug her into a one-armed hug. Sometimes she was sure he could sap her fear away with just the presence of his earth-and-petrichor scent, the way her tears soaked into his cardigan.

"First of all, you've failed no one."

"What about Bells!"

"If anyone failed, it was *me*."

"What—"

"Do you remember what I told you about visions when you were a child?" came her father's rumbled question, changing the topic.

Nicole tried to remember and replied into his shoulder: "You said if you hadn't had the same visions, it wasn't a definite chain of events. That unless *you* Saw a death, it wasn't going to happen."

"Exactly." Her father's face was stony when she pulled back. But the fear about Lynch still hurting Bells and Remi that had been straining inside her relaxed a little. "Lynch has killed, and he will be killed for it, that much I know."

The boat glided in silence for a few moments before he spoke again. "You know, it was exciting for me, the first time your mother and I had to move. The first few times, actually. The idea of dropping everything and going somewhere new, with new identities, new everything. But the excitement only lasted for the first couple of places, and it got harder as we got older. I knew I wanted to be with her for the rest of my life, but after a while the novelty of moving wore off as we had to sacrifice more."

Nicole wiped her damp cheeks. She tugged her coat tighter against the chill. "You've never told me this before."

"I never needed to. It will hurt to move, but you must understand it's necessary. It's who you're with that you have to hold on to. Not the possessions that come and go. And when you feel the strain that makes you think twice about leaving, you need to remember why you're doing what you're doing. Leaving our old home was the hardest decision of my life. But I couldn't lose you all."

Somehow, she remembered snatches of that night. Of driving away from the place her mother had been killed.

It felt eerily similar to this.

"I promised her," continued her father, "that if anything happened to her, I would take you kids away and not look back. I wish I hadn't had to make the choice, but I did. I had to choose between running away with my three babies to keep you hidden, or going after the Empyreal who killed her. Sometimes, it will break your heart to leave, but it will keep you alive."

38 KYAN

It was two o'clock in the morning when Kyan found himself listening to Nicole's soft breathing. He stood in the dark forest surrounding the Palmers' lake house. Her breathing ebbed and flowed like the water lapping against the dock and he found it difficult not to picture her lying in a mess of sheets in the front bedroom.

Lynch's movements within the forest boundary sliced the image away.

Despite the family's impressive evasive maneuvers, Lynch had tracked Bells through the scent of his own venom on her and Kyan had followed.

The fight at the museum had devolved, humans panicking when they realized they were trapped. While Callum had helped the Palmers escape, Lynch had dug his fist into Kyan's wound, reopening it, then swiftly escaped through the bars before they closed, leaving a trail of bitten people in the street. Kyan had to Influence a security guard back to sense to get him to open the gates. Callum had offered to stay behind and Influence the humans.

Kyan gritted his teeth in pain. He'd have time to get the sliver of the crystal out after this. From the rise of his hunter's instincts, he knew that tonight would be the night this chase ended.

He'd known as soon as Nicole and her family planned to get away that Lynch would follow. He was driven. Whether just for answers or the mysteries in the artwork.

Kyan's muscles burned. He wanted this kill *now*. He had proof of Lynch's plans, didn't he? Would that be enough to warrant killing the bastard without his Empyrean power? No prisons had held him, and his deadly calculation was wounding more and more people; risking lives. To Kyan, it was enough.

But his growing hatred was damaging his practicality. He needed to remain level-headed, not get lost in emotions, and yet with every tortured image of Nicole that Lynch played in his mind, a savageness built in Kyan.

He was done playing by the rules.

A distant crack in the brush caught his attention and he stilled, his teeth throbbing with venom, his night hearing amplified.

There was another creature in the woods.

And Lynch was making his way directly to Kyan.

"I know you're there, hunter," came the Specter's voice.

Kyan waited in the forest's darkness, willing his body to complete the transformation, hoping that when he looked in Lynch's eyes he'd see murder, that he'd scent it on the wind.

But when Lynch appeared, Kyan read pure calculation. Ghostly moonlight powdered through the spearing pines and gashed over the Specter, revealing the twisted need in his pale eyes.

But no murder.

"It must be so frustrating," Lynch said. "Knowing that if I just *attempted* to kill something and my body let out that nice little death-scent, you could transform." He bared his teeth in a smile.

"I can kill you in other ways," Kyan warned, stalking around him. "So last chance. Fuck off. Because if you don't, I will hunt you to the ends of this earth."

"I have a few things I need to do before that day comes. And the Wake's dogs can stay out of it."

Agony ripped through Kyan, setting a flare of warning in his mind. He looked down with surprise.

The crystal.

Lynch leered closer as his vision fogged. "Nothing but a surge of magic will get that out of you, not when its poisoning is so intense, not unless you drank a human clean of their blood and plasma. But you wouldn't do that, would you? Because the only humans around here are too far away, and far too *innocent*."

Kyan fought the undertow, buckling. A violent anger forced him to try to stand as Lynch bared his teeth and slipped back into the dark forest.

He wouldn't let the piece of crystal take him out completely. But it would slow him down, and that could make his nightmare of losing someone else a reality.

Because while Lynch still wasn't giving off the kill hormone, he had no idea if the other creature would.

He couldn't get there too late.

Not again.

39 NICOLE

Nicole jerked awake, panic glaring her senses, and took in the unfamiliar surroundings.

Moonlight filtered in through a window to her left and kept the room in a cold glow.

The lake house.

She had no idea what time it had been when they'd arrived, only recognized the dark pines guarding the place like arrowheads, black against the navy sky. She remembered her exhaustion climbing out of the boat.

After coming inside and drifting up to her room, she'd kicked off her lake-soaked clothes and changed into fresh jeans and a T-shirt. Then she'd sat up with the family into the wee hours, watching over Bells and trying to set pieces of the cipher against her mother's bestiary, coming up blank. None of the correlated letters and numbers matched, which meant it wasn't the key they needed to decipher the message.

There were a hundred or more manuscripts in their house that could be the code. But she couldn't figure that out without more options or without it being safe enough to return to Estwood.

And then there was the worrying about Kyan; wondering if she could call him to check in but not sure if Lynch could somehow track it.

She hadn't meant to fall asleep. She'd wanted to plan, to figure out what the hell she was supposed to do in this mess, but she must have drifted off until a vision woke her.

It came back with sudden clarity.

He's found us.

Nicole raced to the window and flung open the curtains. No one stood there, unlike in her vision, and yet she sensed the danger creeping in, on their haven in the forest, and knew the Specter was lurking somewhere. Waiting.

But Kyan was out there, too.

Nicole let the curtain fall, shielding herself from the chill. She scrambled back into her bed and buried herself in the still-warm covers, trying not to think about what she'd Seen.

Lynch was going to kill Kyan to get to her.

She was wrong. She had to be. Kyan would be *fine*. He was perfectly able to figure out the impending attack before the Specter took him by surprise. Even if he'd been hurt by the crystal, it was illogical to consider that Kyan would be defeated by Lynch alone. He was an ancient warrior with years of experience.

But the vision swept over her again. Blurred, frenzied visions of Lynch overpowering Kyan. Kyan lying in the dark, unforgiving forest. Bloodless. *Limbless.* The dawn flickering in his glazed eyes like the dying fire of his soul.

Then the Specter would be free to kill again.

She shoved it away. Surely she was mistaken; perhaps it had been a nightmare? But she'd caught the glimpse of her eyes in the window-pane when she'd opened the curtains: bloodshot from a fading vision.

Not all visions came true, she knew that. Her father had reminded her, and Kyan had mentioned how the Wake use Seers to locate dangerous creatures for Empyreals to hunt. Visions didn't always come to fruition if someone was able to intervene. And yet she couldn't imagine how Kyan would be overpowered. . . .

So why did she See it?

And why did she See two shadows over his body?

Not Callum, some other creature.

Horror steeped through her blood like ice. *That's* how Kyan would be overpowered: he was going to be ambushed. Lynch must have summoned something else, planned something they'd missed.

She had to ask her father if he Saw it, too, then they could warn Kyan.

She pulled on a worn jumper and flung open the bedroom door, a surprised gasp catching in her throat. She raised her fist to attack, but Dylan caught it.

"Jeez, jumpy, are we?" He stood in the doorway like he'd sensed her scrambling around, a sharpened rounders bat under his arm, still dressed. "You didn't think you could get out of the house without one of us realizing, did you? Sorry, I'm not letting you run out into the forest after a psychopathic Specter." Dylan shook his head. "Silly."

"Move, Dylan, this is important, there's something inside me—" Nicole tugged at her jumper uncomfortably. "It's drawing me out there. I need to at least warn him." Kyan needed her, whether he knew it or not. "Help me signal him."

Dylan frowned and Nicole strode past him, pulling the bat out from under his arm. He hastily followed her.

"What is wrong with you?" Dylan hissed.

342

Nicole paused. She didn't know, but the thought of Kyan dying was torturing her.

Dylan jumped in front of her, his face stony. "No."

She didn't have time for this. "Listen to me. Something is wrong, I can feel it."

"If it's wrong, then you know not to go rushing out after it. Where's your sense, Nicole?" His eyes desperately searched hers.

She gripped the bat. Of course he wouldn't understand. He couldn't feel the searing in her chest, building like a fire until it would consume her.

Before he could say he was with her or against her, she hurried past him.

"For god's sake, Nicole—" Dylan began.

But as they came to the ground floor, the front door slammed shut. Nicole froze as Dylan skidded into her.

There, framed by the glass in the door, was Bells, drifting out into the night like a wraith. Her sister's pale-pink pajamas were almost white in the moonlight, her hair half unfurling from her plait.

Nicole blinked. Was it an illusion? She looked into the living room to find her father asleep and Bells missing.

She didn't wait; she ripped open the front door and yelled. "Bells, get in here, *now*!"

But her sister didn't stop.

Hours had passed since Bells had been bitten. The venom had worn off, but Lynch must be drawing her through the short-term connection formed by the bite.

Dylan cursed and ran out toward their sister.

Nicole bolted after him. "Dylan, grab her, it's a trap."

343

"Bells!" boomed their father from the living room.

For the fleeting second before they were ambushed, Nicole felt weightless as she ran with Empyrean speed. She ignored the bite of pain in her elbow. That didn't matter. Nothing mattered like getting to her siblings.

The bone-jarring collision came out of nowhere.

Nicole barely had a moment to understand who she'd run into when she was flung over their hard shoulder. She gagged as the impact jabbed into her stomach, the rounders bat slipping from her fingers. She struggled to gasp in air and thrashed at the person who held her, scenting that vile smell.

Lynch.

Nicole reared back, twisting to see him. His pale skin looked translucent in the moonlight and something about it made her feel viciously sick. She tried to get out of his hold, but he clamped a hand around her injured elbow and she screamed with pain.

Dylan had scooped up Bells and turned back to the house, filling Nicole with relief. But then movement behind him flickered— another creature dressed in black with their hooded head low and it dived for her brother. Its face was sliced with darkness so all Nicole could see was the raw white of its neck.

"Don't you touch him!" she spat, getting her arms around Lynch's neck so she could rip it clean off. "I'll kill you!"

"Nicole!" shouted her father. A gunshot ripped through the woods from the lake house, cracking and echoing off the lake, splintering a tree beside the new creature and allowing Dylan to skid back toward the house with Bells.

She felt a blast of magic rip under her skin—no, "magic" was too gentle a word for the force that crashed through her entire body, slowing the blood, the muscles, the adrenaline. It didn't harm her, just filled her with a dire prophetic feeling.

As if death was here.

It stole through her with such intensity Lynch staggered backward with fear, as if he saw a flash of his own death.

The blast had come from her father, and whatever it was, it wasn't the power of a Seer.

So, with Nicole still over his shoulder, Lynch ran.

Branches whipped past her, and the air was ripped from her lungs. Icy wind seared her bare skin and fury coursed in her veins.

Then she was thrown from Lynch's shoulder. She was momentarily weightless again, her stomach lurching before she crashed hard into the bracken.

"Let's make sure you can't keep running around with that kind of speed, shall we?" Lynch said, before he brought her bat down, and broke her leg.

KYAN

Kyan was close but could sense something terrible. He ran, knowing that with every stride he was wedging the piece of crystal deeper along its meandering journey through his body. He could feel the internal bleeding.

But it didn't matter.

Nicole had been taken.

At first, he didn't recognize the feeling that stung his heart and pushed him to run faster than he ever had.

He hadn't felt panic in centuries.

Twigs scraped at his skin, streaking his arms and face with blood from the speed he moved. The night was a new predator, sinking its teeth into any chance of Nicole escaping.

Now he understood why the Wake encouraged them away from memories and family . . . from partners. If you had family, love, you had fear.

And fear for Nicole felt like the only thing that could kill him.

He could feel the other creature: its dark, unearthly presence mocking him. If only he could have killed Lynch when he first came to Estwood, then none of this would have happened. And somehow another supernatural had gotten past his defenses without him even knowing. It shouldn't have been possible.

Then Nicole screamed such a broken sound of pain that something fundamental in him fractured and turned wild.

When Kyan burst through the trees, Nicole was the first thing he saw, crumpled on the floor, clutching her leg.

Agony lanced into his side like a spear.

"Kyan!" Nicole screamed.

"Ah, my executioner," crooned Lynch, his voice thick with scorn. "Joined us at last. How is that crystal feeling? I'm sure the sliver is taking a nice, long journey through every organ in your body."

"No!" Nicole shouted, thrashing.

Kyan bared his teeth and took a step to go to her, but the pain cut him at his knees and his own strangled cry startled him as the world descended swiftly into darkness.

40 NICOLE

Lynch had brought her to a cliff away from the lake house. Whatever blast of magic her father had sent their way seemed to have deeply unnerved him. He was making up for it by pacing with angry strides and rubbing at his temple, as if to scrub away unwelcome thoughts.

"I must say, your family has been a fucking menace. Daddy's bullets sure were hard to get out."

Nicole bared her teeth in a smile. "Good."

He smiled back. "So the few people I almost drained of plasma to give me strength have you to thank for their wounds."

Nicole felt sick. She needed to get up and get Kyan away from here.

Her leg should be swiftly healing, but it *wasn't*. It must have been the overuse of tonics blocking her Empyrean powers and healing abilities, the same reason why her neck hadn't healed, except these were wounds inflicted without magic. Her elbow at least should be better. Did that mean she wouldn't heal at all until she stopped the tonics?

"What's the goal, here, Lynch?" she asked, hoping to buy time for her and Kyan. "Kill me?" Rage sharpened her instincts, even as she fought against the bone-splintered agony in her leg.

If he tried to kill her, he'd release the kill hormone and it would be near impossible to stop the transformation. But maybe she could resist long enough for Kyan to get that shard of the crystal out. In the meantime, she would fight Lynch every step of the way. She wouldn't make it easy for him.

At least my family is safe. She'd seen them come together as Lynch had taken her.

But Kyan . . .

"Nicole." His voice was ragged with pain. He lay close to the edge of the cliff, gripping his bloodied side as it pulsed, dark and glistening.

The crystal was making its way through his organs. Organs that wouldn't heal because he was in the middle of a transformation.

Nicole's heart smashed against her ribs. Watching him struggle felt out of time with everything else. He was the person she'd come to know as powerful, infuriatingly so. *Immortal.*

Now he was reduced to writhing in the soil. The agony in his face and body strained her more than she thought possible. She could feel the immortal presence of his power waning.

The vision she'd had was coming true. And it showed her how much she'd come to care for him, because she couldn't bear it.

Lynch was in front of her in a second. He gripped her jaw, hand smothering her face as he pulled her up from the ground. Nicole thrashed, but it was useless, he didn't even seem to feel it.

"Don't," he spat. "Or I'll put him in even more pain thanks to your handy little crystal."

The veins in Kyan's neck stood proud under his skin, his stomach, now smeared with blood, pushing out and clenching again with each breath.

"His body's pain and attempts to heal overrode his Empyrean senses just long enough for me to make tonight possible. I've been hunted by Empyreals before, my dear, so I've learned a few tricks. One more reason why being on my side would only help you. *I'm* the one with the answers you need. But tell me, why *have* you been drawn to him? I thought at first it was the danger he posed, but let's be honest, I'm more deadly."

"Perhaps because he's a good man," Nicole said, realizing how true it was.

Lynch laughed and waved a hand toward Kyan. "Goodness is overrated. Besides, he's assassinated thousands of creatures, snuffed them from the earth."

Nicole trembled, her power scorching her insides with an overwhelming, vicious need. "He doesn't kill for sport, he does it to protect. You are *nothing* compared to him. I doubt you've ever been good in your life."

Lynch grabbed her and his moist lips grazed her stinging cheek. "I could be your worst fucking nightmare, Nicole. Don't tempt me. You and I? We're kindred spirits, so don't try to piss me off when I'm trying to help you."

"Help me how?" she gritted out.

"Help you let go. Let go of your disguise. You don't need to hide who you are with me, like you do with him."

Warning bells began in her head. She scrunched her eyes shut as images flickered through her mind: the many ways he planned to destroy the others. Her first vision of him returned with full force and a lance of pain shot through her as power reared under her skin.

Let me take you over, it breathed.

"I brought you a little present," Lynch said.

The other creature moved from the forest; shadows draped over it like a safety net until moonlight slanted over its eyes and confusion pierced her fear.

The . . . *curator?*

"What did you do to him?" she demanded.

Lynch secured her with an iron grip.

The curator didn't look that different, but she could feel it. He wasn't a Specter.

He was something *worse.*

"I made him," Lynch said.

"But . . . Specters don't have that ability." She'd heard of humans mutating and transforming into Empyreals when in grave supernatural danger, but nothing like this. Nothing like humans *becoming* creatures.

"The Wake, my dear, have a lot to answer for. They've developed all sorts of macabre ways to skew this world in their favor. You think *I'm* bad? They made me what I am, and through scoping out their secrets I discovered how to make the curator into something of his own twisted ilk. They'll do anything to make sure they can trigger the Wild Hunt. What else does that hellish landscape in the *Dante* painting look like? A vicious hunt, run by the Wake, killing all manner of creatures, including Empyreals who disobey them?"

"No," Kyan panted, "that's not possible. They wouldn't summon the Wild Hunt; they're trying to prevent it."

"Are they?" Lynch asked, sarcasm dripping from his words. "God, you're so disgustingly naive. Haven't you noticed creatures getting more vicious lately?"

Lynch's words seemed to pierce something in Kyan: he had, she realized. And if this was true, if *Lynch* knew about this from working

351

on the inside of the Wake, it meant that her mother's reconnaissance had been right.

But what was driving the Wake to do this? Who were they? And why were they keeping these realizations from Empyreals . . . unless they didn't trust them not to defect if they found out? The thought both horrified and heartened her. If there were more Empyreals like Kyan, more hunters who might want to resist . . .

And yet, none of it would matter if she couldn't get them out of this.

Nicole looked at the curator. Surely there was some way to heal him, reverse this—this—transformation? But whatever he'd become seemed unstable. She could feel the new pouring waves of horror coming off him—ones that made her body twitch and power lurch around her solar plexus.

"How did you do this?" Kyan growled.

Cold malice and pride glittered in Lynch's eyes as he prowled over to Kyan. Nicole went to crawl closer, worried about Kyan's proximity to the edge of the cliff, but a knife of pain shot through her leg.

"The night I stabbed you with the crystal," Lynch said, "it severed your ability to locate me for a few hours so I infected, for lack of a better word, the curator. But I knew my little experiment wouldn't finalize itself for a few days, and then you organized tonight's little soiree as if just for me, just in time."

That was why he'd said on the night when they got the painting back, that he'd return to her in a few days.

"I'd like to claim I did it solely for this moment," Lynch continued, "but that's not quite true. When I got to Westmoore and found her dead, I couldn't get *inside*. The damned Seer had warded every inch of the manor against theft. Which is why *you* could stroll right in: you didn't want to steal anything. So, I needed someone to get past the supernatural wards. I needed a human. Initially, I only used him to take the painting. Though, I'll admit, getting into his head and using him to kill the Finfolk was an unexpected bonus. The poor creature had dragged itself from the water, across the beach, and up to the manor that night to warn Westmoore of her demise, to warn her about *me*." He smirked. "But it meant I then had the blood I needed for a little art restoration of my own. In the end it felt like it would be a good idea to have a nice backup plan."

Nicole shook her head. Lynch had gotten into the curator's head and walked him through the wards into Westmoore Manor, allowing him to steal the painting and escape.

But surely if he'd killed the Finfolk, she would have smelled the kill hormone on him? *No*, she realized, *because he was still human when he did it*. He wouldn't have had a kill scent.

"So now, my dear lovely Nicole. It's time for the grand finale."

The curator seethed and twitched and a deep, sudden instinct cleaved through her core.

The Empyreal, the truest, deepest part of her, was ready to awaken.

Lynch came back over to her, the tone of his voice turning intimate. He crouched before her and she was struck by his cold grace, his insouciant demeanor.

"Do it," he whispered, eyes dark with longing and fascination. "Show him what you are."

Nicole's stomach dropped. "No," she whispered. "Don't do this."

"Nicole," Lynch tutted, lifting one of his long-fingered hands and tapping it under her chin. "Don't be afraid."

"I'm not afraid," she growled. "I'm *angry*." She was *viciously* angry. How had it come to this? How did he have such a good idea of how desperate her insides were to remake her into something so dangerous?

"I know," he said, lips curving up. He loomed closer in the darkness. "I can scent emotions, and yours are so . . ."—he hissed in a breath—"palpable. I knew you were something special the moment we had our first little chat."

"I can't will a transformation," she whispered.

Lynch came closer, like they were two awful confidants.

She still had a chance to hide this from Kyan. "Just let us go. You have the cipher. You'll figure it out." The part of her that had strived for so long to find her mother's clues twisted to say those words, but she had no choice. The game was up.

"I don't think so, Nicole, and I know the way Empyreals work. That's why I brought *him*."

Lynch glanced at the curator who was pacing in the dark between the trees, as if the moonlight was too much for him.

"*I'm* not going to kill Kyan to trigger your transformation, *he* is. He's too hungry, Nicole, look at his poor face."

Horror turned her blood to ice. "No," she whispered. But she could feel it, like invisible waves that threatened to take her under. The scent that was calling to her Empyrean power was growing more twisted and vicious.

She tried to move away, but Lynch grabbed her, his cold grip bruising.

"Yes," he said.

If she could hold off the sickly rising in her soul until Kyan got the crystal out and killed Lynch, it would all be all right. She just needed to resist attacking, otherwise she'd snap. But it was so hard. So hard not to cry.

To not rip Lynch's head off in pure fury.

"If I transform," she whispered, "he'll just take me away."

"No," Lynch said, stroking the hair from her face. "He'll be dead. No one will know."

"What about Callum?" she tried. "He's another Empyreal."

A flash of fear went through Lynch's eyes, there and gone in an instant. It was the first real glimpse of vulnerability she'd ever seen in him. *Why?* What scared him so much about Callum?

"We'll be gone before he can find us."

KYAN

Knife-sharp pain seared Kyan's abdomen and warnings glared bright in his body, flashing over his vision as he struggled to stay conscious. His fingers kept threatening to go limp over the wound. He felt them as a cool, distant stroke.

Useless.

Nicole was trying to give him time and keep Lynch talking, but it felt like the crystal was seared onto every nerve, only to tear each as it moved. He could feel it getting closer to his heart. It would kill him if he didn't get it out in the next few minutes. But he had no way to, save from stabbing himself in the chest and trying to dig it out.

Kyan glared at the curator, who sneered over him.

He couldn't believe he'd missed it. The *curator*, made into something new? In his entire life Kyan had never heard of a human being turned into a creature. Mutating into an Empyreal, yes. But this? And the suggestion that the Wake had developed the secret to this . . .

Was it possible, or was Lynch lying? But then, why would he? He had the upper hand.

"Why would the Wake want another Dark Age?" Kyan managed, staring up at the curator, trying to figure out what he might be. But his body's senses were too loud with warnings: *Can't heal.*

Can't heal.

"Is that why they want Westmoore's paintings?" Nicole asked, picking up on his desire to bide time. "Because they showed the Wild Hunt?"

He hated that he couldn't move. Hated that memories were coming back to him now, of all moments. Flashes of him racing through the mist to get to the Druids, of the scent of Nicole's blood,

356

her scream still ringing in his ears . . .

He needed a knife, but there was only one strapped to his ankle.

"I knew you were a smart one, Nicole," Lynch said. "Yes. Yes, I think that's it. That, and whatever lovely little message is hidden in the cipher. But of course, Westmoore fucked us over with that, didn't she? Tell me, did it feel good to help her die?"

Confusion struggled through the haze of Kyan's pain. "What?"

"I didn't kill her," Nicole said. Her eyes darted to him, but he read some truth in them, along with the grief.

No. *No*, that couldn't be right. If she'd killed Westmoore, the kill scent would have been all over her. He would have transformed to hunt her; he would have known.

"I suppose you didn't, if you want to play semantics. I'll admit, the storm was smart." Lynch turned, blood glinting on his teeth. "You should have seen it sooner, Empyreal." He tsked.

"You're lying," Kyan said.

"I'm surprised," Lynch said, mock pity in his voice as he came toward Kyan. Kyan stilled his efforts to angle his bloody hand closer to his ankle. "Didn't you check Westmoore's body?"

He hadn't; the Wake had dealt with it since it was a supernatural's body. They hadn't let him see it. "They said Westmoore died of natural causes."

Lynch laughed. "Of course they did. They didn't want you looking too hard." He grinned, swanning back over to Nicole, feeding off their worry. "So, tell us, Nicole. Why did you give her the key to her death?"

A pulse of pain had Kyan convulsing, but he knew it wasn't just this revelation. It was a sense of betrayal. Despite everything she'd kept from him, he hadn't expected this.

"She knew the Wake would send you to torture her; to try and get information from her mind," Nicole said to Lynch, her gaze tracking the curator's increasingly frustrated movements. "So, she asked my father to make a poison. To give her a peaceful death if she ever needed one. So you couldn't kill her first."

No. The Wake wouldn't use a creature assassin. Kyan had doubted their methods before, knew of times when they'd done things and given him missions he'd thought twice about, but this? And yet, deep down, her words stirred the theories; the discomfort he'd felt in their employ for centuries. Always little things he'd mostly brushed off, but filed away because he felt the good outweighed the rest.

"How?" Kyan demanded.

"By brewing a death-flower only a talented herbalist could make," Lynch said. "I'll admit, I wasn't sure who could have made the flower, but the storm that night didn't blow away all the evidence like Westmoore had hoped. Rain splattered the rest of the pollen onto her cuff. A little detail, but a crucial one."

"Why did they send you?" Kyan asked, feeling his grip on consciousness slipping away as his fingers brushed the hilt of the knife. He fought it. He needed to know. He needed to *fight.*

One hand pulled free the weapon, hiding it as the other dug back into the wound at his side, but it only made the pain burn brighter, and he could feel the bleeding worsen inside.

"Westmoore had information they wanted. But when I got there and found the body, I realized they'd send an Empyreal after me to clean up the mess, so, I got myself a little leverage. But you *refused* to tell them. So here we are. Only I know the secret," Lynch taunted. "I know the Wake will pay handsomely to learn what it is.

"And you'll be dead."

41 NICOLE

"But you, my dear," Lynch said, coming back over to Nicole. "Let me tell you how this is going to go. You"—he lowered his voice, amused—"*transform*. And then we decipher the code and use it to be free of the Wake forever. He would never do that. He would never leave them; he's been too indoctrinated. This whole time he could have stopped me, he could have cut off my head to keep you safe, but no."

Kill him, her power urged. She wanted to. *Oh god,* she wanted to. If she did, they'd be safe tonight. But then what? Kyan would take her away.

It was still a damn sight better running from him than allowing him to die.

That she couldn't let happen. Because what she'd said about him before, she meant.

Lynch cupped her face, frowning at her. Imploring. "For five minutes, just think about yourself, Nicole. No one else. Just you and me. You want this. I can feel the huntress shaking you apart from the inside. Don't you want to be free?"

He stroked her cheek, tracing through the tear that had spilled there. She was shuddering, her teeth almost chattering from the *need*. It seemed to crawl through her the longer she was in proximity to the curator.

But if she didn't stop fighting this, Kyan would die.

Another cool tear slid down her face.

She could wait a little longer. Maybe Callum was nearby. Maybe he could save them, and she could keep her secret. Her home. The safety of her family. The promise of a *life* that was hers. And Kyan would be alive.

Impatience flittered through Lynch's pale eyes.

"I could use an Empyreal on my side. The Wake will surely send more Empyreals after me. You could be my huntress. My protector. 'If you will comply with my conditions, I will leave them and you at peace; but if you refuse, I will glut the maw of death, until it be satiated with the blood of your remaining friends.'" The *Frankenstein* quote sharpened his features, his tone. And he must have read the bleakness in hers. The resistance. So he sighed. "I think it's time we begin," Lynch said to the curator.

At that moment, Kyan lifted up a knife to his chest, as if to cut into it and take out the crystal shard. Lynch flashed a hand toward what had once been the curator as if giving him permission and, like a leash had been snapped, the creature started for Kyan.

The curator's foot came down on Kyan's hand before he could use the knife, the blade falling from his grip.

"No, please," she whispered, tears blurring her vision, her throat hot with fear. "I can't. Stop!" She scrambled to get up, gasping in pain.

Lynch watched, his pale eyes full of satisfaction.

"I'll help you with the cipher, we'll do it together!" Nicole tried, scrambling closer.

Lynch's eyes narrowed. "We can do that after, when you're not so . . ." His gaze slid to Kyan. "Distracted."

"The Wake are already hunting you down," she said. "You kill an Empyreal and they'll double their efforts—"

Anger flashed over his face. "You forget, Nicole, I've killed before, I'll kill again. At least I accept what I am."

He nodded to the curator, who turned to Kyan and kicked his bleeding side.

Nicole screamed as the creature's jaw cracked open to reveal Specter-like teeth: needle-like, long, horrific.

One more stomp like that would likely push the crystal into Kyan's heart.

It would kill him.

And the creature knew it.

In that split second, as her instincts narrowed in on that change, as the scent of deathly intention blasted through her exhausted defenses, Nicole realized the extent of the control she'd tried to keep on her life, on everyone around her, on *what happened next*. Maybe she was part Seer, and it knocked the breath out of her and stripped her down to the bones of her fears. But she was also an Empyreal, and that part of her was strong and hungry and powerful.

That part of her would eat Lynch alive if she let it.

And it wanted to.

She could not control her power. She'd smothered herself by pretending to be human; she'd built a cage around her true nature until she'd doubted everything, feared herself. Fought it. And it had caused so many issues, so much pain.

She didn't want to be in control anymore. She didn't want to pretend.

Trust yourself, her mother's books had told her.

This wasn't about giving Lynch what he wanted, this was about not fighting herself anymore.

Nicole didn't feel Lynch's vise grip, or the bursting of blood vessels in her arm, or the searing pain in her broken leg. It was the last daring gaze into Kyan's eyes that reminded her what she was; the imminent threat of his death that gave her body permission. But it was her mind, her soul, that allowed it.

I trust you, she told herself, and that thrashing thing inside her stilled beneath her recognition.

I trust y—

Its unfurling made the world thicken with impulse. Her power contained her suddenly, drawing her into herself until she was burning from its heat. Until a lash of panic made her feel like she was drowning and fear engulfed her so quickly she couldn't breathe.

Then the varnish of her mortal canvas made way for what was really beneath.

Kyan roared, but it sounded distant.

A moment followed that changed her completely. A moment of lost time, of transformation, where she floated in warm and midnight waters. Suddenly her body was no longer heavy with the Empyreal birthing itself in her veins and it flooded her in a bank of warm *rapture.*

Her leg healed with a distant snapping sound.

Molten venom flooded into her mouth; power pumped her muscles with energy and strength, and her mind with knowledge she couldn't have comprehended before. Ice stung her veins as she shoved Lynch so hard, he cracked through the bark of a tree.

She threw herself at the curator with a shattering scream, tackling him away from Kyan. He buckled beneath her as great fangs curved from her mouth, long and sharp and deadly.

Her tears dried; her Empyreal awakened.

And her teeth plunged into the curator's neck.

42 NICOLE

Relief sank through Nicole's fangs and deep into her core as blood flecked across her face.

She muffled the curator's shriek instinctively, crushing her hand to his mouth. Euphoria drugged her, muting his scrambling.

He slashed with sharp nails, kicked her hard enough something cracked inside, but with the blood in her mouth and her venom pulsing into his body, she barely felt it. She barely heard it, either, over her power's urge to—

Protect, protect, protect.

Snatches of Kyan printed in her brain: his eyes wide with horror and a fury that made her blood stagger cold in her veins. She closed her own so she wasn't meeting that gaze as her limbs contracted and held the curator to her like a snake. When her teeth cut his skin and blood gushed into her mouth and over her clothes, she felt *good*. *This* was what she was supposed to do, and all the tension and the pain of resisting slipped away.

But it was a vicious kind of hunger. The tear of skin and tendons and her body's urge to pull them apart.

"Isn't that better?" Lynch asked roughly from where he'd pushed himself up.

Nicole jolted, noticing something wetting the hair at her temple.

The curator's tears.

She pulled back, the sensitive bone of her fangs burning in the cold air, so starkly different from being buried in hot blood. The raw, glistening wound in his neck was coated with clear, burning venom, but would take a little longer to affect him than it would a human.

Somewhere deep inside, she felt a distant horror.

Was he savable?

And yet the kill hormone pulsed and breathed off him.

Nicole got up to go to Kyan, feeling both shaky and energized; more alive than she'd ever been.

"Ah, ah," Lynch warned, coming closer to stop her. He moved choppily, the tree behind him splintered from where she'd thrown him.

She smacked him down with a hard backhand and he crashed into the forest floor, stunned. Nicole pinned him to the bracken and pure bliss gutted through her to *finally* have him in her grip. To be ready to kill after everything he'd done.

"Didn't you think I would fight?" she asked with a laugh that didn't sound like her own. "You actually thought I'd go quietly? Your most idiotic mistake was that you *bit my sister.*"

Lynch rolled his eyes and yet now in this awakened form she could scent something subtle coming off him.

Fear.

"Yes, I did to prove a point. Point proven, too, I think. I'll do whatever it takes to get that answer. Just look." He fanned a hand out at Kyan. "Almost dead. *Him.* The Wake's best Empyreal."

"Your second mistake," Nicole said, leaning closer, "was that you tried to kill Kyan."

No one hurts him, came the Empyrean voice in the back of her mind.

He's mine.

Lynch's eyes narrowed and the curator grabbed her ankle, hauling her backward. He dragged her through the soil and smacked his fist into her kneecap. Pain lanced through her senses.

"Let's not get carried away," Lynch growled. "But if I have to beat some sense into you I will."

Nicole lashed out as Lynch and the curator fought her rabidly, quick and savage, their confusion making them desperate. When they bit her, she bit back with curved, razor teeth, finally ripping into Lynch the way her body had wanted to since she'd sensed him in the alley of the museum. The plasma's power flooded her system, but she had little time to appreciate its strange pleasure.

Her world blurred into the spray of blood and slice of her nails into the meat of muscle, the struggle of limbs and the flash of Lynch's harried fury. She sank into power and impulse, away from all fear and pain, headlong into the rush and flood of everything she had wondered about for years, fighting them as much as they did her with an inner knowledge of where to bite, where to break. Realizing distantly that, though she was tearing through skin and screaming their senses half numb with supernatural shrieks, she wouldn't have survived this as a human.

She would have been dead already.

It was another Baobhan Sith scream lacerating her throat that dimly informed her what her body was doing. It was shifting back and forth between two transformations, merging her into something with the blood hunger of a Specter and death-hunger of a Baobhan Sith, depending on which of her adversaries tried to tear into her.

She couldn't completely comprehend it. Could only feel the immediate viciousness of these new appetites . . . and Kyan. His distress was like a gleaming wire through the dark.

When she came back to herself, Lynch was dragging himself away, and the curator had finally stilled after she'd loosed an ear-splitting Baobhan Sith scream inches from his face. A scream, she knew, that had burst his organs from the inside.

Nicole shoved him off and rose, limbs oiled with supernatural power.

There were strange, deep tugs in her body. As if the muscle and blood and power wanted to congeal in all the places she'd been battered half to death. Her body slowly adjusted to the other creature it needed to kill: Lynch, who still scrabbled gently in the dirt, half-paralyzed by her venom.

But she had something else to do first.

She splashed through puddles of blood until she stood over Kyan.

He was cast in moonlight with a dark spatter over his face and hair. She knelt beside him, cupping his chin gently, vaguely noticing her nails were so long they were like sharp, disjointed fingers.

And they were slick with blood.

He was so handsome. So . . . confused. His jaw was tight; that needling frown in his brow as always. Somewhere inside, she felt a strong, warm emotion that almost hurt. And something else— bright as the Empyrean fire. Epic and loving. Distantly, she thought to smile so he didn't fear her.

"It's okay," she said softly. "I'm here."

Kyan's eyes widened with pain when her other hand met the wound on his chest, finding that he'd used a knife to stab up under his ribs and tried to pull the crystal shard out with his weakening strength. That emotion seared through her so strongly her eyes blurred with wetness.

Nicole bent, pressing a slight kiss to his mouth, leaving a smear of blood and venom on his lips.

Then she pressed her nails into his wound.

Kyan's body arced off the ground with a gritted cry but she held him down with her other hand, and felt it—the crystal. She concentrated as Kyan panted, his eyes dark with pain and wide on hers. Then, as if seeking another Specter, the crystal moved away from his heart and up toward her. Her nails clamped around it, and she sent enough energy into him that his body tissues didn't reattach to it, before pulling it free.

Kyan's eyes rolled back and he fell swiftly unconscious as his body began to heal and his chest wound sealed over. Nicole ripped the burning sliver from where it had sealed to her hand, tearing skin with it, and flung it over the cliff.

Then she turned her attention to Lynch.

The Specter lay prone in the dirt, half in a dark puddle of blood. His body was a mess of severed muscle, torn skin, and bites she didn't even remember making. But he was still alive.

He threw a frantic glance to the curator, who had stopped convulsing, his heartbeat silent. She wanted to feel guilt and hoped that maybe somehow, she did. But it did not make it through the bliss of transformation.

So, she turned all that hatred onto Lynch.

Her body morphed, more slowly this time. She didn't know what Lynch had made the curator, but she knew she'd become some kind of mutated mix of a Specter and a Baobhan Sith to kill it. And now she was transforming again.

It allowed her to appreciate it, stalking toward him in the dark.

Her throat soothed as her teeth extended, as her body transformed into Lynch's predator. A Specter, yes, but there was something beneath it that gave her pause. Lynch's power was a twisted one, so she was matching it.

She couldn't much feel her wounds, only the blood cooling on her body. Sound was becoming sharper: people were running in the woods, shouting for *Nicole*.

"The only way to stop me is to kill me," Nicole said darkly, her throat razoring with borrowed power. She fell onto Lynch, digging her knees into his shoulders to pin him. "Try it. Just think about it. Wouldn't you like to? Wouldn't it make you feel better to rip my throat out? I *bested you*. Playing Frankenstein didn't work out, after all."

He only stared at her with hatred.

She laughed, a torn, sharp sound. "I've realized something about you, Lynch. About me. I always thought being a Seer would mean I would be a weaker Empyreal. But it only made me stronger. Do you know why?"

He bared his teeth.

"Because I've just learned that, while the kill scent of your old victims dissipated after some time, enough that other Empyreals could no longer scent it and transform—allowing you to evade other Empyreals and even Kyan—*I* can scent it on you in those visions. So even if you never decide to kill me, or kill again, I can kill you *right now*."

Her family had no idea her power would be able to do this, because Empyreals like her—Empyreals who also had Seer abilities—were unheard of. But now, after fearing, after wondering, she knew

369

that being both a Seer and Empyreal was not a weakness, but a strength.

"So, before I kill you, I want to know: Are you going to give me the rest of the cipher?"

Even though his eyes were glossed and white with fear, he snarled his answer, "No."

"Are you sure?"

"Are *you*? You go down this path with nothing but your family to help and the Wake will find you. Your Empyreal won't protect you. There's no going back. You were not made by some kindly deity; you were made by the Goddess of Death. And She does not sup once."

Nicole paused. Distantly she felt disturbed by that. That . . . worried her.

But it also felt *right*.

Nicole leaned closer. "Then I hope She takes my offering."

"Wait," Lynch whimpered, his human-sounding plea making it through her killing haze. She frowned at the unfamiliar tone and opened her bloodied mouth to say more, but it choked in her throat at a great wet crack. She looked down at her body, to find Lynch had stabbed the sharpened bat into her stomach.

With a snarl, Nicole ripped it out, and sank her teeth into his neck.

Images and memories seared her mind. Specters were capable of seeing a person's memories, she remembered. And as he began to buck beneath her, she worked backward through his mind; felt him bite her sister with a lurch of her own clear, bright hatred.

Then she rewound back in time to see him smearing the *Dante* painting in Finfolk blood, the emerald liquid turning translucent and the cipher revealing itself beneath, watching as he scratched it down in a little book that he'd memorized days later.

Then he was standing over Westmoore's dead body on the beach at night, swiping his finger through the pollen and thinking, *You smart old bitch.*

Nicole went to pull out of the memories, but they drew her farther back.

Into Lynch's last kills, collectors and artists pleading at him to stop.

Into the minimalistic halls and white rooms of the Wake's secret quarters, with their circular symbol on a fogged glass door. Getting instructions, seeing them use and mutate creatures into worse versions of themselves. Feeling it being done to *him*, and distantly realizing this was how Lynch was so strong, so vicious: he'd been meddled with unnaturally.

Nicole ripped away, blood streaking down her chin and she gasped in a great rattling breath.

"I wish," Lynch said as he began to buck and convulse from her venom, "it didn't have to be this way."

Nicole lifted the bat he'd stabbed into her and brought it down into Lynch's chest. "I don't," she snarled.

Then she grabbed his head, and ripped it off.

43 KYAN

Kyan's eyes burned when they opened and his entire body ached.

He jerked up, finding his wound with a gasp. It was sealing, healing, but it felt like a chunk of him had been pulled out. His stomach. His heart.

His hand lifted to his lips where they tingled with venom. He wiped it off and struggled upright.

Pieces of bodies were strewn over the bloody soil. Lynch's dead eyes, from his headless body, stared off to the edge of the cliff.

To Nicole.

Power throbbed off of her. Kyan could feel the killer in her veins, the body made for metamorphosis.

The Empyreal.

Blood soaked her clothes and her petite figure shook from the withdrawal of abilities that were quickly nestling back into her soul. The hot skin under her nails steaming gently in the autumn air.

Then she turned.

Her eyes were wild and blood-dark, a sated, devilish color. Kyan froze as she shrank into an attack position and venom dripped down her chin from shrinking fangs. They were glossy in the moonlight, sliding back into her mouth.

And yet he was relieved. He was so fucking relieved that she was safe; *alive*. Something had cracked inside him watching her get beaten. He'd managed to retrieve his knife, but hadn't been able to dig out the shard. So he'd tried to claw his way to her, tried not to implode from the force of something stronger than he'd ever felt redesigning him from the inside out.

And now, seeing her there, his mouth went dry as those feelings that had begun to build since they'd met began to solidify.

"Nicole . . ."

"Don't come any closer." Her eyes shifted quickly in the direction of her pursuing family.

"Focus on them, nothing else," Kyan said.

Concentration flittered across her features and he used the break in her defenses to move toward her, but she dodged back, her foot grazing the edge of the cliff. Loose rock scattered downward until it hit the water. Her fury was depleting, and he could feel her fear rushing in.

Her eyes shone with tears. "Kyan, I . . . I killed them. . . ."

He felt a powerful, desperate urge to hold her. "Nicole, come here. Come to me."

She didn't move but a brush of wind picked up, and her scent struck him like a blade.

The scent of a newly changed Empyreal.

Gods. Kyan gritted his teeth as his scar burned and pulsed. Within two days the unearthly fragrance would spread past Estwood. It filled his nostrils: ambrosial, heavy and addictive. A dark scent no perfume could mask. His eyelids flickered as the oath scored his memory, reminding him of his duty to the Wake.

Pain lashed through every vein as he remembered it: "I, hunter of the Wake, declare that I will, to the extent of all my ability, detain and transport to the organization any discovered Empyreal who is unclaimed. No matter how young, no matter whose bloodline, no matter what piece of the earth they inhabit."

And with it that intense feeling in his chest, that sense of belonging, that bind between them drew tight enough to leave him breathless.

Mine.

The visceral nature of the thought wasn't his hunting urge, it was his *Empyreal*.

She's your mate.

Kyan's mind went silent. Even that insistent oath stilled.

But . . . Empyreals didn't *have* mates. He'd spent most of his life relieved by the knowledge that he would never be so connected to someone else and risk losing them.

This—it wasn't possible. Even if it felt the way other mated creatures had described it. Like there was a tether to her he couldn't break, didn't *want* to break, that made sense of the way he'd been so drawn to her from the start.

With a crash, Dylan burst through the trees and didn't even notice Kyan. "Nikki, we need to get out of here. He'll—"

Nicole continued to stare at Kyan. Did she feel it, too?

Her brother spun and flinched. He scanned the place, likely planning how to get her away, but Kyan knew, when Dylan's eyes settled back on him, what the boy's next thought would be.

How do I kill him?

Kyan slid his eyes back to Nicole.

She wouldn't look like herself to her brother. She looked like a wild animal, her eyes wide and glazed. Her fangs sliced her lip as she jittered slightly, too fast for a human to notice.

"She's an Empyreal?" Kyan said, even though he already knew the answer.

Nicole looked between them. Kyan clenched his fists, but it only made the scarred skin on his forearm feel like it was tearing.

Dylan answered anyway. "What do you *think*, Kyan?"

Nicole cringed.

What was he supposed to do? He had a mission, an oath. He *couldn't* resist it. But looking at her there, feeling what he was feeling, he wasn't sure he could obey it, either.

Kyan shook his head. "It's not possible. An Empyreal can't be half something else, it would make them weaker. . . ."

Or stronger.

Nicole had taken on two creatures at the same time; she must have slipped from one transformation into the next. He thought of the times she'd shaken in the presence of Lynch, not just with rage but *power*. What if, as half Seer, she could have made this transformation before Lynch or the curator made that killing decision?

If the Wake found out and were sending other creatures on assassinations that had nothing to do with protecting people and everything to do with political alliances, or whatever the hell they wanted these paintings for, then she would be invaluable to them.

The thunderous crack of a gunshot cleaved through the moment and before he could reach her, Nicole jolted and fled down the cliff.

"No!" he roared. She hadn't been hit, just startled. But if she ran off, she'd be alone as she transformed back, and an Empyreal's first healing process was often the worst and longest.

Suddenly, something slammed into him. No, *through* him.

Confused, he touched his side, and his fingers came away wet with blood.

375

44 NICOLE

Cool water sprayed over Nicole's legs as she raced alongside the lake.

She'd bolted, unable to bear something so loud with her newly sensitive ears, and dropped down some of the cliff, skidding and racing down the rest. But she'd also been afraid of the confrontation; of the struggle in Kyan's eyes. He was awake, he was *alive*. But if he got to her, he was going to take her away. So, she had to get away first.

The water was grounding her, but the tearing power wasn't quelling. Surely it was supposed to after she'd completed the kill?

Kill.

She'd killed the curator.

Nicole's gasp turned into a sob.

Her skin stung from the change. The gashes they'd inflicted on her still open and the blood drenched her clothes and stuck to her wounds. Absentmindedly she wiped her mouth with the back of her sleeve, catching the material with her newly sharp teeth. Everything *hurt*, especially the gaping wound in her stomach.

She fell and the rough pebbles of the shore stabbed into her knees. Nicole threw her hands into the icy water and red flooded into the clear lake.

The curator was a *creature*?

Another image flashed—Kyan's pained eyes after that gunshot.

Was he *dead*? A nauseating horror roared up her throat. *No!* She thrashed at the water as a sinking blackness crept into her mind. What if he was? *Why* did she jump?

Water soaked into her clothes, adding to the internal chill, and as she sat there, she finally allowed herself to cry. The sobs came easily, burning her raw throat. Vaguely, she knew it was an aftereffect of swallowing the blood and screaming a Baobhan Sith's scream, but she couldn't help herself. When Lynch had gripped her, she gave in to the instinct, and the second she made the choice, control had disappeared.

She had not missed it.

When they broke her ribs and kicked her kneecap in, Nicole forgot her pain; she forgot what pain *was*. All she saw was rage and power and felt the warm control of her Empyreal.

She couldn't remember what she did to them next, and she didn't want to. The memories were fading and jarring, rippling away like her shifting reflection in the water. She stared at it: those once-familiar eyes, now too dark. Her mouth was bloodied, teeth dripping with something that ran down her chin, a sticky but clear liquid. It hissed when it dropped to the lake's surface.

Venom.

Nicole spat it out and scrambled farther into the lake. She splashed her face, the cold water burning her teeth, but her soaked clothes just clung to her skin.

The blood wouldn't come off.

Nicole struggled to rise, now heavy with bloodied water, and ran into the forest on weak legs. She staggered in the darkness, tripping and bumping into things, jumping at any sound. Everything was too loud, too easy to see; even the bright moon scorched her eyes.

Was she dying?

What had happened to her family?

How could she find home?

Trembling, she fell against a tree and hugged her legs to her chest. Her body felt like it was shutting down, becoming too *heavy*. It had been so vibrant, so impossibly alive. And now she'd ruined everything.

She rested her head against the bark and closed her stinging eyes.

It was all over now.

They would never be safe again.

45 KYAN

Kyan clutched the gunshot wound. Pain pulsed beneath his bloody fingers. It had nearly healed, but the bullet had been a nightmare to get out.

Nicole's father had shot him, no doubt to try and silence him before he could return to the Wake. Thankfully any Specter poison on the bullets wouldn't affect him now that he was transforming back into an Empyreal. Besides, Kyan didn't *want* to tell their family's secret, not after seeing Nicole standing there, small and scared. He couldn't bring himself to take her away from them, at least not tonight.

He would resist for as long as possible; he could try and fight it.

He'd used most of his energy to quickly go after her before her father could get another shot in. The last thing he wanted was to hurt her family. So, he'd left her father with his gun, and her brother with his barely restrained worry.

She was close. Cold and wet and huddled somewhere. She would be on edge after her transformation and in pain now. He pushed faster when her breathing tapered out and grew less frantic. She'd run fast and far, but after swearing that oath, after this feeling in his chest, he could hunt her anywhere.

He stumbled into a small clearing to find her there, sobbing. Her dark head was bowed over her knees, and she sat curled at the base of a tree like a blood-slick Darksprite.

"Nicole?"

Her head shot up. For a second it looked like she would run from him, but she just stared, her eyes dilated and wary, waiting to see what he would do.

"Come on, I'm taking you back to the lake house."

Her lip trembled and a tear slid down her cheek. He was in front of her quickly and picked her up from the dirt, noticing a great bloody gash in her neck—two deep puncture marks. Her whole throat was full of drying blood and her white T-shirt deep red with it. A dangerous fury swirled in his stomach at the memory of how Lynch and the curator had beaten and bitten her.

He pressed his mouth to her damp forehead and smoothed her wild hair. She pressed her head into the hollow of his shoulder as he lifted her from the ground. That harrowing tension in his chest, that wire of fear, slackening now she was in his arms.

Mine.

"You're safe now," he said thickly.

Nicole gave a tender whimper and her eyes fluttered closed, her hot cheek pressing into his skin. He started back to the lake house with her in his arms, the night whispering a thousand stern words, his oath burning in his chest.

He thought of her smile as he walked: not the one she'd given Callum the day they'd met, but the one she'd had on her face when she met Vera. Nicole had watched the restorer raptly, delighted to learn more about the art, about the supernatural. Her eyes had brightened, her nose wrinkled with a grin. He wanted her to smile at him like that, just once. The need almost choked him. He'd make damn well sure she'd get through this so she had the chance.

It took time, but Kyan got her back to the house.

Bells stumbled toward the door expectantly as he strode up the steps. The venom had left her system and though her neck was bandaged, she looked a sight better now that Lynch was dead and any lingering lure had been snuffed out. Still, panic flew over her features at the sight of Kyan. Then she saw Nicole's blood.

"Oh my god!" Tears filled her eyes and she scrambled toward them.

Nicole's breathing was drawn and labored.

"What did they do to her?" cried Bells.

"She'll be all right when she makes it through the healing process." He didn't say he had no idea if she would. She'd switched between two transformations. Throughout centuries of being around other Empyreals, he'd never seen anyone do that so quickly.

He couldn't think about that now.

"We need to clean her up and make her comfortable. Where can I put her?"

Bells's lip trembled. "Upstairs, her room is on the right."

She stroked Nicole's face, eyes wide with horror, then grabbed her phone. The others were still out looking so she called them as she followed Kyan up the stairs.

He opened Nicole's door and slowly placed her on the bed, gently removing her ruined running shoes. She remained unconscious as her sister ran into the adjoining bathroom.

"Why hasn't she fully transformed back?"

"It's her first transformation, they're the most intense ones we ever go through. It takes time. She may have even gone through it twice."

"I need to clean her up." Bells moved quickly, grabbing everything she thought she would need. "If you can put some warm water in the bath, I'll wash the blood off and get her into some clean clothes."

Kyan nodded silently and did as she asked.

When he came back into the room, Bells had rolled up her sleeves and was sitting on the bed beside her sister, gently peeling away matted hair from Nicole's face. The sticky blood glinted in the dim light until Kyan flicked on a bedside lamp, filling the room with a warm glow, golden like the Empyrean, not the pale blue of moonlight.

Not the color of a corpse.

Bells laid her hand on Nicole's head. "Is it good or bad she's got a fever?"

"Good, for now. Her body's still in a healing flux."

"Can you help me with her?"

Kyan went into the bathroom and grabbed two towels, dipping them into the warm bathwater. Barely wringing them out, he returned and handed one to Bells before placing the other on Nicole's neck wound.

"Do we need antiseptic or anything?" Bells asked.

"No, an Empyreal's body doesn't respond to human medicines, it would either aggravate her or be no use at all. Her immune system will know how to handle this, it just takes time."

Bells started on Nicole's legs, revealing the slash up her calf that had split enough to show the dark red muscle beneath. She slowly and softly worked the blood off, horror on her trembling face each time she pulled a stained towel away. She worked with a constant frown, her lips pressed in worry, running back and forth from the now-red bathwater.

Kyan held Nicole's face as he cleaned her neck, revealing the marks, listening to her breathing. If it wavered even slightly, he would know, but it didn't.

"Will you wait outside while I undress her?" Bells asked quietly.

Kyan got up without a word and closed the bedroom door behind him, pressing the back of his head against the wall. He'd had centuries to learn how to block out negative, unhelpful thoughts. He used all that training now to keep his mind a cool, empty cavern and wait, listening as Bells went back and forth from the bathroom with dripping towels.

And yet several thoughts were screaming loud, and uninhibited: *She's your mate, what does it mean? How can you protect her? Does she know what she is?*

She's your mate.

She's your—

When Bells called him back in, Kyan was beside her in a second.

"How are her wounds?" he asked.

"Several on her tummy and ribs. And a—" Bells seemed to choke the words out. "Some kind of stab wound."

Kyan checked Nicole's legs and stomach. Her skin had been deeply punctured but was slowly attempting to knit itself back together. Raw purple bruises, some shaped like handprints, covered more of her. His mind went blank with fury. They'd put their hands on her. *Stabbed her*, for fuck's sake. He seethed until he felt a cool press on his forearm, and found Bells giving him a soft pat. He soothed his anger carefully.

They're dead. Gone. They couldn't hurt her again.

"Can you help me get her under the covers?" Bells asked.

Kyan gently lifted Nicole, now in fresh pajamas as Bells stripped off the bloodied quilt, then he laid her back down, her skin still too hot. Bells had done a good job getting the worst off Nicole's face, but he could still smell blood in her hair and under her nails.

As he wrapped Nicole back up in a fresh quilt Bells had grabbed from her room, she stirred and brushed his hand. Kyan sank onto the bed, scanning for a sign she was in pain.

The front door crashed open downstairs and two sets of footsteps raced up. Kyan watched Nicole's face contract in a dreaming frown, her eyelids flickering, and heat warped around his chest, almost uncomfortably. He didn't want to leave her, and that was dangerous. He checked her temperature again. She was too hot.

"Put a cold cloth on her head," he said to Bells, and then, to Nicole, "I'll come back."

Dylan crashed into the room, eyes locking on Nicole and then Kyan, who remained at the bedside, Nicole's hand on his. It stalled him.

Her father burst in the room next, spotting Kyan. "I shot you for a reason," Ronan snarled, gun pointed back at him.

"Dad!" Bells shouted, diving in front of Kyan.

"*Isabella!* Get out of the way. Death is the only way to stop the oath." He aimed a look at Kyan. "You're not taking my daughter anywhere."

"Stop it, Dad!" Bells cried. "He brought her back!"

"Is she okay?" Dylan asked.

"She's recovering, I think she has a few broken ribs and one of her knees is shattered. She's got a bad bite and cuts and a . . . a stab wound, but I've cleaned her up. Kyan says she'll be fine. We just need to give her plenty of time to heal."

Ronan moved closer, gun still trained on Kyan while he watched

Nicole. She looked peaceful, despite everything. When her father spotted Nicole's hand on Kyan's the Seer's expression darkened.

"I'm not taking her anywhere," Kyan said.

"And why the hell would we believe that?" Dylan asked.

"The oath compels you," Ronan added. "If you think I'm letting you out of this house given what you know . . ."

"I wouldn't—" Kyan began.

"Oh, *please*," said Dylan. "You're loyal to the Wake, you can't resist the oath."

"She's my *mate*," Kyan growled, a dangerous anger snarling in his chest. "She's not going anywhere."

He hadn't meant to say it, but the suggestion he'd betray her wasn't sitting with him one fucking bit.

Bells spun toward him, eyes wide. *"What?"*

Kyan bit down.

"That's not possible," Ronan said, shaking his head.

"Empyreals don't have mates," Dylan added, his eyes now on his sister.

"I thought that, too," Kyan said. "Evidently, I was wrong."

"Freya would have known," Ronan said softly.

"So, that's what it meant . . . ," Bells softly whispered.

"What do you mean, Bells?" Dylan asked.

"May I?" she asked, and reached for where Nicole and Kyan's hands touched.

He nodded, his own interest piquing. When Bells's cool fingers met his and Nicole's, the young Seer sucked in a breath. Her eyes went bloody, not with a vision, but as if she was *looking* for one.

"I can feel it," she said instead as her eyes slowly went back to normal. "I wonder if that's why she Saw Kyan coming before he arrived."

Ronan strode closer, a multitude of scenarios clearly running behind those storm-dark eyes, but when he took Kyan in, he seemed to have decided something.

He nodded slightly, and with a slow exhale said, "If you're my daughter's mate, that means you protect *her* over anything."

The mere words caused Kyan's chest to ache. *That* he wanted. *That* he would do.

"Let's go downstairs," Ronan said, still watching Kyan carefully. "Bells, you can get her a healing tonic from the fridge, she needs her strength."

Bells walked slowly from the room, nodding to Kyan. He nodded back. Ronan took a last glance at his daughter and motioned with the gun for Kyan to leave. He squeezed Nicole's hand and pulled his from hers. She stirred but settled when they all left.

"I'm going to dispose of the bodies," Kyan said, striding to the door.

Dylan threw a hasty glance toward his father.

Kyan hesitated. Turned. "I'll keep your secret from the Wake for as long as possible, but I need to know what you all are."

Ronan paced toward the living room. It was an enormous, vaulted space that looked out over the dark lake. Thick old beams adorned the ceiling and blankets were strewn over comfortable furniture below.

"I suppose you already know," said Ronan.

"It doesn't matter if I already know, I want to be sure. And I want the *truth*."

Ronan sighed, and Kyan briefly wondered how old the Seer really was.

"Nicole is half Empyreal, half Seer. Dylan is an Empyreal,

unturned. Bells and I are Seers. Their mother, Freya, was also like you. She was killed several years ago."

The woman from 1902. *That* was how she'd changed her face. She *was* an Empyreal. But how had she known what his mother looked like? Unless Freya was also half Seer and Ronan wasn't aware?

Dylan had said their mother had been killed by an Empyreal. But who?

And *why*?

Kyan didn't know what to say anymore. Everything he thought he knew about the Wake was being questioned. They told him there was no such thing as Empyrean mates, and here he was, almost feral with feeling, with the urge to protect. He had never suspected there could be people like the Palmers hiding, but now he'd found and seen them firsthand. It was wrecking the strength of his allegiance. Untethering him. He'd been so lost when he'd first dedicated himself to the Wake. But this was the opposite. He was different now, so irrevocably different.

"Even if I'm able to keep it to myself, she'll be in danger. The scent she gives off is too intoxicating to go unnoticed. Nicole will no longer be safe; your family will no longer be safe. Any Empyreals near here will be able to track her because of the oath, and creatures could be drawn to her."

Ronan rubbed his face.

Dylan paced. "What can we do, Dad?"

"I'll help you keep them at bay," Kyan said. "But I don't know how long I can. You may have to use the help of a witch or another powerful supernatural to try and mask her scent. Not that I think there's anything that can."

Kyan left without another word, striding into the darkness. After he'd cleared away the bodies, he would see Nicole again. He had promised her.

Nothing and no one could keep him from her now.

46 KYAN

Kyan was just about finished burying the bodies when Callum video-called him. He accepted the call with a bloody thumb and stabbed the shovel he'd grabbed from the lake house shed into the ground.

His friend squinted one look at him through the screen before saying, "Mother of— Well, you certainly made a mess. You'll be pleased to know the drama at the museum is in hand. No one remembers a damn thing." Callum grinned.

Some of the tension in Kyan's shoulders relaxed. "Thank you."

If he hadn't had Callum here to help, he would have had to leave the humans un-Influenced, and then who knew how many of the Wake's Empyreals or other creatures with mind-altering abilities would be sent to try and clean it up. Questions would have been asked—*How did this happen? Why didn't you deal with it?*—and he couldn't have that, not knowing it would bring more attention to Nicole and her family. It proved, as so much through their lives had, that he could trust Callum and Callum could trust him.

And yet, he didn't want to tell Callum the news if it would put him in danger or make him complicit, but he didn't want to— and usually *couldn't*—lie to him either, because his friend saw right through him anyway.

"Callum, I need to ask you to leave Estwood tonight and never go near Nicole again. Not to ask about the woman from 1902 and not to ask about tonight."

He arched a brow. "You didn't kill them," he realized.

Kyan's jaw clenched. "What did I just tell you?"

Callum laughed. "I knew it."

Nicole's scent was still rife in the clearing. Kyan had done his best to bury any of the bloody puddles that contained both her newly transformed scent and that of the Specter and curator. But even with the bodies buried and the carnage disguised, the scent would linger. Just as her blood on his shirt and coat would.

And it was driving him half mad.

"Right," Callum said. "Because then I'll scent the transformation and it will trigger my oath."

Kyan nodded, thinking of his own scarred forearm. General knowledge of a newly turned Empyreal didn't trigger the oath; an Empyreal had to encounter them and scent it, which seemed to begin the physical compulsion. Callum could ignore this, but it would mean having to keep it a secret from the Wake. For Kyan, though, he had no idea how he'd resist; he only hoped Ronan's theory about his and Nicole's mating bond would somehow overshadow the worst of the oath's control. But he'd worry about that when Nicole was awake again.

"And Dylan?" Callum asked.

Kyan said nothing, but Callum's lips just inched up slightly.

"You don't even need to say it, I can guess."

"That's not all. I think . . . I think Nicole and I . . . We're mates, Callum."

His friend's brow furrowed slowly. His eyes, always so clever, went through a flash of emotions: surprise, a shot of amusement, and almost disbelief. Then he said carefully, "Empyreals aren't supposed to have mates."

"I know," Kyan said. "How is it even possible? I didn't—"

I didn't want this, he'd nearly said. He'd been solitary for so long, had blocked the promise of love and felt a measure of relief at the idea that he would never be mated, even as a deeper part he tried to repress longed for it.

"Why is it only happening now?" Callum asked.

"I don't know. Perhaps because she had her first transformation and it made her a full Empyreal, able to form that bond? But even beforehand I was drawn to her, so protective of her. I've never been like that, *wanted* like that. It makes sense, looking back." And yet he thrust his hand through his hair.

Callum leaned against something: a wall of artwork in the museum. "Are you going to accept the bond? You haven't had sex yet, have you?"

Just the word in relation to Nicole made him snarl: "None of your business." He caught himself and scrubbed his face. "Jesus, sorry."

Callum's eyes only winked with mirth. "If you can resist it, it will likely make your . . . protectiveness less aggressive."

Part of him thought it would be wise to just leave, go far away and fight the drive that way. And yet he couldn't until he knew she was healed. Until she'd lost that deathly pallor and the fear in her eyes. Gods, that couldn't be the last image he'd have of her. Even now, he could barely stomach it.

"I don't even know what she knows about Empyreals," Kyan said. "I do know neither of us thought mating was possible, so what does it mean for her? Will she feel trapped?"

"I've seen the way she looks at you, Kyan. If anything this will be a shock, but I don't think it comes out of nowhere. It was brewing before, and it doesn't mean the pair of you have snapped into love. If it's like other creatures, it means there's the potential here for a love unlike anything either of you have experienced before, so it's not a prison sentence."

"Still . . . I don't know what to do."

His friend sobered. "When, pray tell, have I ever been beaten by a conundrum?"

"Only once that I know of," Kyan said, thinking of Nicole's mother. *Freya*, Ronan had called her.

The corner of Callum's lips twitched slightly in a smile. "Something tells me that won't be a mystery for much longer."

"That's not the thing to discuss right now."

"No, the oath is." Callum stared off, thinking. "How are you going to fight it? Clearly you were near her when it happened."

"I don't know," Kyan said, looking out into the dark forest as he briefly explained what he'd learned from Lynch about the Wake, thinking of the pull back to Nicole. It was strong, as if his blood was moving through his body in the strangest way, weighted with this new mission: to hunt and bring her in.

But beyond that he felt his own Empyrean power fighting it. He wouldn't take her to the people that had hunted and massacred innocents. He wouldn't take her if she was afraid. And that seemed to quiet the urge.

"Her family doesn't want her to be taken away," Kyan continued, "which I understand. Before I knew about Lynch being sent by the Wake, I might have said she *should* come with me. That I could help her adjust and she could hunt the way we're supposed to. But there's some big reason why they've hidden from the Wake for this long, and before I make any decisions, I need the full truth."

"Well, if there's anything I'm good at, it's finding out the truth."

Kyan smiled slightly for the first time since Nicole had been in his arms. "Let me get her through the healing phase. I'll find something. I have to."

Callum grinned. "I'll stay out of it for a little bit, give you both some time. But I'm not backing away from this. And before you snarl at me, it's not just because of Nicole. We've been lied to, Kyan. I don't mind a lie—hell, I quite like them—but I don't like people lying to *me* and I definitely don't like not knowing *why*."

Kyan returned to the Palmers' lake house nearly two hours later as the sun was rising. Bells had passed out on the couch, Ronan was concocting something in the kitchen, and Dylan was searching through a weapons room under the stairs.

Kyan ignored them all and strode upstairs to see Nicole. Ronan didn't try to stop him. He knew it would be fruitless.

She was fast asleep despite the sun's morning rays, and the sky's pale colors were seeping through the curtains. Her now dry, wavy hair splayed around her head. Her lips were swollen and bruised, the lavender-laced veins of her eyelids dark. He swept a stray curl away and her eyes slowly opened. Kyan knelt beside the bed as relief warmed his chest.

"How are you?"

She seemed surprised to see him and it hurt. Her lips parted to speak, but no sound emerged. He reached for the glass of water on her bedside table, but she shook her head, eyes half closed, and grabbed his arm weakly, giving him a tug. He kicked off his boots and pulled off his jacket, before climbing onto the bed with her and scooping her into his arms. She pressed her hot forehead into his chest.

"How . . ." she croaked. "How do I stop the pain? How do I go back to being normal?"

Kyan held her close as warm tears soaked into his shirt. "Hold on to me. I'll take the pain away. I promise, the pain will go away."

He fought the aching of his oath, hating how the sweet perfume of her was now riddled with a scent that drove him to the deepest recesses of his dedication. But he could help heal her, so for now, it was all he would focus on.

Closing his eyes, he pressed a hand to her back and drew it up and down her spine. Other mated creatures could help heal their partners through closeness. Kyan had no idea if it was some form of survival trait or merely psychological, but he tried anyway, imagining cooling, healing energy flowing from him into her, taking away the agony in her muscles and the strain in her heart. Lifting the worst of the exhaustion.

Her eyelashes tickled his chest as they flickered closed and her pulse grew more stable. Her grip on him weakened and she fell into a deep, peaceful sleep.

They slept for twenty-four hours. Kyan woke once or twice to check she was comfortable and healing, finding each time a different one of her family members sitting or sleeping on the couch they'd dragged into her bedroom. But the rest allowed him to heal his remaining wounds.

When his eyes opened, he was nestled against her back, his arm around her, and the next day was dawning. She was still asleep, her breath warm and steady on his forearm; her mouth and nose pressed against his wrist. Her eyelashes tickled his hand, and her forehead was cupped in his palm. Though she was sleeping, her grip was tight.

He buried his face in her hair and inhaled.

Resist.

He needed to change his clothes and the bedclothes. Slowly, he willed her to relax so he could tug free without her waking. He checked her wounds, relieved to find them mostly healed, save for bruises, then lifted her to the currently empty couch. He located fresh sheets and stripped the bloodied ones. When it was done, he laid her back down and placed a pillow in his place then silently grabbed his things.

She might need blood when she awoke. The first transformation was unpredictable and the claws of the last creature you'd been could linger.

He thought while he strode to where he'd initially parked his car—two nights ago? How quickly life could change.

He needed to figure out a way of keeping this a secret. But how could he protect her? The Wake would call upon him eventually and he would have to go, otherwise they would know something was happening. After all, the mission was over. The Specter was dead, and the painting destroyed.

Twigs cracked under his boots as his mind worked, flashing images of her transformation, of the night that had changed both their lives.

Kyan knew why he had given her his word, why he was breaking his allegiance to the Wake.

He had a new allegiance, and she felt like home.

47 NICOLE

When Nicole's eyes flashed open it was dark. Bells was slumped on the bed beside her, their hands clasped. Her father and brother were asleep on a couch they must have carried into the room.

Thirst scraped her dry throat. She grabbed the water on her bedside table and gulped it down, but the cool fluid just sloshed over the rawness.

Unsatisfied, Nicole got up, searching. The next moment, she retrieved the drawing pad she'd thrown in her bag and started scribbling down the numbers flashing in her mind. Each in a set of three, each meaning something she couldn't remember. Something important. The memories were fading quickly while her body was changing, while her mind was lessening its attachment to . . . what?

She couldn't remember.

She repeated the sequence again and again, and maybe a fourth time until the thirst felt like it had transformed her throat into sandpaper.

It wasn't water she was lusting for.

The cool night air felt better on her scalding skin. Solid soil beneath her bare feet helped the flimsiness of her limbs, but they were still weak and threatened to give out. Leaves rustled in the dry wind. Everything was too dry. Everything was *alive*, and *loud*. It was all talking to her—the rustle of the trees, the scamper of animals in the dark. And that *thing*, that thing drawing her out where she knew she wanted to be.

To *him*.

Nicole walked down the dirt road from their house, until she found herself striding into the beam of headlights.

The approaching car's brakes slammed on.

A smile tugged at her mouth when Kyan flung the car door open and moved toward her eagerly.

"Nicole! What are you doing out here? You need to rest." He stopped when he got a proper look at her.

His powerful form was cast into silhouette by the headlights and he backed up slowly, making her smile grow.

"Okay, I know you're overwhelmed but you need to think. Do you really want this?"

Nicole was in front of him in an instant, her senses craving his skin on hers. Something deeper, something more essential was so glad for his nearness, for that person who had protected her, helped her, told her of his sprawling life and trusted her with those details. All of it roared into a seismic *need*.

"I never thought I could feel so much." She reached out to touch his chest and felt the strong beat of his heart beneath the muscle, even the rhythm of his breathing excited her.

Especially when that breath caught in his throat.

KYAN

Kyan froze when Nicole's fingers grazed his skin. He could see the Empyrean power in her dilated eyes, feel it in the energy pulsing off her. Now she'd made it through her healing, her senses would really kick in. And that heightened everything, especially desire.

Tell her what's happened.

Her hair was a mess of almost-curls all the way down her back. All she wore was a small T-shirt and pajama shorts.

She reached out to his stomach, and she twisted his shirt around her fist, dragging him toward her. He stifled his surprise at her strength. Before she could hook her arms around his neck, he wrestled backward.

"Nicole. Listen to me—"

"Kyan, stop. We've been dancing around this for ages, I can't stand it anymore. All this time I wanted you and it confused me. Now I see clearly. I need this. *You* need this, don't you? I've seen how hard you've tried not to give in to the temptation. I've felt it. You don't have to do that anymore. We can do whatever we want."

He swallowed hard as long-simmering lust strained his body. Images came unbidden to his mind. Nicole beneath him, her legs around his waist or with a wall of paintings at her back. Heart thundering, little breathless sounds ghosting over his cheeks, his lips. No longer fighting the urge to push her skirt slowly up her thighs, or grind into that warm secret place . . .

He grabbed her shoulders before she prowled closer and heat funneled down him, lighting every nerve. He wanted her—fuck, did he want her—but not like this. He hadn't craved like this before.

The sexual urges he could deal with. With Nicole, however, it was the quickening in his chest at the thought of kissing her mouth that stalled him.

He had cared for people since the death of his family, mildly, and carefully. But that had never come with this sort of . . . hunger.

"Think about this, Nicole, your attraction is due to the change in you, it's heightened. You're not yourself."

Her eyes had a moment of swirling clarity. "I'm more myself than I've ever been."

His breath caught and a rush of emotion stopped his mind from working. "I know what it feels like, trust me. . . ."

She stepped closer until he was against the side of the car and she was pressed up against him, a seductive curve on her lips.

Kyan turned toward the still-open car door. Reaching inside, he grabbed a bag of blood and threw it toward her. Her sudden transformation had made her senses wild. If she had human blood, even if it wasn't from the source, it might calm her down.

"Drink, it'll help."

She didn't even try to catch it. It landed instead on the bracken.

"I don't want to drink it. I want you."

Traitorous desire shot through his body.

She took a step closer and he cursed himself as he fell back into the car. She climbed in on top of him, her hands stroking his shoulders with a little sighing sound that spread long-ignored passion into his body in pulses of need. He squeezed his eyes shut, moving backward.

What was he supposed to do here?

Blood. The bags of blood behind him.

"Are you going to hunt me, Kyan?" Nicole asked, her lips

brushing over his, her gentle fingers grazing his cheek as her hips bore down with gentle pressure against his.

A groan stirred at the back of his throat at the action; at the sight of those gorgeous eyes. Trust and complication morphed his feelings into something more dangerous.

"I don't want to hunt you," he said on a sigh, stroking her cheek with his thumb.

His heart expanded as her eyelashes fluttered and she leaned into his touch. But something in him yearned to do just that. To chase her. To throw her over his shoulder and take her away. And *that* he knew wasn't part of the oath. Part of him desperately wanted it. She could be with him. He could train her. He could bring her to the Wake and show her that it wasn't whatever she thought it was.

But that wasn't what cleaved through the idea. It was the realization that, while the urge to keep her with him was *his*, the urge to take her to *them* was as insistent as his burning scar.

He hated it.

They poisoned me, he realized. The Wake's oath had poisoned his Empyrean nature; who he was. It had been the one thing he'd clung to over the centuries, that calmed him if he ever felt that edge of moral despair; reminded him that he couldn't be doing something bad because his power only ever drove him to kill in response to danger. There was no other way for him to use his urges. Except this oath.

He brushed her lip with his thumb.

No, he didn't want to hunt her.

"I could hunt you, too," she whispered. "Baobhan Sith—we like hunters."

He knew why. In this form she could hear his blood, feel every inch of power in his body.

She gripped his shirt, and it tugged over his skin with friction that made him struggle not to lift his hips.

"Kyan, I'm *hungry.*"

He swore viciously, eyes dark and on her mouth. Nicole leaned into him, every soft curve of her body against his.

"You feel this too, don't you? You want this too?" she asked at a whisper, stroking his mouth.

"I do," he said softly, his heart wrenching and filling at the flutter of her eyelids that revealed both relief and desire.

She sank against him even more, running her hands over his shoulders, his back, as if savoring him, then tucked her head against his neck for a moment to hold him. Tears choked at the back of his throat at the sudden affection.

His heaving chest made her lift and sink on him slightly, so he squeezed his eyes shut to try and regain control.

But then she pulled back and whispered against his lips, "I want you."

She kissed him softly, and the surge of desire made his hips jerk up from the seat, but she was already sitting as snugly over him as she could be. His vision almost doubled with the pleasure. Gods help him if she moved an inch.

"Let me take you back to the house," he said roughly.

"To put me back to bed?"

Ah, fuck.

"Yes," he gritted out. "To *sleep.* And rest."

She pondered this, stroking his lips before she softly shook her head. "No."

And then she was kissing him.

Her lips were so soft, still swollen. He could feel the extra blood in them pulse and tingle. His body reacted, muscles flexing, blood redirecting, and he savored it for a moment too long. Long enough that his own desire began to strain; that his jeans grew too damn tight. That his fingers had started a glide toward her shorts, his kiss carnal, turning into tongue and teeth. He grappled with his mind, lurching backward to grab another blood bag.

He ripped himself away and thrust the nozzle of the packet into her mouth.

Her already large pupils flared, eclipsing the brown, then she grasped the bag greedily. He sighed. It had distracted her, but she wouldn't let go of him.

Kyan lifted her out of the car, trying to remember how to walk, and started back down the dirt path to the house, carrying her wrapped around him. She gulped down the blood happily. It would forever be a marvel to him how an Empyreal changed when they became another creature.

Nicole sucked and licked the nozzle of the bag, and he clamped his eyes shut, but her body was slowly eating at his resolve. Her legs tightened around his waist, her feet tucked over his backside. She snuggled closer, her eyes on him as she drank.

"You're thirsty," she said, turning the nozzle around to his mouth. The wet plastic scraped his lip, and he tried not to look into her hungry eyes as blood dribbled over his mouth.

"No, I'm not, but thank you."

Nicole shrugged. "Okay."

She licked the blood off his lips with a slow, hot tongue.

Concentrate, he told himself. But her breathing, the pressure of her tongue on his mouth . . .

"Nicole," he murmured, "*please.*"

She pulled back at the pained word, frowned, but nodded softly. Then bit him gently on the mouth in a way that made every fucking muscle in his body tremble, only to resume drinking her blood, watching him with those dark, lovely eyes.

And he knew he was a goner.

Kyan forced himself to keep walking against the increasing agony. He was more than grateful that her family were asleep when he took her back inside and tucked her into bed.

Three words nearly came out of his mouth as she blinked up at him in the darkness.

So, he stayed, allowing her to stroke patterns into his palm with an idle finger. She drank the blood until her eyes drifted closed and he sat beside her until her family woke and the sun came up.

He had a feeling he'd stay forever.

48 NICOLE

The next morning Nicole stood under the pounding jets of her shower.

It turned out a post-transformation shower was the most blissful thing to ever exist.

Well, beside Kyan's kiss.

She'd awoken to find herself clutching an empty packet of blood, but the feelings hadn't abated; in fact, they seemed to have grown. Was it because the others had told her that he'd said he wouldn't take her away? That he was trying to fight the oath? She'd never even hoped that could be the case, but these deepening feelings worried her more than the transformation.

Nicole stared down the drain, massaging her neck and scalp, wiping away the crust of blood and dirt to reveal smooth but shiny pink skin, almost healed where her wounds had been. Getting rid of the remnants of that night was like a cleansing. A rebirth. Though, she supposed that happened the moment she'd transformed.

The quiver of her Empyreal had quelled, curled and resting in her solar plexus, but now it stained her veins with amber power. She could feel it sitting in her entire body. She felt stronger. Faster. More capable. Everything was louder, brighter. She could hear out to the forest if she didn't block it out, even the epic roaring of the shower was at first like daggers to her ears.

Her skin felt newly sensitive and yet hard as steel—even harder to pierce than before. Nicole ran two fingers along the bite in her neck and the fading wound on her stomach.

She couldn't remember everything that had happened during her transformation, but flashes kept returning. Not just the rip and wet snap of tendon, or crack of bone and scream of pain, but images like memories. *Lynch's* memories.

But how had the Wake *done* it? How did they have the knowledge and power to twist and mutate creatures?

Switching off the water, Nicole grabbed a towel and went into the bedroom. The sheets had been stripped again, the couch moved back out, and the room aired with a slightly biting cold, but she felt so much better. Still, she wanted to be home in Estwood as soon as possible. But before then, she grabbed her sketch pad from the end of the bed and set it on the dresser, looking into the mirror above it.

Her hair was a tangled mess. To think she'd once been so adamant about trying to smooth and control it, just like everything else. For once, she had no urge to curl it into shining waves. There was no more reason to pretend she was in control anymore . . . and yet there was a new, quiet confidence in her body and mind. Was it that she knew she could defend herself from anything now? Or was it some kind of hormonal reward for the awakening of her Empyreal?

Again and again, she sketched her face. Well, what almost looked like her face. The one looking back at her from the mirror still contained echoes of the one she remembered reflected in the lake. It looked bestial. Dangerous. There were only slivers of a Specter left, like her still-eclipsed pupils and the slightly pointed lines of

405

her ears. She supposed they would stay that way for a little longer until her body calmed the urge to snap to attention every time there was an unexpected sound or movement.

Stooping closer she noticed something else—slivers of red that ran through the brown of her irises. She opened her mouth, pulling her lips back just enough that she could see her teeth as she ran her tongue along them carefully. They didn't look nearly as sharp as they were. A spearing line of red grew across her tongue with a sharp wire of pain. She clamped her mouth shut quickly and swallowed the warm shock of blood as her tongue immediately healed.

She noted it down and flicked through the rest of her sketch pad: all images of creatures she'd copied from Westmoore's collection.

Nicole ripped out the page. This one she would add to their family bestiary.

She paused, letting the emotions wash over her. She felt no grief for Lynch. She'd expected to kill creatures. At that, she felt a quiet steadiness, and . . . relief. And yet she hadn't ever expected to kill someone she considered innocent, like the curator, even if he'd been driven to supernatural madness.

Nicole tried, but failed, to smother a sob. She knew, somewhere in the house, her brother would be able to hear her.

As if on cue, a knock sounded on her door.

"Yeah?" Nicole said.

Her door creaked open and Dylan stepped inside, looking worried. He said nothing, just came to hug her and she clamped her lips together to stop herself from crying.

Dylan rubbed a supportive hand on her back. "Your transformation was . . . complicated. But you did the right thing. And even if you don't think so, the Empyreal inside us knows what's right and wrong. It knew the curator was going to kill if you didn't stop him."

"Are you having a hug without me?" Bells asked from the doorway.

Nicole laughed gently before their sister tucked herself into their arms.

"Well, that's just unfair," their father said a few moments later, before wrapping his arms around the lot of them.

Surrounded by their love, their scents, their warmth, and that eternal sense of safety she felt when with her family, Nicole shut her eyes and cried. Cried for the girl she was no longer; for cutting the curator's life short; for the fact Bells had been bitten; for not finding the answer to her mother's clue, the one thing that could guarantee them safety forever.

And for not knowing where they would go from here.

When she opened her eyes again, she saw the next page of her sketchbook, and her sobs hiccupped off.

"Wait . . . what's this?" Nicole detached herself from her family's embrace.

"Oh, it's your sketchbook," Bells said. "You were drawing in it while you were . . ." She let the sentence fall away, likely unsure how to describe the state Nicole had been in.

Nicole took in the scrawled notes on the page and she frowned. "No, what are *these*?"

"All these numbers? I don't know," Bells said.

Nicole's breath caught as she noticed the familiar pattern, beginning with the same digits Lynch had shown her of the cipher.

Was this . . . were these . . .

"I bit him," Nicole said, realizing what that meant. "And I got the code through his memories." She hadn't remembered because the transformation had been so fraught. Breath gusted out of her in a laugh. She snatched the sketchbook up and waved it at her dumbfounded family. "This is the *cipher*!"

"The lost message from the painting Lynch burned?" Bells asked, puzzled.

"Yes!"

49 KYAN

It was ten o'clock in the morning when Kyan arrived at the Palmers' house in Estwood. Nicole had texted to say they'd returned to the town, and as he knocked on the door, she opened it, dressed in a cream woolen jumper, her hair fanned over her shoulders. She looked good. Healthy. He must have stared for a moment because her cheeks pinked and he lost a little breath when she smiled, her eyes bright and soft, her nose wrinkling slightly.

There it is, he thought.

"Hi, come in." She stepped aside.

He was acutely aware this was the first time he'd ever stepped foot in their house. She seemed to notice, too, meeting his eyes briefly before her smile flickered again.

Kyan crossed the threshold and strode in.

Their home was exactly as he'd imagined. Decorated in coastal colors, the space was clean but lived in. There was an unmistakable warmth to it, too, not just from the morning light, but in the air. It was a family house, and as he followed Nicole into the kitchen, he got to see them as a family.

Homely scents permeated the room: golden pancakes, freshly juiced fruit, and a French press with black coffee already sat on the counter. Toast, eggs, and tea were being made. Enough for a family. Even enough for him.

Also spread across every surface were countless pieces of paper scrawled with numbers, books, notes, and open tomes that looked surprisingly ancient.

"Coffee?" Nicole asked, her tone distracted.

Dylan wasn't exactly thrilled he was in the house. He scowled from where he'd been pulling bacon from the fridge when Kyan walked inside, feeling out of place still in shoes while the rest of them were barefoot or in slippers.

Bells, who seemed to be wearing her father's cardigan, silently slid a mug toward him.

"Thanks," he said, earning a smile from her.

"Any news?" Ronan asked.

Nicole sat at one of the barstools, her eyes flying back over the numbers, scribbling something. Kyan perched on the one beside her, feeling a rush of affection.

"It seems a Baobhan Sith has already been drawn here by Nicole's transformed scent. It staked out a perimeter in the trees around the town. I think it was drawn to the sound of her scream when she transformed. They're rare down in England so I imagine it wanted to find another of her kind."

"Did it mark the trees with blood?" Bells asked as she buttered toast, a frown heavy on her fair brow. Evidently, they knew more about creatures than he suspected, which shouldn't have been a surprise given they'd been avoiding them for years, thanks to their secret.

"Yes," he said.

Bells's eyes lifted with concern. It meant the Baobhan Sith was either marking its territory or preparing to kill Nicole.

"But until it comes back into Estwood's boundaries, I can't risk going out to make a move on it."

"Is it the only one out there?" Dylan asked.

"No, there are a couple of other creatures, but they're scavengers, they'll follow whatever scent takes their interest. Usually they're not harmful, but you can never be too careful. I'm heading out again later." He looked back down at the sheets strewn over the table. "What is all this? Are you trying to piece together more of the cipher Lynch found?"

The family seemed to share a look.

Nicole took in a breath, as if deliberating. She opened her mouth to tell him when Dylan cut in.

"You haven't told the Wake about her yet." It wasn't so much a question as it was a statement.

Yet. Kyan steeled at the implication. "No, I haven't."

"How do we know you won't? The oath isn't just going to go away."

"She's my *mate*. I'm not going to—"

Nicole's intake of breath cut through his words. "W-what?"

Kyan's teeth clacked shut. He hadn't meant to tell her here, he'd wanted to tell her when they were alone, to sit with her and try and explain once he had more of an idea of how this had happened. But then, he had almost no way of figuring that out.

Nicole looked around at her family. "You . . . you all knew?"

"We found out when he brought you home," Bells said softly. "You were unconscious, and Kyan . . ." She trailed off, glancing up at him.

"I didn't even know it was possible," he said. "I wanted to try and get some information first."

411

"That's . . ." She seemed to think. "That's why I felt . . ."

"Maybe not," Dylan suggested. "Maybe it's just strong feelings brought on by your transformation."

Nicole seemed to sense the upset. "Dad?"

Her father looked just as torn. "I did some research and there may have been one legend your mother discovered. She thought she'd met a mated Empyreal pair, and while she was fascinated by the supernatural and wanted to chart every truth about our society, she couldn't risk interviewing or approaching many other Empyreals as they had all been inducted into the Wake. These two, however, had not."

"Who were they?" Kyan asked, wondering if there was some chance he knew either of them. Empyreals were rare, but that didn't mean he'd met all of them.

"She didn't write their names down, perhaps to keep them hidden. But she did note that they'd been bound one night under a hunter's moon."

"'To bind a mated Empyreal pair,'" Nicole recited softly. Ronan nodded.

"Bound like other mating ceremonies? Like for Fae and Vampires?" Bells asked, nibbling on her lip.

"Yes, each supernatural and individual brings their own history into the binding," Ronan said.

"And yet none of that helps *this* situation," Dylan said. "The Wake. The now."

"It would if I understood why you didn't want to be a part of the organization," Kyan said. "After what I learned about Lynch being sent to hunt creatures, I can understand that worrying you, but how did you all know this?"

"You didn't have any idea?" Nicole asked.

Kyan shook his head. "We're not privy to other Empyreals' missions, it's a global operation with bases in every country in the world. I couldn't keep track of every hunt if I tried. Let alone ones I didn't know were happening."

Ronan met his gaze. "There are many reasons why we can't be known to the Wake. Not only because of their manipulations but because they'd split us up and send Nicole and Dylan on countless missions. But most importantly, because they killed my wife, their mother. She was the one who found out what we know about them."

"The information Lynch wanted from the paintings," Nicole added. "*This* information."

Kyan looked down to the scrawled sketches. "You have it?"

"I saw the rest of the cipher in his memories when I bit him. But that's not all. When I was in his mind I saw the strangest things: experiments the Wake have been doing on creatures, making them more dangerous. Leading to things like Lynch being able to twist someone into a supernatural."

Kyan shook his head softly. All this time, for *two millennia*, he'd relied on the Wake and their guidance. Now that faith was being shattered in every possible way.

"You know they don't allow people to disobey or spread this information," Ronan said. "We know too much about them. Too many secrets. They would never let us live."

There was no rumor or doubt in Ronan's eyes. Only truth. And condemnation.

And he was right. They'd had others killed that didn't follow their orders: like Alexander.

413

"That's why you were so adamant about getting the painting back? Why you never trusted me?" Kyan asked Nicole.

She nodded. "I couldn't, not without knowing more about you."

Was this why Nicole's mother had tried to deter him from taking the oath? Had she been trying to protect herself and any future children from being drafted into the Wake, from being used, or perhaps killed, for what their mother knew?

He looked at Nicole. A familiar pain cut through centuries of memories, sharp as crystal: the last time someone he loved was killed.

If this was true, if the Wake killed her mother and there was a risk they'd kill Nicole . . .

I'm not going to let that happen.

He vowed it to her wordlessly. When her dark eyes shimmered with tears it scored him sharply, as powerfully as the oath he'd sworn in Lanhydrock's Cornish wood over a hundred years ago.

As breakfast began, Kyan watched the way they moved as a unit, a synchronistic morning routine even his presence hadn't interrupted. He was glad of it. He wondered if he had ever moved like this with his foster fathers and cousins, but it was so long ago he couldn't remember. Seeing the Palmers together also revealed how different Nicole looked from them all. Her hair dark as autumn compared to their blue eyes and light-brown, almost gold hair. He tried to imagine their mysterious mother here, too. How different events would have been if she was.

His muscles grew taut as Nicole brushed close to him, his blood burning with the oath. Their bond. Her scent was dissipating extraordinarily quickly, but it still lingered in her hair and the little fragrant nooks of her neck and behind her ears, the places he wanted to lean closer to. To brush his lips across.

When breakfast was finished, Nicole rose. "I'm going to head to the university."

Kyan put down his coffee, surprised. "You're still going to classes?"

"No, I need to Influence someone in the admissions office. We're leaving soon, after all."

He knew it had to happen, their attempt to flee the place that was now so saturated in her scent. And yet it still made him almost possessive.

"Then I'll drive you," he said numbly.

He followed her as she went to her room to grab her coat, feeling Dylan's eyes on them.

As they got to the top of the stairs, the open library room to the right caught his attention, specifically the portrait above the fireplace. The circular painting showed a woman that looked just like Nicole. Surprise to see that face again cleaved through him. There was the proof Callum needed.

The woman from 1902 *was* Freya, Nicole's mother.

50 RONAN

Ronan stood in the dim of their kitchen, laying out everything he'd need. Nicole hadn't been able to figure out the key for the cipher in the few days they'd been home. They'd split up and checked every book of Freya's but none of them were making sense. Which meant it was time for his backup plan.

Since Kyan had first arrived in Estwood, Ronan had been working on a new tonic that no longer stifled Nicole's Empyrean powers but helped get rid of her scent just in case something like this happened. He and Freya had dabbled with recipes for years, hoping they could use it to help future Empyreals hide from the Wake, but they'd never had a chance to test it.

Now, though, Nicole had been having it with her food, and they'd made scented bags to place in her wardrobe so it could soak into her clothes. He'd even left some at the lake house, which erased any trace of her, and Kyan was dealing with the creatures that had come investigating.

Thankfully, the tonic was already working, swifter than he'd hoped, and he'd figured out how to make it into a perfume.

With any luck, her scent would have stabilized by tomorrow, making it possible for them to finally leave without her being tracked.

Ronan picked up Nicole's bloody T-shirt from the night of her transformation and assessed the objects laid out: scrapings from their portrait of Freya, a map of the world, and his centuries-old mortar and pestle.

He scraped both the blood and paint inside, mixing them with a carrier, then licked his finger and pressed it to the powdered mixture, setting it on his tongue.

This would be the second time he'd used elements of his true power in fifteen years, and it would have to be the last until they were far away from here.

He didn't want to draw the others.

He hadn't been able to risk trying this any sooner—he'd had no substance powerful enough. But the blood of a newly turned Empyreal was one of the most potent supernatural ingredients on earth.

Especially blood from his daughter.

Images flashed behind his closed eyes. Ronan opened them and looked at the world map he'd laid out on the marble counter. One particular location stood out.

That was where he'd find the artist who painted Freya's portrait.

It was the only other lead they had about his wife, and it was a place to start. Because whether or not Kyan could keep their family's secret, they now had the cipher, and if the Wake ever discovered that, they'd do everything in their power to get it. Whether they managed to decode it or not, they would need more information, and this location, this artist, might give them just that.

By being exposed to Kyan, they'd officially tangled with the Wake in a way that Ronan couldn't ignore. The mate bond Freya had discovered between Empyreals was strong, but was it strong enough to override Kyan's oath?

Ronan scribbled down the coordinates.

Once Nicole's scent had dissipated, they would leave Estwood. And never see Kyan again.

51 NICOLE

The half-destroyed *Dante* painting had taken pride of place in West-moore's study.

It hung over the mantel above the fireplace, its burned canvas and the broken, extravagant gold frame gleaming in the firelight. It was a stark, semi-destroyed reminder to Nicole of how much more she had to do, to research and discover.

And how little time she now had in Estwood.

Her scent should be cleared by tomorrow, which meant she had one night left in the town she had come to think of as home.

Nicole paced, ignoring the book on the table—and the chapter within her mother had written about supernatural symbolism and mated Empyreals. After days of searching with Remi and her siblings—after being tearily reunited—Nicole had been *sure* this one would be the key to the cipher. It was not. Neither was any damn book in their house: none of the ancient texts, none of the bestiaries. She had even tried *Dracula* and *Frankenstein*. But *nothing*. She was out of ideas, and she was out of time.

One more night.

Nicole looked out to the dark sea. Tonight, it had a low, moody gold skyline with heavy navy clouds above, only broken by elegant scythes of bright lightning, like the background of the *Wild Hunt* painting.

She'd packed her things but hadn't been able to leave the manor, just as she'd found it near impossible to think of anything but the revelation from the other day.

She's my mate.

Nicole pressed a hand to her solar plexus, the place her power seemed to live like a second heart. She'd always felt it there, slumbering like a living creature of its own, and now it had taken her over. Remade her. Allowed the bond between her and Kyan to strengthen to an almost painful degree. She'd wondered in those hazy, hungry hours between the transformation why she'd craved his touch so much, why when she'd looked at him bleeding on the edge of the cliff, dying, it had felt like part of her was dying, too.

Nicole looked up at the burned painting. She'd come to take it and pack her things. That she'd done. She'd come to check the book. That was useless.

There was one more thing she was here to do.

Nicole listened to the crackle of the fire, the gentle plink of rain against the expansive glass doors, and the sound of Kyan showering. He was in one of the bedrooms he'd chosen in Westmoore's private quarters, reached either by the private corridor outside the ballroom, or a door through the secret library.

She needed to speak to him and say—what? He was supposed to go back to the Wake, and she and her family were supposed to travel on, searching for artists—for answers—while he continued his life as if he'd never met her. Despite the fact they were mates.

There was no other option, yet the thought made her both grievously sad and absolutely furious.

420

It was for the best. It was for everyone's safety. Fae mates often hated to be parted, preferring to wile away the centuries together, but they could do it. Werewolves didn't have that luxury and were more territorial, but she supposed that was because of the more pressing physical urges that took over. The thought of never seeing Kyan again had her scrubbing the heel of her palm against her chest at the ache beneath.

She heard the clank of the pipes when the water shut off and Kyan's steps as he moved quickly through the house.

She should go. Perhaps it was better if they didn't see one another this last time.

But she couldn't make herself move.

She wanted to know how he *felt* about this. Because she . . . she wasn't even sure. She wanted more time with him, to know what this meant, to know more about him and finally share more about herself, things she hadn't been able to because of who and what she was. She'd barely told him a scrap of truth since they'd met. But since that wall had come down, since she'd lain in his arms and he'd carried her home to her family instead of the one place in the world she feared, she knew that she could trust him with more of herself.

She could trust him with her thoughts, her real feelings, her—

Kyan appeared.

Nicole's breath caught. *My body*, she thought. *I can trust him with that, too.*

He wore nothing but a towel around his waist. He'd entered via the secret gallery room, emerging from the darkness as if stepping from the luxurious mural on the wall, but had come quickly enough that the droplets of water on his chest hadn't dried. Neither had the damp towel that outlined . . . *everything.*

A rush of heat went through her and a sudden dryness parched her throat. When she met his eyes, she saw a new kind of hunger there, one that felt infinitely more real than any other time they'd been close and alone. As if that hunger, tonight, might actually be slaked.

It was electric in the almost darkness and her desires spread with immediate liquid warmth.

"Nicole," Kyan said quietly, a slight rasp to the word.

Damn her for the feeling her name on his lips caused.

"I wasn't sure you'd come here again."

"I'm here," she said, a little breathless. "I wasn't sure if you were . . . busy." *And I didn't know what to say.* She avoided looking at him. The power, the height. It was nearly too much.

"I was just showering." He took a step closer with a gentle shake of his head. "I forgot you could probably hear."

Nicole swallowed at the sight of his water-darkened hair, almost curling at the brow. "Any news on the Baobhan Sith that was sniffing around?" She turned to the fire as he stopped beside her with all that steady, masculine heat.

"She decided on the kill an hour or two ago."

So, something else had wanted to kill her. The realization had her rubbing her arms to ward off the chill. She could feel it now: the echo of transformation on Kyan, a tinge of magic which meant he must have become something with magic to hunt, and kill, the Banshee. Now, he'd smoothly transformed back into an Empyreal because his body was so used to the metamorphosis.

"It's over now," Kyan said softly.

I killed her, were the unspoken words. *I've kept you safe.*

Nicole's eyes almost fluttered closed with a sigh at the unprecedented comfort of being *safe*. That deep, crucial feeling in her chest grew. She looked up, her neck craning gently due to their closeness. His eyes were on hers, the hazel of them dark.

"Why did you come here, tonight, Nicole?"

Her gaze didn't stray from his mouth. "I was just . . . going to check a book and the painting."

"You can have it," he said.

Nicole blinked. "What?"

"The *Dante* painting. It's semi-ruined, but you can have it. I'm telling the Wake it was destroyed."

Here he was again, offering her everything she needed.

His voice was smooth and low as he said, "Is that all?"

Don't make me say it, she almost pleaded.

"Well, I wanted to talk about t-the mates thing."

I want you.

Kyan made a thoughtful sound and nodded, brushing the length of her plait over her shoulder.

She'd rushed out of her house tonight to come here, second-guessing herself the entire time, so she'd flung on some leggings, a little strappy vest top beneath a jumper and tied her hair out of the way. But thanks to the warmth of the study from the fire, she'd shucked off the jumper, and her neck and shoulders were now exposed to the thoughtful weight of his gaze. To the brush of his fingers as they stroked her skin.

"I'm glad you came," Kyan said. "I wanted to talk to you, too. Alone."

Shivers spread beneath his touch like magic, making her recall every delicious time his hands, or his mouth, had been on her.

Just the thought of his mouth made that liquid need grow.

"I know that for other supernaturals, a mate bond is a physical compulsion," Nicole said softly.

Kyan's chest grew with a deep breath, and she had a feeling they had ticked the physical compulsion box.

"For other immortals like Fae," Kyan said, "the mating bond forms so they can find a person to spend immortality with. For some supernaturals who are hunted or possess particularly volatile powers, it helps ensure the continuation of their species by enabling them to find their best match in a fierce, obvious way. For us? It feels like all of them. For me"—his fingers spread over his solar plexus—"I can feel it here. Right where my power has its core."

His gaze trailed down her body, to the places she could feel warming. As if he *knew*. The sensations increased in her breasts, between her legs, making everything suddenly eager, suddenly desperate for his touch.

Nicole drew in a shaky breath. "That's where I feel it, too."

If she stayed here tonight, she'd need him. She felt the draw every time they were together and it filled her with a hunger so acute she couldn't think of a single other thing. It felt so *right*, so intense yet soothing.

But the last impulse she'd given into had felt like it ruined her life, even if it had made her who she was meant to be.

"But I want to make something clear," Kyan said, tipping her chin up slightly with a warm finger, making her look him in the eyes. "That before you transformed and this . . . this connection solidified, I wanted you. I was fascinated by you. I wanted to know you. Not just your secrets, not for the mission, but *you*." His lips curved into a gorgeous smile. "I wondered what type of person would charge after a Specter to save someone she didn't even like."

Nicole laughed weakly.

"Who would throw herself into danger at the mere promise of

finding an answer that would keep her family safe."

Her eyes burned with a quick bolt of tears.

"That," Kyan said, stroking one away, "was who I wanted. I don't want you to feel trapped by this bond. We can try to resist it, if that's what you want."

"But I'm leaving," she whispered. Her father had told her of his plan, and she knew he was right. Knew they couldn't stay here forever. But still . . .

A muscle in Kyan's jaw flickered. "When?"

"Tomorrow," she said, even more softly. A wildness stormed in his eyes, there and gone in a moment. "And you've dealt with the Banshee, so everything's . . . done?"

No more reason to stay.

Kyan nodded cautiously. "Your scent drew her here. It makes other creatures want to be around you, it's . . . addictive, but it's fading now. I don't know how."

"Is it addictive to you?"

"Yes."

She was suddenly more aware of how close they'd drifted. "Like how your scent is addictive to me?"

Kyan's brows raised. "You're addicted to my scent?"

She cursed her heated cheeks. "Not *addicted*."

Another smile pulled at his mouth as his gaze grew intent. "What's it like?"

Nicole laughed, suddenly nervous. "I don't know, it's hard to describe."

"Try."

She had tried to avoid getting close for so long. Now, maybe she didn't have to. She reached for his wrist, tugging him softly so that he perched on the edge of the desk, closer to her height. Then she set her lips to his wrist, eyes on his as she inhaled. A frisson of want raced over her skin, tugged at that desire.

"It's . . . subdued and earthy."

Kyan grew very still when she stepped closer, then spread his legs as far as they could go while still wrapped in the towel so she could press her nose to his neck, her lower lip grazing the raised jugular that throbbed against her mouth. He made a contented sound that piqued her interest and had her instincts purring. Her lips paused on his jawline, under his ear. His skin was scorching.

Nicole inhaled and her whole body shuddered. Her hands fell to one of his thighs for support, the damp towel barely stretching across the size of it.

"I don't really have words. I just know it's . . ." Her breath rushed out. "Intoxicating."

Her hand cautiously grazed his stomach, her heartbeat kicking up to find the thick abs that tensed under her touch, the brush of hair. She pressed another gentle kiss to his jaw and leaned into him as places within her began to awaken.

"You," he started roughly, "have an indescribable scent." His lips grazed hers.

"Surely it's like something?" Nicole breathed.

He shook his head in reply. Slowly, he inclined and brought his face to her neck, inhaling. It felt so intimate, so comfortable to have the brush of his hair against her mouth, the warm press of his cheek against her skin. She closed her eyes, relishing the closeness as her fingers stroked the back of his neck and damp hair.

"Euphoria." The word breathed over her collar and her cheeks warmed.

She'd wanted time with him to just be. Just a little bit. Just to see what it was like.

Maybe she could have that tonight.

"Kyan, I'm spending one more night here. And I . . . I don't want to spend it in my room alone."

If she wanted anyone, it was him. He was strong. Protective. Supportive. An Empyreal just like her, who could understand her like no one else. Who'd transformed and killed, who'd honored and wept through the strange alchemy inside them. After today, when they went their separate ways, there would be new tests for the pair of them to face: how to lie to his organization; how to embark on an artistic, historical hunt of her own—one that might give her the answers she needed. Answers not just for her family, for her own life, but for *them*.

"You're newly turned," he said softly, and she could feel his breath on her neck like a live wire. "You'll be more . . . sensitive."

Nicole choked down the small moan. *Sensitive?* She was on *fire*, and he'd only really looked at her.

Kyan shook his head softly and raised a hand to brush his thumb slowly over her lower lip, watching the movement with a raw, sensual attention.

"If we had sex, Nicole . . ."

Just the word shot her through with such intense desire she couldn't breathe.

Yes, that was what she wanted.

". . . it would make it much harder to leave you. And I don't want you to have to feel this need again, without me there to satisfy you."

She was distantly aware of a little desperate sound and realized

427

she'd made it. She felt shaky; like the molten heat of the Empyrean they were fabled to come from.

Kyan stroked both hands over the back of her thighs and then lifted her up against his body as he stood so her legs wrapped around his waist. Pressing against him made that deep pleasure-desperate core that was beginning an intense, delicious throb. Her chest met his—still wet, the skin hot. Then he slid her down slightly in a way that almost made her eyes roll back as every part of her grazed against him until their lips were level.

"So, what," Kyan rasped, "do you want me to do to you, Nicole?"

"Anything," she whispered against his mouth. "I just need you to touch me or I'm going to scream." His eyes darkened as she scraped her hands down the width of his back and he growled, the sound like thunder at the back of his throat.

His hands squeezed her backside tighter to him, grinding her softly up and down his body. She made a choked moan against his mouth.

"I want you like this," he said roughly. "But I'll control myself."

"Don't."

His lips curled up in a smile she'd been desperate to see more of and then her joy and attraction transformed with his kiss.

It was a slow kind of fevered. As if they were both trying to relish it while also feeling the heat and presence building into more.

Kyan carried her through the manor, lit by little but the near full moon. They must have been walking down a window-lined hallway because light flickered in and out behind her eyelids, but all she felt was his mouth and the low, drugging heat between her legs. Nicole shifted, seeking that stunning pleasure that had teased her each time they'd kissed like this.

Then he bent and she felt the soft press of a luxurious quilt at her back.

Her anticipation soared as his weight settled over her and her thighs parted around his hips. She briefly noted the dark luxury of the room—his bedroom. But then his lips were at her neck and his fingers in her hair and warm muscle pressed against her. The waves outside seemed to urge them toward its ancient rhythm, and just the hint of it as he moved against her made her—

A sound came from her mouth that he echoed, groaning into hers as he kissed her again.

She gripped him, wanted that damn towel off.

"Nicole," Kyan breathed.

"Don't stop." She wouldn't be able to bear it. She'd never wanted anyone like this and she might never again. He stirred her in a way no one else did. His lips coasted over hers gently, supporting.

Her fingers reached for the knot of his towel, grazing the warm skin and the dark hair that ran down and disappeared beneath it. Kyan's hand came over hers, emanating heat.

"Nicole." He searched her face and brought her hand to his mouth before kissing her palm, her wrist. "If you take that off . . ." His jaw worked.

She felt the strain in his body, the hardness of his arousal against her leg. Exquisite need flooded her as they sank into another of those slow, erotic kisses. She didn't know it could be like this. That even the hot stroke of his tongue could feel like it was remaking the world into nothing but the two of them. Nothing but her body and all it could feel. No tomorrows, no yesterdays. Just all this sensation and *connection*.

He cursed with a low moan, his oath-scarred forearm levering him above her as his hand fisted in the sheets.

"What?" she whispered, stroking his frowning face. "What if we only have one night?"

He cupped her face. "I will find you again, Nicole, this isn't goodbye."

She bit down, holding back the tears as she tipped her mouth to his. Kissed him.

"I want to," Nicole said, reaching up to stroke his cheek. "I don't think that I can leave without knowing what it would be like."

"Nicole . . . I don't have any protection."

The admission stopped her words. "*Oh.*"

She didn't either. She had never bought any, never thought about this seriously before Kyan. Empyreals were safe from human illnesses, but their fertility . . .

He gave a pained smile. "Trust me when I tell you, I *want you*. The amount I want you . . ."

He tipped his hips and pressed firmly against her, right against her core with the hard length beneath the towel. A moan slipped from her at the sensation—liquid heat rushing to where they were pressed together, that throb deep and aching.

". . . would make you blush."

"Oh my god," she breathed.

Kyan closed his eyes as if he was fighting for control. And she couldn't help but be a little thrilled that he was so controlled in every other aspect, but not this. Not with her.

"And if we ever got to do this," he said, his eyes opening and fixing on hers with sincerity. "I wouldn't want just one night. I'd want you to myself for much longer."

His mouth brushed her cheek, then the side of her parted lips while his hand stroked up her side. It ran slowly up her stomach, taking the edge of her shirt with it, allowing his skin to press against hers. Her legs parted wider, allowing him to tilt his hips in a way that made her mind blank with pleasure. She gripped his back, stunned at the intensity of the feeling.

"I would want you completely undone," Kyan breathed. "Feeling safe, not worried about the next day. Not thinking about anything but my body and yours and the pleasure I can give you. Then I'll make sure your legs are so weak you can't walk straight."

A staggered breath rushed past her lips. *Oh god*, was she going to pass out?

"But," he continued, "we'll take all night. As long as you need me, as long as it takes for me to know your body and what you like most." His lips were moving over hers. "As long as you want me." He ground between her legs again and the satisfaction spread hot and desperate as a dark tide.

"I'll always want you," Nicole whispered, semi-delirious, raking her nails up his back.

He groaned.

"And I do feel safe."

He closed his eyes, as if relishing the words.

She felt shaky, hot and ready. *So ready.*

"But we . . . can't?" she asked against his lips, trying to quell the disappointment, the frustration.

"No," Kyan whispered. "So I suppose that means I'll have to give you something else to remember."

His kiss was deep, as if he could reach something inside her she hadn't even known existed. Her desire bordered on desperation as his hands left trails of sensation as they stroked her shoulders, before

431

slipping beneath the strap of her shirt, and as he tugged it down slightly, she was hyperaware that she may have foregone a bra.

In their previous kisses they'd both been holding something back.

There was nothing to hold back now.

His mouth trailed from her neck down to her breasts as he tugged the fabric lower, just about to bare her. She wove her fingers into his damp hair and tugged. Kyan made a sound that had her thighs clenching around him. Hunger flashed in his eyes, and then his head ducked to stroke his mouth over her nipple through the fabric. Her breath left her in a whoosh.

"That . . ." Kyan murmured against her skin. "I love that sound."

She fisted her hands and he groaned, rising up slightly to kiss her as he tugged the shirt down to her waist. Cool air ran over her bared breasts and her breath caught as his hand stroked over them, once, twice, while he kissed any other thoughts from her mind. His warm palms cupped, squeezed gently, making them turn heavy and aching so that when his head ducked, and his tongue ran over one nipple, Nicole nearly lurched off the bed.

He kissed her like he had all the time in the world, with a growing wild lust.

She expected him to come back up to her mouth, but instead he moved lower. Nicole stopped breathing as one of his hands smoothly slid to stroke between her legs over the cling of her cotton leggings and she almost screamed with the pleasure. Before she had a chance to grasp the rush of sensation, he dipped his head and kissed her there.

Nicole bit down on the shock of feeling something so . . . *intimate.*

Kyan made a rough, delicious sound, pressing another kiss before scraping his teeth against that bundle of nerves. Nicole moaned, loud, feverishly. Then he used his thumb to roll over a wildly sensitive spot. He hit a kind of fluid rhythm between mouth and hand that began to make her delirious, that had her body growing desperately loose and yet tight, as if she shimmered on the edge of release.

He levered himself up slightly, making no move to pull his mouth from her. But his fingers slipped beneath the band of her leggings. Every ounce of her attention shot to the touch; her eyes squeezed shut.

His skin on her skin.

It was nearly too much.

Kyan's mouth traced her stomach. "Breathe, Nicole."

Could she pass out from the sound of his voice? From him murmuring like that?

She drew in a deep breath, scenting the heated physicality of him and something she realized was probably their scents, which only flooded her with more bliss.

And then his fingers slid lower, to cup her, and began to move.

Right.

There.

They were warm and gentle against the throbbing, and yet it felt explicitly intimate as he curled them gently through the slickness.

Nicole gasped at the sensation. How bare and stark and sensual it felt. How exposing.

Kyan rose over her, eyes on hers as he pushed gently, his finger sliding inside, breaking through the short bite of discomfort with such intense bliss, such heat and tightness it almost made her scream. She fisted her hands in the sheets as he growled a curse and ground his body against the bed.

"*Kyan*—"

Nicole dragged him closer with a strangled moan. His mouth clashed with hers as one of his fingers filled her, slowly, with an exquisite control that had a dark flush rushing up her chest and neck. The sound she made was a mix between agony and ecstasy, and had her tearing at his shoulders, gasping at the newness of it.

God, she needed him everywhere. She needed *more*. She wanted to be bare against him everywhere.

"Kyan . . ." She moaned into his mouth.

And then his finger moved smoothly, deeply.

"Nicole," he groaned. His tongue slaked over hers. "Fucking hell."

"Oh god . . . *please*." She scraped her nails down his back, eager, desperate for everything he could give her to help that intense need, liable to clamp his thick forearm between her legs forever.

And the feeling was building as the heel of his palm kept a gentle rolling pressure on that sensitive bud of nerves while his fingers moved with the lurch of her hips.

It was a type of frenzy, made more intense by the thought that all this was happening with *Kyan*. How much she felt for him, how much she knew, how he'd fought everything to be here with her. How he was striving to protect her. How the slow glide of his tongue and the calming, powerful energy of him levered over her made her feel so sensual, so wanted.

The pleasure soared as he dipped a second finger inside and Nicole cried out at the tightness, the sensation. Kyan stole the sound with his tongue, groaning into her mouth as she did his.

She could feel his heart racing, feel the strain in his body with his desire. And she suddenly, desperately, wanted to touch him, but what he was doing to her was so bright, so consuming she could barely get her body to function.

And then the feeling peaked. The intensity of it rang through every limb with such searing, life-changing satisfaction she screamed out, her vision blurring.

She reeled as his hand slowed, as his kisses gentled.

Weakly, she reached for the towel around his waist.

"Later," Kyan said, then kissed her again, more softly.

She made a sound of protest and he smiled against her lips.

He removed his hand from her gently and the sudden emptiness made her reach for him as he tucked her against his body. She could feel his desire still, and from the warm aftershocks, knew her body would be ready. Knew what she wanted.

If just his hand felt like that, what would *he* be like? She wanted to know. Wanted the connection, and for him to feel pleasure.

But his mouth trailed to her temple, soothed her, as the strain of the last few weeks seemed to hit her all at once.

KYAN

Kyan gently righted Nicole's clothes, bunching his towel to distract from the roaring need as he got up and dipped quickly into the adjoining bathroom. He had to fight the urge to strip off this god-forsaken strangling material and slowly undress her with his teeth, bare her properly, show her what he wanted to do to her. Put his mouth back where—

Fucking hell, he couldn't think about that right now or he'd climb back into bed and—

Kyan clamped his hands around the marble counter as he took a moment to calm himself. He couldn't have the scent of Nicole on him or he'd take her up on what they both wanted, so he used the moments to wash his hands and get himself under some control.

When he came back out, Nicole was lying drowsy in the sheets and his need returned. He settled behind her, but didn't tug her close, yet.

"Rest," he murmured. He reached for her hair and untangled the loosened plait, the sound she'd made when he'd had his hands between her legs still ringing in his ears.

So he tried thinking of cords and braids, the bracelet he wove and unwove when he needed to *think*. That pattern never changed no matter what shattered him in life.

He remembered the brick dust in her hair the day Lynch had attacked her and glanced down to see the healing marks on her skin. Kyan took a calming breath and brushed her hair back from her face and neck. Sinking his hands into it he stroked deeply, mas-saging. Her body relaxed further, their legs tangling, and a warm rush of pleasure flooded him, reminding him of the hard lust he was restraining. He bent closer and tilted to brush his lips to her temple and she made a contented sound that brought a smile to his lips.

Kyan separated her hair and began to loosely braid. A flash of memory flared as he did. The cross and dip, the cords of life, of eternity, being taught of these ancient cycles. He felt like Nicole had unraveled all that and more within him. But did she even know the threads of him she'd untangled?

"Will you tell me about this?" Nicole asked quietly, having reached back to stroke the bracelet at his wrist.

He kept the towel between them, willing his mind away from what it would be like to let her remove it.

She was heavy with sleep now but kept fighting it, and when he finished, tying it off, she twisted, slipping her leg over his thigh, notching them closer in a way that had the heavy need rearing. Nicole draped her arms around him and pressed her cheek to his neck, her chest to his chest.

"I don't remember getting it . . ." Kyan said, heart straining. ". . . only feeling like I couldn't let it go." He cupped her to him, pulling a discarded throw over her and stroking her back. "Nicole, I don't know what to do."

His throat thickened when she turned into his shoulder, brushing her lips across it, seeking comfort and giving it.

She looked up at him and touched his cheek, brushing his lips with her fingers. "Neither do I."

He'd hunted, tracked, and killed the Baobhan Sith that had been circling the town and getting closer to her. It had been outside her home tonight, fascinated by her scent and had decided to kill.

So, he'd taken it out and disposed of the body, then washed himself of the blood and the sand.

Part of him had been relieved at the success of some element of this mission. The reminder that he could hunt and protect.

But she was an Empyreal as well as a Seer. That still shook him. Finding any new Empyreal was extremely rare, but ones like her . . . Someone that could survive the vicious creatures in the world with her own strength. Who didn't need him, but wanted him. Someone he could work with, rather than simply worry for. Who might live as long as him, defend herself with the same inherent knowledge . . .

Perhaps that was why they were mates.

He wanted her more than he'd wanted anything. And he knew that if—*when?*—he had her—*gods*, he couldn't think about being inside her without his body lurching to attention—he'd unleash the hunger that had slumbered in him for so long. She awoke all of it with an insistent ferocity that thrilled him with the anticipation of how he could please her. How he could tell her with his body everything he couldn't say out loud without making this impossible situation harder.

She was the person he'd never expected to find. Not after centuries. Not after losing family so long ago that any kind of closeness with another had grown near impossible.

"*Mo ghrá*," he murmured against her temple as she fell asleep, realizing as he drifted with her, that he'd spoken Irish for the first time in . . . longer than he could remember.

He fell asleep with her holding on to him, and him to her, feeling, tonight, that those cords on the bracelet he'd never allowed himself to discard held more promise than bittersweet memory. More love.

More hope.

52 NICOLE

Nicole kept her eyes closed for a few long moments, savoring the feel of waking beside Kyan. Her body stirred, rearing her swiftly when she realized she was lying against his chest and the towel he'd kept between them had twisted away slightly in the night. She pushed up.

He was still asleep, his handsome face cast in morning light, and she got such a gut punch of feeling that her heart almost hurt. He looked so *peaceful*. That arrowed line between his brows had smoothed to nothing and she felt a deep gratitude that she'd gotten to see it.

She'd had no opportunity to really touch him last night, not after he'd—

A rush of desire made her much more aware of how her body felt this morning. Slightly tender, but as if it had paused to sleep, all that want came back with full force.

Her fingers were already on his stomach. Holding her breath, she moved them slightly, finding that his skin was warm and firm, his chest brushed with dark hair. She marveled at the thought of that body against hers with nothing between them.

Kyan stirred, his arms coming up around her waist, sweeping her hand up against his heart. He made a thoughtful sound. Hummed.

"Good morning," he said, voice rough.

Nicole couldn't help her slow smile.

His eyes opened then, scanning her immediately for discomfort before his expression softened and he levered up to brush a kiss just below her collarbone and above her breast, a gentle, intimate thing. Reminding her of what they'd done and *hadn't* done. And how much she still wanted to do.

She could see the same thing in his eyes.

She threaded her arms around him, tipping him back against the bed, her body flush against his. "Good morning," she said against his mouth, before kissing him gently.

Kyan's warm hands stroked up her back and, as she moved her leg between his, he let out another small hum—a noise that set her instincts stirring.

"We should get out of bed," he said, angling his lower body away.

Nicole felt so warm and she smiled against his mouth. *Why—*

The memory of what day it was flew back to her.

She was leaving Estwood. Today.

She reared back with a cold rush of panic.

"I don't want to go," she whispered, sitting up.

Kyan pushed up on his elbows, and she glanced down to where his scarred forearm lay beside her. She pressed her lips into a hard line and stroked a finger over the scar, making him shudder.

How was it that so much had changed in such a short time: art, transformation, death?

Nicole blinked, wondering why those words tugged at her mind, before realizing they were similar to the note her mother had scrawled in her copy of *Metamorphoses*: *The secret art to transformation, is death.*

Nicole wondered where she'd put the book. They'd have to pack it with everything else—

The realization hit her like a truck.

"Oh my god."

"What?" Kyan asked, going on alert.

"The key," she said, scrambling up and searching the room. She stalled, feeling the pattern of Kyan's plait still in her hair. "Let's go, I've got it!"

She looked back at him, half naked, amused, his lips curled up in a smile. And that feeling hit her again square in the chest, so she climbed back on the bed and kissed him, and when she pulled back, she wanted to say something so badly that it nearly spilled from her lips.

Kyan took her hand. "I'll take you home."

Right. Yes. Home.

The morning was warm when they rushed out, eager to tell the others about her revelation, hoping that *this* would be the key.

Nicole checked her phone, reading the news that there'd been a car crash off the main highway. Apparently, a driver had lost control and swerved deep into the surrounding fields, crashing into an old gas lamp and a student who'd been out there. The car had exploded and Mr. Douglas Alborough—the curator—who'd been reported missing, was discovered in the remains, his identity verified by dental records. The other body was believed to be that of a new student, Michael Lynch. Their reasons for being on the highway were still under investigation, though the bodies had been released for burial.

They wouldn't have been the real ones.

"I used my borrowed warlock's powers to make it work," Kyan

said quietly. "The ones from hunting the Baobhan Sith. There hadn't been enough left of either of them to stage anything else."

Nicole swallowed hard. Kyan squeezed her hand.

She looked up at the blue sky to stem her tears and shoved her phone into her pocket. It was the kind of flawless morning she'd come to associate with this dreamy coastal place. The familiar hum of a bike glided past and seagulls cried out above, but the chill of autumn bit at her neck and cheeks.

Where would they go next?

Nicole let them into the house, then came around to discover that Bells and Remi were in the kitchen. They were both sitting on barstools, though Bells's feet barely reached the footrest.

"Hey!" Remi said, examining Nicole and looking over her shoulder to Kyan with skepticism before arching a brow, a smile playing on her mouth. But if she suspected anything from Nicole's night at the manor, she didn't say a word. "Are you packed?"

"Hold that thought," Nicole said before taking the stairs two at a time into her bedroom.

She stared at it for a moment, semi-packed up, the little tape marks on the walls where she'd removed her posters and art prints. This was the place that had been her real childhood bedroom, that had seen her grow into a teenager, into a young woman. Now what? What more would she become?

She pushed the thought aside. Where had she left the book? The last time she'd seen it had been the day she'd heard that Professor Westmoore was dead. She'd had it when the curator had emailed her to say she could no longer work with Westmoore's paintings. . . .

Nicole sank to her knees and found it under her bed. It must have fallen there in her haste to get to the museum.

The page was still open on her mother's quote, and Nicole felt a bite of excitement. She already knew the beginning of the cipher, so began flicking through the pages as she hurried back downstairs.

T-H-E . . .

She rushed back into the kitchen, set the book on the countertop, and carefully scribbled down the next letters.

. . . W-A-K-E-S-T-R-U-E-L-E-A-D-E-R-S

"It's right," Nicole said, heart pounding. "It's *working*!"

Kyan looked at the letters, his expression like steel. "No Empyreal has ever met the Wake's true leaders."

"I'll call in my parents," Remi said.

"Dylan!" Nicole shouted, having heard him boxing things up in his room. "Get Dad, I've found it!"

A moment later, there were thuds upstairs as her brother hastily went across the hall to their father's room, and then two sets of footsteps were coming down the stairs.

"I'll put some coffee on," Kyan said, sounding slightly numb.

Nicole put her pen down. "Do you . . . you don't have to be here if this is too conflicting for you. I know you're already fighting the oath, and knowing this information might not help your situation."

She realized they hadn't really spoken about how he felt about the Wake. He'd learned so much, but had it changed his feelings of loyalty toward them?

Kyan took her in. "After what I've learned and the threat they pose to you, yes. My loyalty has shifted."

Relief and that warm, unnamed emotion swarmed her chest again.

"What more does it say?" Bells asked, craning closer to the words.

Nicole turned back to the book. "I guess we better find out."

It took them two hours. With every word they'd deciphered, every sentence Bells had read out over Dylan's shoulder, the tension had grown, until the passage was complete. When it was done, they all looked at one another: two families hiding from the Wake and one of its hunters.

Nicole read her mother's last message aloud:

The Wake's true leaders are not human, nor any creature I can discern. As such, they can only be killed by one thing: a creature capable of transforming into their unknown predators: Empyreals.

This is why Empyreals have never met the true leaders of the Wake, for they would sense their evil, and transform to kill them.

I wonder if this is the true reason Empyreals were made by the Goddess of Death—to protect the world not just from the range of deadly creatures, but from the leaders of the Wake themselves.

A cure to the oath must be found, but I have yet to discover one. Perhaps only the God of Oaths himself will know.

What I do know is that there are three ancient items that have been goddess-blessed. Items that will help Empyreals destroy the Wake or perhaps break free from their binds: a painting, an artifact, and something of divine provenance. But they must be used in conjunction with the Siren's ancient instrument. I have tried to locate these items, with little success, my last lead hidden with my painter.

If you are reading this, my messages have led you here. Which means I am gone, and I have failed to keep you safe.

Even the thought of it is my greatest shame.

But I trust that if you have come this far, you can complete this crucial mission.

To destroy the Wake and save the world.

Or it will descend into a supernatural oblivion worse than those fabled Dark Ages, and no one, human or creature, will ever be free again.

Silence rang through the room.

Their mother's clues weren't about finding a new safe house, or even giving them information they could use as leverage against the Wake.

This was about *destroying* them.

"'My last lead hidden with my painter,'" Nicole repeated. "The painter of her portrait?"

Her father nodded, evidently unwilling to say the artist's name in front of Kyan.

Nicole sank back on to the stool.

"'The Siren's ancient instrument,'" Nicole said, looking at where Remi's family stood in the kitchen. "That's what you've been looking for."

Adam nodded. "We have a few leads so we're just going to have to follow them. We need to be off the radar now, too, we can't have the Wake knowing our location. Sirens have been searching for it for centuries, just as the Wake have been aware we're looking for it. And while we were away, we discovered that Sirens *have* been disappearing and the Wake's responsible."

"What?" Bells asked, turning her stricken gaze to Remi.

Remi nodded gravely. "We had theories they've been doing it

445

for a while but that's what Mum and Dad were looking for—proof."

The news was like a gut punch. Whatever the Wake's motives, they believed Empyreals and Sirens could stop them, and so were hunting them for it.

"They nearly killed Adam once," Remi's mother said, "which was why we fled to Estwood. We barely escaped. But if I see that little Empyreal bastard again . . ." The shiny scar on Lawna's collarbone stood out in a beam of morning light.

Kyan tensed. "They sent an Empyreal after him even though he'd never killed anyone?"

"Yes," Lawna said. "And if they find out our location, what's to say they won't send someone to finish the job?"

Adam looked at her, full of love, and warning. "I've told you, if we get anywhere near him again, we're out of there. I'm not letting him get another shot at you."

"It was my job—" Lawna began, a frown on her beautiful face.

Nicole had a feeling this was an old argument.

"Who was it? Did you get a name, a visual?" Kyan asked.

"Huge white guy. I couldn't tell anything else, he was wearing a balaclava."

The doorbell rang, jarring through Nicole's thoughts.

She looked up sharply and went to answer.

Only to discover a different Empyreal standing in the entryway.

"Hello, again, Nicole," Callum said.

53 NICOLE

Callum took a deep breath, the silver turtleneck he wore tightening against his chest.

"You're lucky that delicious little scent is gone," he said, letting himself in. Nicole removed her hand from the door handle, finding the metal had morphed under her new strength.

She cursed inwardly. They shouldn't have waited so long to leave. It had given Callum time to discover what she was, and while she trusted that Kyan wouldn't tell the Wake, she didn't know Callum—and he still wanted information about her mother.

"What are you doing here?" Kyan demanded, striding from the kitchen.

"I wanted to have a little chat with our friend Nicole."

Dread twisted her stomach as he moved lazily into her home. He looked around the corner to where everyone stood.

"Hello, loves," he said, addressing them all but focusing his attention on Dylan.

"Callum?" her brother asked, his features steeling.

The Empyreal's teeth flashed in a grin. "And here I thought you'd be happy to see me."

Her brother's hand fisted at his side before he began to rub his fingers against his thumb.

"Don't worry," Callum said. "The newly transformed scent has changed." He looked between Nicole and Kyan meaningfully. "Great way to keep a clear head."

A dark flush stole up her cheeks.

Callum's eyes winked with humor, and knowledge. "I'm not your enemy, Nicole."

"No?" Remi asked, stepping closer, keeping Bells behind her.

"You work for the Wake," Nicole said. "I'd say that makes you one."

"So does Kyan, but he doesn't seem much like your enemy. I'd recognize that pattern anywhere." He nodded to her plait.

She forced herself not to raise her hand to it. "What do you want?"

"For us all to get to know one another better. Who might you all be? Or maybe I should ask *what*?" He squinted at Remi, then her family. "Sirens and a Hearthea. Quite the voices you have, I'm sure, but we have one pressing matter." He turned to face Nicole. "Your darling mother."

There was a note to the way he said it. Something like—worry?

"We can't tell you anything about her," Nicole's father said, stepping forward. "She was just as much of a mystery to me, to all of us, as she was anyone else. And she's gone."

"See, I just don't believe you," Callum said. "That woman was tenacious."

"The Wake killed her," Dylan said sharply.

Callum shook his head gently. "No body, no proof."

Outrage seared in her brother's gaze. "I saw enough proof the night she was *murdered*."

Nicole grabbed his arm.

"You *saw* her murdered?" Callum asked, skeptical.

"With my own two eyes," Dylan said.

"What did her killer look like?"

"I was five years old; I don't remember."

Callum's eyes narrowed thoughtfully.

"You know the Wake have been up to something for years, Callum," Kyan said. "You're the one with more theories than me."

"Even if I did," Callum said, "you can't lie to the Wake. No matter how strongly you feel, you can't get past the pools."

"What pools?" Remi asked.

"We go in them at the end of every mission when we're debriefed," said Kyan. "A cleansing, they call it. It . . . strips us of things. Any lingering trauma, I don't know. Gets the metaphorical blood off. But it also means that we can't lie to them when we're then debriefed. We have to tell them everything, omitting nothing."

Nicole's stomach dropped. "You'd have to tell them about us?"

Kyan gave a terse nod. "Even if I didn't want to. There's no guarantee that what I feel can override that process."

"Can't you just avoid the debriefing?" Dylan asked.

"No," Callum said. Something in his tone made it seem like he'd tried it before.

"You could if there was something strong enough to override it," Bells said, looking between Nicole and Kyan.

"Like a mating bond," Remi realized.

"This is ridiculous," Dylan snarled. "Besides, even if Kyan *was* bound to Nicole, that's no guarantee he'd be able to resist telling them."

"Or that Callum could either," Lawna said, inclining her chin toward the mysterious Empyreal.

Callum had perched himself on the arm of one of their cream couches, legs crossed, the image of ease and elegance while everyone else stood around, between the archway into the kitchen and about the living room.

"Ah," he said, "you're forgetting that I'm not technically on a mission right now, so no debriefing pools for me. Besides, her scent has changed." He shrugged. "I'm not feeling some uncanny urge to tattle or throw her over my shoulder."

"How can we be sure?" Ronan asked.

"Let's just say . . . don't worry about it. Don't you trust me?" Callum asked.

"No," answered everyone but Kyan and Bells, who watched the Empyreal curiously.

Callum smirked, but his eyes were on Kyan, and something burned there—a brotherhood forged by centuries.

Kyan nodded. "I do. You can trust him."

"How convincing," Dylan said flatly.

Callum's smile grew with fondness this time, and then he flashed a look of daring at Dylan. "That leaves us with *you*," he said to Kyan. "Because while the bond means that you may now be even more loyal to Nicole than the Wake, a ceremony might be the only thing to give that loyalty enough weight to bypass the Wake's power."

"What are you talking about?" Nicole asked.

"The Fae and Vampires have their mating ceremonies. For you two, with Kyan's Irish heritage and Nicole's ancestry being . . . Celtic?" he guessed, and she nodded warily. "You're best with a Celtic binding rite. Like the old Druid ones. Three ceremonies in total, each a year and a day apart. This will allow you to make up your minds over time about truly embracing the bond. By the time the third ceremony is done, we should be out of this mess, but it creates enough of a connection and enough *magic*, for lack of a better word, to override the oath. The oath is an external thing, but a mate? That's not external. Besides, correct me if I'm wrong but I imagine that the protective Empyrean urge has . . . tripled around one another?"

Nicole thought of just how she'd felt when Kyan was about to die. How she now felt at the idea of never seeing him again. She swallowed, noting he was already shadowing her, his chest to her back. She nodded softly.

"You don't have to," Kyan said quietly.

Everyone in the room began to make themselves busy, looking at random objects, turning away. All except her father, whose eyes were on her.

Kyan came to take her hands. "Say the word and I'll find another way."

Nicole tried to swallow, but she knew they didn't have time. They had the painting's clues to follow and she knew that the Wake would want to know why Kyan was lingering here, especially knowing this sleepy university town had been hiding a supernatural conspiracy that could change the lives of creatures, and humans, forever.

She looked over at her father, knowing he would kill, maim, and do anything he'd need to, to keep her from the Wake's clutches. Those storm-gray eyes made her feel secure. She knew that if he'd Seen something awful, he would have told her.

So she turned back to Kyan.

"We can just do the first one for now, right? That'll give us time." Even though she was beginning to fear that she didn't need

451

that time, that she already felt something deep and meaningful growing roots. But it made her feel even more secure to know that they didn't *need* to complete all three and be bound unless they *wanted* to.

"It gives us three years," Bells said, "to destroy the Wake."

Callum's brows rose. "To do what now?"

"How about *we* make a deal," Nicole's father said, stepping through the mix of them and approaching Callum.

The Empyreal seemed to admire her father's boldness.

"If you swear to help Kyan find out what the Wake are really up to from the inside, I'll tell you what you want to know about Freya when the next binding comes around in a year and a day."

Callum looked over at Kyan. "You're doing this?"

Kyan's face was set. "I'm going to figure it out."

Callum waited a few long beats and Nicole almost held her breath.

"Fine, I'll do it," he said. "As long as you two"—he gestured between Nicole's siblings—"do something for me. If Dylan saw your mother's killer but can't remember, it's buried in his subconscious. *You*," he said to Bells, "as his sister and a full Seer can help him unearth the memory."

Dylan had gone pale.

"Absolutely not," their father interrupted. "I'm not putting him through that trauma for your own curiosity."

"It's not for my damn curiosity," Callum said. "If there's an Empyreal being used as an assassin for the Wake, Kyan and I need to know who they are."

Nicole thought of the Empyreal Lawna said had tried to kill Adam—had it been the same person? Was there some way they could actually learn the identity of her mother's killer?

"Just how are we supposed to do this?" Bells asked.

"It might take time, several sessions. It could take weeks. But if we have a year and a day, I suppose that's your deadline, though the sooner the better, because if Kyan and I are walking back into a snake pit we need to know who we can trust."

"Why do you want to know about Mum so badly?" Nicole asked.

Callum's attention cut to her and in it she felt how complicated he was, how there were a few millennia of stories behind those eyes. And yet, something about her mother made him desperate.

"She knew things no one should." The words made Nicole uneasy. But the cold feeling of worry was gone in an instant, replaced with Callum's charming smile. "She also had information I need." Then he looked at Kyan. "Are you ready to risk this? If the Wake find out what we're doing, they'll kill you both. Apostasies are non-existent for a reason; you don't just leave the Wake."

"No," Kyan said, "but we can try to lie to them."

"And if anyone tries to hurt my kids, I'll kill them," added her father simply.

Callum took him in. "I can see why that vicious little madam married you."

Lawna looked at Nicole's father. "We've done this for years. I have more than a little experience with wards and protections. What's a few more while we take the bastards down from the inside?"

Nicole turned to her sister, and a look passed between Remi and Bells.

"I'll officiate," Remi said. "In the absence of a Druid, I'm probably your next best bet. I can use the power of my voice to do the ceremony."

"Then, come along, children," said Callum, rising. "We have a binding to attend."

"Now's the best time for it," Bells said.

"Why?" Nicole asked.

"It's an October full moon," Kyan said. "A *hunter's* moon."

To bind a mated Empyreal pair . . .

54 NICOLE

Lanhydrock's Great Wood was quiet this morning. Dry teardrop leaves in all shades of amber and blood crackled underfoot, and the chill of autumn trailed across the back of Nicole's neck while the pale circle of the hunter's moon watched from above, strange and visible even in the daytime sky.

She almost let down her hair as a cape against the cold, but remembered Kyan's braid and couldn't bear to unravel it.

Nicole looked up at him. His eyes were full of concern, even if his body moved surely through the woods, her hand holding his. She tried to memorize the feeling: the warmth that felt like protection; the shape of his fingers and the press of his knuckles against the pads of her fingers. She knew what he was thinking: just over a hundred years ago Empyreals had sworn their oaths to the Wake beneath these trees, spattered the bracken with their blood, and each other's.

This morning there would be more.

Callum and Dylan stood on her left; Bells and Remi faced them.

"This ritual is the first in a set of three, to accept the mating bond between you," Bells said. She seemed so much older despite the subtle purple circles beneath her eyes. "As you know, it needs to be done twice more to be complete, each spaced a year and a day apart."

That meant in a year and a day she would see Kyan again.

Despite everything, despite the unknowns and great conspiracy to hunt ahead, that thought gave her some comfort.

"Are you sure about this?" Kyan asked her.

"What other choice do we have? If you could resist . . ." But she saw the strain in him. Nicole's eyes tracked to Callum. He *wouldn't* resist.

"We could kill them," her brother suggested dryly.

"You could try," Callum added.

"This oath will override your allegiance to the Wake for a year and a day," Remi interrupted. "At which point the second part of the ceremony will need to be performed. But it must be completed a third time to be binding."

The hairs on the back of Nicole's neck rose.

The threefold Goddess of Death, the Morrígan, returned to her mind.

"Ready?" Remi asked Bells.

Bells stepped forward, taking a knife from her belt.

"Careful now," Callum murmured.

"Nicole, Kyan, I need you to swap hands. Nicole, your left one to Kyan's left," Bells instructed. They did so, standing across one another, gripping each other's wrists almost like they had that day in Lanhydrock when she'd first touched his scar.

"With this blood, we bind," Remi said, adopting an ancient tone that stirred Nicole's Empyreal.

Bells went to lift the knife when she paused. "I won't be able to pierce their skin."

"Looks like we can't do the ritual then," Dylan began. "Let's just go."

"Callum," Kyan said.

His friend rolled his eyes before strolling over. "Fine. Knife please, little one."

"I don't think so," Dylan said, striding over, eyeing the blade Bells offered him. The Empyreal gave him a flat look as he came to stand at Kyan's left.

"Callum can make my mark, Dylan can make Nicole's," Kyan suggested.

Nicole nodded, looking up at her worried brother.

Callum tipped the knife to the point in the center of Kyan's circular scar, but paused before he did, meeting Kyan's eyes as if something had just occurred to him, something that concerned him. Nicole didn't have time to ask, because Callum pressed and the knife pierced, leaving a bead of blood.

Dylan swiftly took the blade and tried to do the same for Nicole, but her skin had grown stronger since her transformation and he hesitated to press harder.

"It's okay," she said softly.

Dylan gritted his teeth and put a supportive hand under her elbow, before putting his weight into it and breaking the skin.

Kyan gave her hands a gentle squeeze as she hissed in a breath. He was risking everything so that he wouldn't take her away. So that he could find out the truth and keep them safe. He was not just a hunter, he was so much more. She closed her eyes as her Empyrean power reared up, curious in the presence of something ancient and magical.

Bells pressed a small finger to the blood and copied the Celtic weave pattern of Kyan's bracelet, drawing it down his arm. Then she did the same for Nicole, painting the pattern from her forearm down to her wrist as Remi repeated her words.

"With this blood, we *bind*."

A rushing filled Nicole's ears. Then came a feeling in that place deep in her solar plexus, the place her power emanated from. It turned her blood molten. Her body seemed to sigh, relieved; enchanted by that shining connection.

Kyan bent and brushed his lips across hers as the feeling swirled in her stomach, around her body and into her Empyreal.

"It's done," Remi said.

Nicole blinked up at Kyan.

She didn't know what to say. It seemed he didn't either. She was afraid to think of love. Her logical mind screamed at her that it was impossible, and yet her life wasn't logical, nor was it human. And if this wasn't love, it was the promise of falling in love. She could haul herself away from the feeling, but looking at his gentle eyes she wasn't sure she wanted to, and it would hurt her heart to do it.

Nicole pressed her cheek to his, her tears burning. He was someone she could find solace and calm with. God, the way she could step into the protective circle of his arms . . .

She wound her arms around him, suddenly desperate not to let go.

It wasn't fair.

She hadn't had enough time.

But that was yet another thing the Wake had taken from her.

"I'll find you again," he promised.

She nodded against his chest, because she couldn't speak. She didn't know how to do this. How not to leave a piece of her heart here, with him.

She opened her mouth to speak, but to say what? *I'll see you soon?*
I'll miss you?

I love you?

Pain and a sliver of panic clutched her.

"I . . ." Tears threatened her vision. She swallowed hard.

"I know," Kyan whispered, saying what neither of them could with a light brush of his lips over hers. She lingered, concentrating one last time on his kiss; the scent of him. Then she forced herself to turn and walk away before she said anything more.

"Maybe this will be more fun than I thought," Callum said behind her.

She felt Bells and Remi either side of her and took their hands as Dylan followed tensely behind, the forest floor snapping beneath him. Together, they walked back through the wood to their waiting parents.

Her father was talking to Adam and Lawna when they broke back out of the tree line. Their cars were parked nose to nose and packed with all their key belongings, having left everything else. A small selection of clothes and toiletries resided in the case atop the car or in overnight bags stuffed under seats. Plants and her mother's books pressed against the back windows; their supernatural weapons hidden beneath. They'd tucked their mother's portrait under the seats and the rolled-up, semi-charred canvas of the *Dante* painting laid carefully in the back. "It's better with you than the Wake," he'd said before they'd set off from Estwood. She hadn't known how to thank him.

Nicole paused and turned to her best friend. Remi's eyes were full of false bravado.

Tears filled Nicole's. "Oh god, I'm going to miss you."

Remi laughed sadly and threw her arms around Nicole. She

clung on, memorizing her friend's warm, honey-and-violets scent.

"So much for our first year of uni," Nicole whispered.

Remi laughed, then pulled back and looked at her fondly. "We'll redo it when all this is over, deal?"

Nicole laughed and squeezed Remi's hand as she thought of all she'd be leaving: not just a town and a place she'd called home, but the people. Her best friend.

It was the people she was with that were her home.

"Deal."

Kyan had challenged her belief that all of the Wake's Empyreals were unwavering in their loyalty. Maybe others were, too. Maybe things could be different.

"Where will you go?" Nicole asked.

"We're going back to the Siren archives," Adam said. "As long as the Wake aren't alerted to us before then, we'll find out what we can."

"Is it safe for you?" Bells asked, frowning up at him.

"Possibly not," Lawna answered. "But this is what we've been working toward our whole lives. My sister will help us get in and keep us hidden."

Nicole's father hugged each of them. "I can't think of any way to thank you for your friendship over these years. This place would have held incomparable solitude."

"Wait," Nicole said. "I have something for you." She hurried over to the car, and when she returned, she had the portrait she'd been painting of Remi with the mythical lyre.

"You finished it!"

Nicole smiled. "Yep, so it's still a little wet, but it's done."

Her friend sighed, taking the picture. "I can't believe it."

"You'll find what it is you're looking for, Remi. I have no doubt."

Remi smiled, eyes glittering with faith and power.

"Ready to go?" Nicole's father asked.

Bells hugged her arms around herself and looked up at Dylan. Nicole felt a thrill of worry, but her brother put his arm around them. She'd always feared any day could be their last in Estwood, she only wished they'd had more time.

"Where are we going?" she asked her father.

"To find the painter and discover where those three ancient items are hidden."

Nicole's heart broke a little as she let go of Remi's hand and climbed inside the car. But it was time.

Time to find a way to rid themselves of the Wake, once and for all.

So they could all find a place to settle, and finally keep it.

KYAN

"I don't know if this is one of our best or worst ideas," Callum said, lounging against a tree like some mischievous forest god, watching the Palmers drive away.

"They're using Empyreals to hunt innocent people, Callum. We need to know who we can still trust without getting the Wake's attention."

"We might already have it," Callum said. "They sent you here for the painting, what are you going to say?"

"The truth," Kyan said. "It was burned by Lynch, and in the transformation he was killed, so he never revealed why he wanted it. The evidence is dead and buried."

Kyan looked down at his marked forearm, thinking of Freya's decoded message: *This is why Empyreals have never met the true leaders of the Wake, for they would sense their evil, and transform to kill them.*

If any Empyreals saw through to the Wake's true intentions and developed suspicions, as Kyan had finally done after so long, they couldn't resist or leave.

You couldn't resist a blood oath.

But you could override it with something more ancient.

He traced the new mark, dotted in the center of one that now felt so wrong. This one felt right. It didn't burn or itch and it forged a kind of ghost connection to Nicole. Even though she wasn't here, he didn't feel like she was gone, and it eased a fraction of that protectiveness and the fear over what was to come. Instead he felt a newly kindled desire for family and home that he thought he'd stripped himself of over the centuries.

Only now could he see how poisonous that had been.

"Why do you really want to find their mother?" Kyan asked, turning to Callum. "She came to me in 1902, used my mother's face. Yet you took it upon yourself to hunt her down. You said she has information you need, about what?"

Callum's smile was slow and amused. "Ah, Kyan. You're starting to ask the right questions. I just wish I had answers for you."

"Can you not be cryptic for ten minutes?"

He laughed. "Maybe I just enjoy a little espionage."

"Don't tell me you're going soft in your old age."

Callum scoffed. "Don't tell me you love her."

Kyan turned, frowning after Nicole's dissipating scent.

Mo ghrá, he'd whispered to her last night.

My love.

"Then don't ask me."

55 KYAN

Steam rose from the Wake's Great Bath in gentle tendrils. The metallic-scented water would poison humans unless treated, but it soothed Empyreals.

Stationed around the rectangular open-air pool were honey-colored pillars stuck with flaring torches, and on the terrace overlooking it all were a series of statues, all dressed in Roman garb. Kyan ignored their unseeing gazes and the twilight sky above. He couldn't hear the sounds of the city of Bath—warding always cloaked over the pool when an Empyreal arrived.

On the stone walls, varnished so humans couldn't see, were several frescoes showing the evolution of the Wake; or at least, the Wake's approved version of events. The sequence went through the supernatural Dark Ages—when the Wake hadn't been around to help curtail the dangerous creatures that nearly overran the world—to showing them being hunted and killed by Empyreals. Then finally into an idyllic, supernaturally peaceful world.

He knew this narrative, had even spouted it himself. Yet now he had cause to doubt it. How had the Wake *really* risen to power? And were these paintings even more indoctrination, or the exposed goal of the Wake all along? Not to prevent, but to trigger another Dark Age and Wild Hunt?

Kyan took a long moment, body almost immersed in the waters and their ancient, greenish hue, his skin sheening with sweat.

You've done this a thousand times.

But he'd never omitted as much as he was about to, nor outright lied.

He made sure to keep his oath-scarred forearm out of the pool.

Water rushed down his shoulders and chest as he rose to walk naked up the stone steps. He knelt at the trio of arches under the terraced walkway that circled the bath and water pooled around him, reflecting the dark sky.

Three of the Wake's human-looking apostles stood before him, one in each arch. They all looked different, but each shared the vague eyes of the Wake's Messengers—conduits for the real power of the Wake.

"Tell us of your mission, hunter," said the central one, their voice both flat and resounding.

Kyan's knees dug into the cold stone and he felt the pull of the water's power drag through his body. His jaw clamped. Not once had he lied to the organization that had helped him hone his Empyrean power, that sent him on mission after mission, kill after kill. That had taken him from helplessness and grief and forged him into something with a purpose.

But he had a new mission now.

He would uncover their true motives and tear them down. He would protect Nicole at all costs, as he was made to. He was finished telling himself he was fine alone. This sacred purpose felt right in a way that some of the Wake's missions had not, and he'd smothered that part of his instincts for too long, needing nothing but their guidance.

So, he'd become the Wake's greatest hunter.

And now he'd hunt *them*.

ACKNOWLEDGMENTS

Oh my gosh, where to begin. Firstly, I want to thank you, dear reader. It's one thing writing a book and finally getting a book deal (shakes tiny fist at the twelve-plus years of waiting), but another to actually have it get out into the world, to you. Thank you for picking up the book of my heart. I hope I get to share many more with you and that you love Nicole and Kyan even a fraction of the way I do.

But now, I'm diving into this bad boy chronologically, so prepare yourselves.

To Aisha Curran, who was the assistant at the Christopher Little Literary Agency about thirteen years ago. I sent you my first-ever book and you responded and encouraged me to keep going. I don't know if you'll ever read this, but thank you for being so compassionate.

To Helen Orrett, my English teacher in school. You inspired me every time I saw you. You were the first person outside my family to read my work, and I have two very vivid and fond memories of you helping me with it: us speed-walking to your next class as you told me, "You must doggedly pursue this," and you writing the title "Empyreal" on the whiteboard in your gorgeous, swirling script.

Thank you so much. You are a true light in the world.

To Paul Holden of the National Trust for supplying me with such incredibly detailed research on the real events at Lanhydrock House in 1902 that I even know what was on the menu.

To Cathi Unsworth, the reader at Curtis Brown Creative, who gave such a glowing review of *Empyreal*'s first few pages when it was still in the editing phase.

To Ciannon Smart for dropping into my life at the most timely moment and offering to read this book before I queried. I'm still convinced you're an angel, and a genius.

To my brilliant, sweet, supportive Pitch Wars mentor, Laurie. I couldn't have done this without you. I'll always be grateful for your words of support and love for this book. I'm so grateful to call you my friend and mentor.

To Rachel Griffin for requesting *Empyreal* during Pitch Wars. You have no idea how much that meant to me. Thank you.

To the girls from my Pitch Wars group, Emily, Hanna, Michelle, Tanvi, and Sarah. Thank you for sharing a little of your genius around me.

To Genevieve Gagne-Hawes. Your words about *Empyreal* literally make me smile to this day and I'll never get over you requesting the book.

To Liza DeBlock, I can never thank you enough for your belief in *Empyreal* and for telling me you couldn't wait a year and a day for the next book. *sobs gently*

To my amazing literary agent, Stephanie Thwaites, who believed in this story immediately and brought that passion to the entire team at Curtis Brown. Special thank-you to Isobel Gahan for her support and brilliance; I'll never forget you calling me outside the dentist and telling me we had an offer. Reader: I danced in the middle of the street. And Luke, I'll be forever grateful for your enthusiasm about the Empyreal series as a TV/film project.

To my incredible American agents, Tina Dubois and Abby Walters, but especially Tamara Kawar for getting the Empyreal series such an incredible home.

To Claire Stetzer and Natasha Bardon for being the editors who saw this book and signed those original Empyreal series book deals. You changed my life.

To my Spanish editor, Luis M. Garcerán, and the amazing foreign rights team at Curtis Brown: Roxane, Isobel, and Savanna. Thank you so much for your incredible enthusiasm and for finding *TTOM* a home in Editorial Hidra. I cried when I got the news!

To Erica Sussman for being so accommodating and excited and getting me a new home at HarperCollins US. I can't wait to bring this book to US and Canadian readers!

To Ajebowale Roberts for being the calm in the storm of the last few months. I'm so excited to work on the next books with you. Also, your in-text comments on *TTOM* made me squeal with joy.

To the FairyLoot team, I'm so honored you chose *TTOM*! You have created the most gorgeous edition. I may have screamed when I saw it, and I've been counting down the days till it's revealed!

To my extraordinary copyeditor, Michelle, for your thorough, warm edits. You caught things no one else had and I am thrilled that you loved the Irish elements. Hopefully I can meet you one day soon in Northern Ireland. (I also want you to edit all my upcoming books, okay?)

And of course, to my family, because you're the best in the world and I love you so much that sometimes it hurts. Your support and goodness have made me who and what I am. I'm truly blessed and grateful—YOU'LL NEVER ESCAPE ME NOW! To my mother for telling me to "go write a book" when I was bored at twelve(?) years old and having absolute faith that I could. To my father for, well, everything. To my sister for being my best friend. To my brother and his stoic support. To Nana, because you read pretty much every single draft and were cutthroat about your thoughts every time. To Grandad and Nana Alma, neither of you had any idea what was going on but supported me anyway. And to Jasmine, I'll always remember you reading the book in the middle of Rector's; thank you for making me believe in friendship.

And to anyone else out there who's struggling with writing or pursuing any dream, *I believe in you*. If you can even *conceive* of your dream, it will happen.

And finally, to Pinterest.

I'm joking.

Kind of.